THE DARKEST ROOM

Johan Theorin

Translated from the Swedish
by Marlaine Delargy

BLACK SWAN

TRANSWORLD PUBLISHERS
61–63 Uxbridge Road, London W5 5SA
A Random House Group Company
www.rbooks.co.uk

THE DARKEST ROOM
A BLACK SWAN BOOK: 9780552774611

First published in Great Britain
in 2009 by Doubleday
an imprint of Transworld Publishers
Black Swan edition published 2010

Addresses for Random House Group Ltd companies outside the UK
can be found at: www.randomhouse.co.uk
The Random House Group Ltd Reg. No. 954009

The Random House Group Limited supports The Forest Stewardship
Council (FSC), the leading international forest certification organisation.
All our titles that are printed on Greenpeace approved FSC certified paper
carry the FSC logo. Our paper procurement policy can be found at
www.rbooks.co.uk/environment

Typeset in 11/12.75pt Giovanni Book by
Falcon Oast Graphic Art Ltd.

2 4 6 8 10 9 7 5 3 1

Printed and bound in Great Britain by Clays Ltd, St Ives plc

The dead gather every winter to celebrate Christmas. But on one occasion they were disturbed by an old spinster. Her clock had stopped, so she got up too early and went to church in the middle of the night on Christmas Eve. There was the murmur of voices as if there were a service going on, and the church was full of people. Suddenly the old woman caught sight of her fiancé from the days of her youth. He had drowned many years ago, but there he was, sitting in a pew among the others.

Swedish folk tale from the nineteenth century

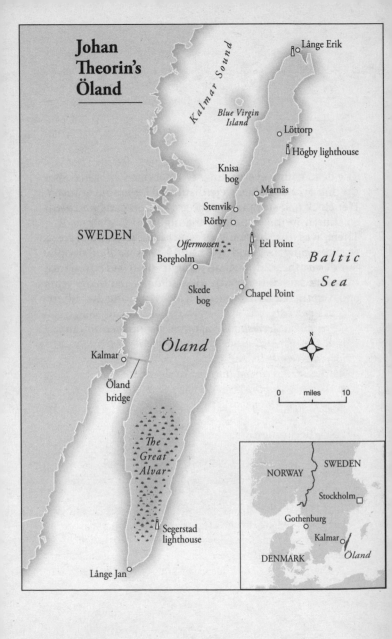

WINTER 1846

*This is where my book begins, Katrine, the year when the
manor house at Eel Point was built. For me the manor
was more than a house where my mother and I lived, it
was the place where I became an adult.*

*Ragnar Davidsson, the eel fisherman, once told me
that large parts of the manor were built with salvaged
cargo from a German vessel carrying timber. I believe
him. On the wall at the far end of the hayloft inside the
barn the words IN MEMORY OF CHRISTIAN
LUDWIG are carved into one of the planks.*

*I have heard the dead whispering in the walls. They
have so much to tell.*

Valter Brommesson is sitting in a little stone house
at Eel Point, praying to God with his hands clasped
together. He prays that the wind and the waves
sweeping in from the sea this night will not destroy
his two lighthouses.

He has experienced bad weather before, but never
a storm like this. A white wall of snow and ice
which has come howling in from the north-east,
stopping all building work.

The towers, O Lord, let us get the towers finished . . .

Brommesson is a builder of lighthouses, but this is the first time he has built a lighthouse with a prism lens in the Baltic. He came to Öland in March the previous year and set to work at once: taking on workmen, ordering clay and limestone and hiring strong draught horses.

The fresh spring, the warm summer and the sunny autumn were glorious on the coast. The work was going well, and the two lighthouses were slowly growing towards the sky.

Then the sun disappeared, winter arrived, and when the temperature dropped people began to talk of blizzards. And in the end it came, the blizzard. Late one night it hurled itself at the coast like a wild animal.

As dawn approaches the wind finally begins to subside.

Then all of a sudden cries are heard from the sea. They come out of the darkness off Eel Point – drawn-out, heart-rending cries for help in a foreign language.

The cries wake Brommesson, and he in his turn wakes the exhausted builders.

'It's a shipwreck,' he says. 'We have to go out.'

The men are sleepy and reluctant, but he gets them on their feet and out into the snow.

They plod down to the shore, their backs bent in the ice-cold headwind. Brommesson turns his head and sees that the half-finished stone towers are actually still standing, down by the water.

In the other direction, to the west, he can see nothing. The flat landscape of the island has become a billowing desert of snow.

The men stop on the shore and gaze out to sea.

They can see nothing in the dark-grey shadows out on the sand bar, but they can still hear faint cries mingled with the roaring of the waves – and the creaking sound of splintering wood and nails being torn free.

A big ship has run aground on the bar, and it is sinking.

In the end the only thing the builders can do is to stand there listening to the sounds and the cries for help from the ship. Three times they try to get one of their boats out to sea, but every attempt fails. The visibility is too poor and the breakers too high, and besides, the water is full of heavy wooden beams.

The grounded vessel must have been carrying a huge load of timber up on deck. When she began to go down the wood was wrenched free by the waves and tumbled overboard. The beams are as long as battering rams and are washed ashore in great shoals. They have begun to fill up the inlets around the point, scraping and banging against each other.

When the sun rises behind the misty grey cloud cover, the first body is discovered. It is a young man, floating in the waves a dozen or so yards from land with his arms outstretched, as if he had still been trying to grab hold of one of the beams around him right up to the very last moment.

Two of the lighthouse-builders wade out into the shallow water, take a firm grip of the rough woollen shirt the body is wearing, and tow the dead man ashore across the sandbank.

At the water's edge each man grabs hold of one ice-cold wrist and pulls hard. The dead man comes up out of the water, but he is tall and broad-shouldered and difficult to carry. He has to be dragged up the snow-covered grassy shore, with the water pouring from his clothes.

The builders gather around the body in silence, without touching it.

In the end Brommesson bends down and turns the body on to its back.

The drowned man is a sailor with thick black hair and a wide mouth which is half-open, as if he had given up in the middle of a breath. His eyes are staring up at the grey sky.

The foreman guesses that the sailor is in his twenties. He hopes he is a bachelor, but he may have a family to provide for. He has died off a foreign shore; he probably didn't even know the name of the island where his ship went down.

'We must fetch the pastor in a little while,' says Brommesson, closing the dead man's eyes so that he will no longer have to meet that empty gaze.

Three hours later the bodies of five sailors have drifted ashore around Eel Point. A broken nameplate has also washed up: CHRISTIAN LUDWIG – HAMBURG.

And timber, lots and lots of timber.

The flotsam is a gift. It belongs to the Swedish Crown now, the same Crown that is paying for the lighthouses on Eel Point. Suddenly the builders have access to top-quality pine worth many hundreds of riksdaler.

'We must all help to bring it ashore,' says Brommesson. 'We'll stack it up out of reach of the waves.'

He nods to himself and looks up towards the snow-covered plain. There is very little in the way of forests on the island, and instead of the small stone house they were planning for the lighthouse-keepers and their families on Eel Point, he can now build a much bigger house made of wood.

Brommesson has a vision of an impressive, enclosed manor with the house itself full of large, airy rooms. A secure home for those who will be looking after his lighthouses here at the end of the world.

But it will be a house built on the spoils of a shipwreck, and that can bring bad luck. Some kind of sacrificial offering will be necessary in order to counteract this bad luck. Perhaps even a prayer room. A memorial room for those who died at Eel Point, for all those poor souls who have not been buried in consecrated ground.

The thought of this bigger house remains in Brommesson's mind. Later that same day he begins to measure out the ground with long strides.

But when the storm has abated and the frozen lighthouse-builders start heaving the timber out of the water and stacking it up on the grass, many of them can still hear the echo of those cries from the drowning men.

I am certain those lighthouse-builders never forgot the cries of the drowning sailors. And I am equally certain that the most superstitious among them questioned Brommesson's decision to build a large house using timber from a shipwreck.

A house built with timber that dying sailors had clung to in despair before the sea took them – should my mother and I have known better than to move in there at the end of the 1950s? Should you and your family really have moved there thirty-five years later, Katrine?

Mirja Rambe

CHANGE YOUR LIFE – MOVE TO THE COUNTRY!

Property: Eel Point estate, north-eastern Öland

Description: Magnificent lighthouse-keeper's manor house from the middle of the 19th century in an isolated and private location with fine views over the Baltic, less than three hundred yards from the shore and with the sky as its nearest neighbour.

Large garden above the shore with flat lawned areas – perfect for children to play – surrounded by sparse deciduous forest to the north, a bird sanctuary to the west (Offermossen), with meadows and fields running down to the sea in the south.

Buildings: Attractive manor house on two floors (no cellar) comprising in total some 280 square yards, in need of renovation and modernization. Wooden frame, joists and facade. Tiled roof. Glass veranda facing east. Five tiled stoves in working order. Pine flooring in all rooms. Communal water supply, separate waste.

Annexe (limestone outhouse) on one floor, ca 80 square yards, water and electricity, ideal rental property after some renovation work.

Outbuilding (barn made of limestone/wood), ca 450 square yards, more basic and in relatively poor condition.

Status: SOLD

OCTOBER

1

A high voice called through the dark rooms.

'Mum-mee?'

The cry made him jump. Sleep was like a cave filled with strange echoes, warm and dark, and waking up quickly was painful. For a second his consciousness could not come up with a name or a place; just confused memories and thoughts. *Ethel? No, not Ethel, but . . . Katrine, Katrine.* And a pair of eyes blinking in bewilderment, seeking light in the blackness.

A second later his own name suddenly floated up from his memory: Joakim Westin. And he was lying in the double bed in Eel Point manor house on northern Öland.

Joakim was at home. He had been living here for one day. His wife Katrine and their two children had been living on the estate for two months, while he himself had only just arrived.

01:23. The red digits on the clock radio provided the only light in the dark room.

The sounds that had woken Joakim could no longer be heard, but he knew they were real. He had heard muffled complaints or whimpers from someone sleeping uneasily in another part of the house.

A motionless body lay beside him in the double bed.

15

It was Katrine; she was sleeping deeply and had crept towards the edge of the bed, taking her coverlet with her. She was lying with her back to him, but he could see the gentle contours of her body and he could feel her warmth. She had been sleeping alone in here for almost two months – Joakim had been living and working in Stockholm, coming to visit every other weekend. Neither of them had found it easy.

He stretched a hand out towards Katrine's back, but then he heard the cry once again.

'Mum-mee?'

This time he recognized Livia's high voice. It made him throw aside the cover and get out of bed.

The tiled stove in one corner of the bedroom was still radiating heat, but the wooden floor was freezing as he put his feet on it. They needed to change things around and insulate the bedroom floor as they had done in the kitchen and the children's rooms, but that would have to be a project for the new year. They could get more rugs to see them through the winter. And wood. They needed to find a supply of cheap wood for the stoves, because there was no forest on the estate where they could go and cut their own.

He and Katrine needed to buy a whole lot of things for the house before the really cold weather set in – tomorrow they would have to start making lists.

Joakim held his breath and listened. Not a sound now.

His dressing gown was hanging over a chair, and he put it on quietly over his pyjama trousers, stepped between two boxes they hadn't unpacked yet, and crept out.

He immediately went the wrong way in the darkness. In their house in Stockholm he always turned right to go to the children's rooms, but here they were to the left.

Joakim and Katrine's bedroom was small, part of the manor house's enormous cave system. Outside was a corridor with several cardboard boxes stacked up against one wall, and it ended in a large hall with several windows. They faced on to the paved inner courtyard, which was flanked by the two wings of the house.

The manor house at Eel Point was closed off to the land, but open towards the sea. Joakim went over to the windows in the hall and looked out towards the coast beyond the fence.

A red light was flashing down there, coming from one of the twin lighthouses on their little islands out at sea. The beam of the southern lighthouse swept over piles of seaweed at the water's edge and far out into the Baltic, while the northern tower was completely dark. Katrine had told him that the northern lighthouse was never lit.

He heard the wind howling around the house and saw restless shadows rising down by the lighthouses. Waves. They always made him think of Ethel, despite the fact that it wasn't the waves but the cold that had killed her.

It was only ten months ago.

The muted sounds in the darkness behind Joakim came again, but they were no longer whimpers. It sounded as if Livia were talking quietly to herself.

Joakim went back towards the corridor. He stepped carefully over a wide wooden threshold and into Livia's bedroom, which had only one window and was pitch dark. A green roller blind with five pink pigs dancing happily in a circle covered the window.

'Away . . .' said a girl's voice in the darkness. 'Away.'

Joakim trod on a small cuddly toy on the floor next to the bed. He picked it up.

'Mummy?'

'No,' said Joakim. 'Just Daddy.'

He heard the faint sound of breathing in the darkness and detected sleepy movements from the small body beneath the flowery coverlet. He leaned over the bed. 'Are you asleep?'

Livia raised her head. 'What?'

Joakim tucked the cuddly toy in the bed, right beside her. 'Foreman had fallen on the floor.'

'Did he hurt himself?'

'Oh no . . . I don't think he even woke up.'

She placed her arm around her favourite toy, a two-legged animal made of fabric that she had bought when they were on Gotland the previous summer. Half sheep, half man. Joakim had named the strange creature Foreman, after the boxer who had made his comeback at the age of forty-five a couple of years earlier.

He reached out and gently stroked Livia's forehead. The skin was cool. She relaxed, her head fell back on to the pillow, then she looked up at him. 'Have you been here long, Daddy?'

'No,' said Joakim.

'There was somebody here,' she said.

'You were just dreaming.'

Livia nodded and closed her eyes. She was already on her way back to sleep.

Joakim straightened up, turned his head and saw the faint glow of the southern lighthouse again, flashing through the blind. He took a step over to the window and lifted the blind an inch or two. The window faced west and the lighthouses weren't visible from here, but the red glow swept over the empty field behind the house.

Livia was breathing evenly again, she was fast asleep. Next morning she wouldn't remember that he'd been there.

He peeped into the other bedroom. It was the one that had been renovated most recently; Katrine had decorated and furnished it while Joakim was in Stockholm taking care of the final move and cleaning the house.

Everything was silent in here. Gabriel, aged two and a half, was lying in his little bed over by the wall, a motionless bundle. For the last year Gabriel had gone to bed around eight o'clock every evening, and slept almost ten hours straight through. The dream of every parent with small children.

Joakim turned away in the silence and crept slowly back along the corridor. The house creaked and knocked quietly around him, the creaks almost sounding like footsteps crossing the floor.

Katrine was still fast asleep when he got back to his own bed.

That morning the family had been visited by a quietly smiling man in his fifties. He had knocked on the kitchen door on the north side of the house. Joakim had opened it quickly, thinking it was a neighbour.

'Hello there,' the man said. 'Bengt Nyberg – I'm from the local paper, *Ölands-Posten*.'

Nyberg was standing there on the porch steps with a camera resting on his fat belly and a notebook in his hand. Joakim had somewhat hesitantly shaken hands with the journalist.

'I heard some big removal vans had come out to Eel Point over the last few weeks,' said Nyberg, 'and I thought I'd take a chance on you being at home.'

'I'm the only one who's just moved in,' said Johan. 'The rest of the family have been living here for a while.'

'Did you move in stages?'

'I'm a teacher,' said Joakim. 'I had to work until now.'

The reporter nodded.

19

'We do have to write about this,' he said, 'as I'm sure you understand. I know we were informed last spring that Eel Point had been sold, but of course now people want to know who's bought it . . .'

'We're just an ordinary family,' said Joakim quickly. 'You can write that.'

'Where are you from?'

'Stockholm.'

'Like the royal family, then,' said Nyberg. He looked at Joakim. 'Are you going to do what the King does, and just stay here when it's warm and sunny?'

'No, we're here all year round.'

Katrine had come into the hall and stood next to Joakim. He glanced at her, she gave a brief nod, and they invited the reporter in. Nyberg shambled over the threshold, taking his time.

They chose to sit in the kitchen; with its new equipment and polished wooden floor it was the room they had done the most work on.

When they had been working in there in August, Katrine and the man laying the floor had found something interesting: a little hiding place under the floorboards, a box made of flat pieces of limestone. Inside lay a silver spoon and a child's shoe that had gone mouldy. It was a house offering, the fitter had told her. It was meant to ensure many children and plenty of food for the inhabitants of the manor house.

Joakim made coffee and Nyberg settled down at the rectangular oak table. He opened his notebook once again.

'How did this all come about, then?'

'Well . . . we like wooden houses,' said Joakim.

'We love them,' said Katrine.

'But wasn't that a big step . . . buying Eel Point and moving here from Stockholm?'

'Not such a big step,' said Katrine. 'We had a house in Bromma, but we wanted to swap it for a house here. We started looking last year.'

'And why northern Öland?'

Joakim answered this time. 'Katrine is from Öland, in a way . . . her family used to live here.'

Katrine glanced at him briefly and he knew what she was thinking – if anybody was going to talk about her background, then it would be her. And she was rarely prepared to do so.

'Oh yes, whereabouts?'

'Various places,' said Katrine without looking at the reporter. 'They moved about quite a bit.'

Joakim could have added that his wife was the daughter of Mirja Rambe and the granddaughter of Torun Rambe – that might have got Nyberg to write a much longer article – but he kept quiet. Katrine and her mother were barely speaking to each other.

'Me, I'm a concrete kid,' he said instead. 'I grew up in an eight-storey apartment block in Jakobsberg, and it was just so ugly, with all the traffic and asphalt. So I really wanted to move out to the country.'

At first Livia sat quietly on Joakim's knee, but she soon got tired of all the chat and ran off to her room. Gabriel, who was sitting with Katrine, jumped down and followed her.

Joakim listened to the little plastic sandals pattering across the floor with such energy, and repeated the same refrain he'd chanted to friends and neighbours in Stockholm over the past few months: 'We know this is a fantastic place for kids too. Meadows and forests, clean air and fresh water. No colds. No cars churning out fumes . . . This is a good place for all of us.'

Bengt Nyberg had written these pearls of wisdom in his notebook. Then they went for a walk around the

21

ground floor of the house, through the renovated rooms and all the areas that still had tattered wallpaper, patched-up ceilings and dirty floors.

'The tiled stoves are great,' said Joakim, pointing. 'And the wooden floors are incredibly well preserved . . . We just need to give them a scrub from time to time.'

His enthusiasm for the manor might have been infectious, because after a while Nyberg started to look around with interest. He insisted on seeing the rest of the place as well – despite the fact that Joakim would have preferred not to be reminded of how much they hadn't yet touched.

'There isn't actually anything else to see,' said Joakim. 'Just a lot of empty rooms.'

'Just a quick look,' said Nyberg.

In the end Joakim nodded and opened the door leading to the upper floor.

Katrine and the reporter followed him up the crooked wooden staircase to an upstairs corridor. It was gloomy up here, despite the fact that there was a row of windows facing the sea, as the panes were covered with pieces of chipboard that let in only narrow strips of daylight.

The howling of the wind could be heard clearly in the dark rooms.

'The air certainly circulates up here,' said Katrine with a wry smile. 'The advantage is that the house has stayed dry – there's very little damage because of damp.'

'Well, that's a good thing . . .' Nyberg contemplated the buckled cork flooring, the stained, tattered wallpaper and the veils of cobwebs hanging from the cornices. 'But you do seem to have plenty left to do.'

'Yes, we know.'

'We can't wait,' said Joakim.

'I'm sure it'll be fantastic when it's finished . . .' said

Nyberg, then asked, 'So what do you actually know about this house?'

'You mean its history?' said Joakim. 'Not much, but the estate agent told us some things. It was built in the middle of the nineteenth century, at the same time as the lighthouses. But there have been quite a lot of alterations . . . the glass veranda at the front looks as if it was added around 1910.'

Then he looked enquiringly at Katrine to see if she wanted to add anything – perhaps what it had been like when her mother and grandmother were tenants here – but she didn't meet his eye.

'We know that the lighthouse-masters and keepers lived in the house with their families and servants,' was all she said, 'so there has been plenty of coming and going in these rooms.'

Nyberg nodded, looking around the dirty upper floor. 'I don't think many people have lived here over the past twenty years,' he said. 'Four or five years ago it was used for refugees, families who had fled from the wars in the Balkans. But that didn't last long. It's a bit of a shame it's stood empty . . . it's such a magnificent place.'

They started back down the stairs. Even the dirtiest rooms on the ground floor suddenly seemed light and warm compared with those upstairs.

'Does it have a name?' Katrine asked, looking at the reporter. 'Do you know if it has a name?'

'What?' said Nyberg.

'This house,' said Katrine. 'Everybody always says Eel Point, but I mean that's the name of the place, not the house.'

'Yes, Eel Point by Eel Shallows, where the eels gather in the summer,' said Nyberg, as if he were reciting a poem. 'No, I don't think the house itself has a name.'

'Houses often have a nickname,' said Joakim. 'We called our place in Bromma the Apple House.'

'This doesn't have a name, at least not that I've heard.' Nyberg stepped down from the bottom stair and added, 'On the other hand, there are plenty of stories about this place.'

'Stories?'

'I've heard a few . . . They say the wind increases off Eel Point when someone sneezes in the manor house.'

Both Katrine and Joakim laughed.

'We'd better make sure we dust often, then,' said Katrine.

'Then of course there are some old ghost stories as well,' said Nyberg.

Silence fell.

'Ghost stories?' said Joakim. 'The agent should have told us.'

He was just about to smile and shake his head, but Katrine got there first: 'I did hear a few stories when I was over at the Carlssons' having coffee – our neighbours. But they told me not to believe them.'

'We haven't really got much time for ghosts,' said Joakim.

Nyberg nodded and took a few steps towards the hall.

'No, but when a house is empty for a while people start talking,' he said. 'Shall we go outside and take a few pictures while it's still light?'

Bengt Nyberg ended his visit by walking across the grass and the stone paths in the inner courtyard and quickly inspecting both wings of the house – on one side the enormous barn, with the ground-floor walls made of limestone and the upper storey of timber painted red, and across the courtyard the smaller, whitewashed outhouse.

'I assume you're going to renovate this as well?' he said after peeping into the outhouse through a dusty window.

'Of course,' said Joakim. 'We're taking one building at a time.'

'And then you can rent it out to summer visitors.'

'Maybe. We've thought about opening a bed and breakfast, in a few years.'

'A lot of people here on the island have had the same idea,' said Nyberg.

Finally the reporter took a couple of dozen pictures of the Westin family on the yellowing grassy slope below the house.

Katrine and Joakim stood beside each other, squinting into the cold wind towards the two lighthouses out at sea. Joakim straightened his back as the camera started clicking, and thought about their neighbours' house in Stockholm, which had merited three double-page spreads in the monthly glossy *Beautiful Homes* the previous year. The Westin family had to make do with an article in the local paper.

Gabriel was perched on Joakim's shoulders, dressed in a green padded jacket that was slightly too big. Livia was standing between her parents, her white crocheted hat pulled well down over her forehead. She was looking suspiciously into the camera.

The manor house at Eel Point rose up behind them like a fortress made of wood and stone, silently watching.

Afterwards, when Nyberg had left, the whole family went down to the shore. The wind was colder than it had been, and the sun was already low in the sky, just above the roof of the house behind them. The smell of seaweed that had been washed ashore hung in the air.

Walking down to the water at Eel Point felt like arriving at the end of the world, the end of a long journey away from everyone. Joakim liked that feeling.

North-eastern Öland seemed to consist of a vast sky above a small strip of yellowish-brown land. The tiny islands looked like grass-covered reefs out in the water. The island's flat coastline, with its deep inlets and narrow points, slipped almost imperceptibly into the water and became a shallow, even seabed of sand and mud, which gradually sank deeper, down into the Baltic Sea.

A hundred yards or so away from them the white towers of the lighthouses rose up towards the dark-blue sky. Eel Point's twin lighthouses. Joakim thought the islands on which they were standing looked as if they were somehow man-made, as if someone had made two piles of stone and gravel out in the water and bound them together with bigger rocks and concrete. Fifty yards to the north of them a breakwater ran out from the shore – a slightly curved jetty made of large blocks of stone, doubtless constructed in order to protect the lighthouses from the winter storms.

Livia had Foreman under her arm, and she suddenly set off towards the wide jetty leading out to the lighthouses.

'Me too! Me too!' shouted Gabriel, but Joakim held him tightly by the hand.

'We'll go together,' he said.

The jetty split in two a dozen or so yards out into the water, like a big letter Y with two narrower arms leading out to the islands where the lighthouses stood. Katrine shouted, 'Don't run, Livia! Be careful of the water!'

Livia stopped, pointed to the southern lighthouse, and shouted in a voice that was only just audible above the wind, 'That one's mine!'

'Mine too!' shouted Gabriel behind her.

'End of story!' shouted Livia.

That was her new favourite expression this autumn, something she had learned in pre-school.

Katrine hurried over to her and nodded towards the northern lighthouse. 'In that case, this one's mine!'

'OK, then I'll take care of the house,' said Joakim. 'It'll be as easy as pie, if you all just pitch in and help a little bit.'

'We will,' said Livia. 'End of story!'

Livia laughed and nodded, but of course for Joakim it was no joke. But he was still looking forward to all the work that was waiting during the course of the winter. He and Katrine were both going to try to find a teaching post on the island, but they would renovate the manor house together in the evenings and at weekends. She had already started, after all.

He stopped in the grass by the shore and took a long look at the buildings behind them.

Isolated and private location, as it had said in the ad.

Joakim still found it difficult to get used to the size of the main house; with its white gables and red wooden walls, it rose up at the top of the sloping grassy plain. Two beautiful chimneys sat on top of the tiled roof like towers, black as soot. A warm yellow light glowed in the kitchen window and on the veranda; the rest of the house was pitch black.

So many families had lived there, toiling away at the walls, doorways and floors over the years – master light-house-keepers and lighthouse-keepers and lighthouse assistants and whatever they were all called. They had all left their mark on the manor house.

Remember, when you take over an old house, the house takes you over at the same time, Joakim had read in a book about renovating wooden houses. For him and Katrine this was not the case – they had had no problem leaving the house in Bromma, after all – but over the years they had met a number of families who looked after their houses like children.

'Shall we go out to the lighthouses?' asked Katrine.

'Yes!' shouted Livia. 'End of story!'

'The stones could be slippery,' said Joakim.

He didn't want Livia and Gabriel to lose their respect for the sea and go down to the water alone. Livia could swim only a few yards, and Gabriel couldn't swim at all.

But Katrine and Livia had already set off along the stone jetty, hand in hand. Joakim picked Gabriel up, held him in the crook of his right arm, and followed them dubiously out on to the uneven blocks of stone.

They weren't as slippery as he had thought, just rough and uneven. In some places the blocks had been eroded by the waves and had broken away from the concrete holding them together. There was only a slight wind today, but Joakim could sense the power of nature. Winter after winter of drift-ice and waves and harsh storms on Eel Point – and still the lighthouses stood firm.

'How tall are they?' wondered Katrine, looking towards the towers.

'Well, I don't have a ruler with me – but maybe sixty feet or so?' said Joakim.

Livia tipped her head back to look up at the top of her lighthouse.

'Why is there no light?'

'It'll come on when it gets dark,' said Katrine.

'Does that one never come on?' asked Joakim, leaning back to look up at the north tower.

'I don't think so,' said Katrine. 'It hasn't done since we've been here.'

When they reached the point where the breakwater

divided, Livia chose the left path, towards her mother's lighthouse.

'Careful, Livia,' said Joakim, looking down into the black water below the stone track.

It might only be five or six feet deep, but he still didn't like the shadows and the chill down there. He was a decent swimmer, but he had never been the type to leap eagerly into the waves in summer, not even on really hot days.

Katrine had reached the island and walked over to the water's edge. She looked in both directions along the coastline. To the north only empty beaches and clumps of trees were visible, to the south meadows and in the distance a few small boathouses.

'Not a soul in sight,' she said. 'I thought we might see a few neighbouring houses, at least.'

'There are too many little islands and headlands in the way,' said Joakim. He pointed to the north shore with his free hand. 'Look over there. Have you seen that?'

It was the wreck of a ship, lying on the stony strip of shore half a mile or so away – so old that all that was left was a battered hull made of sun-bleached planks of wood. Long ago the ship had drifted towards the land in a winter storm; it had been hurled high up on to the shore, where it had remained. The wreck lay to starboard among the stones, and Joakim thought the framework sticking up looked like a giant's ribcage.

'The wreck, yes,' said Katrine.

'Didn't they see the beams from the lighthouses?' said Joakim.

'I think the lighthouses just don't help sometimes . . . not in a storm,' said Katrine. 'Livia and I went over to the wreck a few weeks ago. We were looking for some nice pieces of wood, but everything had been taken.'

The entrance to the lighthouses was a stone archway

some three feet deep, leading to a sturdy door of thick steel, very rusty and with only a few traces of its original white paint. There was no keyhole, just a crossbar with a rusty padlock, and when Joakim got hold of the side of the door and pulled, it didn't move an inch.

'I saw a bunch of old keys in one of the kitchen cupboards,' he said. 'We'll have to try them out some time.'

'Otherwise we can contact the Maritime Board,' said Katrine.

Joakim nodded and took a step away from the door. The lighthouses weren't part of the deal, after all.

'Don't the lighthouses belong to us, Mummy?' said Livia as they made their way back to the shore. She sounded disappointed.

'Well, yes,' said Katrine. 'Sort of. But we don't have to look after them, do we, Kim?'

She smiled at Joakim, and he nodded. 'The house will be quite enough.'

Katrine had turned over in the double bed while Joakim was with Livia, and as he crept beneath the covers she reached out for him in her sleep. He breathed in the scent of her, and closed his eyes.

All of this, only this.

It felt as if they had drawn a line under life in the city. Stockholm had shrunk to a grey mark on the horizon, and the memories of searching for Ethel had faded away.

Peace.

Then he heard the faint whimpering from Livia's room again, and held his breath.

'Mum-mee?'

Her drawn-out cries echoing through the house were louder this time. Joakim breathed out with a tired sigh.

Beside him Katrine raised her head and listened. 'What?' she said groggily.

'Mum-mee?' Livia called again.

Katrine sat up. Unlike Joakim, she could go from deep sleep to wide awake in a couple of seconds.

'I've already tried,' said Joakim quietly. 'I thought she'd gone back to sleep, but—'

'I'll go.'

Katrine got out of bed without hesitating, slid her feet into her slippers and quickly pulled on her dressing gown.

'Mum-mee?'

'I'm coming, brat,' she muttered.

This wasn't good, thought Joakim. It wasn't good that Livia wanted to sleep with her mother beside her every night. But it was a habit that had started the previous year, when Livia had begun to have disturbed nights – perhaps because of Ethel. She found it difficult to fall asleep, and only slept calmly with Katrine lying beside her in her bed. So far they hadn't managed to get Livia to spend a whole night on her own.

'See you, lover boy,' said Katrine, slipping out of the room.

The duties of a parent. Joakim lay there in bed; there was no longer a sound from Livia's room. Katrine had taken over the responsibility, and he relaxed and closed his eyes. Slowly he felt sleep stealing over him once more.

All was silent in the manor house.

His life in the country had begun.

2

The ship inside the bottle was a little work of art, in Henrik's opinion: a three-masted frigate with sails made out of scraps of white fabric, almost six inches long and carved from a single piece of wood. Each sail had ropes made of black thread, knotted and secured to small blocks of balsa wood. With the masts down the ship had been carefully inserted into the old bottle using steel thread and tweezers, then pressed down into a sea of blue-coloured putty. Then the masts had been raised and the sails unfurled with the help of bent sock needles. Finally the bottle had been fastened with a sealed cork.

The ship in the bottle must have taken several weeks to make, but the Serelius brothers destroyed it in a couple of seconds.

Tommy Serelius swept the bottle off the bookshelf, the glass exploding into tiny shards on the new parquet flooring of the cottage. The ship itself survived the fall, but bounced across the floor for a couple of yards before it was stopped by little brother Freddy's boot. He shone his torch on it with curiosity for a few seconds, then lifted his foot and smashed the ship to pieces with three hard stamps.

'Teamwork!' crowed Freddy.

'I hate things like that, fucking handicraft stuff,' said Tommy, scratching his cheek and kicking the remains of the ship across the floor.

Henrik, the third man in the cottage, emerged from one of the bedrooms where he had been searching for anything of value in the wardrobes. He saw what was left of the ship and shook his head. 'Don't smash anything else up, OK?' he said quietly.

Tommy and Freddy liked the sound of breaking glass, of splintering wood – Henrik had realized that the first night they worked together, when they broke into half a dozen closed-up cottages south of Byxelkrok. The brothers liked smashing things; on the way north Tommy had run over a black and white cat that was standing by the side of the road, its eyes glittering. There was a dull thud from the right-hand tyre as the van drove over the cat, and the next second the brothers were laughing out loud.

Henrik never broke anything; he removed the windows carefully so they could get into the cottages. But once the brothers had clambered in they turned into vandals. They upended cocktail cabinets and hurled glass and china to the floor. They also smashed mirrors, but hand-blown vases from Småland survived, because they could be sold.

At least they weren't targeting the residents of the island. From the start Henrik had decided to select only houses owned by those who lived on the mainland.

Henrik wasn't keen on the Serelius brothers, but he was stuck with them – like a couple of relatives who come to call one evening and then refuse to leave.

But Tommy and Freddy weren't from the island, and were neither his friends nor his relatives. They were friends of Morgan Berglund.

33

They had rung the doorbell of Henrik's little apartment in Borgholm at the end of September, at around ten o'clock when he was just thinking of going to bed. He had opened the door to find two men of about his own age standing outside, broad-shouldered and with more or less shaven heads. They had nodded and walked into the hallway without asking permission. They stank of sweat and oil and dirty car seats, and the stench spread through the apartment.

'Hubba bubba, Henke,' said one of them. He was wearing big sunglasses. It should have looked comical, but this was not a person to be laughed at. He had long red marks on his cheeks and chin, as if someone had scratched him. 'How's it going?'

'OK, I suppose,' said Henrik slowly. 'Who are you?'

'Tommy and Freddy. The Serelius brothers. Hell, you must have heard of us, Henrik . . . you must know who we are?'

Tommy adjusted his glasses and scratched his cheek with long, raking strokes. Henrik realized where the marks on his face had come from – he hadn't been in a fight, he had caused them himself.

Then the brothers had taken a quick tour of his one-bedroom flat and slumped down on the sofa in front of the TV.

'Got any crisps?' said Freddy.

He rested his boots on Henrik's glass table. When he unbuttoned his padded jacket his beer belly protruded in a pale blue T-shirt with the slogan SOLDIER OF FORTUNE FOREVER.

'Your pal Mogge says hi,' said big brother Tommy, removing the sunglasses. He was slightly slimmer than Freddy and was staring at Henrik with a little smile playing at the corners of his mouth, a black leather bag in his hand. 'It was Mogge who thought we should come here.'

'To Siberia,' said Freddy, pulling the bowl of crisps Henrik had provided towards him.

'Mogge? Morgan Berglund?'

'Sure thing,' said Tommy, sitting down on the sofa next to his brother. 'You're pals, right?'

'We *were*,' said Henrik. 'Mogge's moved away.'

'We know, he's in Denmark. He was working in a casino in Copenhagen, illegally.'

'Dirty dealing,' said Freddy.

'We've been in Europe,' said Tommy. 'For almost a year. Makes you realize how fucking small Sweden is.'

'Fucking backwater,' said Freddy.

'First of all we were in Germany, Hamburg and Düsseldorf, that was fucking brilliant. Then we went to Copenhagen, and that was pretty cool too.' Tommy looked around again. 'And now we're here.'

He nodded and put a cigarette in the corner of his mouth.

'Don't smoke in here,' said Henrik.

He had been wondering why the Serelius brothers had left the big cities of Europe – if things had indeed been going so bloody well down there – and travelled up to the isolation of small-town Sweden. Had they quarrelled with the wrong people? Probably.

'You can't stay here,' said Henrik, looking around his flat. 'I haven't got room. You can see that.'

Tommy had put the cigarette away. He didn't appear to be listening. 'We're Satanists,' he said. 'Did we mention that?'

'Satanists?' said Henrik.

Tommy and Freddy nodded.

'You mean devil-worshippers?' said Henrik with a smile.

Tommy wasn't smiling. 'We don't worship anyone,' he said. 'Satan stands for the strength within human beings, that's what we believe in.'

35

'*The force*,' said Freddy, finishing off the crisps.

'Exactly,' said Tommy. '*Might makes right* – that's our motto. We take what we want. Have you heard of Aleister Crowley?'

'No.'

'A great philosopher,' said Tommy. 'Crowley saw life as a constant battle between the strong and the weak. Between the clever and the stupid. Where the strongest and cleverest always win.'

'Well, that's logical,' said Henrik, who had never been religious. He had no intention of becoming religious now, either.

Tommy carried on looking around the apartment. 'When did she cut and run?' he asked.

'Who?'

'Your girl. The one who put up curtains and dried flowers and all that crap. You didn't do it, did you?'

'She moved out last spring,' said Henrik.

A memory of Camilla sprang unbidden into his mind, lying reading on the sofa where the Serelius brothers were now sitting. He realized that Tommy was a bit smarter than he looked – he noticed details.

'What was her name?'

'Camilla.'

'Do you miss her?'

'Like dog shit,' he said quickly. 'Anyway, like I said, you can't stay—'

'Chill out, we're staying in Kalmar,' said Tommy. 'That's all sorted, but we're thinking of working here on Öland. So we need a bit of help.'

'With what?'

'Mogge told us what you and he used to do in the winter. He told us about the summer cottages . . .'

'I see.'

'He said you'd be happy to start up again.'

36

Thanks for that, Mogge, thought Henrik. They had quarrelled about the division of the money before Morgan left – perhaps this was his revenge.

'That was a long time ago,' he said. 'Four years . . . and we only did it for two winters, really.'

'And? Mogge said it went well.'

'It went OK,' said Henrik.

Virtually all the break-ins had been problem-free, but a couple of times he and Mogge had been spotted by the people next door and had to make their escape over stone walls, like kids stealing apples. They had always worked out at least two escape routes in advance, one on foot and one in the car.

He went on, 'Sometimes there wasn't anything of value . . . but once we found a cupboard, it was really old. A seventeenth-century German cabinet, we got thirty-five thousand kronor for that in Kalmar.'

Henrik had become more animated as he was talking, almost nostalgic. He had actually had quite a talent for getting in through locked veranda doors and windows without smashing them. His grandfather had been a carpenter in Marnäs, and had been equally proud of his own expertise.

But he also remembered how stressful it had been, driving around northern Öland night after night. It was bitterly cold up there in the winter, both in the wind outdoors and inside the closed-up houses. And the holiday villages were empty and silent.

'Old houses are real treasure troves,' said Tommy. 'So you're in? We need you to find our way round up there.'

Henrik didn't say anything. He was thinking that a person who has a miserable, predictable life must be miserable and predictable themselves. He didn't want to be like that.

'So we're agreed, then,' said Tommy. 'OK?'

'Maybe,' said Henrik.

'That sounds like a yes.'

'Maybe.'

'Hubba bubba,' said Tommy.

Henrik nodded hesitantly.

He wanted to be exciting, to have an exciting life. Now Camilla had moved out the evenings were miserable and the nights were empty, but still he hesitated. It wasn't the risk of being caught that had made Henrik give up the break-ins before, it was a different kind of fear. 'It's dark out in the country,' he said.

'Sounds good,' said Tommy.

'It's *bloody* dark,' said Henrik. 'There are no street lights in the villages, and the power in the cottages is usually switched off. You can hardly see a thing.'

'No problem,' said Tommy. 'We pocketed some torches at a petrol station yesterday.'

Henrik nodded slowly. Torches got rid of the darkness, of course, but only to a certain extent. 'I've got a boathouse we can use,' he said. 'For storage, until we find the right buyer.'

'Great,' said Tommy. 'Then all we have to do is find the right houses. Mogge said you know some good places.'

'Some,' said Henrik. 'It goes with the job.'

'Give us the addresses, then we can check if they're safe.'

'What are you talking about?'

'We'll ask Aleister.'

'What?'

'We usually chat with Aleister Crowley,' said Tommy, placing his bag on the table. He opened it and took out a narrow, flat box, made of dark wood. 'We contact him using this.'

Henrik looked on in silence as Tommy unfolded the

box and placed it on the table. Letters, words and numbers were seared into the wood on the inside of the box. The entire alphabet was there, plus numbers from zero to ten and the words YES and NO. Then Tommy took a small glass out of his bag.

'I tried this out when I was a kid,' said Henrik. 'The spirit in the glass, isn't it?'

'Like fuck it is, this is serious.' Tommy placed the glass on the unfolded box. 'This is a ouija board.'

'A ouija board?'

'That's what it's called,' said Tommy. 'The wood is from the lid of an old coffin. Can you turn the lights down a little?'

Henrik smiled to himself, but went over to the light switch anyway.

All three sat around the table. Tommy placed his little finger on the glass and closed his eyes. The room fell silent. He scratched his throat slowly and seemed to be listening for something. 'Who's there?' he asked. 'Is Aleister there?'

Nothing happened for a few seconds. Then the glass began to move beneath Tommy's finger.

Henrik had gone out to his grandfather's boathouse the very next evening, at twilight, to get it ready.

The little wooden hut was painted red and stood in a meadow a dozen or so yards from the shore, close to two other small cottages owned by summer visitors; no one came near them after the middle of August. You could be left in peace here.

He had inherited the boathouse from his grandfather, Algot. When he was alive they would both go out to sea several times every summer to put out nets, then spend the night in the boathouse and get up at five to check them.

Out here on the Baltic shore he missed those days, and thought it was sad that his grandfather was no longer around. Algot had carried on with his carpentry and little bits of building after his retirement, and had seemed perfectly content with his life right up until the last heart attack, despite the fact that he had left the island only a few times.

Henrik undid the padlock and peered into the darkness inside. Everything looked more or less as it had done when his grandfather passed away six years earlier. Nets hung along the walls, the workbench was still standing on the floor and the iron stove was rusting away in one corner. Camilla had wanted to clear everything out and paint the inside walls white, but Henrik thought it was fine just the way it was.

He cleared away oil cans, toolboxes and other things that were on the wooden floor and spread out a tarpaulin ready for the stolen goods. Then he went out on to the jetty on the point and breathed in the smell of seaweed and brackish salt water. To the north he could see the twin lighthouses at Eel Point rising up out at sea.

Down below the jetty was his motor boat, an open launch, and when he looked into it he could see that the floor was covered in rain water. He climbed down into the boat and began baling out.

As he was working he thought back over what had happened the previous evening, when he and the Serelius brothers had sat down in the kitchen and held a séance. Or whatever it might have been.

The glass had moved constantly across the board, providing answers to every question – but of course it was Tommy himself who had been moving it. He had closed his eyes, but he must have been peeping to make sure the glass ended up in the right place.

At any rate, it had turned out that the spirit of Aleister

wholeheartedly supported their plans to break into summer cottages. When Tommy asked about the village of Stenvik, which Henrik had suggested, the glass had moved to YES, and when he asked if there were valuable things in the cottages up there he had been given the same answer: YES.

Finally Tommy had asked, 'Aleister, what do you think . . . can the three of us trust each other?'

The little glass had remained still for a few seconds. Then it had slowly moved to NO.

Tommy gave a brief, hoarse laugh. 'That's OK,' he said, looking at Henrik. 'I don't trust anybody.'

Four days later, Henrik and the Serelius brothers had made their first trip north, to the cluster of summer cottages which Henrik had selected and Aleister had approved. There were only closed-up houses there, pitch black in the darkness.

Henrik and the brothers weren't looking for small, expensive objects when they broke open a window and got into a cottage – they knew no summer visitors were stupid enough to leave cash, designer watches or gold necklaces behind in their cottages over the winter. But certain things were too difficult to transport home from the country when the holiday was over: televisions, music systems, bottles of spirits, boxes of cigarettes and golf clubs. And in the outhouses there could be chain-saws, cans of petrol and electric drills.

After Tommy and Freddy had smashed the ship in the bottle and Henrik had finished muttering about it, they split up and carried on searching for treasures.

Henrik carried on into the smaller rooms. The front of the house faced the rocky coastline and the sound, and through a picture window he could see the chalk-white half-moon suspended above the water. Stenvik was one of the small, empty fishing villages on the west coast of the island.

Every room he went into met him with silence, but Henrik still had the feeling that the walls and the floor were watching him. For that reason he moved carefully, without making any mess.

'Hello? Henke?'

It was Tommy, and Henrik called back, 'Where are you?'

'Here, just off the kitchen . . . it's some kind of office.'

Henrik followed Tommy's voice through the narrow kitchen. He was standing by the wall in a windowless room, pointing with his gloved right hand.

'What do you think about this?'

He wasn't smiling – Tommy hardly ever smiled – but he was looking up at the wall with the expression of someone who might have made a real find. A large wall clock was hanging there, made of dark wood, with Roman numerals behind the glass covering the clock face.

Henrik nodded. 'Yes . . . could be worth something. Is it old?'

'I think so,' said Tommy, opening the glass door. 'If we're lucky it'll be an antique. German or French.'

'It's not ticking.'

'Probably needs winding up.' He closed the door and shouted, 'Freddy!'

After a few seconds the younger brother came clomping into the kitchen. 'What?'

'Give me a hand with this,' said Tommy.

Freddy had the longest arms of the three of them. He unhooked the clock and lifted it down. Then Henrik helped to carry it.

'Come on, let's get it outside,' said Tommy.

The van was parked close to the house, in the

shadows at the back. It had KALMAR PIPES & WELDING on the sides. Tommy had bought plastic letters and stuck them on himself. There was no such welding company in Kalmar, but driving around in a company van at night looked less suspicious than in some anonymous old delivery van.

'They're opening a police station in Marnäs next week,' said Henrik as they were lifting the clock out through the veranda window. There was almost no wind tonight, but the air was fresh and cold.

'How do you know?' said Tommy.

'It was in the paper this morning.'

He heard Freddy's hoarse laugh in the darkness.

'Oh, well, that's it then,' said Tommy. 'You might as well ring them and shop the two of us, then you might get a reduced sentence.'

He dropped his lower lip, showing his teeth; that was his way of smiling.

Henrik smiled back in the darkness. There were thousands of summer cottages all over the island for the police to keep an eye on, besides which they usually worked only during the day.

They placed the clock in the back of the van, along-side a collapsible exercise bike, two large vases made of polished limestone, a video player, a small outboard motor, a computer, printer and television with stereo speakers that were already in there.

'Shall we call it a night?' said Tommy when he had closed the back door of the van.

'Yes. I don't think there's anything else.'

Henrik went back to the house briefly anyway, to close the window. He picked up a couple of small pieces of shale from the ground and pushed them into the gaps in the wooden frame to hold the window in place.

'Come on,' shouted Tommy behind him.

The brothers thought it was a waste of time, closing the place up after a break-in. But Henrik knew it could be months before anyone came to the cottage, and with the window open the rain and snow would destroy the décor.

Tommy started the engine as Henrik climbed into the passenger seat. Then he lifted off a section of the door panel and reached inside. Wrapped in small pieces of kitchen paper was ice – crystal meth.

'Want another?' said Tommy.

'No. I've had enough.'

The brothers had brought the ice with them from the continent, both to sell and for personal use. The crystals were like a kick up the backside, but if Henrik took more than one hit per night he started quivering like a flagpole, and found it difficult to think logically. The thoughts thudded around in his head, and he couldn't get to sleep.

He wasn't a junkie, after all – but nor was he boring. One hit was fine.

Tommy and Freddy didn't seem to have the same problem, or else they were planning to stay awake all night when they got back to Kalmar. They stuffed the crystals in their mouths, paper and all, and washed the whole lot down with water from a plastic bottle on the back seat. Then Tommy put his foot down. He swung round the house and out on to the empty village road.

Henrik looked at his watch – it was almost twelve thirty. 'OK, let's go to the boathouse,' he said.

Up by the main road Tommy pulled up obediently at the Stop sign, despite the fact that the road was completely clear, then turned south.

'Turn off here,' said Henrik after ten minutes, when the sign for Enslunda appeared.

44

There was no sign of any other cars or people. The gravel track ended at the boathouses, and Tommy backed the van up as close as possible. It was as dark as a cave down here by the sea, but up in the north the lighthouse at Eel Point was flashing.

Henrik opened the van door and heard the rushing of the waves. The sound drifted in from the coal-black sea. It made him think of his grandfather. He had actually died here, six years ago. Algot had been eighty-five years old and suffering from heart disease, but he had still crawled out of bed and taken a taxi out here one windy winter's day. The driver had dropped him off on the road, and soon after that he must have had a major heart attack. But Algot had managed to get to his boathouse, and he had been found dead just by the door.

'I've got an idea,' said Tommy as they were unloading the stolen goods by the beam of the torches. 'A suggestion. Listen up and tell me what you think.'

'What?'

Tommy didn't reply. He just reached into the van and pulled something out. It looked like a large black woollen cap. 'We found this in Copenhagen,' he said. Then he held the black fabric up to the torch, and Henrik could see that it wasn't a cap. It was the kind of hood robbers wear, a balaclava, with holes for the eyes and the mouth. 'My suggestion is that we put these on next time,' said Tommy, 'and move on from the summer cottages.'

'Move on? Move on to what?'

'Houses that aren't empty.'

There was silence for a few moments in the shadows by the shore.

'Great idea,' said Freddy.

Henrik looked at the hood without saying anything. He was thinking.

45

'I know . . . the risks increase,' said Tommy. 'But so do the gains. We'll never find cash or jewellery in the summer cottages . . . only in houses where people live all year round.' He dropped the hood back in the van and went on, 'Of course, we need to check with Aleister that everything's OK. And we need to choose safe houses that are a bit out of the way, with no alarms.'

'And no dogs,' said Freddy.

'Correct. No bloody dogs either. And nobody will recognize us with the hoods on,' said Tommy, looking at Henrik. 'So what do you think, then?'

'I don't know.'

It wasn't really about the money – Henrik had a good trade these days – it was mostly the excitement he was after. It chased away the tedium of everyday life.

'Freddy and I will go solo, then,' said Tommy. 'It'll bring in more money, so that's no problem.'

Henrik shook his head quickly. There might not be many more outings with Tommy and Freddy, but he wanted to decide for himself when to stop.

He thought about the ship in the bottle, smashed to pieces on the floor earlier that evening, and said, 'I'm in . . . if we take it easy. And nobody gets hurt.'

'Who would we hurt?' said Tommy.

'The house owners.'

'They'll be asleep, for fuck's sake. And if anybody wakes up we'll just speak English. Then they'll think we're foreigners.'

Henrik nodded, not completely convinced. He pulled the tarpaulin over the stolen items and fastened the padlock on the boathouse door.

They jumped into the van and set off south across the island, back towards Borgholm.

After twenty minutes they were in town, where rows of street lamps drove away the October darkness. But the pavements were just as empty as the country roads. Tommy slowed down and pulled in by the apartment block where Henrik lived. 'Good,' he said. 'In a week, then? Tuesday night next week?'

'Sure . . . but I'll probably go out there before then.'

'You like living out here in the middle of nowhere?'

Henrik nodded.

'OK,' said Tommy, 'but don't start trying to do any deals of your own with the stuff. We'll find a buyer in Kalmar.'

'Fine,' said Henrik, closing the door of the van.

He walked towards the dark doorway and looked at his watch. Half past one. It was pretty early despite everything, and he would be able to sleep in his lonely bed for five hours before the alarm woke him for his ordinary job.

He thought about all the houses on the island where people lay sleeping. Settled.

He'd get out if anything happened. If anyone woke up when they broke in, he'd just get out of there. The brothers and their fucking spirit in the glass could fend for themselves.

3

Tilda Davidsson was sitting with her bag containing the tape recorder in a corridor at the residential home for the elderly in Marnäs, outside the room of her relative Gerlof Davidsson. She wasn't alone; on a sofa further down the corridor two small white-haired ladies had sat down, perhaps waiting for afternoon coffee.

The women were talking non-stop, and Tilda found herself listening to their quiet conversation. It was conducted in a discontented, troubled tone, like a long series of drawn-out sighs.

'They're always on the move, flying all over the place,' said the woman closest to Tilda. 'One trip abroad after another. The further away the better.'

'You're absolutely right, they certainly don't begrudge themselves anything these days,' said the other woman, 'indeed they don't . . .'

'And the money they spend . . . when they're buying things for themselves,' said the first one. 'I rang my youngest daughter last week and she told me she and her husband were buying another new car. "But you've got a lovely car," I said. "Yes, but everybody else in our street has changed their car this year," she said.'

'That's all they do, buy, buy, buy, all the time.'

48

'That's right. And they don't keep in touch, either.'

'No, they don't . . . My son *never* rings, not even on my birthday. It's always me who rings him, and then he never has time to chat. He's always on his way somewhere, or there's something he wants to watch on TV.'

'And that's another thing – they're always buying television sets, and they have to be the size of a house these days . . .'

'And new fridges.'

'And cookers.'

Tilda didn't get to hear any more, because the door to Gerlof's room opened.

Gerlof's long back was slightly bent and his legs were shaking just a little – but he was smiling at Tilda like an old man without a care in the world, and she thought he looked more alert today than when she had seen him the previous winter.

Gerlof, who was born in 1915, had celebrated his eightieth birthday in the summer cottage down in Stenvik. Both his daughters had been there, his eldest daughter Lena with her husband and children, and her younger sister Julia with her new husband and his three children. That day Gerlof's rheumatism had meant that he had to sit in the same armchair all afternoon. But now he was standing in the doorway leaning on his stick, wearing a waistcoat and dark-grey gabardine trousers.

'OK, the weather forecast has finished,' he said quietly.

'Great.'

Tilda got up. She had had to wait before going into Gerlof's room, because he had to listen to the weather forecast. Tilda didn't really understand why it was so important – he was hardly likely to be going out in this cold – but presumably keeping an eye on the wind and the weather was a routine left over from his days as captain of a cargo ship on the Baltic.

'Come in, come in.'

He shook hands with her just inside the door – Gerlof wasn't the kind of person who hugged people. Tilda had never even seen him pat anyone on the shoulder.

His hand was firm as it grasped hers. Gerlof had gone to sea as a teenager, and despite the fact that he had come ashore twenty-five years ago, the calluses were still there from all the ropes he'd hauled, all the boxes of cargo he'd lifted and the chains that had torn the skin from his fingers.

'So what's the weather got in store, then?' she asked.

'Don't ask.' Gerlof sighed and sat down on one of the chairs by his small coffee table, his legs stiff. 'The radio station has changed the time when the forecast starts yet again, so I missed the local temperatures. But in Norrland it's going to get colder, so I should imagine it will down here too.' He cast a suspicious glance at the barometer next to the bookcase, then looked out of the window towards the bare trees and added, 'It's going to be a hard winter this year, a cold, early winter. You can see that by the way the stars shine so brightly at night, especially the Plough. And by the summer.'

'The summer?'

'A wet summer means a hard winter,' said Gerlof. 'Everybody knows that.'

'I didn't,' said Tilda. 'But will it make any difference to us?'

'It certainly will. A long, hard winter influences just about everything. The shipping on the Baltic, for example. The ice delays the ships and the profits fall.'

Tilda moved into the room and was confronted by all the memories of Gerlof's time at sea. On the walls were black and white pictures of his ships, oiled nameplates and framed ship's certificates. There were also small photographs of his late parents and his wife.

Time stood still in here, thought Tilda.

She sat down opposite Gerlof and placed the tape recorder on the table between them. Then she plugged in the flat table microphone.

Gerlof gave the recording equipment the same look as the barometer. The tape recorder wasn't very big, but Tilda could see his eyes flicking back and forth between it and her.

'Are we just going to . . . talk?' he said. 'About my brother?'

'Among other things,' said Tilda. 'That's pretty straightforward, isn't it?'

'But *why*?'

'Well, to preserve the memories and stories . . . before they disappear,' said Tilda, and added quickly, 'Of course, you're going to be around for years yet, Gerlof, that's not what I mean. I just want to record them to be on the safe side. My dad didn't tell me much about Grandfather before he died, you know.'

Gerlof nodded. 'We can talk. But when something's being recorded you have to be careful what you say.'

'There's no problem,' said Tilda. 'You can always record over a cassette tape.'

Gerlof had agreed to the recording almost without thinking when she had called him in August and said she was moving to Marnäs, but it still seemed to be making him a bit tense. 'Is it on?' he said quietly. 'Is the tape running?'

'No, not yet,' said Tilda. 'I'll tell you when.'

She pressed down the Record button, saw that the tape was running and nodded encouragingly at Gerlof. 'Right . . . we've started.' Tilda straightened up and it seemed to her that her voice was more tense and formal than usual as she went on: 'This is Tilda Davidsson and I am in Marnäs with my grandfather Ragnar's brother Gerlof, to talk about our family . . . and about my grandfather here in Marnäs.'

Gerlof leaned forward a little stiffly towards the microphone and corrected her in a clear voice. 'My brother Ragnar did not live in Marnäs. He lived on the coast outside Rörby, south of Marnäs.'

'Thank you, Gerlof . . . and what are your memories of Ragnar?'

Gerlof hesitated for a few seconds.

'There are a lot of good memories,' he said eventually. 'We grew up together in Stenvik in the twenties, but then of course we chose completely different professions . . . he bought a little cottage and became a farmer and a fisherman, and I moved down to Borgholm and got married. And bought my first cargo ship.'

'How often did you see each other?'

'Well, whenever I was home from sea, a couple of times a year. Around Christmas and some time in the summer. Ragnar usually came down to us in town.'

'Were there celebrations then?'

'Yes, especially at Christmas.'

'What was it like?'

'Crowded, but good fun. Lots of food. Herring and potatoes and ham and pigs' trotters and dumplings. And of course Ragnar always brought plenty of eel with him, both smoked and pickled, and lots of cod soaked in lye . . .'

The more Gerlof talked, the more he relaxed. And so did Tilda.

They carried on talking for another half-hour or so. But after a long story about a windmill fire in Stenvik,

Gerlof raised a hand and waved feebly. Tilda realized he was tired, and quickly switched off the tape recorder.

'Fantastic,' she said. 'It's amazing how much you remember, Gerlof.'

'The old family stories are still in my head, I've heard them so many times. Telling stories like this is good for the memory.' He looked at the tape recorder. 'Do you think it got anything?'

'Of course.'

She rewound the tape and pressed Play. Gerlof's recorded voice was quiet and slightly grumpy and repetitive, but it could be heard clearly.

'Good,' he said. 'That'll be something for those researchers into ordinary people's lives to listen to.'

'It's mostly for me,' said Tilda. 'I wasn't even born when Grandfather died, and Dad was no good at telling stories about the family. So I'm curious.'

'That comes with the years, as you acquire more and more of a past to look back on,' said Gerlof. 'You start to get interested in where you came from, I've noticed that with my daughters too . . . How old are you now?'

'Twenty-seven.'

'And you're going to be working here on Öland?'

'I am. I've finished all my training.'

'How long for?'

'We'll see. Until next summer, at any rate.'

'That's nice. It's always good when young people come here and find work. And you're living here in Marnäs?'

'I've got a one-bedroom place just by the square. You can see south along the coast . . . I can almost see Grandfather's cottage.'

'It's owned by another family now,' said Gerlof, 'but we can go down there and take a look at it. And at my cottage in Stenvik, of course.'

Tilda left the Marnäs home just after half past four, with the tape recorder in her rucksack.

When she had fastened her jacket and set off on the road towards the small centre of Marnäs, a young lad drove past her on a pale-blue puttering moped heading in the opposite direction. She shook her head at him to show what she thought of mopeds driving fast, but he didn't catch her eye. Twenty seconds later he was gone.

Once upon a time Tilda had thought that fifteen-year-old boys on mopeds were the coolest thing in the world. Nowadays they were more like mosquitoes, she thought – small and irritating.

She adjusted her rucksack and carried on towards Marnäs. She was intending to call in at work for a while, even though she didn't officially start until the following day, and then go back to her little apartment and carry on unpacking. And ring Martin.

The puttering of the moped behind her hadn't completely died out, and now it was getting louder again. The young rider had turned around somewhere over by the church and was on his way back into town.

This time he had to pass Tilda on the pavement. He slowed down slightly, but revved the engine menacingly and tried to swing past her. She looked him in the eye and positioned herself directly in his way. The moped stopped.

'What?' yelled the boy over the noise of the engine.

'You're not allowed to ride a moped on the pavement,' said Tilda just as loudly. 'It's illegal.'

'Yeah, right.' The boy nodded. 'But you can drive faster along here.'

'You can also run someone over.'

'Whatever,' said the boy, giving her a bored look. 'Are you going to call the police?'

Tilda shook her head. 'No, I'm not, because—'

'The police aren't around here any more.' The boy twisted the accelerator on the handle of the moped. 'They shut the police station two years ago. There are no police anywhere in the north of Öland.'

Tilda was tired of trying to shout over the puttering engine. She leaned forward quickly and pulled the cable out of the ignition. The moped immediately fell silent.

'There are now,' she said, quietly and calmly. 'I'm a police officer and I'm here.'

'You?'

'I start today.'

The boy stared at her. Tilda took her wallet out of her jacket pocket, opened it up and showed him her ID. He looked at it for a long time, then he looked back at her with a respectful expression.

People always looked differently at someone when they knew they were a police officer. When Tilda was in uniform, she even looked at herself differently.

'Name?'

'Stefan.'

'Stefan what?'

'Stefan Ekström.'

Tilda got out her notebook and wrote down his name.

'This is just a warning, but next time it'll be a fine,' she said. 'Your moped has been modified. Have you bored out the cylinder?'

Stefan nodded.

'Then you'd better get off and walk home with it,' said Tilda. 'Then you can sort out the engine so that it's legal.'

Stefan climbed off.

They walked in silence side by side towards the square in Marnäs.

'Tell your pals the police are back in Marnäs,' said

Tilda. 'The next modified moped I see will be impounded, and there'll be a fine.'

Stefan nodded again. Now he'd been caught he seemed to regard it as something of a coup.

'You got a gun?' he asked as they arrived in town.

'Yes,' said Tilda. 'Under lock and key.'

'What kind?'

'A SIG-Sauer.'

'Have you shot anybody with it?'

'No,' said Tilda. 'And I'm not intending to use it here.'

Stefan looked disappointed.

She had agreed with Martin that she would call him around six, before he went home from work. Before that she had time to take a look at her future workplace.

The new police station in Marnäs was in a side street a couple of blocks from the square, the police shield above the door still wrapped in white plastic.

Tilda took the station keys out of her pocket. She had collected them the previous day from the police station in Borgholm, but when she got to the front door it was already unlocked. She could hear men's voices inside.

The station consisted of just one room, with no reception area. Tilda vaguely remembered that there used to be a sweet shop here when she visited Marnäs as a child. The walls were bare, there were no curtains, and no rugs on the wooden floor.

Two burly middle-aged men were standing inside, wearing jackets and outdoor shoes. One of them was in the dark-blue police uniform, the other in civilian clothes with a green padded jacket. They fell silent and quickly turned towards Tilda, as if she had interrupted them in the middle of an inappropriate joke.

Tilda had met one of them before, the one in civilian clothes – Inspector Göte Holmblad, who was in charge of the local police. He had short grey hair and a permanent smile playing around the corners of his mouth. He seemed to recognize her.

'Hello there,' he said. 'Welcome to the new district.'

'Thank you.' She shook hands with her boss and turned to the other man, who had thinner black hair, bushy eyebrows, and was in his fifties. 'Tilda Davidsson.'

'Hans Majner.' His handshake was firm, dry and brief. 'I guess the two of us will be working together up here.'

He didn't sound completely convinced that this would work out well, thought Tilda. She opened her mouth to say something in agreement, but Majner carried straight on.

'Of course I won't be around too much to start with. I'll look in now and again, but I'll be working mostly from Borgholm. I'm keeping my desk there.'

He smiled at the local police chief.

'Right,' said Tilda, suddenly realizing that she was going to be more alone as a police officer on northern Öland than she had thought. 'Are you working on a particular project?'

'You could say that,' said Majner, looking out of the window at the street, as if he could see something suspicious out there. 'Drugs, of course. That kind of crap comes on to the island, just like everywhere else.'

'This is your desk, Tilda,' said Holmblad from over by the window. 'We'll be getting computers installed, of course, a fax machine . . . and a police radio unit over here. For the time being you'll just have to manage with the telephone.'

'OK.'

'In any case, you're not going to be sitting around in the office much. Quite the opposite, in fact,' said Holmblad. 'That's the idea of the local policing reforms: you need to be out there, a visible presence on the

57

streets. The focus is traffic offences, criminal damage, petty theft and break-ins. The less complex investigations. And youth crime, of course.'

'Suits me,' said Tilda. 'I stopped a modified moped on the way here.'

'Good, good.' Her boss nodded. 'So you've shown that there's a police presence here again. And next week is the official opening ceremony. The press have been invited. Newspapers, local radio . . . You'll be available then?'

'Of course.'

'Good. And I expect your work here will be . . . well, I know you've just come from Växjö, and here on the island you're bound to be working more independently. For better or worse. More freedom to organize your working day as you wish, but also more responsibility. I mean, it takes half an hour to get here from Borgholm, and the station there isn't manned all the time. So if anything happens it could take a while before you get any help.'

Tilda nodded. 'At the police training academy we often practised situations where back-up was delayed. My tutors were very keen on—'

Majner snorted over by his desk. 'The tutors at the training academy haven't got a clue about the reality of the situation,' he said. 'It's a long time since they were out on the job.'

'They were very competent in Växjö,' said Tilda quickly.

This was like sitting right at the back in the police van as a new recruit – you were expected to keep your mouth shut and let the older ones do the talking. Tilda had hated it.

Holmblad looked at her and said, 'All I'm saying is that it's important for you to bear in mind the long distances here on the island before you go into a problematic situation alone.'

She nodded. 'I hope I'll be able to deal with any problems that arise.'

The police chief opened his mouth again, possibly to continue his lecture – but at that moment the telephone on the wall rang.

'I'll get that,' he said, striding over to the desk. 'It might be from Kalmar.'

He picked up the phone. 'Marnäs police station, Holmblad.' Then he listened. 'Where?' He was silent again. 'Right,' he said eventually. 'We'd better get out there.' He put the phone down. 'That was Borgholm. The emergency number has had a call about an accidental death on northern Öland.'

Majner got up from his empty desk. 'Local?'

'By the lighthouses off Eel Point,' said Holmblad. 'Anyone know where that is?'

'Eel Point is south of here,' said Majner. 'Four or five miles, maybe.'

'OK, we need to take the car,' said the chief of police. 'The ambulance is already on its way. Evidently it's a drowning.'

WINTER 1868

Once the two lighthouses had been built, there was a sense of security around Eel Point, for both ships and people. At least that's what the men who built them believed – they believed that life on the coast was safe and secure for all time. The women knew this was not always the case.

Death was closer in those days, it came into the houses.

In the hayloft of the old barn there is a woman's name, hastily carved into the wall: BELOVED CAROLINA 1868. Carolina has been dead for more than 120 years, but she has whispered to me through the wall about what could happen at Eel Point – in what are sometimes referred to as the good old days.

Mirja Rambe

The manor house is large, so large. Kerstin goes from room to room, searching for Carolina, but there are so many places to look. Too many places on Eel Point, too many rooms in the house.

And the blizzard is on its way, it feels like a weight in the air outside, and Kerstin knows there isn't much time.

The manor house is solidly built and will not suffer in the storm, but the question is how the people will be affected. A blizzard makes everyone gather around the stoves like lost birds, waiting for it to pass.

A difficult summer with a poor harvest on the island has been followed by a harsh winter. It is the first week in February, and so bitterly cold on the coast that no one goes outside unless they have to. But the lighthouse-keepers and the iron-workers still have to do their shifts over in the towers, and today every fit man except Karlsson, the master lighthouse-keeper, is out on the point getting the lighthouses ready for the snowstorm.

The women have remained in the house, but Carolina is nowhere to be found. Kerstin has searched every room on both floors, and has been up among the beams in the attic. She cannot talk to any of the other maids or the wives of the lighthouse-keepers, because they are not aware of Carolina's condition. They may have their suspicions, but they do not know for certain.

Carolina is eighteen, two years younger than Kerstin. They are both housemaids working for Sven Karlsson, the master lighthouse-keeper. Kerstin regards herself as the one who thinks things through and is more careful. Carolina is more lively and more trust-ing – in some ways she is just as adventurous as Kerstin's older sister Fina, who went to America last year – and that means she sometimes has problems. Recently Carolina's troubles have increased, and she has told only Kerstin about them.

If Carolina has left the manor and gone out into the forest or off towards the peat bog, Kerstin will not be able to find her. Carolina knew there was a blizzard on the way – is she still so desperate?

Kerstin goes outside. In the snow-covered inner courtyard the wind comes sweeping down from the sky, whirling between the buildings, unable to make its escape. The blizzard is approaching, this is just a premonition.

She hears a scream which quickly falls silent. That wasn't the wind.

It was a woman screaming.

The wind tears at Kerstin's kerchief and pinafore, making her lean forward. She forces open the door of the barn and steps inside.

The cows moo and move uneasily as she searches among them. Nothing. Then she climbs the steep staircase up to the big hayloft. The air is freezing up here.

Something is moving over by one of the walls, below the big mound of hay. Faint movements in the dust and the shadows.

It is Carolina. She is lying on the hay-covered floor, her legs immobile beneath a dirty blanket. Her breathing is weak and wheezing as Kerstin comes closer, her expression full of shame.

'Kerstin . . . I think it just happened,' she says. 'I think it came out.'

Kerstin walks over to the blanket, full of fore-boding, and kneels down.

'Is there anything there?' whispers Carolina. 'Or is it just blood?'

The blanket over Carolina's knees is sticky and wet. But Kerstin lifts one corner and nods. 'Yes,' she says. 'It's come out.'

'Is it alive?'

'No. It's not . . . complete.'

Kerstin leans over her friend's pale face. 'How are you feeling?'

Carolina's eyes are flickering all over the place. 'It died without being baptized,' she mumbles. 'We have to . . . we have to bury it in consecrated ground so that it won't walk again . . . It will be a lost soul if we don't bury it.'

'We can't,' says Kerstin. 'The blizzard is here. We'll die if we go out on the road.'

'We have to hide it,' whispers Carolina, struggling to breathe. 'They'll think I've been whoring . . . that I tried to get rid of it.'

'It doesn't matter what they think.' Kerstin places her hand on Carolina's burning forehead and says quietly, 'I've had another letter from my sister. She wants me to go to America, to Chicago.'

Carolina doesn't seem to be listening any longer, she is just panting faintly, but Kerstin goes on anyway. 'I'm going to go across the Atlantic to New York, then travel on from there. She's even deposited the money for the ticket in Gothenburg.' She leans closer. 'And you can come with me, Carolina. Would you like to do that?'

Carolina does not reply. She is no longer struggling to breathe. The air is simply seeping out of her, barely audible.

In the end she is lying there motionless in the hay, her eyes wide open. Everything is silent in the barn.

'I'll be back soon,' whispers Kerstin, her voice full of tears.

She pushes the thing lying in the hay into the blanket, then folds it over several times to hide the marks of the blood and the birth fluid. Then she stands up and takes the bundle in her arms.

63

She goes out into the courtyard, where the wind is still increasing in strength, and battles her way back to the main house, pressed against the stone wall of the barn. She goes straight to her little room, packs her few possessions and Carolina's, then puts on layer after layer of clothes, ready for the difficult journey that awaits her when the blizzard has abated.

Then Kerstin walks without hesitation to the large drawing room, where oil lamps and the tiled stove spread warmth and light through the winter darkness. Master lighthouse-keeper Sven Karlsson is sitting in an armchair by the table in the centre of the room, his black uniform straining at the seams over his belly.

As a servant of the Crown Karlsson is one of the privileged members of the parish. He has almost half the rooms in the manor house at his disposal, and has his own pew in the church over in Rörby. Beside him his wife Anna is enthroned on a fine chair. A few maids are hovering in the background, waiting for the blizzard to pass, and in a dark corner sits Old Sara, who came from the poorhouse in Rörby after the master lighthouse-keeper put in the lowest bid at the auction to establish who would take care of her.

'Where have you been?' says Anna when she sees Kerstin.

Her voice is always loud and sharp, but now it is shriller than usual in order to be heard above the howling wind.

Kerstin curtseys, positions herself in silence in front of the table and waits until everyone's eyes are on her. She thinks about her older sister over in America. Then she places the bundle she has brought with her on the table, right in front of Sven Karlsson.

'Good evening, sir,' says Kerstin loudly, unfolding the blanket. 'I have something here . . . something you appear to have lost.'

4

Joakim's third morning in the manor house at Eel Point was his last completely happy start to the day for many years – perhaps ever.

Unfortunately he was too stressed to register how good he felt.

He and Katrine had had a late night. Once the children had gone to sleep they had walked through the south-facing rooms on the ground floor, pondering how each room's different personality could best be brought out with their choice of colours. White would of course be the base colour throughout the whole of the ground floor, both on the walls and ceiling, while the wooden details like cornices and doorframes could vary from room to room.

They had gone to bed at half past eleven. The house had been silent then, but a couple of hours later Livia had started calling out again. Katrine had merely sighed and got out of bed without a word.

The whole family got up just after six. The horizon in the east was still pitch black. The great winter darkness was drawing closer, Joakim realized. Only two months to go until Christmas.

The family gathered at half past six in the kitchen. Joakim wanted to make a quick getaway to Stockholm, and had finished his cup of tea almost before Katrine and the children had sat down. As he placed his cup in the dishwasher he saw an orange strip of light from the sun, which was still hidden by the sea, and higher up in the sky the V-shaped formation of a flock of birds, bobbing slightly as they flew out over the Baltic. Geese or cranes? It was still too dark to see them clearly, and he wasn't very good at identifying birds in flight.

'Can you see those birds out there?' he said over his shoulder. 'They're doing just what we've done . . . moving south.'

Nobody answered. Katrine and Livia were munching their sandwiches, Gabriel was drinking milk from his cup.

The two lighthouses down by the water rose up towards the sky like fairy-tale castles, the south tower regularly flashing its red glow. From the panes of glass at the top of the north tower came a fainter white light that didn't flash. This was slightly odd, because the northern lighthouse hadn't shown a light before. Joakim leaned closer to the window. The white glow might have been a reflection of the sunrise, but it appeared to be coming from inside the tower.

'Are there more birds moving south, Daddy?' said Livia behind him.

'No.'

Joakim stopped looking at the lighthouses. He went back to the breakfast table to clear away.

The migrating birds had a long journey ahead of them, just like Joakim. He would be driving some two hundred and seventy miles today, to pick up the last of their possessions from the house in Bromma. He would stay the night with his mother Ingrid in Jakobsberg, then drive back to Öland the next day.

This was his last trip to the capital, at least for this year.

Gabriel seemed bright and cheerful, but Livia looked as if she was in a bad mood. She had got up with Katrine's help, but was still sleepy and quiet. She was holding her sandwich in one hand, elbows on the table, staring down into her glass of milk.

'Eat up now, Livia.'

'Mmm.'

She certainly wasn't a morning person, but when she got to nursery she usually cheered up. She had changed to an older playgroup the previous week, and seemed happy there.

'So what are you going to do at nursery today?'

'It's not a nursery, Daddy.' She looked up at him with a truculent expression. 'Gabriel goes to nursery. I go to school.'

'Pre-school,' said Joakim. 'Isn't that right?'

'School,' said Livia.

'OK . . . so what are you going to do today?'

'Don't know,' said Livia, staring down at the table again.

'Are you going to play with a new friend?'

'Don't know.'

'OK, but drink up your milk now. We're off into Marnäs soon . . . to school.'

'Mmm.'

By twenty past seven the sun was on its way up over the horizon. Its yellow beams were feeling their way cautiously across the calm sea, without giving any warmth. It would be a sunny but cold day – the thermometer on the wall of the house was showing plus three degrees.

Joakim was out in the courtyard scraping frost from

the windows of the Volvo. Then he opened the back door for the children.

Livia settled herself in her child seat with Foreman in her arms. Joakim fastened Gabriel into the smaller seat beside her. Then he got into the driver's seat. 'Wasn't Mum going to wave us off?' he asked.

'She's gone to the bathroom,' said Livia. 'She's gone to do a big one. She likes to sit there for a while when she does a big one.'

Livia had quickly cheered up after breakfast and become more talkative. Once she got to playgroup she would have tons of energy.

Joakim leaned back in his seat and looked at Livia's little red two-wheeler and Gabriel's three-wheeler, standing out in the courtyard. He noticed the bikes weren't locked. This wasn't the big city.

Katrine came out a couple of minutes later, turned off the light in the hallway and locked the door behind her. She was wearing a bright-red winter jacket with a hood, and jeans. In Stockholm she had usually dressed in black, but here on Öland she had begun to go for roomier and slightly more colourful clothes. She waved to them and gave the red-painted wooden wall next to the door a friendly pat. Lack of sleep had smudged dark shadows beneath her eyes, but she still smiled towards the car.

Their manor house. Joakim waved at Katrine and smiled back.

'OK, let's go,' said Livia from the back seat.

'Go! Go!' yelled Gabriel, waving goodbye to the house.

Joakim started the engine and the headlights came on, illuminating the house. A thin layer of glittering frost covered the ground, an early sign of winter. He would soon have to change over to studded tyres.

Livia quickly pulled on her headphones so that she could listen to the adventures of Bamse the bear – she had been given a tape recorder of her own, and had quickly learned how the buttons worked. When there were songs on the tape she let Gabriel listen too.

The route to the main coast road was a gravel-covered track running between a small, dense deciduous wood and a ditch along the bottom of an old stone wall. The track was narrow and twisting, and Joakim kept his speed down, gripping the wheel firmly. He hadn't got to know all the bends yet.

Out by the main road their new metal mailbox was hanging on a post. Joakim slowed down and looked to see if there was any sign of lights from other cars. But everything was dark and silent in both directions. Just as deserted as the opposite side of the road, where a yellowish-brown bog extended into the distance.

They didn't meet any other cars on their way into Marnäs through the little village of Rörby, and there weren't many people out and about when they drove into town. A fish van drove past them and a couple of schoolchildren aged about ten were running towards the school, their rucksacks bumping on their backs.

Joakim turned on to the main street and headed for the empty square. A few hundred yards further on was Marnäs school, and next door, in an enclosed yard with slides and sandpits and a few trees, was Livia and Gabriel's pre-school. It was a low wooden building with a warm yellow light shining from the big windows.

Several parents were dropping off their children on the pavement in front of the school, and Joakim stopped at the end of the row of vehicles without switching off the engine.

Some of the other parents smiled and nodded at

him – after the previous day's article in *Ölands-Posten* many people in Marnäs now knew who he was.

'Watch out for the cars,' said Joakim. 'Stay on the pavement.'

'Bye!' said Livia, opening the car door and manoeuvring herself out of the child seat. It wasn't a protracted farewell; she was used to him being away.

Gabriel said nothing; when Joakim helped him out of the seat he just charged away.

'Bye then!' Joakim called after them. 'See you tomorrow!'

By the time the doors closed Livia was already several yards away, with Gabriel right behind her. Joakim put the car in gear and swung across the road, back towards Eel Point.

Joakim parked next to Katrine's car in front of the house and got out to pick up his overnight bag and say goodbye.

'Hello?' he called out in the porch. 'Katrine?'

No reply. The house was completely silent.

He went into the bedroom, picked up his case and went outside again. He stopped on the gravel.

'Katrine?'

There was silence for a few moments, then he heard a muted scraping from the inner courtyard.

Joakim turned his head. It was the sound of the big black wooden barn door being opened. Katrine stepped out of the darkness and waved to him.

'Hi there!'

He waved back and she came over.

'What were you doing?' he asked.

'Nothing,' she said. 'Are you leaving now?'

Joakim nodded.

'Drive carefully.'

Katrine leaned over and quickly pressed her mouth against his – a warm kiss in the cold. He breathed in the scent of her skin and her hair for one last time.

'Say hello to Stockholm from me,' she said, giving him a long look. 'When you get home I'll tell you about the loft.'

'The loft?' said Joakim.

'The hayloft in the barn,' said Katrine.

'What about it?'

'I'll show you tomorrow,' she said.

He looked at her. 'OK . . . I'll call you from Mum's tonight.' He opened the car door. 'Don't forget to pick up our little lambs.'

At twenty past eight he pulled into the petrol station by the turning for Borgholm to pick up the rented trailer. It was already booked and paid for, so all he had to do was hook it up and set off.

The traffic was heavier after Borgholm and Joakim ended up in the middle of a long line of cars – most were presumably commuters who lived on the island but worked in Kalmar, on the mainland. They maintained a leisurely country speed.

The road curved to the west and when the ground disappeared beneath it he was up on the bridge. He liked driving across it, over the span between island and mainland, high above the water in the sound. This morning it was difficult to see the surface of the water down below; it was still too dark. By the time he came off the bridge and joined the coast road towards Stockholm, the sun was rising higher above the Baltic. Joakim could feel its warmth through the side window.

He switched on a radio station playing rock music, put his foot down and headed north at speed, past the small communities along the coast. It was a winding road, beautiful even on a cold, overcast day. It passed through dense pine forests and airy groves of deciduous trees by the water, past inlets and streams that headed out to sea and disappeared.

The road continued to curve gradually westwards, and left the coast to head in towards Norrköping. Just outside the town Joakim stopped for a couple of sandwiches in an empty hotel restaurant. He had a choice of seven different bottled mineral waters in the chilled counter – Swedish, Norwegian, Italian and French; he realized he was back in civilization, but chose tap water.

After he'd eaten he carried on, first towards Södertälje and then into Stockholm. He reached the tall apartment blocks in the south-west suburbs of the city at around half past one, and his Volvo and trailer became just one of a multitude of vehicles, large and small, heading for the city centre in lane upon lane of traffic, past long rows of storage depots, apartment blocks and stations used by the commuter trains.

Stockholm looked beautiful from a distance, a big city on the Baltic, built on a series of large and small islands, but Joakim felt no real pleasure at being back in the city of his childhood. All he could think of were the crowds and the queues and the struggle to get in first. There was a constant lack of space here; too few places to live, not enough parking, inadequate daycare provision – even a shortage of burial plots. Joakim had read in the paper that people were being encouraged to cremate their dead nowadays, so that they would take up less space in the churchyard.

He was already missing Eel Point.

The busy road split repeatedly into a boundless labyrinth of bridges and junctions. Joakim chose one of the exits, turned off and entered the network of the city, with its traffic lights and noise and dug-up streets. At one junction he sat trapped between a bus and a dustbin lorry and watched a woman pushing a child in a buggy across the street. The child was asking something, but the woman was just staring straight ahead with a sullen expression.

Joakim had a couple of things to do in the capital. The first was to call in at a small gallery in Östermalm to pick up a landscape painting, an inheritance he didn't really want to be responsible for.

The owner wasn't in, but his elderly mother was there and recognized Joakim. When he had given her his receipt she went off to unlock a security door and bring out the Rambe painting. It was in a flat wooden box, fastened with screws.

'We looked at it yesterday before we packed it,' said the woman. 'Incomparable.'

'Yes, we've missed it,' said Joakim, although that wasn't strictly true.

'Are there any of the others left on Öland?'

'I don't know. The royal family has one, I think, but it's hardly likely to be hanging in some drawing room at Solliden.'

With the painting safe in the boot Joakim drove west towards Bromma. It was half past two and the rush-hour traffic hadn't yet begun to snarl up. It took him just about quarter of an hour to get out of the city and turn off towards the area where the Apple House lay.

The sight of his old home awoke a greater sense of nostalgia within him than Stockholm had done. The house was only a few hundred yards from the water, in a big garden surrounded by a fence and thick lilac hedges. There were five other big houses on the same street, but only one of them was visible through the trees.

The Apple House was a tall, airy wooden house that had been built for the director of a bank at the beginning of the twentieth century. But before Joakim and Katrine bought the house it had been lived in for many years by a collective of New Age individuals, young relatives of the owner who had allowed people to rent rooms and had clearly been more interested in meditating than in decorating or general maintenance.

No one in the collective had shown any kind of staying power or respect for the house, and the neighbours had fought for many years to get rid of them. When Joakim and Katrine finally took it on, the house was dilapidated and the garden almost completely overgrown – but they had both tackled the renovation of the Apple House with the same energy as they had devoted to their first shared apartment on Rörstrandsgatan, where a crazy eighty-two-year-old had lived with her seven cats.

Joakim had been working as a craft teacher and had devoted himself to the house in the evenings and at weekends; Katrine had still been working part-time as an art teacher, and had spent the rest of the time on the house.

They had celebrated Livia's second birthday along with Ethel and Ingrid in a chaotic mess of ripped-up floorboards, tins of paint, rolls of wallpaper and various power tools – with only cold water because the hot-water system had broken down that same weekend.

By the time Livia turned three, however, they had been able to have a proper old-fashioned children's party on newly stripped wooden floors, with walls that had been smoothed down and papered, and staircases and banisters that had been repaired and oiled. And when Gabriel celebrated his first birthday, the house had been more or less finished.

These days the place looked like a turn-of-the-century house again, and could be handed over in good order, apart from the leaves in the garden and the lawn that needed mowing. It was waiting for its new owners, the Stenbergs – a couple in their thirties with no children, who both worked in the city centre but wanted to live on the outskirts.

Joakim pulled up on the gravel drive and reversed so that the trailer ended up by the garage. Then he got out and took a look around.

Everything was quiet. The only neighbours whose house was in sight were the Hesslins, Lisa and Michael, and they had become good friends with Katrine and Joakim – but there were no cars on their drive this afternoon. They had repainted their house last summer, this time in yellow. When *Beautiful Homes* had done a feature about it two years ago, it had been white.

Joakim turned to look over at the wooden gate and the gravel path leading to the Apple House. His thoughts turned involuntarily to Ethel. Almost a year had passed, but he could still remember her calling out.

Beside the fence a narrow track led through a grove of trees. No one had seen Ethel walking down the track that evening, but it was the shortest route down to the water.

He started to walk up to the house, and looked up at the white facade. The lustre was still there, and he remembered all those long brushstrokes when he had gone over it with linseed oil two summers ago.

He unlocked the door, opened up and walked in. When he had closed the door behind him, he stopped again. He had cleaned up over the last few weeks ready for the move, and the floors still looked free of dust. All the furniture, rugs and pictures from the hallway and the rooms were gone – but the memories remained.

There were so many of them. For more than three years he and Katrine had put their souls into this house.

You could have heard a pin drop in the rooms around Joakim, but inside his head he could hear all the hammering and sawing. He took off his shoes and moved into the hallway, where a faint smell of cleaning fluid still hung in the air.

He wandered through the rooms, perhaps for the very last time. Upstairs he stopped in the doorway of one of the two guest bedrooms for a few seconds. A small room, with just one window. Plain white wallpaper and an empty floor. Ethel had slept here when she was living with them.

Some of their things were still down in the cellar, the ones there hadn't been room for in the removal van. Joakim went down the narrow, steep staircase and started gathering them together: an armchair, a few dining chairs, a couple of mattresses, a small ladder and a dusty birdcage – a souvenir of William the budgerigar, who had died several years ago. They hadn't managed to finish cleaning properly down here, but one of their vacuum cleaners had been left behind. He plugged it in and quickly vacuumed the painted cement floor, then wiped down the cupboards and ledges.

The house was empty and clean.

Then he collected up the cleaning equipment – the vacuum cleaner, buckets, cleaning fluid and cloths – and placed them at the foot of the cellar stairs.

In the carpentry workshop on the left many of his spare tools were still hanging. Joakim started packing them into a cardboard box. Hammers, files, pliers, drills, set squares, screwdrivers. Modern screwdrivers might be better, but they weren't as solid as the old-fashioned ones.

Brushes, handsaws, spirit level, folding rule . . .

Joakim was holding a plane in his hand when he suddenly heard the front door opening on the floor above. He straightened up and listened.

'Hello?' came a woman's voice. 'Kim?'

It was Katrine, and she sounded anxious. He heard her close the front door behind her and walk into the hallway.

'Down here!' he shouted. 'In the cellar!'

He listened, but there was no reply.

He took a step towards the cellar stairs, still listening. When everything remained deathly silent up above, he quickly went upstairs, realizing at the same time how improbable it was that he would see Katrine standing there in the hallway.

And of course she wasn't there. The hallway was just as empty as when he had come into the house half an hour before. And the front door was closed.

He went over and tried the handle. It was unlocked.

'Hello?' he shouted into the house.

No reply.

Joakim spent the next ten minutes going through the entire house, room by room – despite the fact that he knew he wasn't going to find Katrine anywhere. It was impossible, she was still on Öland.

Why would she have taken her car and driven after him all the way to Stockholm, without even calling him first?

He'd misheard. He must have misheard.

Joakim looked at the clock. Ten past four. It was almost dark outside the window.

He took out his mobile and keyed in the number for Eel Point. Katrine should have picked up Livia and Gabriel and be back home by now.

The phone rang out six times, seven, eight. No reply.

He rang her mobile. No reply.

Joakim tried not to worry as he packed the last of his tools and carried them out to the trailer along with the furniture. But when everything was done and he'd turned out all the lights in the house and locked up, he took out his mobile again and rang a local number.

'Westin.'

His mother Ingrid always sounded worried when she answered the phone, Joakim thought.

'Hi Mum, it's me.'

'Hello, Joakim. Are you in Stockholm now?'

'Yes, but—'

'When will you be here?'

He heard the pleasure in her voice when she realized it was him, and just as clearly the disappointment when he explained that he couldn't come over and see her this evening.

'But why not? Has something happened?'

'No, no,' he said quickly. 'I just think it's safer if I drive back to Öland tonight. I've got our Rambe painting with me in the boot and a load of tools in the trailer. I don't want to leave them out overnight.'

'I see,' said Ingrid quietly.

'Mum . . . has Katrine called you today?'

'Today? No.'

'Good,' he said quickly. 'I was just wondering.'

'So when are you coming to see me?'

'I don't know,' he said. 'We live on Öland now, Mum.'

As soon as they'd hung up he rang Eel Point.

Still no reply. It was half past four. He started the engine and pulled out on to the street.

The last thing Joakim did before he headed south was to hand the keys of the Apple House in at the estate agent's office. Now he and Katrine were no longer property owners in Stockholm.

The rush-hour traffic heading for the suburbs was in

full swing when he hit the main road, and it took him forty-five minutes to get out of the city. By the time the traffic finally thinned out it was quarter to six, and Joakim pulled into a car park in Södertälje to call Katrine one more time.

The phone rang four times, then it was picked up.

'Tilda Davidsson.'

It was a woman's voice – but he didn't recognize the name.

'Hello?' said Joakim.

He must have keyed in the wrong number.

'Who's calling?' said the woman.

'This is Joakim Westin,' he said slowly. 'I live in the manor house at Eel Point.'

'I see.'

She didn't say anything else.

'Is my wife there, or my children?' asked Joakim.

A pause at the other end of the phone.

'No.'

'And who are you?'

'I'm a police officer,' said the woman. 'I'd like you to—'

'Where's my wife?' said Joakim quickly.

Another pause.

'Where are you, Joakim? Are you here on the island?'

The policewoman sounded young and slightly tense, and he didn't have much confidence in her.

'I'm in Stockholm,' he said. 'Or rather on the way out . . . I'm outside Södertälje.'

'So you're on your way down to Öland?'

'Yes,' he said. 'I've been to pick up the last of our stuff from our house in Stockholm.' He wanted to sound clear and lucid and make the policewoman start answering questions. 'Can you tell me what's happened? Have any of—'

'No,' she interrupted him. 'I can't say anything. But it would be best if you got here as quickly as possible.'

'Is it—'

'Watch your speed,' said the policewoman, breaking off the conversation.

Joakim sat there with the silent mobile to his ear, staring out at the empty car park. Cars with their headlights on and lone drivers whizzed past him out on the motorway.

He put the car in gear, pulled out on to the road and carried on heading south, doing twelve miles above the speed limit. But when he began to see pictures in his head of Katrine and the children waving to him outside the house at Eel Point, he pulled off the road and stopped the car again.

The phone rang only three times on this occasion.

'Davidsson.'

Joakim didn't bother saying hello or introducing himself.

'Has there been an accident?' he asked.

The policewoman didn't speak.

'You have to tell me,' Joakim went on.

'Are you still driving?' asked the woman.

'Not right now.'

There was silence at the other end of the phone for a few seconds, then she replied, 'There's been an accident. A drowning.'

'A . . . a death?' said Joakim.

The policewoman was once again silent for a few seconds. Then she spoke, sounding as if she were reciting a formula she'd learned by heart.

'We never give out that kind of information over the telephone.'

The little mobile in Joakim's hand seemed to weigh

two hundred pounds, the muscles in his right arm were trembling as he held it.

'Possibly. But this time you have to,' he said slowly. 'I want a name. If someone in my family has drowned, you have to give me the name. Otherwise I'll just keep on calling.'

Silence at the other end of the phone.

'Just a moment.'

The woman disappeared again; it felt to Joakim as if several minutes passed. He shivered in the car. Then there was a scraping noise on the phone.

'I have a name now,' said the woman quietly.

'Whose?'

The policewoman's voice was mechanical, as if she were reading out loud.

'The victim's name is Livia Westin.'

Joakim held his breath and bowed his head. As soon as he had heard the name he wanted to get away from this moment, away from this evening.

The victim.

'Hello?' said the policewoman.

Joakim closed his eyes. He wanted to put his hands over his ears and silence every sound.

'Joakim?'

'I'm here,' he said. 'I heard the name.'

'Good, so we can—'

'I have one more question,' he interrupted her. 'Where are Katrine and Gabriel?'

'They're with the neighbours, over at the farm.'

'OK, I'm on my way. I'm setting off now. Just tell . . . tell Katrine I'm on my way.'

'We'll be here all evening,' said the policewoman. 'Someone will meet you.'

'OK.'

'Do you want us to send for a priest? I can—'

'That won't be necessary,' he said. 'We'll sort things out.'

Joakim switched off his phone, started the car and pulled quickly out on to the road again.

He didn't want to spend any more time talking to some policewoman or priest, he just wanted to get to Katrine right now.

She was with the neighbours, the policewoman had said. That must be the big farm to the south-west of Eel Point, whose cows grazed on the meadows down by the shore – but he didn't have the telephone number, right now he couldn't even remember the name of the family who lived there. Evidently Katrine must have had some kind of contact with them. But why hadn't she called him herself? Was she in shock?

Suddenly Joakim realized he was sitting there thinking about the wrong person.

He could no longer see anything. The tears started pouring down his cheeks and he had to pull over to the side of the road, switch on his hazard lights and rest his forehead on the steering wheel.

He closed his eyes.

Livia was gone. She had sat behind him in the car listening to music this morning, and now she was gone.

He snivelled and looked out through the windscreen. The road was dark.

Joakim thought about Eel Point, and about wells. She must have fallen down a well. Wasn't there a well lid in the inner courtyard? Old wells with cracked lids – why hadn't he checked to see if there were any around the place? Livia and Gabriel had run about wherever they wanted between the buildings, he ought to have talked to Katrine about the risks.

Too late now.

He coughed and started up the Volvo. He wouldn't stop again. Katrine was waiting.

When he was back out on the road he could see her face before him. It had all started when they met while they were viewing the same apartment. Then Livia had come along.

Becoming responsible for Livia had been a big step, he recalled. They both wanted children, but not quite yet. Katrine wanted to do things in the right order. They had intended to sell the apartment and buy a house outside the city in plenty of time before the first child came along.

He remembered how he and Katrine had sat at the kitchen table talking quietly about Livia for several hours.

'What are we going to do?' said Katrine.

'I'd love to take care of her,' Joakim had said. 'I'm just not sure the timing is quite right.'

'It *isn't* right,' Katrine had said crossly. 'Far from it. But we're stuck with it.'

In the end they had decided to say yes to Livia. They had bought the house anyway, and three years later Katrine had fallen pregnant. Gabriel had been planned, unlike Livia.

But just as Joakim had predicted, he had loved watching her grow up. Loved her bright voice, her energy and her curiosity.

Katrine.

How must she be feeling right now? She had called to him inside his head, he had heard her.

Joakim changed gear and put his foot down. With the trailer behind the car he couldn't drive to Öland at top speed, but almost.

The most important thing now was to get to the manor house on the island as quickly as possible – home to his wife and son. They needed to be together.

He could see Katrine's bright face floating in the darkness in front of the car.

5

By eight o'clock in the evening everything was quiet again around the lighthouses at Eel Point. Tilda Davidsson was standing in the big kitchen of the manor house. The whole house was absolutely silent. Even the slight breeze from the sea had died away.

Tilda looked around and got the feeling she was in the wrong century. Apart from the modern kitchen equipment it was like travelling back to a household at the end of the nineteenth century. A wealthy household. The dining table was large and heavy, made of oak. On the shelves stood copper pans, porcelain from the East Indies and hand-blown glass bottles. The walls and ceiling were painted white, but the cupboards and wooden cornices were pale blue.

Tilda would have loved to walk into a Carl Larsson kitchen like this every morning, instead of the little kitchenette in her rooms on the square in Marnäs.

She was completely alone in the house now. Hans Majner and two other colleagues who had travelled from Borgholm up to the scene of the accident had left Eel Point at around seven. Her boss Göte Holmblad had come along with them to the scene, but had kept a low profile and left at five, almost at the same time as the ambulance.

The father of the family who lived at Eel Point, Joakim Westin, was due to arrive by car from Stockholm late that evening – and it had been obvious that Tilda was going to be the one to stay behind and wait for him. She was the only one who had offered, and her colleagues had quickly agreed.

It wasn't because she was a woman, Tilda hoped, but because she was the youngest and had the shortest service record.

The evening shift was OK. The only thing she had needed to do all afternoon, apart from answering the radio and the telephone, was to stop a reporter from *Ölands-Posten* approaching the scene of the accident with his camera. She had referred him to the duty press officer in Kalmar.

When the paramedics went down to the shore with their stretcher she had followed them, stood out by the jetty and watched as they slowly lifted the body out of the water between the jetty and the northern lighthouse. The arms hung there lifeless, water pouring from the clothes. This was the fifth death Tilda had been involved in during her time with the police, but she would never get used to seeing lifeless bodies pulled out of the water or out of smashed-up cars.

It was also Tilda who had answered when Joakim Westin rang. It was really against police procedure to inform relatives of a death over the telephone, but it had gone OK. The news had been bad – the worst imaginable – but Westin's voice had sounded calm and collected throughout the conversation. It was often better to hear bad news as quickly as possible. *Give both the victims and the relatives as much accurate information as possible, as quickly as possible*, she had learned from Martin at the police training academy.

She left the kitchen and went into the main house. There was a faint smell of paint here. The room closest to the kitchen had new wallpaper and a newly polished floor and was warm and cosy, but when she went along the corridor she could see rooms that were cold and dark, with no furniture. It made her think of condemned apartments she had been into shortly after she became a policewoman, apartments with no heating where people lived like rats.

The house at Eel Point wasn't really a house Tilda would want to live in, particularly not at this time of year, in the winter. It was too big. No doubt the coast was lovely when the sun was shining, but in the evening the desolation was complete. Marnäs, with its single shopping street, felt like a densely populated metropolis in comparison to the emptiness of Eel Point.

She left the light on, went out on to the glassed-in veranda and opened the outside door.

A damp chill was drifting in off the sea. There was just one lamp outside, a single light bulb covered with a cracked glass shade, casting a yellow glow over the cobbles and rough tufts of grass in the inner courtyard.

Tilda stood in the shelter of the big barn's stone wall, next to a pile of wet leaves, and took out her mobile. She really wanted to hear another voice, but she hadn't got around to ringing Martin this evening, and now it was several hours too late – he would already have gone home from work. Instead she rang the number of the neighbours, the Carlsson family. The mother picked up after two rings.

'How are they?' asked Tilda.

'I've just had a look at them and they're both asleep,' said Maria Carlsson quietly. 'They're in our guest room.'

'That's good,' said Tilda. 'How long will you be up

tonight? I was intending to come over with Joakim Westin, but I don't think he'll be back from Stockholm for three or four hours.'

'Just come over. Roger and I will stay up for as long as necessary.'

When Tilda had switched off her phone she immediately felt lonely again. It was eight thirty now. She thought about going home to Marnäs to rest for an hour or so, but of course there was the risk that Westin or someone else might telephone here.

She went back into the house.

This time she continued along the short corridor and stopped in the doorway of one of the bedrooms. This was a small, cosy room, like a bright chapel in a dark castle. The wallpaper was yellow with red stars, and along the walls sat a dozen or so cuddly toys on small wooden chairs.

This must be the daughter's room.

Tilda went in cautiously and stood on the soft rug in the centre of the room. She guessed that the parents had fixed up the children's rooms first, so that their son and daughter would quickly feel at home in the manor house. She thought about the room she had grown up in, a small room she had shared with one of her brothers in a rented apartment in Kalmar. She had always longed for a bedroom of her own.

The bed in this room was short but wide, with a pale-yellow coverlet and lots of fluffy cushions with cartoon figures on them: elephants and lions wearing nightcaps and lying in their own little beds.

Tilda sat down on the bed. It creaked slightly, but it was soft.

The house was still completely silent around her.

She leaned back, was received by the pile of cushions and relaxed, her gaze fixed on the ceiling. If she let her thoughts run free the white surface could become like a movie screen, showing pictures from her memory.

Tilda could see Martin on the ceiling, the way he had looked when he had slept beside her in bed for the last time. It had been in her old apartment in Växjö almost a month ago, and she hoped he would come over to visit her soon.

Nothing is as warm and cosy as a child's bedroom.

She breathed out slowly and closed her eyes.

If you don't come to me, then I'll have to come to you . . .

Tilda sat up with a start, in the middle of a breath, with no idea where she was. But her father was with her, she could hear his voice.

She opened her eyes.

No, her father was dead, his car had gone off the road eleven years ago.

Tilda blinked, looked around and realized she had been asleep.

She smelled the aroma of newly polished wood and saw a freshly painted ceiling above her, and remembered that she was lying on a little bed in the manor house at Eel Point. And straight after that an unpleasant memory of running water flashed into her mind – the water pouring from the clothes on the body down by the shore.

She had fallen asleep in a child's bedroom.

Tilda blinked away the sleep, glanced quickly at the clock and saw that it was ten past eleven. She had slept for over two hours and dreamed strange dreams about her father. He had been there with her, in the child's bedroom.

She heard something, and raised her head.

The house was no longer completely silent. She heard faint noises that rose and fell, as if someone – or more than one person – was talking.

89

It was the sound of low voices.

It sounded like muted mumbling. A group of people talking, quietly and intensely, somewhere outside the house.

Tilda got up silently from the bed, with the feeling that she was eavesdropping. She held her breath so that she could hear better, and took a couple of silent steps towards the door, out of the bedroom, and listened again. Perhaps it was just the wind between the buildings.

She went out on to the veranda again – and just when she thought she could distinguish the voices clearly through the glass, they suddenly fell silent. Everything was dark and still between the large buildings of the manor.

The next moment a bright light swept through the rooms – the headlights of a car. She heard the faint sound of an engine approaching, and realized that Joakim Westin had arrived back at Eel Point.

Tilda took a final glance back into the house to make sure everything looked as it should. She thought about the sounds she had heard and had a vague feeling of having done something forbidden – despite the fact that waiting for the owner inside the warm house had seemed like the obvious thing to do. Then she pulled on her boots and went out into the darkness again.

As she stepped outside, the car with its trailer was just swinging around to stop in the turning area. The driver switched off the engine and got out. Joakim Westin. A tall, slim man aged about thirty-five, dressed in jeans and a winter jacket. Tilda could barely make out his face in the darkness, but she thought he was looking at her with a grim expression. His movements as he left the car were rapid and tense.

He closed the car door and came over to her. 'Hi,'

he said. He nodded, but without extending his hand.

'Hi.' She nodded too. 'Tilda Davidsson, local police . . . we spoke earlier.'

She wished she had been wearing her police uniform, not civilian clothes. It would have felt more appropriate on this dark night.

'Is there only you here?' said Westin.

'Yes. My colleagues have left,' said Tilda. 'And the ambulance.'

There was silence. Westin just stood there, somehow indecisive, and she couldn't think of a single decent question to ask.

'Livia,' said Westin eventually, gazing up at the lit windows of the house. 'Is she . . . is she not here?'

'She's being taken care of,' said Tilda. 'They've taken her to Kalmar.'

'What happened?' asked Westin, looking at her. 'Where did it happen?'

'By the shore . . . next to the lighthouses.'

'Did she go out to the lighthouses?'

'No, or rather . . . we don't know yet.'

Westin's eyes were flicking between Tilda and the house. 'And Katrine and Gabriel? Are they still at the neighbours'?'

Tilda nodded. 'They've fallen asleep. I rang and checked a while ago.'

'Is that the place over there?' said Westin, looking towards the lights in the south-west. 'The farm?'

'Yes.'

'I'm going over there.'

'I can drive you,' said Tilda. 'We can—'

'No, thank you. I need to walk.'

He walked past her, clambered over a stone wall and strode off into the darkness.

The bereaved should never be left alone, Tilda had

91

learned during her training, and she quickly set off after him. It was hardly appropriate to try to lighten the situation with questions about his journey from Stockholm or other small talk, so she just walked in silence across the field towards the lights in the distance.

They should have brought a torch or lantern; it was pitch black out here. But Westin seemed able to find his way.

Tilda thought he had forgotten she was behind him, but suddenly he turned his head and said quietly, 'Careful . . . there's barbed wire here.'

He led them around the fence and closer to the road. Tilda could hear the faint rushing of the sea to the east. It sounded almost like whispering, and it made her remember the sounds back at the house. The quiet voices through the walls.

'Does anyone else live in the manor house?' she asked.

'No,' said Westin tersely.

He didn't ask what she meant, and Tilda didn't say any more.

After a few hundred yards they came up on to a gravel track that led them straight to the farm. They walked past some kind of silo and a row of parked tractors. Tilda could smell manure, and she heard the sound of faint lowing from a dark barn on the other side of the farmyard.

They arrived at the Carlsson family house. A black cat walked down the steps and slunk off round the corner, and Westin asked quietly, 'Who found her? Was it Katrine?'

'No,' said Tilda. 'I think it was one of the staff from the day nursery.'

Joakim Westin turned his head and gave her a long

look, as if he didn't understand what she was talking about.

Tilda realized later that she should have stopped on the steps and talked more to him then. Instead she took two more steps up to the door and tapped gently on one of the panes of glass.

After a minute or so a blonde woman dressed in a skirt and sweater came and opened the door. It was Maria Carlsson. 'Come in,' she said. 'I'll go and wake them up.'

'You can let Gabriel sleep,' said Joakim.

Maria Carlsson nodded and turned away, and they both followed her slowly through the hallway. They stopped just inside the door of the large room, which was a combination of a dining room and TV room. Candles had been lit in the windows, and quiet flute music was playing on the stereo.

There was a kind of ceremonial, funereal atmosphere in the air, thought Tilda, as if someone had died here in the house, not over by the lighthouses on Eel Point.

Maria Carlsson disappeared into a dark room. It took a minute or two, then the little girl came out into the light.

She was wearing trousers and a sweater, clutching a cuddly toy firmly under her arm, and her expression was sleepy and uninterested as she looked at them. But when she realized who was standing on the other side of the room, she quickly brightened up and began to smile.

'Daddy!' she shouted, scampering across the floor.

The daughter didn't know anything, Tilda realized. Nobody had told her yet that her mother had drowned.

Even more remarkable was the fact that her father, Joakim Westin, was standing stiffly by the door, making no attempt to move towards his daughter.

93

Tilda looked at him and saw that he no longer looked tense, but frightened and confused – almost terrified.

Joakim Westin's voice was filled with panic.

'But this is Livia,' he said, looking at Tilda. 'But what about Katrine? My wife, where's . . . where's Katrine?'

NOVEMBER

6

Joakim was sitting waiting on a wooden bench outside a low building at the district hospital in Kalmar. The weather was cold and sunny. Beside him sat a young hospital chaplain dressed in a blue winter jacket, a Bible in his hand. Neither of the men spoke.

Inside the building there was a room where Katrine was waiting. Beside the entrance was a sign with the words CHAPEL OF REST.

Joakim was refusing to go in.

'I'd really like you to see her,' the junior doctor had said when she met Joakim. 'If you can cope with that.'

Joakim shook his head.

'I can tell you what you'll see in there,' said the junior doctor. 'It's very dignified and respectful, with low lighting and candles. The deceased will be lying on a bier, with a sheet covering—'

'—a sheet covering the body, leaving the face visible,' said Joakim. 'I know.'

He knew, he had seen Ethel in a room like this the previous year. But he couldn't look at Katrine lying there like that. He lowered his eyes and silently shook his head.

Eventually the junior doctor nodded. 'Wait here, then. It will take a little while.'

She went into the building, and Joakim sat down in the pale November sunshine and waited, gazing up at the blue sky. The hospital chaplain next to him was moving uneasily in his thick jacket, as if the silence were unpleasant.

'Were you married long?' he said eventually.

'Seven years,' said Joakim, 'and three months.'

'Have you any children?'

'Two. A boy and a girl.'

'Children are always welcome to come along and say goodbye,' said the priest quietly. 'It can be good for them . . . help them to move on.'

Joakim shook his head again. 'They're not going through this.'

Then there was silence on the bench again.

After a few minutes the doctor came back with some Polaroid photographs and a large brown package. 'It took a little while to find the camera,' she said. Then she held out the photographs to Joakim.

He took them and saw that they were close-ups of Katrine's face. Two were taken from the front, two from the side. Katrine's eyes were closed, but Joakim couldn't fool himself into thinking she was just sleeping. Her skin was white and lifeless, and she had small wounds on her forehead and on one cheek.

'She's injured,' he said quietly.

'It's from the fall,' said the doctor. 'She slipped on the rocks out on the jetty and hit her face, before she ended up in the water.'

'But she . . . drowned?'

'It was hypothermia . . . the shock of the cold water. This late in the year the temperature of the Baltic is below ten degrees,' said the doctor. 'She took water into her lungs when she went below the surface.'

'But she fell in the water,' said Joakim. 'Why did she fall?'

He didn't get a reply.

'These are her clothes,' said the doctor, handing over the package. 'You don't want to see her?'

'No.'

'To say goodbye?'

'No.'

The children fell asleep in their bedrooms every night in the week following Katrine's death. They had lots of questions about why she wasn't at home, but eventually they fell asleep anyway.

Joakim, however, lay there in the double bed gazing up at the ceiling, hour after hour. And when he did fall asleep there was no rest. The same dream recurred night after night.

He dreamed that he was back at Eel Point. He had been gone for a long time, perhaps for several years, and now he had returned.

He was standing beneath a grey sky on the deserted shore by the lighthouses, then he began to walk up towards the house. It looked desolate and completely dilapidated. The rain and snow had washed away the red, leaving the facade pale grey.

The windows of the veranda were broken and the door was standing ajar. Everything was dark inside. The oblong stones forming the steps up to the veranda were cracked and askew. Joakim walked slowly up them and into the darkness.

He shivered and looked around in the darkness of the porch, but everything was just as shabby and run-down inside as outside. The wallpaper was ripped, gravel and dust covered the wooden floors, all the furniture was gone. There was no trace of the renovation he and Katrine had made a start on.

He could hear noises from several of the rooms.

From the kitchen came the murmur of voices and scraping sounds.

Joakim walked along the corridor and stopped in the doorway.

At the kitchen table sat Livia and Gabriel, bent over a game of cards. His children were still small, but their faces had a network of fine wrinkles around the mouth and eyes.

Is Mum home? asked Joakim.

Livia nodded. *She's in the barn.*

She lives in the hayloft, said Gabriel.

Joakim nodded and backed slowly out of the kitchen. His children stayed where they were, in silence.

He went back outside, across the grass-covered inner courtyard, and pushed open the door of the barn.

Hello?

There was no reply, but he went in anyway.

At the steep wooden staircase leading up to the hayloft he stopped. Then he began to climb. The steps were cold and damp.

When he got to the top he couldn't see any hay, just pools of water on the wooden floor.

Katrine was standing over by the wall, with her back to him. She was wearing her white nightgown, but it was soaking wet.

Are you cold? he asked.

She shook her head without turning round.

What happened down by the shore?

Don't ask, she said, and slowly began to sink through the gaps in the wooden floor.

Joakim walked over to her.

Mum-mee? called a voice in the distance.

Katrine stood motionless by the wall.

Livia has woken up, she said. *You need to take care of her, Kim.*

Joakim woke up with a start. The sound that had woken him up was no dream. It was Livia calling out.

'Mum-mee?'

He opened his eyes in the darkness, but stayed in bed. Alone.

Everything was silent once again.

The clock by the side of the bed was showing quarter past three. Joakim was certain he had fallen asleep just a few minutes ago – and yet the dream about Katrine had lasted an eternity.

He closed his eyes. If he stayed where he was and didn't do anything, perhaps Livia would go back to sleep.

Like a reply the call echoed through the house once more.

'Mum-mee?'

After that he knew it was pointless to stay in bed. Livia was awake and wouldn't stop calling until her mother came in and lay down beside her.

Joakim sat up slowly and switched on the lamp on the bedside table. The house was cold, and he felt a crippling loneliness.

'Mum-mee?'

He knew he had to take care of the children. He didn't want to, he didn't have the strength, but there was no one else to share the responsibility with. He left his warm bed and moved quietly out of his bedroom and over to Livia's room.

She raised her head when he bent over her bed. He stroked her forehead, without saying anything.

'Mummy?' she mumbled.

'No, it's just me,' he said. 'Go to sleep now, Livia.'

She didn't reply, but sank slowly back on to her pillow.

Joakim stood there in the darkness until she was breathing evenly again. He took a step backwards, then another. Then he turned towards the door.

'Don't go, Daddy.'

Her clear voice made him stop dead on the cold floor.

She sounded wide awake, despite the fact that she was lying in bed like a motionless shadow. He turned slowly to face her. 'Why not?' he asked quietly.

'Stay here,' said Livia.

Joakim didn't reply. He held his breath and listened. She had sounded awake, but he still thought it seemed as if she were asleep.

When he had been standing there, silent and motionless, for a minute or so he began to feel like a blind man in the dark room.

'Livia?' he whispered.

He got no answer, but her breathing was tense and irregular. He knew she would soon call out again.

An idea suddenly came into his head. At first it felt unpleasant, then he decided to try it out.

He crept out of the door and into the dark bathroom. He groped his way forward, bumped into the hand basin, then felt the wooden laundry basket next to the bathtub. The basket was almost full; nobody had done any washing for almost a week. Joakim hadn't had the strength.

Then he heard the call from Livia's room, as expected.

'Mum-mee?'

Joakim knew she would carry on calling for Katrine. This was how it was going to be, night after night. It would never end.

'Quiet,' he muttered by the laundry basket. He opened the lid and started burrowing among the clothes.

102

Different aromas rose up to meet him. Most of the items were *hers*; all the sweaters and trousers and underclothes she had worn in the final days before the accident. Joakim pulled out a few things: a pair of jeans, a red woollen sweater, a white cotton skirt. He couldn't resist pressing them against his face.

Katrine.

He wanted to linger there among the vivid memories the scent of her brought into his mind – they were both blissful and painful – but Livia's plaintive cry made him hurry.

'Mum-mee?'

Joakim took the red woollen sweater with him. He went past Gabriel's room and back into Livia's.

She had kicked off the coverlet and was waking up – she raised her head when he came in and stared at him in bewildered silence.

'Sleep now, Livia,' said Joakim. 'Mummy's here.' He placed Katrine's thick sweater close to Livia's face and pulled the coverlet up to her chin. He tucked her in closely, like a cocoon. 'Sleep now,' he repeated, more quietly this time.

'Mmm.'

She mumbled something in her sleep, and gradually relaxed. Her breathing was calmer now; she had placed her arm around her mother's sweater and buried her face in the thick wool. Her sheep from Gotland was lying on the other side of the pillow, but she ignored it.

Livia was asleep again.

The danger was past and Joakim knew that next morning she wouldn't even remember that she had been awake. He breathed out and sat down on the edge of her bed, his head drooping.

A darkened room, a bed, the blinds pulled down.

He wanted to fall asleep, to sleep as deeply as Livia

and forget himself. He just couldn't think any more; he had no strength left.

And yet he couldn't sleep.

He thought about the laundry basket, about Katrine's clothes, and after a couple of minutes he got up and went back into the bathroom. To the laundry basket.

The thing he was looking for was right at the bottom: Katrine's nightgown, white with a red heart on the front. He took it out of the basket.

Out in the corridor he stopped and listened outside both the children's rooms, but all remained silent. Joakim went into his room, put the light on and remade the double bed. He shook and smoothed the sheets, plumped up the pillows and folded back the coverlet. Then he got back in, closed his eyes and breathed in the smell of Katrine.

He reached out and touched the soft fabric.

Morning again. Joakim woke to the stubborn beep of the alarm clock – which meant that he must have slept.

Katrine is dead, he said to himself.

He could hear Gabriel and Livia starting to move about in their beds – and then he heard one of them padding barefoot over the wooden floor to the bathroom – and he realized that he could smell the scent of his wife. His hands were holding on to something thin and soft.

The nightgown.

In the darkness he stared at it with something close to embarrassment. He remembered what he had done in the bathroom during the night, and quickly pulled up the coverlet to hide it.

Joakim got up, took a shower and got dressed, then dressed the children and settled them at the breakfast table. He glanced at them to see if they were watching him, but they were both concentrating on their plates.

The darkness and the cold in the mornings seemed to make Livia more lively. When Gabriel had left the kitchen to go to the bathroom she looked at her father. 'When is Mummy coming back?'

Joakim closed his eyes. He was standing at the worktop with his back to her, warming his hands on his coffee mug.

The question hung there in the air. He couldn't bear it, but Livia had asked the same question every morning and evening since Katrine's death.

'I don't really know,' he replied slowly. 'I don't know when Mummy's coming back.'

'But *when?*' said Livia more loudly.

She was waiting for his answer.

Joakim didn't speak, but eventually he turned around. The right time to tell her would never come. He looked at Livia. 'Actually . . . I don't think Mummy will be coming back,' he said. 'She's gone, Livia.'

Livia stared at him. 'No,' she said firmly and decisively. 'She has *not.*'

'Livia, Mummy isn't coming—'

'She is too!' screamed Livia across the table. 'She *is* coming back! End of story!' Then she went back to eating her sandwich.

Joakim lowered his eyes and drank his coffee; he was beaten.

He drove the children into Marnäs at around eight each morning, away from the silence of Eel Point.

The sound of joyous laughter and screams met them as they walked into Gabriel's nursery. Joakim had no strength whatsoever. He just gave his son a tired hug as they said goodbye. Gabriel quickly turned away and ran

105

off towards the cheerful voices of his friends in the soft-play room.

But the children's energy would disappear with time, Joakim thought; they would grow old and their faces would become grey and sunken. Behind those bright faces lay pale skulls with empty eye sockets.

He shook his head to push the thought away.

'Bye, Daddy,' said Livia when he left her in the cloakroom at pre-school. 'Is Mummy coming home tonight?'

It was as if she hadn't heard what he had said at the breakfast table.

'No, not tonight,' he said. 'But I'll come and pick you up.'

'Early?'

Livia always said she wanted to be picked up early – but when Joakim did turn up early, she never wanted to leave her friends to go home.

'Of course,' he said. 'I'll come early.'

He nodded, and Livia ran off to join the other children. At the same time a grey-haired woman looked out of the cloakroom.

'Hello, Joakim,' she said, her expression sympathetic.

'Hello.'

He recognized her; it was Marianne, the head of the pre-school unit.

'How's it going?'

'Not so good,' said Joakim.

He had to be at the funeral director's office in Borgholm in twenty minutes, and moved towards the door. But Marianne took a step towards him. 'I understand,' she said. 'We all do.'

'Does she talk?' said Joakim, nodding towards the other room.

'Livia? Yes, she—'

'I mean, does she talk about her mother?'

106

'Not much. And nor do we. Or rather, what I mean is . . .' Marianne stopped for a second or two, then went on: 'If it's OK with you, the staff are no different with Livia now than they were before. She's just like all the other children in the class.'

Joakim nodded.

'If you didn't already know . . . I was the one who found her in the water,' said Marianne.

'Right.'

Joakim had no questions, but she carried on talking anyway, as if she needed to tell him.

'There was just Livia and Gabriel left here that day. It was after five, and still no one had come to pick them up. And there was no answer when I telephoned. So I put them in my car and drove out to Eel Point. The children ran into the house, the door wasn't locked . . . but the place was silent and empty. I went out looking, and then I saw something red down in the water, by the lighthouses. A red jacket.'

Joakim was listening and at the same time wondering what Marianne's head looked like beneath the thin skin. A fairly narrow cranium, he thought, with high white cheekbones.

She went on: 'I saw the jacket, and then I saw a pair of jeans . . . and then I realized there was someone floating out there. So I rang the emergency number, then I ran down to the water. But I could see it was too late. It just seems so strange . . . I mean, I'd been talking to her the day before.'

Marianne lowered her eyes and fell silent.

'And there was no one else there?' said Joakim.

'What do you mean?'

'The children weren't there? They didn't see Katrine?'

'No, they were still in the house. Then I took them over to the neighbours. They didn't see anything.'

107

'Good.'

'Children live in the present, they adapt,' said Marianne. 'They . . . they forget.'

As Joakim walked back out to the car, he knew one thing for certain: he didn't want Livia to forget Katrine.

And he mustn't forget her either. To forget Katrine would be unforgivable.

WINTER 1884

The light in the northern lighthouse at Eel Point went out this year. As far as I know, it has never been lit since.

But Ragnar Davidsson told me that a light can still be seen in the tower sometimes – the night before someone is going to die.

Perhaps it is an old fire that sometimes flares up in the lighthouse. The memory of a terrible accident.

Mirja Rambe

Two hours after sunset, the light in the northern lighthouse at Eel Point goes out.

It is the sixteenth of December 1884. The storm that has swept in across the island during the afternoon has reached its peak, and the thunderous roar of the wind and the crashing waves brushes aside any other sound in the area around the lighthouses.

Mats Bengtsson, the lighthouse-keeper, is on his way out into the storm, heading for the southern lighthouse; it is only because he is outside looking towards the shore that he can see through the thickly falling snow that something has happened. The southern lighthouse is flashing as usual, but there is no light in the northern tower – it has gone out, just as if someone has blown out a candle.

Bengtsson just stares. Then he turns back and runs across the inner courtyard, up the steps to the manor house. He tears open the porch door. 'The light is gone!' he yells into the house. 'The northern light is out!'

Bengtsson hears someone reply from the kitchen – perhaps his own wife, Lisa – but he doesn't linger in the warmth. He goes back outside into the blizzard.

Down in the meadow by the shore, blasted by the snow, he has to lean forward like a cripple; it feels as if the Arctic wind is blowing straight through him.

Up in the tower the assistant keeper, Jan Klackman, is on watch alone; his shift began at four o'clock. Klackman is Bengtsson's best friend. Bengtsson knows that he might need help to get the light going again, whatever has happened.

At the beginning of winter a rope was attached to a line of iron posts to show the way from the house down to the lighthouses, and Bengtsson clings to it with both hands, like a lifeline. He fights his way down to the shore, straight into the wind, and makes his way out on to the jetty leading to the lighthouses. Out here there is a chain he can hold on to, but the stones are as slippery as soap and covered in ice.

When he finally reaches the little island where the northern lighthouse stands, he looks up at the dark tower. Despite the fact that the lamp has gone out, he can see a faint yellow glow from the large panes of glass at the top of the tower.

Something is burning up there, or glowing. The paraffin. The new fuel that has replaced coal –

the paraffin must have caught fire.

Bengtsson manages to open the steel door leading into the tower, and goes inside. The door slams shut behind him. Everything is still but not silent, because the storm is still roaring outside.

He hurries up the stone staircase that runs along the wall in a spiral.

Bengtsson begins to pant. There are 164 steps – he has run up them innumerable times and counted them. On the way up he can feel the storm shaking the thick walls the whole time. The lighthouse seems to be swaying in the blizzard.

Halfway up the stairs an acrid stench hits his nostrils.

The stench of burnt meat.

'Jan?' shouts Bengtsson. 'Jan!'

Twenty steps further up he sees the body. It is lying with its head pointing down the steep staircase, like a rag that has been cast aside. The black uniform is still burning. Somehow Klackman has lost his balance up in the lighthouse, and ended up with the burning paraffin all over him.

Bengtsson takes the final steps towards him, takes off his coat and begins to put out the fire.

Someone is coming up the steps behind him and Bengtsson calls out, without looking round, 'He's burning!'

He carries on smothering the fire on Klackman's body, to get rid of the burning paraffin.

'Here!' He feels a hand on his shoulder. It is assistant keeper Westerberg; he has a rope with him and quickly loops it under Klackman's arms. 'Now we can lift him!'

Westerberg and Bengtsson quickly start carrying Klackman's smoking body down the spiral staircase.

At the bottom it is possible to breathe almost normally again. But is Klackman breathing? Westerberg has brought a lantern which is standing on the floor, and in its glow Bengtsson can see how badly burned his friend is. Several of his fingers are blackened, and the flames have reached his hair and face.

'We have to get him outside,' says Bengtsson.

They push open the door of the lighthouse and stagger out into the storm, with Klackman between them. Bengtsson breathes in the fresh, ice-cold air. The snowstorm has begun to subside, but the waves are still high.

Their strength gives out when they reach the shore. Westerberg lets go of Klackman's legs and sinks to his knees in the snow, panting. Bengtsson also lets go, but leans over his face. 'Jan? Can you hear me? Jan?'

It is too late to do anything. Klackman's badly burnt body lies there motionless on the ground. His soul has departed.

Bengtsson hears cries and anxious voices approaching, and looks up. He sees master lighthouse-keeper Jonsson and the other four keepers hurrying through the wind. Following behind them are the women from the house. Bengtsson sees that one of them is Klackman's wife, Anne-Marie.

His head feels completely empty. He must say something to her, but what do you say when the worst has happened?

'No!'

A woman comes running. She is beside herself with grief and bends over Klackman, shaking him in desperation. But it is not Anne-Marie Klackman – it is Bengtsson's wife, Lisa, who is lying there weeping beside the lifeless body.

Mats Bengtsson realizes that nothing is as he thought.

He meets his wife's eyes as she gets up. Lisa has come to her senses now and realizes what she has done, but Bengtsson nods.

'He was my friend,' is all he says, as he turns his gaze towards the dark tower of the lighthouse.

7

'So you think everything was better in the old days, Gerlof?' said Maja Nyman.

Gerlof lowered his cup on to the coffee table in the home at Marnäs and pondered his reply for a few seconds, as he always did.

'Not everything. And not always. But a great deal was certainly . . . better planned,' he said eventually. 'We had time to think before we did something. These days they don't.'

'Better planned?' said Maja. 'Is that what you think? Don't you remember the shoemaker down in Stenvik? The one who was in the village when we were little?'

'You mean Shoe-Paulsson?'

'Arne Paulsson, that's right,' said Maja. 'The worst shoemaker in the world. He had never learned how to tell the difference between right shoes and left shoes, or else he thought it was unnecessary. So he just made one kind of shoe.'

'So he did,' said Gerlof quietly. 'I remember them.'

'You remember the pain, if nothing else,' said Maja with a smile. 'Paulsson's wooden clogs managed to pinch and fit too loosely at the same time. And they always came off when you ran. Was that better?'

Tilda was sitting at the table in the dining room at the

home, listening in total fascination. She had almost forgotten her troubles at work. Conversations like these about the old days should be preserved, she thought, but the tape recorder was in the drawer of Gerlof's desk.

'No, no,' said Gerlof, picking up his coffee cup. 'Perhaps people didn't think ahead too much in the old days. But at least they *thought*.'

Twenty minutes later, Tilda and Gerlof were back in his room, and her tape recorder was up and running once again. The wall clock was ticking in the background as Gerlof began to talk about his early days as a teenage skipper on the Baltic.

Life wasn't dreary and uneventful at the home, Tilda realized – it was restful. She felt more and more contented in Gerlof's little room, because there she could almost forget what had happened over the last few days. Everything that had gone wrong at Eel Point.

Wrong name, wrong information about the deceased, wrong approach – a grieving husband who was refusing to speak to her and doubtless plenty of gossip among her colleagues in her first few days as a local police officer.

And yet she wasn't the only one who'd done something wrong.

She suddenly noticed that Gerlof had stopped chatting and was looking at her.

'That's the way it is,' he said. 'Everything changes.'

The cassette tape was turning in the machine on the table.

'Yes, these are modern times,' said Tilda loudly. 'And the old times . . . what do you think about when you remember the old times?'

'Well . . . for me it's shipping, of course,' said Gerlof, looking suspiciously at the tape recorder. 'All the beautiful cargo ships slipping in and out of the harbour at Borgholm. The smell when you went aboard . . . wood tar and paint and fuel oil, stagnant bilge water from the hold and frying food from the galley.'

'So what was the best thing about those days?' said Tilda.

'The calmness . . . and the silence. The fact that things could take their own time. When I sailed on the cargo ships there were small engines on most of them, of course, but on those that had only sails there was nothing to be done when the wind dropped of an evening. You dropped anchor and waited for the wind to get up again next day. And nobody knew exactly where the cargo ships were, before the telephone and short-wave radio came in. One day they would just turn up off the coast again, on their way to their home harbour in full sail. And then the wives could relax, for this time.'

Tilda nodded. Then she thought again about the information she'd got wrong the previous week, and asked, 'What do you know about the manor house at Eel Point, Gerlof?'

'Eel Point? Well, a little. It was on the wrong side of the island from Stenvik, but your grandfather was a neighbour, after all.'

'Was he?'

'More or less. His cottage was a mile or so further north. Ragnar used to fish for eels off the point, and he was a watchman for the lighthouses.'

'Are there any special stories about the place?'

'Well, the manor house does have something of a reputation,' said Gerlof. 'They say that the foundations are made of granite from an old abandoned chapel, and that the timber in the house came from ships wrecked on the rocks. They were recycling even in those days.'

'Why is there only a light in one tower?' said Tilda.

'There was some kind of accident there, I think it was a fire . . . The twin lighthouses were built to distinguish Eel Point from other lighthouse locations around Öland, but in the end I suppose it got too expensive to have them both working every night. One was enough.' Gerlof thought for a while, then added, 'And of course these days ships navigate with the help of satellites, so even that one is no longer necessary.'

'Modern times,' said Tilda.

'Exactly. Right shoes and left shoes.'

There was silence in the room.

'Have you been out to the point?' asked Gerlof.

Tilda nodded. They had finished talking about the Davidsson family now, so she switched off the tape recorder. 'I was at the house last week,' she said. 'Someone drowned.'

'Yes, I read about it in *Ölands-Posten*. A young woman. I suppose it was the mother of the family who bought the manor house?'

'Yes.'

'So who found her?'

Tilda hesitated. 'I shouldn't really say much.'

'No, of course not. It's a police matter, after all. And a tragedy.'

'Yes. Especially for the husband and children.'

In the end Tilda told him most of it anyway. How she'd been called out to the scene of the accident. The body being pulled out of the water by the lighthouses. 'This woman, Katrine Westin, was alone. She had her lunch and put the dishwasher on. Then she walked down to the shore and out along the jetty. And slipped, or threw herself in the water.'

'And drowned,' said Gerlof.

117

'Yes. She drowned straight away, despite the fact that the water is shallow there.'

'Not everywhere. It's deeper out by the jetty, I've seen sailing boats moor there. Did anyone see it happen, this accident?'

Tilda shook her head. 'No witnesses have come forward, at any rate. The coast was deserted.'

'The Öland coast is almost always deserted in the winter,' said Gerlof. 'And there was no trace of anyone else at Eel Point? Someone who could have pushed her?'

'No, she was alone out on it. You have to go across the shore to get on to it, and there were no other footprints in the sand.' Tilda looked at the tape recorder. 'Shall we talk about Ragnar now?'

Gerlof didn't seem to be listening to her. He got up with some difficulty and went over to the desk. He took a black notebook out of one of the drawers.

'I always make a note of the weather,' he said. He flicked through to the page he wanted. 'There was hardly any wind that day. It was blowing at between three and six feet per second.'

'Yes, I suppose it was. It was calm out at Eel Point.'

'So no waves can have raced up the shore and wiped out any traces,' said Gerlof.

'No. And the footprints from the woman's shoes were still there in the sand – I saw them myself.'

'Was she injured in any way?'

Tilda hesitated before answering. Pictures she didn't want to see came into her mind. 'I only saw her briefly, but she had a small wound on her forehead.'

'A graze?'

'Yes. It was probably from the fall – she probably hit her head on the stone jetty when she fell.'

Gerlof slowly sat down again. 'Any enemies?'

'What?'

'Did she have any enemies ... the woman who drowned?'

Tilda sighed. 'How am I supposed to know that, Gerlof? Do mothers with small children usually have mortal enemies here on the island?'

'I was just thinking that—'

'We need to change the subject now.' Tilda looked at her elderly relative with a serious expression. 'I know you like mulling things over, but I shouldn't be talking to you about this sort of thing.'

'No, no, you're a police officer, after all,' said Gerlof.

'Local police, yes. Not a murder investigator.' She added quickly, 'And there is no murder inquiry, anyway. There is nothing to suggest a crime has been committed – no motive. Her husband doesn't seem to believe it was an accident, but even he can't come up with a reason why anyone should have killed her.'

'Yes, well, I'm just doing a bit of thinking,' said Gerlof. 'I enjoy it, as you said.'

'Good. But now we need to do a bit more recording.'

Gerlof was silent.

'I'm switching the tape recorder on now. OK?' said Tilda.

'What about from the sea?' said Gerlof.

'What?'

'If someone came along the coast in a boat and moored by the jetty on Eel Point, then there wouldn't be any footprints in the sand.'

Tilda sighed. 'OK, so I'd better start looking for a boat, then.' She looked at him and asked, 'Gerlof, are you finding these recordings difficult?'

Gerlof hesitated.

'I find it a bit difficult to talk about relatives who have

119

died,' he said eventually. 'It feels as if they're sitting and listening in the walls.'

'I think they'd be proud.'

'Maybe. Maybe not,' said Gerlof. 'I suppose it depends what I'm saying about them.'

'It's mostly Grandfather I want to talk about,' said Tilda.

'I know.' Gerlof nodded seriously. 'But he might be listening too.'

'Was he hard work as an older brother, Ragnar?'

Gerlof didn't speak for a few seconds.

'He had his moments. He had a long memory. If he felt someone had cheated him he would never do business with that person again . . . He never forgot an injustice.'

'I don't remember him,' said Tilda. 'Dad hardly remembered him either. At any rate, he never talked about him.'

Silence once again.

'Ragnar froze to death in a winter storm,' Gerlof went on. 'The body was found on the shore to the south of his cottage. Did your dad tell you that?'

'Oh yes, he was the one who found Grandfather. He was going out fishing, wasn't he? That's what Dad said.'

'He'd been checking his nets on the seabed that day,' said Gerlof, 'and then when the wind got up he had gone ashore at Eel Point. He was the watchman, after all, and people had seen him out by the lighthouses. The boat must have broken up in the waves, because Ragnar walked home along the shore . . . and then the blizzard came. Ragnar died in the snow.'

'Nobody is dead until they are warm and dead,' said Tilda. 'People have been found frozen stiff and with no pulse in snowdrifts, but they've come back to life when they've been brought into the warmth.'

'Who told you that?'

'Martin.'

'Martin? Who's he?'

'My . . . boyfriend,' said Tilda.

She immediately regretted using that word. Martin would not have liked being described as her boyfriend.

'So you've got a boyfriend?'

'Yes . . . or whatever you want to call it.'

'I should think boyfriend will do perfectly well. What's his surname?'

'His name is Martin Ahlquist.'

'Nice,' said Gerlof. 'Does he live here on the island, your Martin?'

My Martin, thought Tilda.

'He lives in Växjö. He's a teacher.'

'But perhaps he'll come and visit you sometimes.'

'I hope so. He has talked about it.'

'Nice.' Gerlof smiled. 'You look as if you're in love.'

'Do I?'

'Your face lights up when we talk about Martin. It's lovely.'

He smiled encouragingly across the table, and Tilda smiled back. Everything seemed so simple when she was sitting here with Gerlof talking about Martin. Not complicated at all.

8

Livia fell asleep each night with Katrine's red woollen sweater beside her in the bed, and Joakim lay with her nightgown under his pillow. It gave him a feeling of calmness.

Life at Eel Point went on at half speed. The children had to be taken into Marnäs and picked up each weekday, and Joakim took care of that job. In between he was alone at the manor for seven hours, but there was no peace. The funeral director called him several times with different questions before the funeral, and he had to contact banks and various companies to get Katrine's name removed from their records. Relatives got in touch, both Katrine's and Joakim's, and friends from Stockholm sent flowers. Several of them wanted to come to the funeral.

What Joakim really wanted was to unplug all the telephones and lock himself in at Eel Point. Shut down.

Of course, there was a huge amount of renovation to be done inside the house, and in the garden and to the outside of the house – but all he really wanted to do was to lie in bed, breathe in the scent of Katrine's clothes, and stare up at the white ceiling.

And then there was the police. If he had been able to find the strength, he would have spoken to them to find out who was responsible for internal investigations, if there was such a person – but he just couldn't do it.

The only one who got in touch from that particular authority was the young local policewoman from Marnäs, Tilda Davidsson.

'I'm sorry,' she said. 'I really am very sorry.'

She didn't ask how he was feeling, just kept on apologizing for the mix-up over the names. The wrong name was on the note she was reading from, she said – it was a misunderstanding.

A misunderstanding? Joakim had come home to console his wife, but had found her dead.

He listened to Davidsson in silence, answered in monosyllables and asked no follow-up questions. The conversation was a short one.

When it was over he sat down at the family computer and wrote a letter to *Ölands-Posten*, giving a brief outline of what had happened after Katrine's death. In conclusion he wrote:

> For several hours I believed that my daughter had drowned and my wife was alive, when in fact the reverse was true. Is it too much to ask that the police should be able to distinguish between the living and the dead?
>
> I don't think it is; that's what the relatives have to do, after all.
>
> Joakim Westin, Eel Point

He hadn't expected anyone in the police to accept responsibility after that, either, and he wasn't disappointed.

Two days later he met Åke Högström, the priest in Marnäs who was to bury his wife.

'How are you sleeping?' the priest had asked over coffee after they had gone through the ceremony one last time.

'Fine,' Joakim had replied.

He tried to remember what they had decided. They had called the cantor to choose which hymns were to be played, he remembered that, but he'd already forgotten what they had decided on.

The parish priest from Marnäs was in his fifties, with a gentle smile, a little beard, a black jacket and a grey polo-neck sweater. The walls in his study at the vicarage were covered with shelves full of books of all kinds, and on the desk stood a picture of the priest holding a gleaming perch up to the camera.

'The light from the lighthouse doesn't disturb you?' he asked.

'The light?' said Joakim.

'The constant flashing at night, from the lighthouse tower out on Eel Point?'

Joakim had shaken his head.

'I suppose you get used to it,' said Högström. 'It's probably similar to having traffic noise just outside your window. You lived in the middle of Stockholm before you came here, didn't you?'

'A little way out,' said Joakim.

It was only small talk, an attempt to lighten the heavy conversation, but for Joakim it was still a huge effort to find the words.

'So it's hymn number 289 to begin with, 256 after the prayers and 297 to finish off,' said Högström. 'That was what we said, wasn't it?'

'That'll be fine.'

A dozen or so guests from Stockholm arrived the evening before the funeral: Joakim's mother, his uncle, two cousins and some close friends of his and Katrine's. They moved cautiously around the house and talked mostly to each other. Livia and Gabriel were excited by all the visitors, but didn't ask why everyone had come.

The funeral took place at eleven o'clock on a Thursday in Marnäs church. The children weren't there – Joakim had dropped them off at pre-school as usual at eight o'clock, without saying anything. For them today was just like any other, but Joakim had driven home, put on his black suit and lain down on the double bed again.

The wall clock was ticking out in the corridor, and Joakim remembered that it was his wife who had wound it up. It shouldn't be ticking now she was gone, but it was.

He had stared at the bedroom ceiling, thinking about all that was left of Katrine in and around the house. Inside his head he could hear her calling to him.

An hour later, Joakim was sitting on an uncomfortable wooden pew, his eyes fixed on a large mural. It showed a man of his own age nailed to a Roman instrument of torture. A cross. The church in Marnäs was high and filled with echoes. The sound of quiet weeping hovered beneath the vaulted stone ceiling.

Joakim was sitting right at the front next to his mother, who was wearing a black veil and weeping with small, careful sniffles, her head bowed. He knew he wasn't going to cry at all, just as he hadn't shed a single tear at Ethel's funeral last year. The tears always came later, late at night.

It was two minutes to eleven when the church door opened and a tall, broad-shouldered woman strode in. She was wearing a black coat and a black veil which concealed her eyes, but her lips were painted with bright-red lipstick. Her heels echoed on the stone floor, and many heads turned in the church. The woman marched up and sat down in the pew at the front on the right, next to Katrine's four half-sisters and brothers.

She was their mother and Katrine's mother: Mirja Rambe, Joakim's mother-in-law, the artist and singer. He hadn't seen Mirja since their wedding seven years earlier. In contrast to that particular day she appeared to be sober now.

Just as Mirja sat down, the bells began to toll up in the church tower.

Less than forty-five minutes later it was all over, and Joakim could hardly remember anything Pastor Högström had said, or what hymns they had sung in the church. His head had been filled with images and sounds of crashing waves and running water.

Afterwards, when they had crossed the bitterly cold churchyard and gathered in the community hall, lots of people came over to talk to him.

'I'm so sorry, Joakim,' said a bearded man, patting him on the shoulder. 'We were very fond of her.'

Joakim focused his gaze and suddenly recognized the man – it was his uncle from Stockholm.

'Thank you . . . thank you very much.'

There wasn't much else to say.

Several other people wanted to stroke his back or give him a stiff embrace. He let them carry on, he was every-body's pet.

'It's so awful . . . I was only talking to her a few days ago,' said a weeping girl aged about twenty-five.

He recognized her behind the handkerchief she was using to wipe her eyes; it was Katrine's younger sister. Her name was Solros – Sunrose – he recalled. Mirja had given all five of her children unusual second names;

Katrine's was Månstråle, Moonbeam, but she'd hated it.

'And she'd been so much happier lately,' Solros went on.

'I know. She was glad we'd moved down here.'

'Yes, and she was pleased she'd found out about her father as well.'

Joakim looked at her. 'Her father?' he said. 'Katrine never had any contact with her father.'

'I know,' said Solros. 'But Mum's written a book and revealed who he was.'

The tears came again. She hugged him and went off to join her brothers and sister.

Joakim stayed where he was and saw Albin and Viktoria Malm, friends from the centre of Stockholm, sitting at a table with the Hesslin family, their neighbours from Bromma. He also saw his mother, sitting alone at another table with a cup of coffee, but didn't go over to her.

When he turned around Pastor Högström was talking to a small, grey-haired woman on the other side of the room. He went to join them.

Högström turned his kindly gaze in his direction. 'Joakim,' he said, 'how are you feeling?'

Joakim just nodded several times. It was an appropriate response, it could mean anything. The little elderly lady smiled up at him expectantly and nodded as well, but didn't seem to know what to say either. Then she took two tentative steps backwards and disappeared.

That's the thing about the bereaved, thought Joakim, they smell of death and are best avoided.

'I've been thinking something over,' he said seriously to Högström.

'Oh yes?'

'If you hear someone calling for help here on the

island, when you yourself are on the mainland, miles and miles away, what does that mean?'

The priest looked at him blankly. 'Miles and miles away . . . how could you possibly hear that?'

Joakim shook his head. 'But that's what happened,' he said. 'I heard my wife – Katrine – when she died. I was in Stockholm at the time, but I heard her when she drowned. She called out to me.'

The priest looked down into his coffee cup. 'Perhaps you heard someone else?' He had lowered his voice, as if they were talking about forbidden matters.

'No,' said Joakim. 'It was Katrine's voice.'

'I understand.'

'I *know* I heard her,' said Joakim. 'So what does it mean?'

'Who knows, who knows,' was all Högström said, patting him gently on the shoulder. 'Get some rest now, Joakim. We can talk again in a few days.'

Then he left.

Joakim stood there staring at a poster on the wall, advertising a charity collection for those affected by radiation in Chernobyl. Ten years had passed since the catastrophe.

Our daily bread for the victims of the radiation, said the heading on the poster.

Our daily Chernobyl, thought Joakim.

Finally it was evening again and he was back at Eel Point. This long day was coming to an end.

Inside the house Livia and Gabriel were being put to bed by their grandmother. Lisa and Michael Hesslin were standing by their car out at the front. It was late and they had a long journey back to Stockholm, but they had still come back to the house with him.

'Thanks for coming,' said Joakim.

'No problem,' said Michael, placing his black suit in its plastic covering on the back seat.

There was a tense silence.

'Come up to Stockholm soon,' said Lisa. 'Or come over to Gotland with the children, to our cottage.'

'Maybe.'

'We'll be in touch, Joakim,' said Michael.

Joakim nodded. Gotland sounded better than Stockholm. He never wanted to go there again.

Lisa and Michael got into the car and Joakim took a step back as they drove off.

When the car had pulled out on to the road and the glow of its lights had disappeared, he turned and looked down towards the lighthouses. Out on its little island the southern tower flashed its red light across the water. But the northern tower, Katrine's tower, was just a black pillar in the darkness. He had only seen a light in it once.

After a few attempts he found the path down to the shore and followed the same route he had taken with Katrine and the children several times during the autumn. He could hear the sea in the darkness, feel the bitterly cold wind. Carefully he made his way down to the water, across the tufts of grass on the shore and the strip of sand, out on to the big blocks of stone that protected the lighthouses from the waves.

The waves were like slow breaths in the darkness tonight, thought Joakim. Like Katrine when they were making love – she would pull him down towards her in bed, holding him tight and breathing in his ear. She had been stronger than him. It was Katrine who had decided they were moving here.

Joakim remembered how beautiful it had been on the coast when they came here for the first time. It had been a clear, sunny day at the beginning of May, and the manor house had looked like a wooden palace up above the glittering water.

When they had finished looking round the house they had walked down to the shore hand in hand, along a narrow path through a field of wood anemones in full bloom.

Beneath the open sky on the coast the flat islands in the north were floating out at sea like something magical, covered in fresh grass. There were birds everywhere: flocks of flycatchers, oystercatchers and larks, soaring and diving. Small groups of black and white tufted ducks were bobbing along beyond the lighthouses, and closer to the shore swam mallard and grebe.

Joakim remembered Katrine's face in the bright sunshine.

I really want to stay here, she had said.

He shivered. Then he clambered cautiously out on to the furthest block in the jetty and looked down into the black water.

This is where she'd stood.

The footprints in the sand had shown that Katrine had gone out on to the jetty alone. Then she had fallen or thrown herself in the water, and quickly sunk beneath the surface.

Why?

He had no answers. He only knew that at the moment when Katrine drowned, he had been standing in a cellar in Stockholm and had heard her come in through the door. Joakim had heard her calling. He was sure of it, and that meant that the world was even more incomprehensible than he had thought.

After half an hour or so in the cold he went back up to the house.

His mother Ingrid was the only member of the family left after the funeral. She was sitting at the kitchen table and turned her head with a start when Joakim came in, a furrow of anxiety on her forehead. The furrow had got deeper and deeper over the years, first of all during her husband's illness and then with every new crisis Ethel brought home.

'They've all left now,' said Joakim. 'Have the children gone to sleep?'

'I think so. Gabriel finished his milk and fell asleep straight away. But Livia was restless . . . she raised her head and called out to me when I crept out the first time.'

Joakim nodded and went over to the worktop to make a pot of tea. 'She plays possum sometimes,' he said. 'She pretends to be asleep to fool us.'

'She talked about Katrine.'

'Right. Do you want some tea?'

'No, I'm fine, thank you. Does she often do that, Joakim?'

'Not when she's going to sleep.'

'What have you told her?'

'About Katrine?' said Joakim. 'Not much. I've told her . . . that Mummy's away.'

'Away?'

'That she's gone away for a while . . . just like when I stayed in Stockholm while Katrine and the children were here. I can't cope with telling her any more right now.' He looked at Ingrid and suddenly felt uneasy. 'And what did you tell her tonight?'

'Nothing. That's your job, Joakim.'

'I will tell her,' he said. 'When you've gone . . . when there's only me and the children here.'

Mummy's dead, Livia. She drowned.

When would he be ready for that? It was just as

131

impossible as the idea of slapping Livia across the face.

'Will you move back now?' asked Ingrid.

Joakim stared at her. He knew she wanted him to give up, but he still pretended to be surprised.

'Back? Back to Stockholm, you mean?'

Leave Katrine? he thought.

'Yes . . . I mean, I'm there, after all,' said Ingrid.

'There's nothing for me in Stockholm,' said Joakim.

'But you could buy back the house in Bromma, couldn't you?'

'I can't buy anything,' he said. 'I haven't got the money, Mum, even if I wanted to. All the money went into this place.'

'But you could sell . . .' Ingrid stopped and looked around the kitchen.

'Sell Eel Point?' said Joakim. 'Who'd want the place in this state? It needs fixing up first . . . and Katrine and I were going to do that together.'

His mother said nothing as she gazed out of the window, her expression morose. Then she asked, 'That woman at the funeral, the one who arrived late – was that Katrine's mother? The artist?'

Joakim nodded. 'That was Mirja Rambe.'

'I thought I recognized her from your wedding.'

'I didn't know if she would turn up.'

'Well, of course she was going to turn up,' said Ingrid. 'Katrine was her daughter, after all.'

'But they hardly had any contact with each other. I haven't seen her once since the wedding.'

'Had they fallen out?'

'No . . . but I don't think they were exactly friends. They called each other from time to time, but Katrine hardly ever talked about Mirja.'

'Does she live here?'

'No. She lives in Kalmar, I think.'

'Aren't you going to get in touch with her?' said Ingrid. 'I think you should.'

'I don't think so,' said Joakim. 'But we might bump into each other some time. This is a small island, after all.'

He looked out of the window at the darkness of the inner courtyard. He didn't want to see anyone at all. He wanted to lock himself in here in the manor house at Eel Point and never go out again. He didn't want to look for a new teaching post, and nor did he want to carry on working on the house.

He just wanted to sleep for the rest of his life, next to Katrine.

9

The November night was dry, but it was cold, dark and foggy. The only light in the sky came from a pale half-moon behind a film of cloud as fine as silk.

Perfect weather for break-ins.

The house on the rocky north-west coast of the island lay up on the ridge and had been built recently; it was only a couple of years old. It had been designed by an architect, with lots of wood and glass. Commissioned and built by summer visitors with too much money, thought Henrik. He remembered that his grandfather had called rich people from the mainland 'Stockholmers', wherever they came from.

'Hubba bubba,' said Tommy, scratching his neck. 'Let's go.'

Freddy and Henrik followed him in the direction of the gravelled slope below the house. All three were dressed in jeans and dark jackets, and Tommy and Henrik were carrying black rucksacks.

Before they had set off northwards from Borgholm the Serelius brothers had had another session with the ouija board in Henrik's kitchen. An hour and a half before midnight they had lit three candles, and Tommy had set up the board on the kitchen table with the glass in the middle.

Everything went quiet; the atmosphere thickened.

'Is there anybody there?' asked Tommy with his finger on the glass.

The question hung in the air for perhaps ten or fifteen seconds, then the glass jerked and moved to the side. It stopped on the word YES.

'Is it Aleister?'

The glass didn't move.

'Is it a good night tonight, Aleister?' asked Tommy.

The glass remained on YES for a few more seconds. Then it began to move towards the letters.

'Write it down!' Tommy hissed at Henrik.

Henrik wrote, with a cold, unpleasant feeling in his stomach.

E-E-L-P-O-I

Finally the glass was still again in the middle of the board. He looked down at the paper and read what he'd written:

'EEL POINT EEL POINT WORKS OF ART EEL POINT ALONE WALKS THERE,' he read.

'Eel Point?' said Tommy. 'What the fuck is that?'

Henrik looked at the board. 'I've been there . . . it's the site of a lighthouse.'

'Is there a lot of art there?'

'Not that I saw.'

At around midnight Henrik and the Serelius brothers had parked the van behind a boathouse five hundred yards away, then remained among the rocks down by the shore until the last of the lights were switched off behind the shining picture windows on the upper floor. Then they had waited for almost another half-hour and each swallowed a dose of ice crystals before pulling the black hoods over their heads and beginning to move towards the house.

135

Henrik was a bit cold, but the ice had increased his pulse rate. The greater the risk, the greater the excitement. He hardly thought about Camilla at all on a night like this.

The sound of the waves, rhythmically swirling in over the gravel behind them, muffled the sound of their footsteps as they made their way almost silently up the steep slope. An iron fence surrounded the whole garden, but Henrik knew there was an unlocked gate on the side facing the sea. They were soon in the shadows by the wall of the house.

The sliding door to the ground floor was made of glass, fastened with a simple catch, and Henrik took a hammer and chisel out of his rucksack. All it needed was a short sharp blow, and the catch was open.

The small wheels squeaked faintly as Tommy pushed the door to one side on its steel track, but the sound was barely louder than the sighing of the wind.

No alarm reverberated through the darkness.

Tommy stuck his masked head through the doorway. Then he turned and nodded to Henrik.

While Freddy stood guard by the door they went into the warmth. The sound of the wind from the sea faded away, and the shadows in the house enveloped them.

They walked across a painted concrete floor into a fairly large games room. There was a table in the middle of the room, a billiard table. There was plenty of stuff here.

Like a commando Tommy indicated with a hand signal that they should split up, and Henrik nodded and went off to the left. There was a small bar along one side of the room with a dozen or so bottles lined up. Five of them were unopened, and he carefully pushed them down into his rucksack, one after the other. Then he carried on into the house, past the wooden staircase leading to the upper floor.

He went into a living room with a leather sofa. The sofa was facing a small television and video, and he carried those over to Freddy by the outside door. Then he went back and took a look under the sofa.

There was something large and shiny under there. A set of golf clubs?

He bent down and pulled out a folded tarpaulin, with some effort. On top of it lay a complete set of diving equipment, with flippers, yellow oxygen tanks, some kind of pressure meter and a black wetsuit. The stuff looked as if it had never been used; perhaps it had been bought the previous summer for some bored teenager who wanted to learn to dive but had changed their mind.

There was something else on the tarpaulin as well: an old hunting gun.

The rifle seemed to be well looked after, with a polished wooden butt and a shoulder strap of well-oiled leather. A small red cardboard box containing cartridges lay beside it.

Henrik took one thing at a time. He started by carrying out the oxygen tanks and bumped into Tommy, who was carrying a computer monitor to the outside door. Tommy saw the tanks and nodded his approval.

'There's more,' whispered Henrik, and went back.

He put the rest of the diving equipment under one arm and slung the gun over his shoulder. He pushed the box of cartridges into his rucksack. Then he went back to the sliding door, where Tommy was busy carrying out an exercise bike. That looked brand-new as well, but Henrik shook his head.

'No room,' he whispered.

'It'll fit,' said Tommy. 'We'll take it apart and—'

They heard a thud in the darkness.

A thud, followed by footsteps. The noise came from upstairs.

Then the light on the staircase was switched on.

'Hello?' called a man's voice.

'Forget the bike!' hissed Henrik.

They all took to their heels at the same time. Out through the glass door, across the lawn, out through the gate and down to the shore. All three were laden with stolen goods, but it wasn't far to the van across the pebbles.

Henrik put down what he was carrying, took a deep breath and looked around. There were lights everywhere in the house now, but no one seemed to be following them.

'Load up!' shouted Tommy, pulling off his hood and climbing in behind the wheel. He started the engine without putting the headlights on.

Henrik and Freddy quickly pushed everything into the back of the van – rucksacks, TV, diving equipment. They had managed to bring everything down from the house, everything except the exercise bike. Henrik still had the gun over his shoulder.

Tommy floored the accelerator and the van shot away. Up on to the road and south along the coast. Not until they were out of sight of the house did he switch on the lights.

'Take the east road,' said Henrik.

'What are you scared of?' said Tommy. 'Roadblocks?'

Henrik shook his head. 'Take it anyway.'

It was one thirty now, but Henrik was wide awake, his heart pounding. They had done it. They had found gold on the coast. It was almost like before, like his outings with Mogge.

'We must do this again,' said Tommy once they

were out on the main road. 'It was so fucking easy!'

'Reasonably easy,' said Henrik beside him. 'We woke them up.'

'So what?' said Tommy. 'What could he do? We were quicker, straight in and out.'

They came to a sign pointing down a side track, and Tommy slammed on the brakes. Then he turned the wheel.

'Where are you going?'

'Just one last thing. Something really simple, before we go home.'

A tall white stone building appeared among the trees to the left of the track. Long and narrow and illuminated by spotlights.

A church, Henrik realized.

It was the white medieval church in Marnäs. He vaguely remembered that his grandparents had got married there many decades ago.

'Is it open?' said Tommy, pulling over by the churchyard wall. He carried on for a few yards on to a small gravelled track next to the church, and braked in the shelter of some dense trees. 'You can usually walk straight in.'

'Not at night,' said Henrik.

'So? In that case we'll just have to break in.'

Henrik shook his head as Tommy switched off the engine. 'I'm not coming in,' he said.

'Why not?'

'You two can do this on your own.'

Henrik had no intention of saying anything about his grandparents' wedding. He just stared at Tommy, who nodded.

'OK, you sit there and keep an eye open, then,' he said. 'But if we find anything in there, it's ours. Mine and my brother's.'

139

Tommy took out the rucksack containing the tools, slammed the door of the van and disappeared into the darkness, heading for the church, with Freddy trailing along behind.

Henrik leaned back and waited. The darkness was suffocating among the trees. He thought about his grandmother, who had grown up around here.

The door of the van suddenly opened, and Henrik jumped.

It was Freddy. His eyes were shining, as they did after a particularly successful raid, and he was talking fast.

'Tommy's on his way,' he said. 'But look at this! There was a cupboard in the sacres— . . . sacarest— . . . What the fuck is it called?'

'The sacristy,' said Henrik.

'What do you think these might be worth?'

Henrik looked at the old candlesticks Freddy was holding out. Four of them, they looked like silver. Had they been there when his grandparents got married? There was a good chance.

Now Tommy was back at the van, sweaty and excited. 'You can drive,' he said to Henrik. 'I need to count all this.' He jumped into the passenger seat to the sound of clinking.

He had a plastic bag in his hand, which he emptied on to the seat between his legs. Coins and notes came pouring out.

'Their collection box was made of wood,' he said with a laugh. 'It was right by the door, all I had to do was give it a kick.'

'Hundred-kronor notes,' said Freddy, leaning forward between the seats.

'I'm going to count them,' said Tommy, with a look at Henrik. 'Just remember this belongs to us.'

'You keep it,' said Henrik quietly.

140

He didn't feel so good now. It was just too much, breaking into churches and stealing money that was meant to go to pensioners or people in Somalia with leprosy or whatever. Too fucking much. But what was done was done.

'What's this?' said Tommy, bending down.

He had discovered the gun on the floor under the seat.

'I found it in the house,' said Henrik.

'Fucking hell.' Tommy picked it up. 'It's an old Mauser. Collectors love this sort of thing, but people still use them for hunting. They're very reliable.' He looked curiously along the barrel and pulled back the bolt.

'Take it easy with that thing,' said Henrik.

'It's fine . . . the safety catch is on.'

'So you know about guns?'

'Of course,' said Tommy. 'I used to hunt elk. When Dad was sober we were always out in the forest.'

'You might as well take care of it, then,' said Henrik.

He started up the van and switched on the lights. He swung around and slowly drove out of the trees.

'Not too many more,' he said when they were back on the road.

'What?'

'These trips, I can't cope with many more.'

'We have to do a few more. Four more.'

'Two,' said Henrik. 'I'll go out with you twice more.'

'OK. Where?'

Henrik was silent behind the wheel.

'A couple of places I know,' he said. 'A priest's house where there could be some jewellery. And maybe the manor house at Eel Point.'

'Eel Point?' said Tommy. 'The one Aleister gave us a tip about?'

Henrik nodded, even though he believed that the person moving the glass around the board was called Tommy, not Aleister.

'We can go up there and see if he was right,' said Tommy.

'OK . . . but then that's enough.'

Henrik stared gloomily at the empty road. Fuck. This was completely out of control – not at all like the trips with Mogge.

He should have tried harder to stop that last break-in. Stealing from churches brought bad luck.

10

'The police are back in Marnäs now, and we've got our eye on every criminal. I want everyone in northern Öland to be aware of that fact.'

Inspector Holmblad certainly had a gift for public speaking, Tilda realized as she listened to him, and he seemed to like being in the centre of things. He gazed out over the audience of a dozen or so who had gathered in the cold wind on the street outside the new police station in Marnäs – journalists, colleagues and perhaps a couple of ordinary residents – and continued his inaugural speech.

'The local police are a new aspect of police work, a more personal police force . . . comparable with the beat constables in the old days, who knew everyone in the community where they worked. Of course, our society has become more complex since then, there are more networks, but our local police officers here in northern Öland are well prepared. They will be working together with clubs and companies and will be devoting particular attention to crimes committed by young people.'

He paused. 'Any questions?'

'What are you going to do about the graffiti around the square?' said an elderly man. 'It's a disgrace.'

'The police will be bringing in anyone who is caught spraying graffiti,' replied Holmblad. 'We have the right to search them and to confiscate any aerosols, and we will of course be applying a zero-tolerance approach in this matter. But vandalism is equally an issue for schools and parents.'

'And what about the thieving, then?' asked another male voice. 'All these break-ins into churches and summer cottages?'

'Breaking and entering is one of the key targets for the local police force,' said Holmblad. 'We will be making it a priority to solve these cases and to bring the perpetrators to justice.'

Tilda was standing behind her boss like a dummy, her back stiff and her eyes fixed firmly ahead. She was the only woman present, but would have preferred to be anywhere but Marnäs on this particular day. She would also have preferred to be someone else – not a police officer, at any rate. The uniform was too thick and too tight, it was suffocating her.

And she didn't want to stand so close to her new colleague, Hans Majner.

The father of the family over on Eel Point, Joakim Westin, had written a critical letter to *Ölands-Posten* three days ago, about the police mix-up between his dead wife and his living daughter. He hadn't mentioned anyone in particular by name, but after the letter had appeared Tilda thought that people on the streets of Marnäs had begun to stare at her in a different way, scrutinizing and judging her. And last night Holmblad had called her to say that she had to go out to Eel Point with him – to apologize.

'. . . And finally I have a couple of items for our new local police team, Hans Majner and Tilda Davidsson. The keys to the station and this . . .' Inspector Holmblad picked up a rectangular brown parcel that had been leaning against a desk. He opened it and took out an oil painting of a sailing ship, a three-masted ship out at sea in the middle of a violent storm. 'This is a gift from Borgholm, a symbolic way of showing that we are all in the same boat.'

Holmblad handed over the painting and a bunch of keys each to Majner and Tilda with great ceremony. Majner unlocked the station door and invited everyone in with a sweeping gesture.

Tilda stepped to one side and let the men go in first.

The office had recently been cleaned, and the floor was spotless. On the walls were maps of Öland and the Baltic. Holmblad had ordered open prawn sandwiches, which were laid out on a coffee table between Majner's and Tilda's work stations.

There were already several piles of paper on Tilda's desk. She picked up one of the plastic folders and went over to her colleague.

Majner was standing by his own desk tucking into the sandwiches. He was talking to two male colleagues from Borgholm, who were laughing at something he'd just said.

'Hans, could you spare a moment?'

'Absolutely, Tilda.' Majner smiled at his colleagues and turned to her. 'What is it?'

'I'd really like to talk about your message.'

'What message?'

'The message about the death at Eel Point.' Tilda moved to one side and Majner followed her. 'You recognize this, I presume?' She held up the piece of paper she had placed in the folder the day after she had received it from Majner. This was her proof.

Three names were written in ink on the note. The first was LIVIA WESTIN. The second was KATRINE WESTIN.

The third was GABRIEL WESTIN. Next to Livia's name was a cross: †

'So?' said Majner, nodding. 'That was the name I got from the emergency call centre.'

'Exactly,' said Tilda. 'And you were supposed to mark the name of the person who drowned. That's what I asked you to do.'

Majner was no longer smiling. 'And?'

'You put the cross in front of Livia Westin's name.'

'Yes?'

'But that was wrong. It was the mother, Katrine Westin, who had drowned.'

Majner speared a few prawns on his fork and stuffed them in his mouth. He seemed completely uninterested in the conversation.

'OK,' he said, munching on his prawns. 'A mistake. Even the police make a mistake sometimes.'

'Yes, but it was your mistake,' said Tilda. 'Not mine.'

Majner looked up at her. 'So you don't trust me?' he said.

'Well yes, but . . .'

'Good,' said Majner. 'And just remember—'

'Are you two getting to know one another?' a voice interrupted them. Inspector Holmblad had come to join them.

Tilda nodded. 'We're trying,' she said.

'Good. Don't forget we're going out after this, Tilda.'

Holmblad nodded and smiled and moved on, over to the reporter and photographer from the local paper.

Majner patted Tilda on the shoulder. 'It's important to be able to rely on a colleague, Davidsson,' he said. 'Don't you agree?'

She nodded.

'Good,' said Majner. 'Right or wrong . . . a police

146

officer must be sure that he or she will always have back-up. If anything happens.'

Then he turned his back on her and returned to his colleagues.

Tilda stood there, still wishing she was somewhere else.

'Right, Davidsson,' said Göte Holmblad half an hour later, when three-quarters of the sandwiches had been eaten and the rest put away in the fridge. 'We'd better get to our little meeting. We'll take my car.'

At this point Tilda and the inspector were alone in the newly opened police station. Hans Majner had been one of the first to leave.

By this stage Tilda had decided she wasn't even going to try to like him.

She put on her uniform cap, locked the station door and went out to the car with Holmblad.

'We're under no obligation to make a visit like this,' Holmblad explained when they were sitting in the car. 'But Westin has called Kalmar a couple of times wanting to speak to me or someone else in authority, so I thought it would be a good idea to have a conversation with him face to face.' He started the car, pulled away from the kerb and went on, 'The important thing is to avoid official complaints and investigations. A visit like this isn't an official gesture, but it usually clears up most misunderstandings.'

'I contacted Westin a few days after his wife's death,' said Tilda, 'but he wasn't interested in talking at the time.'

'I can try to reason with him on this occasion,' said Holmblad. 'That might work better. I mean, it isn't a question of apologizing, but rather—'

'I have nothing to apologize for,' said Tilda. 'I wasn't the one who supplied the wrong information.'

'No?'

'It was a colleague who gave me a note with a mark next to the wrong name. I just read it out.'

'Oh? But as you know, it's best not to inform relatives of a death over the telephone. I think we all have to accept responsibility for the fact that routine procedure wasn't followed on this occasion.'

'That's what my colleague said,' said Tilda.

They left Marnäs and drove along the coast road, south towards Eel Point. The road was completely deserted this afternoon.

'I've been thinking about buying myself a house on the island for a long time,' said Holmblad, glancing across at the meadows along the shoreline. 'Here on the eastern side.'

'Oh yes?'

'It really is beautiful here.'

'Yes,' said Tilda. 'This is where my family comes from, the villages around Marnäs. My father's side of the family.'

'I see. Was that why you came back?'

'One of the reasons,' said Tilda. 'The job was attractive too.'

'The job, yes,' said Holmblad. 'Today it begins in earnest.'

A few minutes later they reached the yellow sign for Eel Point, and Holmblad turned off on to the winding gravel track.

They could see the lighthouses now, and the red buildings. This time Tilda was able to see the lighthouse-keepers' estate in daylight, even if grey cloud cover was hiding the sun.

Holmblad pulled up in front of the house and turned off the engine. 'Remember,' he said, 'you don't have to say anything if you don't want to.'

Tilda nodded. Bottom of the heap – so keep quiet. Just like when she was little, at the dining table with her two older brothers.

In daylight the house at Eel Point seemed more appealing, thought Tilda, but it was still much too big for her to like the idea of living there.

Holmblad knocked on the glass pane in the kitchen door; the door opened after a minute or so. 'Good afternoon,' said Holmblad. 'Here we are.'

Joakim Westin's face had become even more grey, Tilda thought. She knew he was thirty-four, but he looked like a fifty-year-old. His eyes were dark and tired. He simply nodded at Holmblad, but didn't acknowledge Tilda. Not even with a glance. 'Come in.'

Westin disappeared into the darkness, and they followed him. Everything was neat and clean, no dust bunnies, but when Tilda looked around it was as if a grey film had settled over everything.

'Coffee?' asked Westin.

'Thank you, that would be good,' said Holmblad.

Westin went over to the coffee-maker.

'Are you on your own here now . . . you and the children?' asked Holmblad. 'No relatives?'

'My mother has been staying with us,' said Westin, 'but she's gone back home to Stockholm.'

There was a silence. Holmblad adjusted his uniform. 'We'd very much like to start by expressing our regrets . . . and saying that this sort of thing simply shouldn't happen,' he said. 'The procedures with regard to informing relatives about a death fell down somewhat in this case.'

'You've got that right,' said Westin.

'Yes, we do regret what happened. But—'

'I thought it was my daughter,' said Westin.

'I'm sorry?'

'I thought my daughter had drowned. I thought that for several hours, all the way from Stockholm to Öland. And the only consolation . . . it wasn't much of a consolation, but the only consolation was that my wife Katrine would be there when I arrived, and she would be feeling even worse than me. Then at least I would be able to try and console her, for the rest of our lives.' Westin paused, then went on very quietly, 'We would have each other, at least.'

He fell silent, gazing out of the window.

'As I said, our sincere regrets,' said Holmblad. 'But it's happened now . . . and we have to make sure that it doesn't happen again. To a relative of someone else, I mean.'

Westin hardly seemed to be listening. He was studying his hands as Holmblad stopped speaking, then he asked, 'How's the investigation going?'

'The investigation?'

'The police investigation. Into my wife's death.'

'There is no investigation,' said the inspector quickly. 'We carry out investigations or preliminary investigations only when a crime is suspected, and in this case there are no grounds for suspicion.'

Westin looked up from the table. 'So what happened was nothing out of the ordinary?'

'Well, of course it wasn't exactly normal,' said Holmblad, 'but—'

Westin took a deep breath and continued, 'My wife said goodbye to me outside the house that morning. Then she went inside and scraped windows. Then she made herself some lunch, and after that she went down to the shore. And then she walked right to the end of the jetty and jumped into the water. Does that seem normal to you?'

'Nobody's saying it was suicide,' said Holmblad. 'But

as I said, there are no grounds to suspect any kind of crime. For example, if she'd had a couple of glasses of wine with her lunch and then walked along stones that were slippery—'

'Do you see any bottles around here?' Westin interrupted him.

Tilda looked around. There were in fact no bottles of wine in the kitchen.

'Katrine didn't drink,' Westin went on. 'She didn't drink alcohol. You could have checked that out with a blood test.'

'Yes, but—'

'I don't drink either. There is no alcohol here at all.'

'May I ask why?' said Holmblad. 'Are you religious?'

Joakim looked at him, as if the questions were insolent. And perhaps they were, thought Tilda.

'We have seen what drink and drugs can do,' he said eventually. 'We don't want that kind of stuff in our house.'

'I understand,' said Holmblad.

There was silence in the big kitchen. Tilda looked out of the window towards the lighthouses and the sea. She thought about Gerlof, about his constant curiosity.

'Did your wife have any enemies?' she asked suddenly.

From the corner of her eye Tilda could see Holmblad looking at her as if she had suddenly appeared out of nowhere at the kitchen table.

Joakim Westin also seemed surprised by the question. Not annoyed, just surprised. 'No,' he said. 'Neither of us has any enemies.'

But Tilda thought he seemed hesitant, as if there were more to say.

'So she hadn't been threatened by anyone here on the island?'

Westin shook his head. 'Not as far as I know . . . Katrine has been living here alone with the children over the past few months. I've only come down from Stockholm at the weekends. But she hasn't mentioned anything like that.'

'So she seemed perfectly normal before she died?'

'More or less,' said Joakim Westin, looking down into his coffee cup. 'A bit tired and low, maybe . . . Katrine was finding it quite hard to be alone while I was working in Stockholm.'

Silence fell again.

'May I use your bathroom?' said Tilda.

Westin nodded. 'Out through the porch and it's to the right along the corridor.'

Tilda left the kitchen. She found her way easily; after all, she had been in the house before.

The smell of paint had almost gone from the porch and corridors now, and the house felt a little more lived in.

In the corridor leading to the bedrooms a painting had been hung up recently. It was an oil painting depicting a greyish-white landscape – it looked like northern Öland in the winter. A snowstorm was swirling over the island, blurring all the contours. Tilda couldn't remember having seen the island depicted in such a dark, forbidding way before, and remained standing in front of the picture for a while before she carried on to the bathroom.

It was small but warm, tiled from floor to ceiling, with a thick blue rug on the floor and an old-fashioned bathtub standing on four lion's paws made of cast iron. When she had finished she went back into the corridor and past the closed doors leading to the children's rooms. She stopped at the next bedroom along; the door was half-open.

A quick look?

Tilda poked her head in and glimpsed a small room with a big double bed. There was a small bureau next to the bed, with a framed photograph of Katrine Westin, waving from a window.

Then Tilda saw the clothes.

A dozen or so hangers with women's clothes on them were hung around the bedroom walls like pictures. Sweaters, trousers, tops, blouses.

The double bed had been neatly made, and a white nightgown lay tidily folded on one pillow – as if it had been placed there in the expectation that the woman who owned it would come and put it on when darkness fell. Tilda looked at the strange collection of clothes for a long time, then backed out of the bedroom.

On the way back to the kitchen she heard the inspector's voice: 'Well, time we were getting back to our duties.'

Göte Holmblad had finished his coffee and got up from the table.

The atmosphere in the room seemed less tense now. Joakim Westin stood up and glanced briefly at both Tilda and Holmblad.

'Fine,' he said. 'Thank you for coming.'

'No problem,' said Holmblad, and added, 'Of course, you are at liberty to pursue this matter, I want you to know that, but we would very much appreciate it if—'

Westin shook his head. 'I won't be taking it any further. It's over.'

He accompanied them into the hallway. Out on the steps he shook hands with both officers.

'Thanks for the coffee,' said Tilda.

Dusk had fallen, and there was a smell of burning leaves in the air. Down by the shore the lighthouse was flashing.

'Our constant companion,' said Westin, nodding towards the light.

'Do you have to take care of the lighthouses in any way?' asked Holmblad.

'No, they're automated.'

'I heard the stones they used to build them were taken from an old abandoned chapel,' said Tilda, pointing towards the forest in the north. 'It was somewhere down by the point.'

It felt as if she were showing off and trying to play the tourist guide, but Westin was actually listening.

'Who told you that?'

'Gerlof,' said Tilda, and explained, 'He's in the local-history society over in Marnäs; he knows quite a bit about Eel Point. If you want to know more I can ask him.'

'That would be good,' said Westin. 'Tell him he's welcome to come over for coffee some time.'

When they were back in the car Tilda looked over at the big house. She thought about all those silent rooms. Then she thought about the clothes hanging on the walls in the bedroom.

'He's not feeling too good,' she said.

'Of course he isn't,' said Holmblad. 'He's grieving, after all.'

'I wonder how the children are doing?'

'Small children forget pretty quickly,' said Holmblad. He pulled out on to the coast road heading for Marnäs, and glanced over at Tilda. 'Those questions you asked in the kitchen were a little . . . unexpected, Davidsson. Did you have something in particular in mind?'

'No, it was really just a way of making contact with him.'

'Well, maybe it worked.'

'We could probably have asked him a lot more.'

'Oh?'

'I think he had things to tell us.'

'About what?'

'I don't know,' said Tilda. 'Maybe . . . family secrets.'

'Everybody has secrets,' said Holmblad. 'Suicide or accident? That's the question. But it's not our job to investigate.'

'But we could look for traces,' said Tilda, 'quite impartially.'

'Traces of what?'

'Well . . . of someone else at the scene.'

'The only traces that were found were of the dead woman,' said Holmblad. 'Besides which, Westin was the last person to see his wife. He said that, after all. In which case, if we're going to look for a murderer, we need to start with him.'

'I was thinking, if I have time to—'

'You're not going to have any time, Davidsson,' Holmblad went on. 'Local police officers are always short of time. You'll be visiting schools, picking up drunks, stopping the graffiti, investigating break-ins, patrolling the streets of Marnäs and keeping an eye on the traffic on the roads outside town. And you'll also be sending reports to Borgholm.'

Tilda thought for a moment. 'In other words,' she said, 'if there's any time left after all that, I can knock on doors in the properties around Eel Point and look for witnesses to Katrine Westin's death. That would be OK, wouldn't it?'

Holmblad looked out through the windscreen, without a smile. 'I suspect I've got a future inspector sitting next to me,' he said.

155

'Thanks,' said Tilda, 'but I'm not looking for promotion.'

'That's what they all say.' Holmblad sighed, as if he were contemplating his own career choices. 'Do what you want,' he said eventually. 'As I said, you're responsible for organizing your own time, Davidsson, but if you find anything you must hand it over to the experts. The important thing is that you report all activities to Borgholm.'

'I love paperwork,' said Tilda.

WINTER 1900

When the abyss suddenly opens up, Katrine – what do you do then? Stay where you are, or jump?

At the end of the 1950s I was sitting on a train in northern Öland next to an old woman on her way to Borgholm. Her name was Ebba Lind; she was the daughter of a lighthouse-keeper, and when she heard that I lived at Eel Point, she told me a story about the manor house. It was about what happened the day before she went up into the loft with a knife and carved her brother's name and dates into a plank in the wall: PETTER LIND 1885–1900.

Mirja Rambe

It is the first year of the new century. There is not a breath of wind on this sunny Wednesday, the last in January, but Eel Point is completely cut off from the outside world.

The blizzard moved in across Öland the previous week, and for twelve hours the entire coast was covered in snow. Now the wind has died away, but the temperature outside is minus fifteen degrees. The road has disappeared under great mounds of snow several feet deep, and the families at the manor have received neither post nor visitors for six days. The animals still have plenty of fodder in the barn, but there aren't many potatoes left and as usual there isn't much wood.

Brother and sister Petter and Ebba Lind have gone out to chop up blocks of ice, which will be buried in the food cellar at the manor to keep the food cool when the spring comes. They clambered over the white ramparts of ice and snow down by the shore at Eel Point after breakfast. The sun was just coming up, shining over an unbroken sea of ice covered in snow. They went past the last island at about nine o'clock, out into a sparkling world of great expanses of snow and sunbeams.

They are walking on the water now, just as Jesus did. The snow that covers the ice crunches beneath their boots.

Petter is fifteen, two years older than Ebba. He leads the way, but stops and looks back from time to time.

'OK?' he asks.

'Fine,' says Ebba.

'Are you warm enough?'

She nods, almost too out of breath to talk. 'Do you think we'll be able to see southern Gotland out there?' she asks.

Petter shakes his head. 'I think it's too flat . . . and a bit too far away.'

After another half-hour or so they can finally see open water beyond the ice. The crests of the waves glitter in the sun, but the sea is coal-black.

There are many birds out here. Flocks of long-tailed ducks have gathered out at sea, and closer to the ice a pair of swans are swimming. A sea eagle is circling above the line dividing the water and the ice. Ebba thinks it is watching something, perhaps the ducks – but suddenly the eagle swoops and soars upwards again with something slender and black in its talons. She shouts to Petter, 'Look at that!'

Eels, there are lots and lots of shiny eels wriggling on the ice. Hundreds of eels that have crawled up out of the sea and can't get back. Petter hurries over to them and puts his ice saw down in the snow.

'We'll catch some,' he calls, bending down and opening his rucksack. The eels slither away from him, try to wriggle away, but he follows them and grabs hold of one. Then he picks up more, half a dozen, and his rucksack comes to life and starts writhing around as the eels wind themselves around each other, trying to find a way out.

Ebba moves further north and starts to collect some eels of her own. She picks them up by their flat tails to avoid their sharp little teeth, but they are slimy and difficult to get hold of. But there is plenty of meat on them, every female weighs several pounds.

She pushes two into her rucksack and chases a third, which she also manages to catch eventually.

The air has grown colder. She looks up and sees that the feathery cirrus clouds have drifted west from the horizon and settled like a veil over the sun. Lower, darker rain clouds have followed them, and the wind has got up once again. Ebba has not noticed that the wind has increased, but now she hears the sound of breaking waves out in the open sea.

'Petter!' she shouts. 'Petter, we have to go back!'

He is over a hundred yards away among the eels on the ice, and doesn't seem to hear her.

The waves are getting higher and higher, they are beginning to swirl in across the white edge, making the ice cover slowly begin to rise and fall. Ebba can feel it swaying.

She lets go of the eel she has caught and begins to run towards Petter. But then she hears a terrible sound. Cracks like thunder – not from the clouds in the sky, but from the ice beneath her feet. It is the deep roar that comes when the waves and the wind make the ice cover break apart.

'Petter!' she shouts again, more afraid than ever.

He has stopped catching eels now and turned around. But he is still almost a hundred yards away from her.

Then Ebba hears a sharp explosion like a shot from a cannon very close by, and she sees the ice opening up. A black crack has appeared in all that whiteness, a dozen or so yards closer inland.

The water is pushing the ice apart. The crack is widening rapidly.

Instinctively Ebba forgets everything else and begins to run. When she stops at the crack it is almost three feet wide, and it is growing all the time.

Ebba cannot swim, and is afraid of water. She looks at the crack and turns around in despair.

Petter is on his way to her, he is running with his hand over his rucksack but is still more than fifty steps away. He waves towards the land. 'Jump, Ebba!'

She leaps, straight over the black water.

She just manages to land on the far edge of the ice, stumbles and rolls over.

Petter is left alone on the big ice floe. He reaches the edge just thirty seconds or so after Ebba, but by now the crack is several yards wide. He stops and hesitates, and it grows even wider.

The brother and sister stare at each other in terror. Petter shakes his head and points towards the shore. 'You have to fetch help, Ebba! They need to get a boat out!'

Ebba nods and turns away. She races off across the ice.

The wind and the waves continue to break up the ice, and the cracks pursue her. Twice new abysses open up in front of her, but she manages to leap across.

She turns around and sees Petter one last time. He is standing alone on a gigantic ice floe beyond a black gulf that is growing all the time.

Then she has to start running again. The thundering roar as the ice breaks up echoes along the coastline.

Ebba runs and runs with the increasing wind at her back, and now finally she can see the manor between the lighthouses – her home. But the big estate is just a little dark-red clump on the land, she is still far out on the ice. She prays to God, for Petter and for herself, and begs Him to forgive them for going so far out.

She leaps across a fresh crack, slips, but carries on running.

Eventually she reaches the ramparts of ice at the edge of the sea. She gets down on all fours and scrambles over them, snivelling and sobbing. She's safe now.

Ebba gets up and looks back. The horizon has disappeared behind a veil of fog. The ice floes have gone too. They have drifted east, off towards Finland and Russia.

Ebba carries on up the shore, sobbing. She knows she must hurry back to the house now and get the lighthouse-keepers to put out to sea in their boats. But where are they to look for Petter?

The last of her strength gives out, and she falls to her knees in the snow.

Up on the hill the house at Eel Point looks down on her. The roof of the manor house is white with snow, but the windows are as black as coal.

As black as holes in the ice, or as black as angry eyes. Ebba imagines that God has eyes like that.

11

One day at a time.

They never talked about it, but Livia and Gabriel seemed to be under the impression that their mother had simply gone away, and would be back. It wasn't good, but at the same time Joakim had almost begun to believe it himself.

Katrine had gone away on holiday, but perhaps she would come back to the manor house.

The day after the police officers' visit to Eel Point he was standing in the kitchen looking out of the window. There were no birds heading south over the house on this November day, just a few stray gulls circling over the sea.

He had driven the children into Marnäs a couple of hours earlier and had planned to do some food shopping afterwards. He had gone into the shop on the square, but had just stood there.

So many things for sale, so many advertisements.

A poster over by the meat counter seemed to be offering LEAN BONE FEVER, ONLY 39.50 A POUND.

Lean bone fever? He must have misread it, but he was suddenly afraid to go closer and find out what it really said. He backed slowly out of the shop.

Joakim couldn't cope with shopping for food.

He had driven back home. He had walked into the vast silence and taken off his outdoor clothes. Then he had gone over to stand by the window. He had no plans other than to stand here as long as possible.

In front of him on the pale wood of the kitchen work-top lay a forgotten lettuce on a dish. Had he bought it, or Katrine? He couldn't remember, but over the past few days it had begun to turn black inside its plastic bag. Putrefaction in the kitchen wasn't a good sign, he ought to throw it away.

He hadn't the energy.

He took a last glance out of the kitchen window, towards all the greyness that was empty water and an overcast sky off Eel Point, and came up with a new plan: he would go and lie down, and never leave his bed again.

Joakim went into the bedroom and lay down on the double bed. He stared up at the ceiling. Katrine had taken down the ugly sheets of plasterboard that had been nailed up there, and had re-created the original white ceiling that had been there before, perhaps since the nineteenth century.

The ceiling looked good, it was like lying beneath a white cloud.

Suddenly he heard a tentative knocking through the silence. Hard knuckles against rattling glass.

Joakim turned his head.

Bad news? He was always ready for more bad news.

The knocking came again, more energetic this time.

It was coming from the kitchen door.

Slowly he got up from the bed, went through the kitchen and out into the hallway. Through the glass he could see two people dressed in dark clothes standing on the steps outside.

It was a woman and a man of Joakim and Katrine's

age. The man was wearing a suit, the woman a dark-blue coat and skirt. Both smiled pleasantly at him as he opened the door.

'Good morning,' said the woman. 'We're Filip and Marianne. May we come in?'

He nodded and opened the door wide. Were they from the funeral director's office in Marnäs? He didn't recognize them, but several people from the office had been in touch over the past few weeks. They'd all been very nice.

'Oh, this is lovely,' said the woman as they walked into the kitchen.

The man looked around, nodded and turned to Joakim. 'We're travelling round the island this month,' he said, 'and we noticed someone was home.'

'We live here all year round . . . my wife and I and our two children,' said Joakim. 'Would you like some coffee?'

'Thank you, but we don't use caffeine,' said Filip, sitting down at the kitchen table.

'What's your name?' said Marianne. 'If you don't mind my asking.'

'Joakim.'

'Joakim, we would really like to give you something. Something important.'

Marianne took something out of her bag and placed it on the table in front of Joakim. It was a brochure. 'Look at that. Isn't it beautiful?'

Joakim looked at the slim brochure. On the cover was a drawing of a green meadow beneath a blue sky. In the meadow sat a man and a woman in white clothes. The man had his arm around a lamb which had lain down on the grass, and the woman had her arm around a big lion. They were smiling at one another.

'Isn't that paradise?' said Marianne.

Joakim looked up at her. 'I thought this place was paradise,' he said. 'Not now, but before.'

Marianne looked at him in confusion for a few seconds. Then she began to smile again. 'Jesus died for us,' she said. 'He died so that things could be as wonderful as this for us.'

Joakim looked at the drawing again and nodded. 'Wonderful.' He pointed at the huge mountains in the background. 'Fantastic mountains.'

'It's the kingdom of heaven,' said Marianne.

'We go on living after death, Joakim,' said Filip, leaning across the table as if he were revealing a great secret. 'Eternal life . . . isn't that fantastic?'

Joakim nodded. He couldn't stop looking at the drawing. He had seen brochures like this before, but had never realized how beautiful the pictures of paradise were. 'I'd really like to live in those mountains,' he said.

Fresh mountain air. He could have lived there with Katrine. But the island they had moved to was completely flat, there were no mountains. And no Katrine . . .

Joakim suddenly found it difficult to breathe. He leaned forward, feeling thick tears welling up in his throat.

'Don't you feel . . . don't you feel well?' said Marianne.

He shook his head, leaned over the table and began to cry. No, he didn't feel well. He wasn't well, he was suffering from lean bone fever.

Oh, Katrine . . . and Ethel . . .

He wept and snivelled uncontrollably for several minutes at the kitchen table, shut off from the outside world. Somewhere in the distance he could hear whispering voices and the gentle scraping of chairs, but he couldn't stop weeping. He felt a warm hand on his shoulder which remained there for a few seconds before

166

it was removed. Then the outside door closed gently.

When he finally blinked away the tears he was alone. He heard the sound of a car starting up outside. The brochure with the people and the animals in the meadow was still on the table. When the sound of the engine had died away, Joakim snivelled in the silence and looked at the drawing.

He had to do something. Anything.

With a tired sigh he stood up and threw the brochure in the rubbish bin under the sink.

The house was completely silent around him. He went along the corridor into the empty drawing room and looked for a long time at the tins, bottles and rags that were lined up on the floor. Katrine had obviously started cleaning down the window frames the week before.

She had had much clearer views on the décor than Joakim, and had chosen all the colours, wallpaper and wooden detailing throughout. And the material had already been bought, it was lying on the floor by the walls waiting to be used.

Joakim sighed again.

Then he opened a bottle of sugar soap and picked up a rag. He started working on the window frames, stubborn and focused. The sound of the rag rubbing against the wood sounded desolate in the silence.

Don't press too hard, Kim, he heard Katrine saying in the back of his head.

The weekend came. The children were at home, playing in Livia's room.

Joakim had finished the windows in the big room, and now he was going to start wallpapering the room in the south-west corner. He had set up a table and mixed a bucket of wallpaper paste after breakfast.

This was a smaller bedroom which, like many of the others, had a 120-year-old tiled stove in one corner. The flower-patterned wallpaper in most of the rooms looked as if it dated from the beginning of the twentieth century, but unfortunately it was too badly damaged to be preserved. There were a huge number of damp stains, and in some places the paper had been hanging off in long strips. Katrine had pulled them away earlier in the autumn and then smoothed down the walls, filled in the holes and prepared everything ready for wallpapering.

Katrine had particularly liked this little corner room.

But Joakim wasn't going to call up any more memories of her right now. He wasn't going to think, he was just going to wallpaper.

He picked up the rolls of zinc-white paper, a heavy English handmade wallpaper of the same type they had used in the Apple House. Then he picked up the knife and the long ruler and started cutting lengths.

He and Katrine had always done the wallpapering together.

Joakim sighed, but started working. It wasn't possible to get stressed out when you were wallpapering, and so the work turned into something close to meditation. He was a monk, the house was his monastery.

When he had put up the first four lengths and smoothed them down with a brush, Joakim suddenly heard a faint thudding noise. He got down from the ladder and listened. The thuds were regular, with a few seconds in between, and they were coming from outside.

He went over to the window facing out from the back of the house and opened it. Bitterly cold air swept in.

A boy was standing on the grass down below, perhaps a year or two older than Livia. At his feet he had a yellow plastic football. The boy had curly brown hair, poking out from underneath a woollen winter hat; his padded jacket was inaccurately buttoned, and he was looking up at Joakim with some curiosity.

'Hi,' said Joakim.

'Hi,' said the boy.

'It's not a good idea to kick your ball around here,' said Joakim. 'You could break a window if your aim isn't great.'

'I'm aiming at the wall,' said the boy. 'I always hit what I'm aiming at.'

'Good. What's your name?'

'Andreas.'

The boy rubbed his nose, red with the cold, with the palm of his hand.

'Where do you live?'

'Over there.'

He pointed towards the farm. So Andreas was one of the Carlsson family's children, out and about on his own this Saturday morning.

'Would you like to come in?' said Joakim.

'Why?'

'You can say hello to Livia and Gabriel,' said Joakim. 'They're my children. Livia's the same age as you.'

'I'm seven,' said Andreas. 'Is she seven?'

'No. But she's *almost* the same age as you.'

Andreas nodded. He rubbed his nose again, then made a decision. 'For a little while. We'll be eating soon.' He picked up his ball and disappeared around the side of the house.

Joakim closed the window and went out of the room. 'Livia! Gabriel!' he shouted. 'We've got a visitor.'

After a few seconds his daughter appeared, clutching Foreman in her hand. 'What?'

'There's someone here who wants to meet you.'

169

'Who?'

'A boy.'

'A boy?' Livia opened her eyes wide. 'I don't want to meet him. What's his name?'

'Andreas. He lives on the farm next door.'

'But Daddy, I don't know him.'

There was panic in her voice, but before Joakim had the chance to say something sensible about the fact that meeting new people isn't going to make you ill, the outside door opened and Andreas walked into the porch. He stopped on the doormat.

'Come on in, Andreas,' said Joakim. 'Take off your hat and your jacket.'

'OK.'

The boy took off his outdoor clothes and dropped them on the floor.

'Have you been in this house before?'

'No. It's always locked.'

'Not now, it's open now. We live here now.'

Andreas looked at Livia and she looked back, but neither of them said hello.

Gabriel was peeping out shyly from his sister's room, but he didn't say anything either.

'I helped bring our cows in,' said Andreas after a while, looking round the room. 'From the enclosure out there.'

'Today?' said Joakim.

'No, last week. They have to stay in now. Otherwise they'd freeze to death.'

'That's true, everybody needs heat in the winter time,' said Joakim. 'Cows and birds and people.'

Livia was still staring curiously at Andreas without joining in the conversation. Joakim had also been shy when he was little; it was a shame if she had inherited that particular characteristic.

'You could kick the football around for a while,' he said. 'I know a great room you could use.'

He led the way into the house with the children following along behind. They came to the large drawing room, which was still almost completely unfurnished; there were just a couple of dining chairs and a few cardboard boxes on the floor.

'You can play in here,' said Joakim, stacking three of the boxes in front of the window to protect it.

Andreas dropped the football, dribbled it tentatively then kicked it across the wooden floor to Livia. Dust swirled up like a fine grey mist.

Livia kicked at the ball as it came speeding towards her. She missed. Gabriel scampered after it, but couldn't catch up.

'Stop it with your foot first,' said Joakim to the children, 'then you'll be able to control it.'

Livia gave him a sour look, as if she could do without the advice, thank you. Then she quickly turned and captured the ball between her feet in one corner of the room and kicked it back hard.

'Good shot,' said Andreas.

Little flirt, thought Joakim, but Livia was smiling contentedly.

'Go and stand over there,' said Andreas, pointing to the other doorway. 'You can be in goal and we'll shoot.'

Livia quickly ran over to the double doors, and Joakim left the room and went back along the corridor to his wallpapering. He could hear the ball bouncing across the floor behind him.

'Goal!' he heard Andreas shout, and Livia and Gabriel shrieked before all three of them started laughing.

Joakim loved the happy noises spreading through the house. Very good, he had sorted out a friend for his children.

He stuck his brush in the bucket of paste, stirred it around and made a start on the long wall. Length after length of paper went up; the room changed colour and gradually became lighter. Joakim smoothed out the bubbles and wiped away the excess paste with a damp sponge.

When only a couple of feet of unpapered wall remained he realized that the echoing children's voices could no longer be heard from the drawing room. The house was completely silent again.

Joakim climbed down from his ladder and listened.

'Livia?' he called. 'Gabriel? Would you like some juice? And biscuits?'

No reply.

He listened for a while longer, then went out of the room and along the corridor. But halfway to the drawing room he looked out of the window into the courtyard and stopped.

The door to the big barn was standing ajar.

It had been shut before, hadn't it?

Then he saw that Andreas Carlsson's outdoor clothes had gone from the floor.

Joakim pulled on a jacket and a pair of boots and went out into the courtyard. The children must have pulled the heavy door open together. Maybe they had gone inside too, into the darkness.

Joakim went across and stopped in the doorway of the barn.

'Hello?'

No reply.

Were they playing hide and seek? He walked across the stone floor, breathing in the smell of old hay.

They had talked about turning the barn into a gallery, he and Katrine, some time in the future when they had cleared out all the hay, the dung and all the other traces of the animals who had lived there.

He was thinking about Katrine again, although he shouldn't. But on the morning of the day she drowned he had seen her coming out of the barn. She had looked embarrassed, as if he had caught her out.

Nothing was moving inside the barn, but Joakim thought he could hear a tapping or creaking noise from the hayloft up above, like footsteps. A narrow, steep wooden staircase led up to the loft, and he grabbed hold of the sides and began to climb.

Coming into the loft from the dark passageways and stalls down below was almost like walking into a church, he thought. Up here there was just a big open space for the hay to dry – an open-plan solution, as the agents liked to call it – and the roof arched high above him in the darkness. Thick beams ran the length of the loft, several feet above Joakim's head.

Unlike the upper floor of the main house, it was impossible to get lost up here, even if it was difficult to pick your way through all the rubbish that had been piled up on the floor. Heaps of newspapers, flowerpots, broken chairs, old sewing machines – the hayloft had become a dumping ground. A couple of tractor tyres, almost as tall as a man, were leaning up against a wall. How had they got those up here?

When he saw the untidy loft, Joakim suddenly remembered dreaming that Katrine was standing up here. But the floor had been clean, and she had been standing over by the far wall with her back to him. He had been afraid to go over to her.

The winter wind was like a faint whisper above the roof of the barn. He didn't really like being alone up here in the cold.

'Livia?' he shouted.

The wooden floor creaked in front of him, but he got

173

no other answer. Perhaps the children had hidden in the darkness; they were probably spying on him from the shadows. They were hiding from him.

He looked around and listened.

'Katrine?' he said quietly.

No reply. He waited in the darkness for several minutes, but when the silence in the hayloft remained unbroken, he turned and went back down the steps.

When he got back into the house he found his children where he should have looked in the first place – in Livia's bedroom.

Livia was sitting on the floor drawing, as if nothing had happened. Gabriel had obviously been given permission by his big sister to stay in there, because he had fetched some toy cars from his room and was sitting beside her.

'Where have you been?' Joakim asked, more sharply than he had intended.

Livia looked up from her drawing. Katrine had never painted for pleasure, even though she was an art teacher, but Livia enjoyed drawing.

'Here,' she said, as if it were perfectly obvious.

'But before . . . Did you go outside? You and Andreas and Gabriel?'

'For a little while.'

'You mustn't go in the barn,' said Joakim. 'Did you hide in there?'

'No. There's nothing to do in the barn.'

'Where's Andreas?'

'He went home. They were going to eat.'

'OK. We'll be eating soon too. But don't go outside again without telling me, Livia.'

'No.'

* * *

The night after Joakim had been out in the barn, Livia started talking in her sleep again.

She had gone to bed with no trouble that night. Gabriel had fallen asleep at around seven, and while Joakim was helping Livia to brush her teeth in the bathroom she had studied his head at close quarters with considerable curiosity.

'You've got funny ears, Daddy,' she said eventually.

Joakim put his daughter's mug and toothbrush back on the shelf and asked, 'What do you mean?'

'Your ears look so . . . old.'

'I see. But they're no older than I am. Have they got hair in them?'

'Not much.'

'Good,' said Joakim. 'Hair in your nose and ears isn't exactly cool.'

Livia wanted to stay in front of the mirror for a while, pulling faces, but Joakim gently led her out of the bathroom. He put her to bed, and read the story twice about Emil getting his head stuck in the soup bowl, then turned off the light. As he was leaving the room he could hear her wriggling further down the bed and snuggling her head into the pillow. Katrine's woollen sweater still lay beside her in the bed.

He went into the kitchen, made himself a couple of sandwiches and switched on the dishwasher. Then he turned out all the lights. In the darkness he groped his way back to his own bedroom and switched on the main light.

There it stood, the cold, empty double bed. And on the walls above it hung clothes. Katrine's clothes, which by now had lost all trace of her scent. Joakim ought to take them down, but not tonight.

He turned off the light, got into bed and lay there motionless in the darkness.

175

'Mum-mee?'

Livia's voice made Joakim raise his head, wide awake.

He listened. The dishwasher in the kitchen had finished, and the clock radio was showing 23:52. He had slept for over an hour.

'Mum-mee?'

The cry came again; Joakim got out of bed and went back to Livia's room. He stood in the doorway until he heard her again.

'Mum-mee?'

He went over to the bed. Livia was lying under the covers with her eyes closed, but by the glow of the light out in the corridor Joakim could see her head moving restlessly on the pillow. Her hand was clutching Katrine's sweater, and he carefully released it.

'Mummy isn't here,' he said quietly, folding up the sweater.

'Yes, she is.'

'Go to sleep now, Livia.'

She opened her eyes and recognized him.

'I can't sleep, Daddy.'

'Yes, you can.'

'No,' said Livia. 'You have to sleep here.'

Joakim sighed, but Livia was wide awake now, and there was nothing else for it. This had always been Katrine's job.

Cautiously he lay down on the edge of the bed. It was too short, he'd never be able to get to sleep.

He fell asleep after two minutes.

There was someone outside the house.

Joakim opened his eyes in the darkness. He couldn't hear anything, but he could feel that they had a visitor.

He was fully awake again.

What time was it? He had no idea. He might have slept for several hours.

He raised his head and listened. The house was silent and still. The only sound was the faint ticking of a clock – and the barely audible breathing in the darkness beside him.

He sat up silently and carefully and got off the bed. But after only three steps he heard the voice behind him.

'Don't go, Daddy.'

He stopped and turned around. 'Why not?'

'Don't go.'

Livia was lying motionless, facing the wall. But was she awake?

Joakim couldn't see her face, just her blonde hair. He went back to the bed and sat down cautiously beside her. 'Are you asleep, Livia?' he asked quietly.

After a few seconds came the reply: 'No.'

She sounded awake, but relaxed.

'Are you sleeping?'

'No . . . I can see things.'

'Where?'

'In the wall.'

She was talking in a monotone, her breathing slow and calm. Joakim leaned closer to her head in the darkness. 'What can you see?'

'Lights, water . . . shadows.'

'Anything else?'

'It's light.'

'Can you see any people?'

She was silent again, before the reply came: 'Mummy.'

Joakim stiffened. He held his breath, suddenly afraid that this was serious – that Livia was asleep, and really could see things through the wall. *Don't ask any more questions*, he thought. *Go to bed.*

But he had to carry on.

'Where can you see Mummy?' he asked.

'Behind the light.'

'Can you see—'

Livia interrupted him, speaking with greater intensity. 'Everybody's standing there waiting. And Mummy's with them.'

'Who? Who's waiting?'

She didn't reply.

Livia had talked in her sleep before, but never as clearly as this. Joakim still suspected that she was awake, that she was just playing games with him. But he still couldn't stop asking questions.

'How's Mummy feeling?'

'She's sad.'

'Sad?'

'She wants to come in.'

'Tell her . . .' Joakim swallowed, his mouth dry. 'Tell her she can come in any time.'

'She can't.'

'Can't she get to us?'

'Not in the house.'

'Can you talk to her?'

Silence.

Joakim spoke slowly and clearly. 'Can you ask Mummy . . . what she was doing down by the water?'

Livia lay motionless in the bed. There was no response, but he still didn't want to give up.

'Livia? Can you talk to Mummy?'

'She wants to come in.'

Joakim straightened up in the darkness and didn't ask any more. The whole thing felt hopeless.

'You must try . . .'

'She wants to talk,' Livia broke in.

'Does she?' he asked. 'About what? What does Mummy want to say?'

178

But Livia said nothing more.

Joakim said nothing either, he just got up slowly from the bed. His knees creaked; he had been sitting in the same position with his back rigid for too long.

He moved silently over to the blind and peeked out from the back of the house. He could see his own transparent reflection in the window pane, like a misty shape – but not much beyond it.

There was no moon, no stars. Clouds covered the sky. The grass in the meadow rippled slightly in the wind, but nothing else was moving.

Was there anyone out there? Joakim let go of the blind. To go outside and take a look he would have to leave Livia and Gabriel alone, and he didn't want to do that. He stayed by the window, unsure what to do, and eventually turned his head.

'Livia?'

No reply. He took a step back towards the bed, but saw that she was fast asleep.

He wanted to carry on asking questions. Perhaps even wake her up to find out if she could remember anything about what she'd seen in her sleep, but of course it wasn't a good idea to press her. Joakim pulled the flowery coverlet up over her narrow shoulders and tucked her in.

He returned silently to his own bed. The covers felt like a shield against the darkness as he crept in. He listened anxiously for noises from the corridor and from Livia's room. The house was silent, but Joakim was thinking of Katrine. It was several hours before he managed to fall asleep.

12

A Friday night at the end of November.

The big vicarage at Hagelby was almost two hundred years old, and lay at the end of a forest track half a mile or so outside the village. The Swedish church no longer owned the vicarage. Henrik knew it had been sold to a retired doctor and his wife from Emmaboda.

Henrik and the Serelius brothers had parked their van in a grove of trees up by the main road. They had left everything in it except for two rucksacks containing just a few tools, with plenty of room for anything they might pick up. Before they set off through the forest, past the stone wall by the church and the graveyard, they had each knocked back a dose of crystal meth and washed it down with beer.

Henrik had drunk more beer than usual; his nerves were at breaking point tonight. It was all the fault of that fucking board – the Serelius brothers' ouija board.

They had conducted a quick session in Henrik's kitchen at around eleven o'clock. He had turned off the main light, and Freddy had lit the candles.

Tommy placed his index finger on the glass. 'Is there anybody there?'

The glass began to move straight away. It ended up on the word YES.

Tommy leaned forward. 'Is it Aleister?'

The glass moved over to the letter A, then L . . .

'He's here,' said Tommy quietly.

But the glass carried on to G, then to O and T. Then it stopped.

'Algot?' said Tommy. 'Who the fuck is that?'

Henrik stiffened. The glass had begun to move across the board again, and he quickly reached for a piece of paper and wrote down what it was spelling out.

ALGOT ALGOT NOT GOOD ALONE HENRIK NOT GOOD NOT LIVING NOT GOOD HENRIK NOT

Henrik stopped writing. 'I can't do this any more,' he said quickly, pushing the piece of paper away. He took a deep breath, got up and switched on the main light, then breathed out.

Tommy took his finger off the glass and looked at him. 'OK, chill out,' he said. 'The board is just supposed to be a help . . . let's go.'

It was twelve thirty when they finally arrived at the vicarage. It was a cloudy night, and the house was in darkness.

Henrik was still pondering over the board's message. Algot? His grandfather's name had been Algot.

'Are they home?' whispered Tommy in the shadows among the birch trees in the lower part of the garden. Just like Freddy and Henrik, he had pulled the black hood over his head.

Henrik shook himself. He must pull himself together, focus on the job. 'I'm sure they are,' he said. 'But they sleep upstairs. Up there, where the window's open.' He pointed up at a window that was slightly ajar in one of the corner rooms.

'Good, let's go,' said Tommy. 'Hubba bubba.'

181

He led the way up the stone path and the steps. Then he leaned forward and peered thoughtfully at the lock. 'Looks pretty solid,' he whispered to Henrik. 'Shall we go for a window instead?'

Henrik shook his head. 'This is the country,' he whispered back. 'And they're pensioners. Look.'

He reached out, silently pushed down the handle and opened the door. It wasn't locked.

Tommy said nothing, he simply nodded and went inside. Henrik followed, with Freddy right behind him.

This wasn't good – three men inside the house was one too many. He signalled that Freddy should stay and keep watch outside, but he just shook his head and walked in.

Tommy opened the next door and disappeared into the house itself. Henrik followed.

They were in a big, dark hallway. It was warm inside – pensioners were a chilly breed, thought Henrik, and they always had the heating turned up high. The floor was covered with a dark-red Persian carpet that muffled the sound of their footsteps, and on one of the walls hung a huge mirror with a gold frame.

Henrik stopped. A thick black leather wallet was lying on the marble table below the mirror. He quickly reached out and tucked the wallet into his jacket pocket.

When he looked up he could see himself in profile: a hunched figure in dark clothes, with a black hood covering his head and a big bag on his back. *Thief*, he thought. He could almost hear Grandfather Algot's voice in the back of his head. It was all down to the hood – it would make anyone look dangerous.

There were three doors leading off the hallway, two of them ajar. Tommy had stopped by the middle door. He listened, shook his head and opted for the right-hand one.

Henrik followed him. He could hear Freddy's breathing and heavy footsteps right behind him.

The door led into a drawing room – an elegant room, with several small wooden tables crowded with objects. It looked as though a lot of it was rubbish, but on one of the tables stood a large Småland crystal vase. Good. Henrik pushed it into his rucksack.

'Henrik?'

Tommy was whispering from the other side of the room. He had opened a bureau, pulled out the drawers and made a real find, Henrik saw: rows of silver cutlery and a dozen or so napkin rings made of gold; necklaces and brooches; even some bundles of hundred-kronor notes and foreign currency.

A treasure trove.

They all pitched in to empty the bureau, without saying a word. The cutlery clinked slightly as they gathered it up, and Henrik wrapped it in some linen serviettes from the bureau to muffle the sound.

Their rucksacks were heavy and well filled by now.

Anything else that might need a new owner?

Paintings covered the walls, but they were too big. Henrik caught sight of something tall and narrow in one of the windows. He pulled back the curtain.

It was some kind of old lantern with panes of glass and lacquered wood, perhaps twelve inches high and six inches wide. Rather charming. It would go nicely in his flat if a fence didn't want to buy it. He wrapped a tablecloth around the lantern and pushed it into his rucksack.

Enough.

There was no sign of Freddy when they emerged into the hallway. Had he gone further into the house?

A door opened slowly – it was the door leading to the kitchen, and Henrik was so sure it was Freddy that he

183

didn't even turn his head – but suddenly he heard Tommy gasp.

Henrik turned and saw a white-haired gnome standing in the doorway.

The man was wearing brown pyjamas and was just putting on a pair of thick glasses.

Fuck. Caught again.

'What are you doing?'

A stupid question that didn't get a reply. But Henrik felt Tommy stiffen beside him, like a robot switching to attack mode.

'I'm calling the police,' said the man.

'Shut up!' Tommy moved. He was a head taller than the man, and pushed him back into the kitchen. 'Don't move!' shouted Tommy, kicking out.

The old man dropped his glasses as he stumbled in the doorway and collapsed just inside. The only sound he made was a long drawn-out wheezing.

Tommy followed him; there was something sharp in his hand. A knife or a screwdriver.

'That's enough!' Henrik hurried over to try and stop Tommy but stumbled over a rag rug, and ended up standing on the old man's hand with his heavy boot. There was a crunching sound.

'Come on!' somebody shouted – perhaps Henrik himself.

Henrik stumbled backwards and banged into the marble table in the hallway. The big mirror fell to the floor with a series of crashes. Fuck. Everything was blurred like on a dance floor, fast and unplanned. It was impossible to control things any more. And where the hell was Freddy?

Then he heard a high-pitched voice behind him.

'Get out!'

Henrik whirled around. He saw a woman standing by

the man on the floor. She was even shorter, and looked terrified.

'Gunnar?' she called, bending down. 'Gunnar, I've called the police.'

'Come on!' Henrik fled, without even looking to see whether Tommy was obeying his order or not. There was still no sign of Freddy. Through the veranda and out into the night.

Henrik ran across the grass, hard with frost, came around the corner of the house and raced into the forest. Branches tore at his face, his rucksack was chafing his shoulders and he couldn't find the track, but he still kept on running.

Something grabbed hold of his foot and suddenly he was flying through the air. Straight down into the shadows, where the wet leaves and undergrowth received him. Something hit the back of his head hard. The night became blurred.

He felt really bad.

When Henrik came to he was crawling on all fours. He was moving slowly forwards across the ground, his head aching, aiming for a black shadow that was growing up ahead of him. A little cave. He crept in through the opening and curled up. Someone was after him, but in here he was safe.

It took several minutes for his mind to clear. He raised his head and looked around.

Silence. Total darkness. Where the fuck had he ended up?

He felt earth beneath his fingers and realized that he had crawled into an old stone-covered cellar in the forest near the vicarage. It was cold and damp. It smelt of fungus, kind of mouldy.

Suddenly he got the idea that he was lying in an old

death chamber. An earth cellar for the dead, where they lay waiting to be buried over in the graveyard.

Some kind of insect with long legs landed on his ear. A spider that had just woken up. He knocked it away quickly with his hand.

Henrik was beginning to feel claustrophobic, and slowly crawled out of the cellar. His rucksack got hooked on the roof, but he turned sideways and made it out on to the frozen ground.

Fresh winter air.

He got up and set off through the undergrowth, away from the lights shimmering in the windows of the vicarage through the trees. When he reached the wall of the graveyard he knew he was heading the right way.

Suddenly he heard a van door slam. He listened. An engine started up far away in the darkness.

Henrik moved more quickly through the trees, came out on to a broad path and began to run. The trees thinned out and he saw the Serelius brothers' van. It was just reversing out on to the road.

He got there just in time and tore open the side door.

Freddy and Tommy turned their heads quickly, and realized who it was.

Henrik jumped in and slammed the door. 'Drive!'

Once the van was moving he finally breathed out and leaned back, his head pounding.

'What the fuck happened to you?' asked Tommy over his shoulder. He was breathing heavily, clutching the wheel very tightly. The stiff rage was still there in his shoulders.

'I got lost,' said Henrik, shrugging off his rucksack. 'Fell over a tree root.'

Freddy chuckled to himself. 'I had to jump out of a window!' he said. 'Straight down into the shrubbery.'

'Still, we got some good stuff,' said Tommy.

Henrik nodded, his jaws rigid with tension. The old guy Tommy had knocked down – what had happened to him? He didn't want to think about that right now. 'Take the east road,' he said. 'To my boathouse.'

'Why?'

'The police are going to be out this way tonight,' said Henrik. 'When there's violence involved they come tearing over from Kalmar . . . I don't want to bump into them up on the main road.'

Tommy sighed, but took the turning down to the eastern coast road.

It took them a good half-hour to unload everything and hide it in the boathouse, but it was worth it to feel safer. All Henrik had left in his rucksack when they got back in the van was the money and the old glass lantern.

They took a detour along the east coast to Borgholm, but didn't see any police activity. On the outskirts of the town Tommy ran over a cat or a hare, but this time he seemed too tired to take any pleasure in it.

'We'll take a break,' said Tommy as they reached the streetlights of the town. 'A little bit of time off.'

They pulled in by Henrik's apartment block. It was quarter past three.

'OK,' said Henrik, opening the door. 'And we need to go through the money . . . make sure it's all sorted.'

He wasn't about to forget that the Serelius brothers had been ready to drive off and leave him up in the forest.

'We'll be in touch,' said Tommy through the open window of the van.

Henrik nodded and walked towards the building.

It wasn't until he was inside his flat that he realized how filthy he was. His jeans and jacket were covered in black stains from the soil. He threw them in the laundry

187

basket, drank a glass of milk and stared blankly through the window.

His recollections of the night in the vicarage were vague from start to finish, and he had no desire to go over them again. Unfortunately his clearest memory was of the old man's hand crunching beneath his boot. He hadn't meant to do that, but . . .

He turned the light off and went to bed.

It was difficult to get to sleep; his forehead was aching and his nerves were buzzing throughout his body, but some time after four he drifted off into the mists of sleep.

A couple of hours later Henrik was woken by the sound of knocking in the apartment. The sound of knocking on glass. Then silence.

He raised his head from the pillow and looked around the dark room in confusion.

The soft sound of knocking came again. It seemed to be coming from the hallway.

Henrik left the warmth of his bed and staggered out into the shadows to listen.

The knocking was coming from his rucksack. Three knocks, then silence. Then a couple more knocks.

He bent down and unzipped the bag. The old lantern from the vicarage was inside, still wrapped in the tablecloth.

Henrik lifted it out.

The wooden frame of the lantern had cooled down in the van, presumably. Now it was getting back up to room temperature. That's why it was clicking and knocking.

He placed the lantern on the kitchen table, closed the door and went back to bed.

The sound of faint knocking could be heard from the

kitchen from time to time. It was just as irritating as a dripping tap, but Henrik was so tired he eventually went to sleep anyway.

13

The important thing was never to forget Katrine.

Every time Joakim forgot her, even if it was only for a moment, the pain returned inexorably when he suddenly remembered that she no longer existed. For that reason he tried to keep her in his thoughts all the time – just beyond the border where grief took over, but keeping her constantly present.

On the Sunday three weeks after the accident he took the children on a long trek in the area around the manor house. They started by heading west, inland, and Joakim could feel the presence of Eel Point behind him; he imagined that Katrine had stayed behind indoors to put up some wallpaper. Maybe she would soon come out into the fields and catch them up.

It was a windy but sunny November day, and they had cinnamon buns and hot chocolate with them. Joakim's rucksack had a built-in child's carrying seat where Gabriel could sit when he was tired, but most of the time he was running across the meadows with Livia.

When they reached the main road Joakim shouted to them to stop, and they all crossed over together after looking in both directions, as Livia and Gabriel had learned.

Livia had slept more peacefully for the last few nights

and didn't seem the least bit tired, but Joakim could feel the constant lack of sleep like a swollen weight behind his eyes. He felt slightly better during the day now he had set to work on the house again, but the nights were still difficult. Even when Livia was fast asleep he lay there awake in the darkness, waiting. Listening.

Talking in her sleep didn't seem to have any negative effects on Livia; almost the reverse. But she had started bringing home drawings she'd done at pre-school. Many of them showed a woman with yellow hair, sometimes standing in front of a blue sea, sometimes in front of a big red house. Above the pictures she had written MUMMY in sprawling letters.

Livia still asked almost every morning and evening when Katrine was coming home, and Joakim always gave the same answer: 'I don't know.'

An old stone wall ran along the other side of the road, and when they had climbed over it they found themselves at the edge of a flat, grey landscape with open water between patches of reeds and clumps of pale-yellow grass. The water was black and still; it was impossible to tell how deep it was.

'This is called a peat bog,' said Joakim.

'Can you drown here?' asked Livia.

She tried pushing a stick down into a muddy puddle, and didn't notice that the question had made Joakim tense up.

'No . . . only if you can't swim.'

'I can swim!' shouted Livia.

She had been to four swimming lessons in Stockholm during the summer.

Gabriel suddenly screamed and started to cry – he had sunk down and got his Wellingtons stuck in the grass by the water. The muddy ground let him go with a disappointed slurp when Joakim pulled him out. He put Gabriel down on firm ground, looked out over the black water and suddenly remembered something the agent who showed them round the house at Eel Point had told them as they were driving past the peat bog.

'Do you know what they used to do out here in the Iron Age?' he asked. 'Hundreds and hundreds of years ago?'

'What?' said Livia.

'I've heard that they used to *sacrifice* things to the gods.'

'Sacrifice – what does that mean?'

'It means that you give away things you like,' said Joakim, 'in order to get even more back.'

'So what did they give away, then?' asked Livia.

'Silver and gold and swords and that kind of thing. They threw them into the water as a gift to the gods.'

According to the agent, animals and human beings had also been sacrificed sometimes – but stories like that were definitely not for the ears of the children.

'Why?' said Livia.

'I don't know ... but I suppose they believed it would make the gods happy, and they would make life easier.'

'What kind of gods were they?' said Livia.

'Pagan gods.'

'What does that mean?'

'Well, it means they were ... a bit nasty sometimes,' said Joakim, who wasn't too good on the history of religion. 'Norse gods like Odin and Freya. And nature gods in the earth and the trees. But they don't exist any longer.'

'Why not?'

'Because people stopped believing in them,' said

Joakim, setting off again. 'Let's go. Do you want to sit in the rucksack seat, Gabriel?'

His son shook his head cheerfully and scampered off after Livia again.

A narrow path which was drier ran along the side of the bog, and they followed it northwards. At the end of the bog lay fields, and beyond them was Rörby with its white church rising up on the horizon.

Joakim would have liked to walk much further, but by the time they got to the fields the children had slowed down considerably. He took off his rucksack. 'Time for a snack.'

It took them quarter of an hour to empty the flask of hot chocolate and eat up all the buns. They found dry rocks to sit on, and everything was silent all around them. Joakim knew that the peat bog was a bird sanctuary, but they didn't see a single bird all day.

After they had eaten they crossed back over the main road. Joakim chose a path alongside the little wood that grew north-west of Eel Point. The wood was low-growing and bushy, like all the woods he had seen on the island. It consisted of pine trees, all leaning slightly inland, away from the harsh winds coming off the sea. Among them grew thickets of hazel and hawthorn.

They carried on down to the sea, where the wind grew stronger and colder. The sun was starting to set, and the sky had lost its blue glow.

'There's the wreck!' shouted Livia when they had almost reached the shore.

'The wreck!' echoed Gabriel.

'Can we go out there, Daddy?'

From a distance it still bore some resemblance to the hull of a ship, but as they got closer it looked more like a pile of broken old planks of wood. The only thing that hadn't been smashed to pieces was the keel: a warped wooden beam half-buried in the sand.

Livia and Gabriel walked all the way around the wreck, but came back disappointed.

'It can't be fixed, Daddy,' said Livia.

'No,' said Joakim, 'I think it's had it.'

'Did everybody on the boat drown?'

She was always talking about people drowning, thought Joakim.

'No, they survived,' he said. 'I'm sure the lighthouse-keepers helped them get ashore.'

They carried on southwards along the damp shore. The waves swirled up on to the sand, and Livia and Gabriel tried to walk as close to them as possible without getting soaked. When a big wave came rushing towards them they jumped out of the way, screaming and laughing.

After quarter of an hour they had reached the stone jetty that sheltered the lighthouses. Livia ran over to it across the sand and clambered up on to the first block of stone.

This was where Katrine had gone just three weeks ago. Straight along the jetty and down into the water.

'Don't go up there, Livia,' called Joakim.

She turned and looked down at him. 'Why not?'

'You might slip.'

'I won't.'

'You might. Come down, please!'

In the end she climbed down again, silent and sullen. Gabriel looked at his sister and his father, unsure which of them was right.

They walked past the stone pathway out to the light-houses, and Joakim had an idea that might put Livia back in a good mood. 'Maybe we could go and look inside one of the lighthouses,' he said.

Livia turned her head quickly. 'Can we?'

'Of course we can,' said Joakim, 'as long as we can unlock the door. But I know where there's a bunch of keys.'

He led the way back up to the house, unlocked the kitchen door and as usual quelled the impulse to call out to Katrine as he walked in.

In one of the kitchen cupboards was a metal box that the agent had passed on, containing documents relating to the history of the house. The old bunch of keys was also in the box – an iron ring with a dozen or so keys, some of them larger and heavier than any he had seen before.

Gabriel wanted to stay indoors where it was warm; he wanted to watch a video of Pingu the penguin. Joakim inserted it into the machine. 'We won't be long,' he said.

Gabriel just nodded, already caught up in the film.

Joakim picked up the clanking bunch of keys and went out into the cold again, with Livia beside him. 'So which one shall we choose?'

Livia thought it over and pointed. 'That one,' she said. 'Mummy's lighthouse.'

Joakim looked at the north tower. That was the one that no longer flashed – even though he did think he had seen a light there just once, at dawn on the day Katrine had walked out along the stone jetty. 'OK,' he said. 'We'll try that one.'

So they walked out into the sea along the stone pathway and took the left fork where it split. They reached the little island. In front of the metal door of the lighthouse stood a polished slab of limestone, big enough for both father and daughter to stand on.

'OK, let's see if we can get in, Livia . . .'

Joakim looked at the padlock and chose a key that looked as if it might fit, but it was too big for the keyhole. The second key he chose fitted into the hole, but wouldn't turn. The third key fitted too, and when Joakim got a firm grip he was actually able to turn it, even though the padlock was stiff. He pulled on the handle as hard as he could. The door opened slowly on stiff hinges, but stopped after six or seven inches.

It was because of the big limestone slab. The winter waves and ice – or perhaps the grass growing around it – had pushed it upwards over the years, and the bottom of the door was catching on it.

When Joakim grabbed hold of the upper part of the steel door it bent outwards an inch or two more, but refused to open. He peered inside, with the sense that he was looking into a black mountain crevice.

'What's inside?' asked Livia behind him.

'Wow', he said, 'there's a skeleton on the floor.'

'What?'

He turned and smiled at her wide-eyed expression. 'I'm only joking. I can't see much . . . it's almost pitch black.'

He stepped back on to the stone slab and let Livia take a look.

'I can see some stairs,' she said.

'Yes, that's the staircase leading up into the tower.'

'It's curved,' said Livia. 'It goes round . . . and up.'

'Right up to the top,' said Joakim, and added, 'Wait here.'

He had spotted a rectangular piece of rock down by the water, and went down and fetched it. This gave him a good threshold to stand on.

'Can you move back a bit, Livia?' he said. 'I'm going to try and climb in and push the door open from the inside.'

'I want to come in as well!'

'After me, maybe,' said Joakim.

He stood on top of the rock, bent the upper part of the door outwards as far as he could, and squeezed in through the opening. He just managed it – he was glad he didn't have a beer gut.

The daylight disappeared once he was inside the lighthouse, and he could no longer hear the wind from the sea. He stepped down on to a flat cement floor, and felt thick, curved stone walls around him.

Slowly he got used to the darkness and looked around. How long was it since anyone had been inside the lighthouse? Several decades, perhaps. The air was dry, as in all buildings made of limestone, and every surface was covered with powdery grey dust.

The stone staircase Livia had seen started almost at his feet and spiralled up along the walls, around a thick pillar in the centre of the tower. It disappeared up into the darkness, but somewhere up there he had the impression of a faint light, presumably from the narrow windows in the tower.

Someone had left things on the floor. A couple of empty beer bottles, a pile of newspapers, a red and white metal can with the word CALTEX on it. Next to the stone staircase was a low wooden door, and when Joakim pushed it open a little way he saw even more rubbish: old wooden boxes piled on top of one another, empty bottles, and dark-green fishing nets on the walls. There was even something that looked like an old mangle in there. Someone had been using the lighthouse as a dumping ground.

'Daddy?'

Livia was calling him.

'Yes?' he replied, and heard the echo of his voice bouncing up the spiral staircase.

Her face peered in through the doorway. 'Can I come in too?'

'We can try . . . Can you climb up on to the rock, then I can try and pull you in?'

As soon as she began to squeeze herself through the opening he realized he wouldn't be able to bend the door outwards and pull her inside at the same time. She could easily get stuck.

'I don't think this is going to work, Livia.'

'But I want to come inside!'

'We can go over to the southern lighthouse,' he said, 'and maybe we can—'

Suddenly Joakim heard scraping noises from above. He turned his head and listened.

Footsteps. It sounded like echoing footsteps high up on the spiral staircase.

The noise was coming from the tower. It must be his imagination, but it *sounded* like heavy footsteps – and it sounded as if they were slowly but surely coming down the stairs.

This wasn't Katrine, this was someone else.

Heavy footsteps . . . it sounded like a man.

'Livia?' called Joakim.

'Yes?'

She was still outside, and Joakim thought about how close she was to the water. If she took a couple of steps back and happened to fall . . . And Gabriel, Gabriel was alone up in the house. How could he have left him?

'Livia?' he called again. 'Stay where you are, I'm coming out.'

He grabbed the doorframe and heaved himself up. The steel door seemed to want to keep him there, but he forced his way through the opening. It might have looked quite funny, like a parody of a birth, but his heart was pounding and Livia was standing there looking at him with fear in her eyes.

Joakim climbed down on to the stone outside and breathed in the fresh, cold sea air.

'There we are,' he said, and quickly pushed the steel door shut behind him. 'Let's get back to Gabriel. We can look inside the other lighthouse another day.'

As he quickly replaced the padlock and locked the door he was expecting protests, but Livia said nothing. She took his hand in silence and they walked back along the jetty and up on to the shore. It was almost twilight.

Joakim thought about the noises in the lighthouse.

It must have been the wind from the sea blowing around the tower, or the beak of a gull scraping against the glass. Not footsteps.

WINTER 1916

The dead are trying to reach us, Katrine. They want to talk to us, they want us to listen.

What do they want to say to us? Perhaps that we should not seek death too early.

In the loft above the barn there is a date from the time of the First World War carved into the wall: December 7th 1916. After that there is a cross, and the beginning of a name: † GEOR

Mirja Rambe

Alma Ljunggren, the wife of the master lighthouse-keeper, is sitting at her loom in the room at the back of the house. A wall clock is ticking behind her. Alma cannot see the sea from here, and that suits her very well. She doesn't want to see what her husband Georg and the other lighthouse-keepers are doing down by the shore.

There are no voices to be heard in the house; all the other women are down on the shore. Alma knows that she too should be there to support the men, but she dare not go. She hasn't the strength to be any kind of support, she barely has the courage to breathe.

200

The wall clock continues to tick.

A sea monster has drifted ashore at Eel Point this winter morning, in the third year of the Great War. The monster was discovered after last night's fierce snowstorm: a black monster with pointed steel spikes all over its round body.

Sweden is a neutral country as far as the Great War on the continent is concerned, but is still affected by it.

The monster on the shore is a mine. Presumably Russian, dropped the previous year in order to stop the Germans transporting ore across the Baltic. But of course it doesn't matter what country it comes from, it is just as dangerous anyway.

The ticking in the room suddenly stops.

Alma turns her head.

The wall clock behind her has stopped. The pendulum is hanging straight down.

Alma picks up a pair of black sheep shears from a basket beside her loom, gets up and goes out of the room. She throws a shawl around her shoulders and walks out on to the veranda at the front of the manor house. She still refuses to look down towards the shore.

The waves must have torn the mine free of its mooring out at sea during the blizzard over the past few days, and slowly washed it towards the land. Now it is stuck fast in the sandy seabed and the slushy ice only fifty yards or so from the southern lighthouse.

The year before, a German torpedo drifted ashore just north of Marnäs. It was shot to pieces, and the naval authorities now insist that mines are dealt with in the same way. The Russian mine must be destroyed, but it is not possible to blow it up so close to the lighthouses. It must be towed away. The lighthouse-keepers are going to place a rope around the mine and then carefully tow it away from the lighthouses.

Master lighthouse-keeper Georg Ljunggren is leading the work at sea. He is standing in the prow of an open motor boat, and up on the veranda Alma can hear her husband's booming orders echoing out across the shore, all the way up to the house.

When she opens the door, she can hear him very clearly.

Alma goes out into the cold and walks across the courtyard, recently cleared of snow, towards the barn, without looking down towards the shore.

There is no one in the barn, but when she opens the heavy door and walks in the cows and horses start to move in the darkness. The storm makes them uneasy.

Alma slowly walks up the steps to the hayloft. There is no one here either.

The hay reaches almost to the roof, but there is a small passageway along the wall so that she can make her way across the wooden floor. She walks over to the far wall and stops. She has stood here several times over the past few years, but now she reads the names once again. Then she takes the sheep shears, places the point against one of the planks of wood and begins to carve today's date: December 7th 1916. And a name.

The shouts from the shore fall silent.

Everything is quite still, and up in the loft Alma drops the shears. She clasps her hands together by the wall and prays to God.

Everything is silent at Eel Point.

Then comes the explosion.

It is as if the air all around the manor house is compressed, and at the same time the thundering roar from the shore rolls inland. The blast wave comes a second later; it cracks several window panes in the barn and deafens Alma. She closes her eyes, sinks back into the hay.

The mine has exploded too soon. Alma knows it.

When the blast wave has passed she gets to her feet in the hayloft. After a few frozen seconds the cows begin to bellow down in the barn. Then comes the sound of loud voices from the meadow by the shore. They are approaching the house very quickly.

Alma hurries down the steps.

Both lighthouses are still standing, she sees, they haven't been touched. But the mine is gone. All that is left is grey, murky water where it lay. And there is no sign of the lighthouse-keepers' boat.

Alma sees the other women coming: Ragnhild and Eivor, the wives of the lighthouse-keepers. They stare at her, their expressions numb.

'The master?' asks Alma.

Ragnhild shakes her head stiffly, and now Alma can see that her pinafore is wet with blood. 'My Albert . . . was standing in the prow.'

Her knees give way. Alma rushes towards her along the stone path and catches her as she falls.

14

Livia slept peacefully on the Sunday night. Joakim woke up as dawn was breaking after three hours of dreamless sleep. He could never sleep any longer than that at a stretch these days, and he woke with his head pounding with exhaustion.

In the morning he drove the children to Marnäs as usual, and when he got home the house was silent and empty. He carried on wallpapering one of the bedrooms at the southern end of the house.

At around one o'clock he heard the muted sound of a car engine approaching Eel Point. He looked out. A large wine-red Mercedes was driving up the gravel track at high speed. Joakim recognized it; he had seen it leaving the church in Marnäs, one of the first cars to depart after the funeral.

Katrine's mother had come to visit.

Even though the car was big, the woman who was driving it seemed even bigger, somehow. She struggled to get out of the door, as if she were stuck between the steering wheel and the driver's seat. But eventually she was standing in front of the house, dressed in skin-tight jeans, pointed boots and a leather jacket covered in buckles. A woman of about fifty-five, wearing red lipstick and thick black eyeliner and mascara.

She adjusted her pink silk scarf and looked over at the house with a forbidding expression. Then she lit a cigarette.

Mirja Rambe, his mother-in-law from Kalmar. She hadn't been in touch at all since the funeral.

Joakim took a deep breath, let the air out slowly, then went through the house to open the kitchen door.

'Hello, Joakim,' she said, blowing smoke out of the corner of her mouth.

'Hi there, Mirja.'

'I'm glad you're home. How are you?'

'Not so great.'

'I can understand that . . . this sort of thing makes you feel like shit.'

That was all the sympathy he got from her. Mirja dropped her cigarette on the gravel and moved towards the kitchen door; he stepped aside and she swept past in a miasma of tobacco and perfume.

In the kitchen she stopped and looked around. Joakim knew it was completely different from when she had lived in the house more than thirty years ago – but when she made no comment on all the work they had put in, he felt compelled to ask, 'Katrine redid most of this room last summer. What do you think?'

'It's good,' said Mirja. 'When Torun and I rented one of the rooms in the outhouse, there were single men living in here, in the main house. It just looked like shit. Dirt everywhere.'

'Did they work in the lighthouses?' asked Joakim.

'The lighthouse-keepers were gone by then,' said Mirja tersely. 'These were just drifters.'

She shook herself, as if she wanted to change the subject, and asked, 'So where are my little grandchildren, then?'

'Livia and Gabriel are at school. In Marnäs.'

'Already?'

'Well, it's pre-school. Livia's doing activities for six-year-olds.'

Mirja nodded, but without smiling. 'New names,' she said. 'Same dog kennel.'

'Pre-school isn't a dog kennel,' said Joakim. 'They love it.'

'I'm sure they do,' said Mirja. 'In my day it was called little school. Same old crap . . . day after day.'

Suddenly she turned around again. 'Speaking of animals . . .' She went back outside.

Joakim stayed in the kitchen, wondering how long Mirja was intending to stay. The house felt much smaller when his mother-in-law was there, as if there weren't enough air.

He heard a car door slam and she came back into the kitchen carrying something in each hand. She held up a grey box with a handle.

'It was free. I got it from my neighbour,' she said. 'I had to buy all the bits and pieces.'

Joakim realized that the box was a cat basket, and it wasn't empty.

'Are you joking?' he said.

Mirja shook her head and opened the basket. A fully grown grey tomcat with black stripes jumped out and stretched on the wooden floor. He looked mistrustfully at Joakim.

'This is Rasputin,' said Mirja. 'He'll live like a Russian monk here, won't he?'

She opened a big bag and took out several tins of cat food, a dish, and a tray with some cat litter.

'We can't have him here,' said Joakim.

'Of course you can,' said Mirja. 'He'll liven things up.'

Rasputin rubbed up against Joakim's legs and went out into the hallway. When Mirja opened the outside door he shot off.

'He's gone looking for rats,' she said.

'I haven't seen a single rat here,' said Joakim.

'That's because they're smarter than you.' Mirja took an apple out of the bowl on the kitchen table and went on, 'So when are you coming to Kalmar to visit me?'

'I didn't know we were invited.'

'Of course you are.' She bit into the apple. 'Come whenever you like.'

'Katrine never got an invitation, as far as I know,' said Joakim.

'Katrine wouldn't have come anyway,' said Mirja. 'But we called each other sometimes.'

'Once a year,' Joakim corrected her. 'She rang you at Christmas, but she always closed the door when she was on the phone to you.'

Mirja shook her head. 'I talked to her just a month ago.'

'What about?'

'Nothing special . . . my latest exhibition in Kalmar. And my new boyfriend, Ulf.'

'The two of you talked about you, in other words.'

'And about her.'

'So what did she say?'

'She felt lonely here,' said Mirja. 'She said she didn't miss Stockholm . . . but she did miss you.'

'I had to carry on working there for a while.'

He could of course have resigned from his teaching post earlier. He could have done a whole lot of things differently, but that wasn't something he wanted to discuss with Mirja.

She wandered further into the house, but stopped at the Rambe painting outside Joakim's bedroom.

'I gave this to Katrine for her twentieth birthday,' she said. 'Something to remember her grandmother by.'

'She really liked it.'

'It shouldn't be hanging here,' said Mirja. 'The last

picture by Torun that was sold at auction went for three hundred thousand kronor.'

'Really? But nobody knows we've got it here.'

Mirja stared intently at the picture, following the grey-black lines of the oil paints with her eyes. 'There are no horizontal lines at all, that's why it's so difficult to look at,' she said. 'This is the way you paint if you've been out in the blizzard.'

'And Torun had?'

'Yes. It was our first winter here. They had issued a warning about snowstorms, but Torun went off to the peat bog anyway. She liked walking inland and then sitting down to paint.'

'We were there yesterday,' said Joakim. 'It's lovely by the bog.'

'Not when the blizzard comes,' said Mirja. 'Torun's easel blew away before she had time to take it down, and suddenly she could see only a few yards in front of her. The sun disappeared. There was nothing but snow, everywhere.'

'But she survived?'

'She was on her way out on to the bog and stumbled into the water, but then the snow eased for a moment and she caught sight of the flashing light of the lighthouse.' Mirja looked at the painting and went on quietly, 'It was just in the nick of time. She said that when she was squelching about on the bog she could see the dead . . . those who were sacrificed during the Iron Age. They rose up out of the water and reached out for her.'

Joakim was listening intently. He was beginning to understand where the atmosphere in Torun's paintings came from.

'She had problems with her eyesight after that,' Mirja went on. 'That was when it started. And of course she went blind in the end.'

'Because of the blizzard?'

'Maybe . . . at any rate, she couldn't open her eyes for several days. The blizzard lifted sand from the fields and mixed it with the snow. It was like having pins stuck in your eyes.'

Mirja took a step away from the painting.

'People don't want dark paintings like this,' she said. 'Here on Öland it has to be an open sky, blue sea and great big fields full of yellow flowers, nothing else. Bright pictures in white frames.'

'The kind of thing you produce,' said Joakim.

'Absolutely.' Mirja nodded energetically, apparently not in the least annoyed. 'Sunny summer paintings for the summer people.' She looked around. 'But you don't seem to have any Mirja Rambe paintings here. Or have you?'

'No. Katrine has postcards of some of them somewhere.'

'That's good, postcards bring the money in too.'

Joakim wanted to leave the vicinity of the bedrooms – it felt too private. He moved back in the direction of the kitchen.

'How many of Torun's paintings were there to start with?' he asked.

'A lot. There must have been fifty.'

'And now there are only six, is that right?'

'Six, yes.' Mirja's expression was grim. 'The six that were saved.'

'And people say—'

Mirja interrupted crossly, 'I know what people say – that her daughter destroyed them. A collection that would be worth several million today. They say I put them in the stove one cold winter and burned them so we wouldn't freeze to death.'

'Katrine said that wasn't true,' said Joakim.

'Oh yes?'

'She said you were envious of Torun, and that you threw her paintings in the sea.'

'Katrine was born the year after it happened, so she wasn't there.' Mirja sighed. 'I hear the gossip here on the island: Mirja Rambe is a difficult old woman . . . her boyfriends are too young for her, she's an alcoholic . . . I suppose that's what Katrine said as well?'

Joakim shook his head, but he remembered how Mirja had staggered around at their wedding in Borgholm, trying to seduce his younger cousin.

They were out on the veranda now. Mirja fastened her leather jacket. 'Come with me,' she said. 'I want to show you something.'

Joakim followed her into the courtyard. He saw Rasputin slinking through the fence, heading down towards the sea.

'This hasn't changed much,' said Mirja as they walked over the uneven stones. 'Just as many weeds.'

She stopped, lit a fresh cigarette, then looked in through the dusty windows of the outhouse. 'Nobody home,' she said.

'The agent called it the guest house,' said Joakim. 'We're going to fix it up in the spring . . . at least, that was the plan.'

From the outside the whitewashed building looked like a rectangular single-storey block with a tiled roof. Inside was a wood store, a carpentry workshop, a laundry room with a floor damaged by damp, a sauna built in the 1970s and two guest rooms, each with a shower. In the past families had stayed in the guest rooms in the summer, when it got too hot in the main house.

Mirja looked at the building and shook her head. 'We lived out here for three years, Torun and I. Among the mice and the dust bunnies. It was like living in a fridge in the winter.'

Mirja turned her back on the outhouse. 'This is what I wanted to show you . . . over here.' She went over to the barn and pulled open the door leading into the vast darkness.

Mirja stubbed out her cigarette and switched on the lights, and Joakim followed her over the stone floor. She pointed towards the loft. 'It's up there,' she said.

Joakim hesitated for a few moments. Then he followed Mirja up the steep steps. Everything was just as untidy as the last time he'd been up in the loft.

'You can't get through here,' he said.

'Nonsense,' said Mirja.

She made her way without hesitation among all the suitcases, boxes, old pieces of furniture and bits of rusty machinery. She found narrow passageways between the rubbish and went over to the wall on the far side of the loft. Then she stopped and pointed at the broad planks of wood. 'Look . . . I found this thirty-five years ago.'

Joakim moved closer. By the faint light from the window he could see that someone had carved letters into the bare wood of the wall. A series of names and dates, and sometimes a cross or a biblical reference.

BELOVED CAROLINA 1868 was carved into a plank just below the ceiling. Beneath it came JAN, MUCH MISSED, GONE TO THE LORD 1883, and a little further down IN MEMORY OF ARTHUR CARLSSON, DROWNED JUNE 3RD 1911, JOHN 3:16.

There were many more names on the wall, but Joakim stopped reading and turned to Mirja. 'What is this?'

'These are the people from the manor house who have died,' said Mirja. Her voice, which had been quite loud, was now much quieter, almost reverential. 'Those who were close to them have carved their names. They were already here when I was young . . . but these are new.' She pointed to a couple of names close to the floor: it said CIKI in thin letters in one place, and SLAVKO in another.

'They could be refugees,' said Joakim. 'Eel Point was a camp some years ago.' He looked at Mirja. 'But why did people carve them here?'

'Well,' said Mirja, 'why do people put up gravestones?'

Joakim thought about the granite block he had chosen for Katrine the previous week. It would be delivered before Christmas, the stonemason had promised. He looked at Mirja. 'So that . . . they won't forget,' he said.

'Exactly,' said Mirja.

'Did you talk to Katrine about this wall?'

'Oh yes, way back in the summer. She was definitely interested, but I don't know if she came up here.'

'I think she did,' said Joakim.

Mirja ran her fingers over the characters carved into the wood. 'When I found these names as a teenager I read them over and over again,' she said. 'And then I began to wonder who they were. Why they had lived here and why they died. It's difficult to stop thinking about the dead, isn't it?'

Joakim looked at the wall and nodded silently.

'And I used to hear them,' Mirja went on.

'Who?'

'The dead.' Mirja leaned closer to the wall. 'If you just listen . . . you can hear them whispering.'

Joakim kept quiet, but couldn't hear a thing.

'I wrote a book about Eel Point last summer,' said Mirja as they were on their way back through the loft.

'I see,' said Joakim.

'I gave it to Katrine when she moved in here.'

'Did you? She never mentioned it.'

Suddenly Mirja stopped; she seemed to be looking for something on the floor. She moved a broken box and looked down. Beneath the box two names had been carved into the floor, very close together, along with a year: MIRJA & MARKUS 1961

'Mirja . . .' Joakim read, and looked at her. 'So you carved this?'

She nodded. 'We didn't want to carve our names into the wall, so we did it here instead.'

'So who's Markus?'

'He was my boyfriend. Markus Landkvist.'

Mirja didn't say any more. She merely sighed and strode over the two names, back towards the steps.

They said goodbye in front of the house. Mirja's energy was almost gone by now. She took a last long look at the house.

'I might come again,' she said.

'You do that,' said Joakim.

'And as I said, you must come to Kalmar with the children. I can find them some juice.'

'Fine . . . and if the cat doesn't settle, I'll bring him with me.'

Mirja smirked. 'Just you try it.'

Then she got into the Mercedes and started the engine.

When Mirja had disappeared in the direction of the coast road, Joakim walked slowly back across the court-yard. He looked down towards the sea – where had the cat gone?

The big door to the barn was still ajar; they hadn't closed it properly behind them. Joakim was drawn

213

towards it, and in the end he went back inside, into the darkness. The silence in here was like a cathedral.

He climbed up the steps again and went over to the far side of the loft. He read all the names on the wall, one after another.

He put his ear close to the wall and listened, but heard no whispering.

Then he picked up a nail that was lying on the floor and carefully carved the name KATRINE WESTIN and her dates into one of the lower planks.

When he had finished he stepped back to look at the whole wall. The memory of Katrine was preserved here now. It felt good.

The children loved Rasputin, of course. Gabriel patted him and Livia gave him a saucer of milk. They didn't want to be separated from the cat for a minute, but the evening after Mirja Rambe's visit the family were invited, without the cat, to visit their neighbours at the farm to the south. The older children weren't at home, but seven-year-old Andreas joined them at the dinner table before he and the Westin children went into the kitchen for some ice cream.

Joakim stayed in the dining room, drinking coffee with Roger and Maria Carlsson. The topic of conversation was fairly inevitable: looking after and renovating houses by the sea that were exposed to all kinds of weather. But he also had another question, which he eventually asked:

'I wondered if you'd heard any stories about our place? About Eel Point?'

'Stories?' said Roger Carlsson.

'Yes, ghost stories or other tales,' said Joakim. 'Katrine said she'd talked to you last summer about . . . about the fact that it was haunted.'

That was the first time he had mentioned her name all evening – he took care not to talk too much about his late wife. He didn't want to seem obsessed, after all. He *wasn't* obsessed.

'She didn't talk to me about any ghosts,' said Roger.

'She did talk to me about it when she came over for coffee,' said Maria. 'She was just wondering whether Eel Point had a bad reputation.' She looked at her husband. 'I mean, when we were little the adults used to talk about a secret room at Eel Point that was haunted . . . do you remember, Roger?'

Her husband just shook his head – obviously ghosts weren't one of his major interests – but Joakim leaned forward. 'Where was this room? Do you know?'

'No idea,' said Roger, drinking his coffee.

'No, I don't know either,' said Maria. 'But my grandfather said something about the ghosts haunting this room every Christmas. The dead came back to the manor and gathered in a particular room. And then they took—'

'That's just ridiculous nonsense,' said Roger, picking up the coffee pot and offering it to Joakim. 'More coffee?'

15

Tilda Davidsson lay naked and sweaty on her thin mattress. 'Was that good?' she asked.

Martin was sitting on the edge of the bed with his back to her. 'Yes . . . I suppose it was.'

As he quickly pulled on his pants and jeans after getting out of bed that Sunday morning, Tilda should have realized what was coming, but she didn't.

He had sat down on the edge of the bed and was looking out of the window.

'I don't think we can do this,' he said eventually.

'Do what?' she asked, still naked under the covers.

'This . . . all this. It's not working.' He was still looking out of the window. 'Karin's asking questions.'

'About what?'

Tilda still didn't realize she was in the process of being dumped. Screwed and then dumped – classic.

Martin had arrived late on Friday, and everything had seemed just the same as usual. Tilda hadn't asked what he'd told his wife – she never did. That evening they had stayed in her small apartment; she had made fish stew. Martin had seemed relaxed, telling her about the new cohort of recruits that had started at the police training academy this term, some good and some less suitable.

'But I expect we'll knock them into shape,' he said.

Tilda nodded, thinking back to her early days at the academy; she had been one of twenty recruits. Mostly boys, just a few girls. They had quickly divided their new tutors into three categories: old tutors who were members of the police force, nice but a little fusty; civilian tutors who taught law and hadn't a clue about real police work – and then the young police tutors who were mainly responsible for the practical work. They came from the field and had exciting stories to tell; they were the role models for the students. Martin Ahlquist was one of them.

On the Saturday they had travelled north in Martin's car, right up to the most northerly point of the island. Tilda hadn't been there since she was little, but she remembered the feeling of having reached the end of the world. Now, in November, a bitterly cold wind was blowing off the sea, and there wasn't a soul in sight around the lighthouses. The chalk-white tower rising above the point, Long Erik, had reminded her of the twin lighthouses at Eel Point. She wanted to discuss the case with Martin, but didn't bring it up – this was her weekend off.

They ate a late lunch at the only restaurant in Byxelkrok that was open in the winter, then went back to Marnäs and stayed in for the rest of the evening.

It was after that that Martin became more reserved, Tilda thought, despite the fact that she tried to keep the conversation going.

They fell asleep in silence, but then in the morning Martin sat down on the edge of the bed and started talking. Without looking at Tilda once he said he had done a lot of thinking since she moved to Öland. He had thought about the choices in his life. And

217

now he had decided. It felt like the right decision.

'It'll be good for you too,' he said. 'Good for everyone.'

'You mean . . . you're leaving me?' she said quietly.

'No. We're leaving each other.'

'I moved here for your sake.' Tilda looked at Martin's naked, hairy back. 'I didn't want to leave Växjö, but I did it for you. I just want you to know that.'

'What do you mean?'

'People were talking about us. I wanted to put a stop to it.'

Martin nodded. 'Everybody likes gossip,' he said. 'But now there's nothing for them to talk about.'

There wasn't really anything more to say. Five minutes later, Martin was dressed; he picked up his bag from the floor without looking at her.

'Right then,' he said.

'So it wasn't worth it?' she asked.

'Yes, it was,' he said. 'For quite a long time. But not now.'

'You're so afraid of conflict,' she said.

Martin didn't respond. He opened the front door.

Tilda suppressed the impulse to send her best wishes to his wife.

She heard the door close, and footsteps disappearing down the stairs. He would go out to his car in the square and drive home to his family as if nothing had happened.

Tilda was still in bed, naked.

Everything was silent. A used condom lay on the floor.

'Are you good enough?' she asked her blurred reflection in the window pane.

No, did you think you were? You're just the Other Woman.

After sitting there feeling sorry for herself for more

218

than half an hour, and getting over the urge to shave off all her blonde hair, Tilda got up. She had a shower, got dressed and decided to go over to the home to see Gerlof. Old people without romantic complications were what she needed right now.

But before she could set off the telephone rang. It was the duty officer in Borgholm calling her out; there had been a break-in at a vicarage north of Marnäs over the weekend. A retired couple living in the house had surprised the burglars, and the man was in hospital with head injuries and several fractures.

Work dulled Tilda's pain.

She got to the house around two, when the daylight was already beginning to fade over the island.

The first person she met at the scene was Hans Majner. Unlike her, he was dressed in full uniform, and was walking around with a roll of blue and white tape and signs that said POLICE NO ENTRY in his hand.

'So where were you yesterday?' he asked.

'I wasn't working,' said Tilda. 'Nobody called me out.'

'You have to check for yourself whether there's anything going on that you need to know about.'

Tilda slammed the car door. 'Shut your mouth,' she said.

Majner turned around. 'What did you say?'

'I told you to shut your mouth,' said Tilda. 'Stop criticizing me all the time.'

She had definitely ruined things with Majner now, but she didn't care.

He stood there motionless for several seconds, as if he didn't really understand what she had said.

'I'm not criticizing you,' he said.

'Really? Give me the tape.'

Silently she began to cordon off the back of the

vicarage, looking for impressions left by shoes to cover up out in the garden. The scene-of-crime technicians would be over from Kalmar on Monday morning.

There were in fact several prints left by shoes in the muddy ground around the house. They looked as if they came from men's boots or shoes with grooves in the soles – and further in among the trees there were traces in the undergrowth indicating that someone had fallen head-first, then crept along on their hands and knees.

Tilda counted the tracks. It looked as if there had been three visitors to the vicarage.

A woman came out from the veranda. It was the lady from next door; she had a key to the house and was keeping an eye on it for the elderly couple who were in hospital in Kalmar. She asked if they would like to come over to her house for a cup of coffee.

A coffee break with Majner?

'I'd rather take a quick look inside, thanks,' said Tilda.

When she had sent the neighbour home she went up the stone steps. On the floor of the hallway past the veranda lay a mosaic of shards of glass from a mirror that had fallen down. The rug was in a heap and blood had splashed across the doorway and over the wooden floor.

The door to the large drawing room was half-open, and she stepped over the broken glass and looked in.

It was a mess. The doors of glass-fronted cabinets stood wide open, and every drawer in an old bureau had been pulled out. Tilda could see the marks left on the polished wooden floor by muddy shoes – the technicians would have plenty to work with here.

When they had finished at the vicarage the two police officers went their separate ways, without exchanging a single word. Tilda got into her car and drove down to the home where Gerlof lived.

'A break-in,' said Tilda to explain why she was late.

'Really?' said Gerlof. 'Where?'

'The vicarage at Hagelby. They beat up the owner.'

'Badly?'

'Pretty badly – he was stabbed as well. But I'm sure you'll be able to read more about it in the paper tomorrow.'

She sat down at his little coffee table, took out her tape recorder and thought about Martin. He would be home by now. He would have walked in through the door, hugged Karin and the kids and complained about how dull the police conference in Kalmar had been.

Gerlof said something.

'Sorry?'

Tilda hadn't been listening. She'd been thinking about how Martin had walked out of the door without looking back.

'Have you been looking for traces of the people who did it?'

Tilda nodded, without going into details.

'The scene-of-crime team will go over the place tomorrow.' She switched on the microphone. 'Shall we talk about the family now?'

Gerlof nodded, but still asked, 'So what do you do, then, at the scene of a crime?'

'Well . . . the technicians preserve any traces,' said Tilda. 'They take photographs and film what's there. They look for fingerprints and hairs and traces of textiles – fibres from clothing. And for biological traces like blood, of course. And then they make plaster casts of any footprints outdoors. They can preserve prints left inside the house from shoes as well, if they make an electrostatic—'

'You're very conscientious,' Gerlof interrupted her.

Tilda nodded. 'We try to work methodically. We're assuming they came in a car, a large people carrier or a van. But we don't have much to go on at the moment.'

'And of course it's important that you find these villains.'

'Absolutely.'

'Could you get me a piece of paper from the desk?'

Tilda did as he asked and looked on silently as Gerlof wrote a few short lines on the piece of paper. Then he handed it to her.

There were three names, in Gerlof's neat handwriting:
John Hagman
Dagmar Karlsson
Edla Gustafsson

Tilda read through them and looked up at Gerlof. 'OK,' she said. 'Are these the burglars?'

'No. They're old friends of mine.'

'Right . . .'

'They can help you,' said Gerlof.

'How?'

'They see things.'

'OK . . .'

'They all live near the road, and they keep an eye on the traffic,' said Gerlof. 'For John and Edla and Dagmar a car is still a big event, particularly at this time of year, in the winter. Edla and Dagmar drop whatever they're doing to look out and see who's driving past.'

'OK. Then I'd better have a chat with them,' said Tilda. 'We're grateful for any information.'

'Quite. Start with John down in Stenvik. We're friends . . . say hello from me.'

'And ask about strange cars,' said Tilda.

'Exactly. John's bound to have seen a few driving along the coast. Then you can go over to Dagmar – she lives by the turning for Altorp – and ask her the same thing. And Edla Gustafsson – Edla in Hultet – is also worth talking to. She lives on the main road, near Speteby on the way to Borgholm.'

Tilda looked at the list of names. 'Thanks,' she said. 'I'll call in if I'm in the neighbourhood.'

Then she pressed Record.

'Gerlof . . . when you think about your brother Ragnar, what comes into your mind?'

Gerlof was silent, mulling the question over.

'Eels,' he said eventually. 'He liked to be out in his little motor boat checking his nets on the seabed in the autumn. He liked to dupe the eels as well . . . to try out different kinds of bait to lure the females into the nets at night and get them into the pots.'

'The females?'

'You only catch female eels.' Gerlof smiled at her. 'Nobody wants the males, they're too small and feeble.'

'So are a lot of men,' said Tilda.

16

'When will it be Christmas Eve, Daddy?' asked Livia one evening when Joakim was putting her to bed.

'Soon . . . in a month.'

'How many days?'

'In . .' Joakim looked at the Pippi Longstocking calendar above her bed and counted, 'twenty-eight days.'

Livia nodded and looked thoughtful.

'What are you puzzling out?' he asked. 'Are you thinking about Christmas presents?'

'No,' said Livia. 'But Mummy will be home then, won't she?'

Joakim didn't say anything at first.

'I'm not so sure about that,' he said slowly.

'She will.'

'No, I don't think we should get our hopes—'

'She will,' said Livia more loudly. 'Mummy will come back then.'

Then she pulled the coverlet up to her nose and refused to talk any more.

Livia had developed a new sleep pattern – Joakim had discovered this after just a couple of weeks at Eel Point. She would sleep peacefully for two nights, but on the third she would become restless and start calling out for him.

'Dad-dee?'

It would usually start an hour or so after midnight, and however deeply Joakim was sleeping, he was instantly wide awake.

Livia's cries also woke the cat, Rasputin. He would jump up on to a windowsill and stare out into the darkness, as if he could see something moving between the buildings.

'Dad-dee?'

At least there was some progress, thought Joakim as he went towards his daughter's room. She no longer called out for Katrine.

This Thursday night he sat down on the edge of Livia's bed and stroked her back. She didn't wake up, just turned to face the wall and slowly relaxed again.

Joakim stayed where he was, waiting for her to start talking. After a couple of minutes she began, in a calm and slightly monotonous voice.

'Daddy?'

'Yes?' he answered quietly. 'Can you see anyone, Livia?'

She was still lying with her back to him.

'Mummy,' she said.

He was prepared now. But he was still unsure if she was really asleep, or simply lying in some kind of half-awake trance – and he was just as unsure if this conversation was really any good for her. Or for him.

'Where is she?' he asked. 'Where's Mummy?'

Joakim watched her lift her right hand from the coverlet and wave it feebly. He turned his head, but of course saw nothing in the shadows. He looked down at his daughter again. 'Can Katrine . . . does Mummy want to say anything to me?'

No reply. When he asked longer questions there was hardly ever a reply.

225

'Where is she?' he asked again. 'Where's Mummy, Livia?'

Still no reply.

Joakim thought for a moment, then asked slowly, 'What was Mummy doing on the jetty? Why did she go down to the sea?'

'She wanted to . . . find out.'

'Find out what?'

'The truth.'

'The truth? Who from?'

Livia was silent.

'Where's Mummy now?' he asked.

'Close.'

'Has she . . . is she in the house?'

Livia didn't respond. Joakim could feel that Katrine was not in the house. She was staying away.

'Can you talk to her now?' he asked. 'Is she listening?'

'She's watching.'

'Can she see us?'

'Maybe.'

Joakim held his breath. He searched for the right questions.

'What can you see now, Livia?'

'There's someone on the shore . . . by the lighthouses.'

'That must be Mummy. Has she—'

'No,' said Livia. 'Ethel.'

'What?'

'It's Ethel.'

Joakim went completely cold.

'No,' he said. 'That can't be her name.'

'Yes.'

'No, Livia.'

He had raised his voice, almost yelled.

'Yes. Ethel wants to talk.'

Joakim was still sitting on the bed, incapable of moving.

'I . . . don't want to talk,' he said. 'Not to her.'

'She wants—'

'No,' said Joakim quickly. His heart was pounding, his mouth was dry. 'Ethel can't be here.'

Livia was silent again.

He couldn't breathe any more, he just wanted to escape from this room. But he stayed there on the edge of Livia's bed, stiff and terrified. And all the time his eyes were flicking over towards the half-open door.

The house was completely silent.

Livia lay motionless beneath the covers now, her head still turned away from Joakim. He could hear the faint sound of her breathing.

In the end he managed to stand up, and forced himself to go out into the dark corridor.

The night outside was light; the full moon had found itself a place between the clouds and was shining in through the freshly painted windows. But Joakim didn't want to look out; he was afraid he might see the thin face of a woman staring in at him, her expression filled with hatred.

He kept his eyes firmly fixed on the floor and went into the porch, where he saw that the outside door to the veranda was not locked. Why could he never remember to lock it before he went to bed?

Well, from now on he would definitely remember.

He walked quickly over and turned the key, with a brief glance towards the shadows in the inner courtyard.

Then he turned around and crept back to bed. He pulled Katrine's soft nightgown from under his pillow, clutching it tightly beneath the covers.

* * *

After that night Joakim decided not to ask Livia about her dreams any more. He didn't want to encourage her any longer, and had begun to be afraid of her answers.

On the Friday morning, after driving the children to Marnäs and before carrying on with the renovation of the ground floor, he did something that felt ridiculous, yet at the same time important. He went around the manor talking to his dead older sister.

He went into the kitchen and stood by the table. 'Ethel,' he said, 'you can't stay here.'

Talking to her should have made him feel foolish, but all Joakim felt was grief and loneliness.

Then he went outside, blinking against the cold wind blowing off the sea, and said quietly, 'Ethel . . . I'm sorry, but you're not welcome here.'

Finally he went over to the barn, pulled open the big door and stood in the doorway.

'Ethel, go away.'

He didn't expect a reply from his dead sister, and he didn't get one. But he felt better, just a little bit better – as if he were keeping her at a distance.

On Saturday the family had visitors: their former neighbours from Stockholm, Lisa and Michael Hesslin. They had called a few days earlier and asked if they could stay over on Öland on their way back from Denmark. Joakim had been pleased – both he and Katrine had enjoyed having Lisa and Michael as their neighbours.

'Joakim,' said Lisa when they had parked the car and come into the hallway. She hugged him, for a long time. 'We really wanted to come and see how . . . Are you tired?'

'A little,' he said, patting her.

'You *look* a little tired. You must make sure you get some sleep.'

228

Joakim just nodded.

Michael patted him on the shoulder and moved into the house, his expression curious. 'I see you've been carrying on with the work here,' he said. 'Fantastic skirting boards.'

'They're original,' said Joakim, following him out into the corridor. 'I've just sanded them down and painted them.'

'And you've chosen exactly the right wallpaper border. It really fits in with the soul of the house.'

'Thanks, that was the idea.'

'Are you doing all the rooms in white?'

'Down here on the ground floor, yes.'

'Looks good,' said Michael. 'Cool and harmonious.'

For the first time Joakim felt a faint pride in what they had achieved so far. He had carried on with what Katrine had started, in spite of everything.

Lisa walked into the kitchen and nodded approvingly. 'Wonderful . . . but have you had a feng shui consultant here?'

'Feng shui?' said Joakim. 'I don't think so. Is it important?'

'Absolutely. It's really important to know how the flow of energy works, particularly here on the coast.' Lisa looked around and placed a hand on her chest. 'There are powerful earth energies here too . . . I can feel them. And they must be able to flow without any kind of impediment, in and out of the house.'

'I'll bear it in mind.'

'We've got a fantastic feng shui consultant who re-organized our cottage on Gotland. I'll give you her number.'

Joakim nodded and heard Katrine giggling inside his head. She had always laughed at Lisa's spirituality.

* * *

They had an excellent dinner at the kitchen table that evening. Joakim fried some plaice, which he had bought in Marnäs. The guests had brought a bottle of white wine, and he drank a glass for the first time in many years. It didn't taste particularly good, but he relaxed a little and was almost able to forget Livia's talk of his dead sister in her sleep.

Livia herself was bright and cheerful this evening. She sat at the table with them and told Lisa about her three teachers at pre-school – how two of them would nip outside for a secret cigarette, although they told the children they were just going out for some fresh air.

Michael told the children about a female elk and her calf they had seen running along the road as they were driving through Småland. Gabriel and Livia listened avidly.

Both children were excited by the visit from the big city, and it was difficult to get them to change into their pyjamas and go to bed. Gabriel fell asleep straight away, but Livia asked Lisa to read her a story about Emil's mischievous adventures.

After twenty minutes Lisa came back into the kitchen.

'Has she gone to sleep?' asked Joakim.

'Yes, she was worn out. She'll sleep like a log all night.'

'I hope so.'

He stayed in the kitchen chatting to Lisa and Michael for another hour, then helped them take their bags to the corner bedroom beyond the large drawing room.

'I've just finished this room,' he said. 'You can be the inaugural guests.'

He had lit the tiled stove earlier in the day, and the guest room felt warm and welcoming.

Half an hour later they had all gone to bed. Joakim lay in the darkness listening to the murmur of Lisa and Michael's voices from the guest room. It felt really good to have them here. Eel Point needed more guests.

Living guests.

He thought about the stories the Carlsson family had told him about the dead at the manor house. And Livia had said the same thing about Katrine – that she would come home on Christmas Eve.

To see her again. To be able to talk to her.

No. He mustn't think that way.

After a few minutes there was silence in the house.

Joakim closed his eyes and fell asleep.

Loud cries could be heard throughout the house.

Joakim woke up with a start and an instant thought: *Livia?*

No, it was a man's voice.

He stayed in bed, sleepy and confused, then remembered he had guests staying.

It was Michael Hesslin calling out in the darkness.

Then he heard the sound of rapid footsteps and Lisa's questioning voice in the corridor.

It was twenty to two when Joakim got out of bed, but first he went to check on the children. Both Livia and Gabriel were fast asleep, but of course Rasputin had jumped out of his basket and was slinking uneasily along the walls.

Joakim went towards the kitchen. The light was on in the hallway, and when he got there Lisa was just putting on her coat and boots. She wasn't smiling now.

'What's happened?' he asked.

'I don't know. Michael woke up and started yelling. He ran out to the car.' Lisa buttoned her coat. 'I'd better go and see what's wrong.'

She went outside and Joakim went into the kitchen, still half-asleep.

Rasputin had disappeared and the house was

231

completely silent now. He put on some water to make tea.

When the tea was ready he stood by the window with his cup and saw Lisa sitting next to Michael in the car. It was snowing lightly, the flakes glittering as they fell through the air.

Lisa seemed to be asking Michael questions; he was sitting behind the wheel just staring out through the windscreen and shaking his head.

After a few minutes Lisa came back inside. She looked at Joakim. 'Michael had a nightmare . . . He says someone was standing next to the bed watching him.'

Joakim held his breath. He nodded and asked quietly, 'Is he coming back inside?'

'I think he wants to stay in the car for a while,' said Lisa, and added, 'I think we'll probably drive down and stay the night at the hotel in Borgholm. It is open in the winter, isn't it?'

'I think so.' Joakim paused, then asked, 'Does he usually . . . sleep badly?'

'No,' said Lisa. 'Not in Stockholm. But he has been a bit on edge. Work isn't going too well right now. He doesn't say much about it, but . . .'

'There's nothing dangerous around here,' said Joakim.

Then he thought about what Livia had said in her sleep. He added, 'Of course, things have been pretty miserable here over the last few weeks. But we wouldn't stay here if we didn't feel . . . safe.'

Lisa glanced around quickly. 'There are powerful energies here,' she said, then asked tentatively, 'Have you felt as if Katrine were still here? As if she were watching over you all?'

Joakim hesitated before nodding.

'Yes,' he said. 'I do feel something at times.'

He fell silent again. He would have liked to talk

about the things he'd experienced, but Lisa Hesslin wasn't the right person to talk to.

'I have to pack,' she said.

Quarter of an hour later Joakim was back at the kitchen window watching the Hesslins' big car driving away. He watched them for a long time, until the tail lights had disappeared up on the main road.

The house was still silent.

Joakim left the light on in the hall and went back to his bedroom, after checking that the children were still sleeping peacefully. He climbed back into bed and lay there in the darkness, his eyes open.

On Monday morning he drove the children into Marnäs, then started sanding down, painting and wall-papering the penultimate bedroom still to be renovated on the ground floor. As he worked he listened for noises, but heard nothing.

It took five hours, including a short lunch break, to finish three of the walls. At around two o'clock he stopped for the day and made some coffee. He went out on to the veranda with his cup, breathed in the cold air and saw that the sun had already gone down behind the outhouse.

The inner courtyard lay in darkness, but Joakim could see that the door to the barn was half-open. Hadn't he closed it on Friday, before the Hesslins arrived?

He pulled on a jacket and opened the outside door.

It was twenty steps over to the barn. When he got there, Joakim pushed the huge door open wide and stepped into the darkness. The old black switch was in the middle of the shorter wall. When he turned it, two small bulbs spread a pale-yellow light across the stone floor, the empty stalls and feeding troughs.

Everything was silent. It didn't look as if any rats had moved in, despite the cold.

Every time he came in here he discovered something new, and now he noticed that the floor near the door looked as if it had been freshly swept. Katrine had mentioned something about the fact that she had been cleaning the barn when they were discussing the various buildings in the autumn.

Joakim looked over towards the wooden steps up to the hayloft and thought about the day he had been up there with Mirja Rambe. He would like to see the wall she had shown him again, the memorial to the dead.

Just a quick look.

When he got up there he could see the rays of the sun again. It was just above the roof of the outhouse, shining in through the small panes on the southern side of the barn.

Joakim moved slowly across the floor, picking his way among all the rubbish.

Finally he was standing in front of the far wall. In the glow of the yellow winter sun the names carved in the wood stood out sharply, their contours filled with shadows.

And on a plank almost at the very bottom were Katrine's name and dates.

His Katrine. Joakim read the name over and over again.

The gaps between the boards were narrow and pitch black, but as he stood beside the broad planks he had a sense of darkness behind them. He suddenly got the feeling that this was not in fact the outside wall of the barn he was standing next to.

Despite the fact that it was almost time to go and pick up Livia and Gabriel, he quickly went outside again. He took a few steps away from the barn and counted the small windows on the upper floor. One, two, three, four, five. Then he went up into the loft again.

There were four windows, high up below the roof. The last one must be on the other side of the wall.

There was no door or gap in the wall. Joakim pressed several of the thick planks, but none of them moved.

17

Dear Karin,

This is a letter from someone who wishes you no ill,
but simply wants to open your eyes. This is the way
things are: Martin has been deceiving you for a long
time. More than three years ago he took over
responsibility for a class at the police training academy
in Växjö; there was a woman in this class who was
almost ten years younger than him. After a party at
the end of the first academic year, Martin started a
relationship with her which has continued until now.

It ended just a few days ago.

I know this for certain because I am the younger
woman in question. I couldn't put up with Martin's
lies any longer in the end, and I hope you won't either
when you find out the truth.

Perhaps you need some kind of proof to convince
you completely? I don't want to get too intimate, but I
can for example describe the two-inch scar above his
right groin after the hernia operation he had a few
years ago. He had been moving rocks at your country
place outside Orrefors when it happened, isn't that
right?

And don't you agree that he ought to wax his hairy

*back and arse now and again, when he's so vain
about the rest of his perfectly honed body?*

*As I said I don't want to hurt anyone, even though I
know it will be painful for you to find out the truth.
There are so many lies in the world and so many
treacherous liars. But together you and I can at least
fix one of them.*

*Best wishes from
'The other woman'*

Tilda leaned back in her chair and read through the
letter on her computer screen one last time.

It was quarter to eight in the morning. She had
arrived at the police station at seven in order to produce
a clean copy from the draft she had scribbled down on
a piece of paper the previous evening. The station was
empty – as usual, Hans Majner wasn't in this early. He
usually arrived about ten, if he bothered to turn up at
all.

Tilda had seen Karin Ahlquist only once. It was when
Martin had had to have his son Anton with him at the
police academy for a few hours before Karin could pick
him up. At about four o'clock she had come out to the
exercise area where they were practising traffic control.
She was a head taller than Tilda, with dark, curly hair.
She remembered how Martin's wife had smiled at her
husband, proud and loving, as they said goodbye that
day.

Tilda looked out of the station window at the empty
street.

Did she feel better now? Was her revenge on Martin
really sweet?

Yes.

She was tired, but she did actually feel better now

the letter was written. She quickly printed off a copy.

When she had taken out a plain white envelope, she felt unsure again. Martin had told her that Karin worked in the county environmental department, and Tilda thought about sending the letter there so that it wouldn't fall into Martin's hands. But post that came to the county office was usually opened and noted in the diary, so in the end she put Karin Ahlquist's home address, printing it neatly in capital letters; she didn't think Martin would recognize her writing. No sender's name.

She pushed the letter into her cotton bag along with the tape recorder, put on her jacket and police cap, and left the station.

There was a yellow postbox on the pavement near the police car. Tilda stopped, but didn't take the letter out of her bag. She hadn't sealed it or put a stamp on it, and she didn't want to post it just yet.

Today she was giving talks on law and order to three school classes after lunch, but before that she had time to go out in the car for a while, check the traffic and knock on a few doors out in the country.

Edla Gustafsson lived near Speteby, in a little red house with a view across the alvar. There weren't many trees around, and the main road went right past her house.

Time had stood still here. This is how people ought to live, thought Tilda – in the wilderness far away from all men.

She took her rucksack with her and rang the doorbell. A sturdy-looking woman opened the door.

'Hi, my name is Tilda . . .'

'Yes, yes, that's fine,' the woman interrupted her. 'Gerlof said you'd be calling. Come in, come in.'

Two black cats slipped away into the kitchen, but Edla Gustafsson seemed pleased to have a visit from a

238

relative of Gerlof. Edla was cheerful and energetic, hardly bothering to listen to Tilda's explanation of why she was there. She quickly put some coffee on and fetched some small cakes from the larder. Cakes with jam, with pearl sugar, with chocolate – ten different kinds altogether on a silver dish, all laid out beautifully in the small parlour.

Tilda stared at the coffee table as she sat down. 'I don't think I've ever seen this many cakes.'

'Really?' said Edla in surprise. 'Have you never been to a cake shop?'

'Well, yes, but . . .'

Tilda looked at a black and white wedding photograph on the wall and thought about the letter to Martin's wife. She had decided to send it that evening. Then Karin Ahlquist would receive it at the end of the week, and have all weekend to kick Martin out.

She cleared her throat.

'I have one or two questions, Edla. I don't know if you've seen the newspaper, but there has been a break-in with serious violence in Hagelby, and the police could do with some help.'

'I've had a break-in as well,' said Edla. 'They got into the garage and took a petrol can.'

'Really?' said Tilda. 'And when was this?'

'It was the autumn of '73.'

'Right . . .'

'I remember, because my husband was still alive and we still had the car.'

'OK, but we're looking at more recent break-ins at the moment, over the last few months.' Tilda held up her notepad. 'So I have a few questions about unfamiliar cars on the main road. Gerlof tells me that you keep an eye on the traffic.'

'Through the window, that's right. I always have done,

I can hear them getting closer. But there are so many nowadays.'

'But I don't suppose there are too many cars at this time of year, in winter?'

'No, it's easier now than when the tourists come. But I don't write the numbers down any more, I haven't time. They drive past so quickly. And I'm no good at identifying the make of a car.'

'But have you seen any cars you didn't recognize over the past few days? Late at night . . . last Friday, for example?'

Edla gave it some thought. 'Big cars?'

'Probably. In some cases they have stolen quite a lot, so they would have needed a car with plenty of space to stow everything.'

'Trucks often drive past here. Dustbin lorries too, and tractors.'

'I don't think they're driving a lorry,' said Tilda.

'A big black car came past here last Thursday. It was heading north.'

'Like a van? Was it late at night?'

'Yes, it was just before twelve, after I'd switched the lights off up in the bedroom,' said Edla. 'A big black van, that's what it was.'

'Good. Did it look new or old?'

'Not particularly new. And there was some kind of writing on the side. "Kalmar", and something to do with welding.'

Tilda made a note of that. 'Great. Thank you so much for your help.'

'Will there be a reward if you catch them?'

Tilda lowered her notepad and shook her head sadly.

After her visit to Edla, Tilda headed back towards the north and turned on to the coast road south of Marnäs.

It went past Eel Point, but that wasn't where she was going. She wanted to take a quick look at her grandfather Ragnar's old place in Saltfjärden before she went back to the police station.

PRIVATE ROAD, it said on a piece of wood by the side of the road. An icy, overgrown track led down towards the sea, and Tilda's police car bounced along in the wheel ruts.

The track led past an old Iron Age burial ground covered in round stones, and ended at a closed gate in front of a white cottage. She could just catch a glimpse of the sea through a grove of pine trees.

Tilda parked by the gate and walked in among the overgrown grass in the garden. Her memories were vague, and everything seemed smaller than when she had last been here with her father, fifteen years earlier. At that time Ragnar was long dead and Tilda's grandmother had been taken into hospital. The house had been for sale. She vaguely remembered the smell of tar, and that there had been several old eel tanks in the yard. They were gone now.

'Hello?' she called out into the soughing wind.

No reply.

The house itself was small, but it was just one of several buildings. There was a boathouse with closed shutters at the windows, a wood store, a barn and something that might have been a sauna. It was a fantastic location, right by the shore, but the whole place needed painting and there was an air of gloom and abandonment about it all.

She knocked on the door of the cottage. No reply there either, as expected. The house was probably just a summer residence now. All traces of the Davidsson family were gone.

Eel Point wasn't visible from here, but when Tilda

241

had passed the pine trees and walked out on to the meadow by the shore, she could see the old wreck a few hundred yards away, and the twin lighthouses on the horizon to the south.

She moved closer to the water, and a large bird that had been sitting on a rock on the shore took off slowly, its wings beating heavily. A bird of prey.

On the edge of the wood there was another cottage, she noticed, and in front of it on the lawn was a chair where someone had placed a pile of blankets.

Then the blankets moved. A head poked out and Tilda realized there was a person wrapped up in them. She went closer and saw that it was an elderly man with a grey beard and a woolly hat, with a Thermos flask beside him and a long, dark-green telescope in his hands.

'You scared off my *Haliaetus albicilla*,' he called out.

Tilda went over to him. 'Sorry?'

'The sea eagle,' said the man. 'Didn't you see it?'

'I did, yes,' said Tilda.

A birdwatcher. They turned up along the coast at all times of the year.

'It was watching the tufted ducks,' said the ornithologist. He pointed his telescope out to sea, where a dozen or so black and white birds were bobbing along on the waves. 'They swim here all year round and hang out with the birds of prey. They're tough little devils.'

'Very exciting,' said Tilda.

'It certainly is.' The man in the blankets looked at her uniform and said, 'This has to be the first time we've ever had the police out here.'

'Well, it does seem very quiet out here.'

'It is. In the winter, at least. Just cargo ships passing by, and a few motor boats now and again.'

'This late in the year?'

'I haven't seen any here this winter,' said the man. 'But I've heard them further down the coast.'

Tilda gave a start. 'You mean around Eel Point?'

'Yes, or even further south. You can hear the sound of an engine several miles away, if the wind is in the right direction.'

'A woman drowned over by the lighthouses at Eel Point a few weeks ago,' said Tilda. 'Were you here then?'

'I think so.'

Tilda looked at him, her expression serious. 'You remember the case?'

'Yes. I read about it . . . but I didn't see anything. You can't see the point through the trees.'

'But can you remember if you heard the sound of an engine on that particular day?'

The ornithologist thought it over. 'Maybe,' he said.

'If a boat went past going south out in the bay, would you have seen it?'

'It's possible. I often sit out here.'

It was a vague testimony. Edla Gustafsson's super-vision of the road was much better than this birdwatcher's monitoring of the Baltic. She thanked him for his help and set off back to the car.

'Perhaps we could keep in touch?'

Tilda turned around. 'Sorry?'

'It's a bit lonely here.' He smiled at her. 'Beautiful but lonely. Perhaps you'd like to come back some time?'

She shook her head. 'I don't think so,' she said. 'You'll have to find a whooper swan to keep you company.'

After lunch Tilda spent almost three hours at the school talking about law and order with the pupils. She had several traffic reports to write up when she got back to the station, but couldn't quite let go of the drowning at

243

Eel Point. She collected her thoughts, then picked up the telephone and rang the manor house.

Joakim Westin picked up after three signals. Tilda could hear the sound of a ball thudding and happy children's voices in the background – a good sign. But Westin himself sounded tired and distant when he answered. Not angry – it was just that there was no strength in his voice.

Tilda didn't bother with any small talk.

'I need to ask you something,' she said. 'Did your wife know anyone who has a boat here on Öland? A boat owner close to your place?'

'I don't know anyone at all who has a boat here,' said Westin. 'And Katrine . . . she never mentioned anyone with a boat either.'

'What did she do during the week when you were in Stockholm? Did she talk about it?'

'She was renovating the house and furnishing it, and looking after the children. She had her hands full.'

'Did she ever have any visitors?'

'Only me. As far as I know.'

'OK, thanks,' said Tilda. 'I'll be in touch if—'

'I have a question too,' Westin interrupted her.

'Yes?'

'When you were here you said something about a relative of yours who knew Eel Point . . . someone from the local-history society in Marnäs.'

'That's right – Gerlof,' said Tilda. 'He's my grandfather's brother. He's written a few things for the society's yearbook.'

'I'd really like to have a chat with him.'

'About the manor?'

'About its history . . . and about a particular story about Eel Point.'

'A story?'

'A story about the dead,' said Westin.

'Right. I don't know how much he knows about folk stories,' said Tilda, 'but I can ask. Gerlof usually likes telling stories.'

'Tell him he's very welcome to come over.'

By the time Tilda hung up it was four thirty. She switched on the computer to do some work on new cases and her own reports, including the one about the black van. It was a reasonably concrete piece of information in the investigation into the break-ins. Everything the birdwatcher had told her about the sound of motor-boat engines around Eel Point was too vague to put in a report. She wrote and wrote, and when she had finished the reports it was quarter to eight.

Hard work – that was the best way to avoid thinking about Martin Ahlquist. To drive him out of her body and soul.

Tilda still hadn't posted the letter to his wife.

WINTER 1943

When the Second World War broke out, the manor at
Eel Point was taken over by the military. The lighthouses
were extinguished and soldiers moved into the house to
guard the coast.

In the loft in the barn there is one name preserved
from this time, but it is not a man's name.

IN MEMORY OF GRETA 1943 it says, carved in
thin letters.

Mirja Rambe

The alarm is raised at the air-monitoring station at
Eel Point the day after the great blizzard has passed
by – a sixteen-year-old girl is missing.

'Lost in the blizzard,' says the director of the
station, Stovey, when the seven men gather in the
kitchen in the morning, wearing the grey uniform of
the Crown. Stovey's real name is Bengtsson, but he
has acquired his new name because he prefers to sit
indoors next to the iron stove when there's a cold
wind outside. And there is almost always a cold
wind outside in the winter at Eel Point. 'I shouldn't
think there's much hope,' he goes on. 'But we'd
better search anyway.'

Stovey himself stays inside to coordinate the search – everyone else sets off in the snow. Eskil Nilsson and Ludvig Rucker, who is nineteen years old and the youngest at the station, are sent off to the west to search in the area around the peat bog, Offermossen.

It is only fifteen degrees below zero and there is just a light breeze today – considerably milder than previous winters during the war, when the thermometer has sometimes dropped to somewhere between minus thirty and minus forty.

Apart from the blizzard the previous night, it has been a quiet winter at Eel Point. The German Messerschmitts have more or less stopped appearing along the coast, and after Stalingrad it is the Soviet Union's supremacy over the Baltic that Sweden fears most.

One of Eskil's older brothers has been sent over to Gotland to live in a tent all the year round. Eel Point is in radio contact with southern Gotland – if the Soviet fleet attacks, they will be the first to know.

Ludvig quickly lights a cigarette when they get outside, and starts ploughing through the snowdrifts in his boots. Ludvig smokes like a chimney, but never offers anyone else a cigarette. Eskil wonders where he gets hold of all his supplies.

Most things have been rationed at the manor for a long time. They can get fish from the sea and milk from the two cows at the manor, but there is a severe shortage of fuel, eggs, potatoes, cloth, and real coffee. Worst of all is the tobacco rationing, which is now down to three cigarettes a day.

But Ludvig seems able to get hold of tobacco with no problem, either in the post or from someone in the villages around Eel Point. How can he afford it?

The conscripts' pay is just one krona per day.

When they have gone a few hundred yards Eskil stops and looks for the main road. He can't see it – the blizzard has made it magically disappear. Bundles of fir branches had been pushed into the ground to mark out the route for the sledge teams, but they must have blown away during the night.

'I wonder where she came from?' says Eskil, clambering over a snowdrift.

'She came from Malmtorp, outside Rörby,' says Ludvig.

'Are you sure?'

'I know her name too,' says Ludvig. 'Greta Friberg.'

'Greta? How do you know that?'

Ludvig merely smiles and takes out a fresh cigarette.

Now Eskil can see the western watchtower. A rope has been fixed up to lead the way there from the road. The tower is built of wood, insulated with pine branches and camouflaged with grey-green sheets of fabric. The snow has been driven up into an almost vertical wall against the eastern side by the blizzard.

The other air-monitoring watchtower at Eel Point is the southern lighthouse, which was converted to electricity just before the war broke out; it has heating and is a very comfortable place to sit and watch for foreign aircraft. But he knows that Ludvig prefers to be alone out here on the peat bog.

Of course, Eskil suspects that he is not always alone in the watchtower. The Rörby boys hate Ludvig, and Eskil thinks he knows why. The girls from Rörby like him too much.

Ludvig goes over to the tower. He sweeps the snow from the steps with his glove, climbs up and disappears for a minute or so. Then he comes back down again. 'Here,' he says, handing over a bottle to Eskil.

It's schnapps. The alcohol content is high, it hasn't frozen and Eskil unscrews the cork and takes a warming gulp. Then he looks at the bottle, which is less than half-full.

'Were you drinking in the tower yesterday?' he asks.

'Last night,' says Ludvig.

'So you walked home in the blizzard?'

Ludvig nods. 'More like crawling, really. You couldn't see your hand in front of your face . . . good job the rope was there.'

He puts the bottle back in the tower, then they plough on northwards through the snow, towards Rörby.

Fifteen minutes later they find the girl's body.

In the middle of a vast expanse of snow north of Offermossen something which could be the slender stump of a birch tree is sticking up. Eskil peers at it and moves closer.

Suddenly he sees that it is a little hand.

Greta Friberg had almost reached Rörby when the snow caught her. Her rigid face is staring up at the sky when they scrape away the snow, and even her eyes are covered in ice crystals.

Eskil can't stop looking at her. He falls to his knees in silence.

Ludvig stands behind him, smoking.

'Is this her?' says Eskil quietly.

Ludvig knocks the ash off his cigarette and leans over for a quick look.

'Yes, that's Greta.'

'She was with you, wasn't she?' says Eskil. 'Yesterday, up in the tower.'

'Maybe,' says Ludvig, and adds, 'I'd better varnish the truth a bit for Stovey about all this.'

Eskil gets to his feet. 'Don't lie to me, Ludvig,' he says.

Ludvig shrugs his shoulders and stubs out his cigarette. 'She wanted to go home. She was freezing cold, and she was terrified of getting stuck in the tower with me all night. So she went her way in the blizzard and I went mine.'

Eskil looks at him, then at the body in the snow. 'We have to fetch help. She can't stay here.'

'We'll use the tow sledge,' says Ludvig. 'We can put her on that. We'll go and fetch it.'

He turns and heads back towards Eel Point. Eskil walks slowly backwards so that he won't be turning his back on the dead girl too quickly, then catches up with Ludvig. They plough along silently in the snow, side by side.

'Are you going to carve her name up in the barn?' he asks. 'Like we did with Werner?'

Werner was a seventeen-year-old who had been called up for military service; he fell into the water from a boat and drowned off the point in the summer of 1942. Greta's name should be carved next to his up in the hayloft, in Eskil's opinion.

But Ludvig shakes his head. 'I hardly knew her.'

'But—'

'It was her own fault,' says Ludvig. 'She should have stayed with me in the tower. I'd have warmed her up.'

Eskil says nothing.

'But there are plenty of girls in the villages,' Ludvig goes on, looking across the far side of

Offermossen. 'That's the best thing about girls, they never run out.'

Eskil nods, but he can't think about girls right now. He can only think of the dead.

DECEMBER

18

It was a new month, the month of Christmas, and it was Friday afternoon. Joakim had returned to the hayloft in the ice-cold barn, and was standing in front of the wall with the names of the dead carved in it. In his hands he held a hammer and a newly sharpened chisel.

He had gone up into the loft an hour or so before he was due to pick up Livia and Gabriel, just as the sun was going down and the shadows were gathering in the inner courtyard. It was a kind of reward that he allowed himself if the renovation work had gone well.

Sitting up here in the loft felt quiet and restful, despite the cold, and he liked studying the names on the wall. He read Katrine's name over and over again, of course, like a mantra.

As he began to learn many of the names off by heart, so the wall itself, with its knot holes and the convoluted rings in the wood, was becoming familiar to him. On the left, in the corner, a deeper split ran along one of the middle planks, and in the end it tempted Joakim to go and take a closer look.

The plank had split along one of the rings showing the age of the original tree. The crack had then widened downwards in a diagonal line, and when he pressed his hand against it the wood cracked and gave way.

That was when Joakim had gone to fetch his tools.

He pushed the chisel into the crack, hit it with the hammer and the sharp metal went straight through the wood. All it took was a dozen or so hard blows with the hammer to loosen the end of the plank. It fell inwards, and the dull thud when it landed proved that the wooden floor continued on the other side of the wall. But it was impossible to see what was in there.

When Joakim bent down to look through the hole, just a couple of inches wide, a definite smell struck him. It rushed towards his face, making him close his eyes and lean against the wall.

It was Katrine's smell.

He got down on his knees and pushed his left hand into the opening. First his fingers, then his wrist and finally the whole of his forearm. He groped about, but could feel nothing.

But when he lowered his fingers they touched something in there, something soft.

It felt like coarse fabric – like someone's jeans or jacket.

Joakim quickly withdrew his hand.

The next moment he heard a dull rumbling on the track outside, and a beam of light illuminated the windows of the barn, white with frost. A car was driving into the courtyard.

Joakim cast a final glance at the opening in the wall, then went over to the steps leading down from the loft.

In the courtyard he was dazzled by the headlights of a car. A door slammed.

'Hi there, Joakim.'

It was a brisk voice that he recognized. Marianne, the head of the pre-school.

'Has something happened?' she asked.

He stared at her in confusion, then pulled up his

sleeve and looked at his watch. In the beam of the head-lights he could see that it was already half past five. The school closed at five. He had forgotten to pick up Gabriel and Livia.

'I missed . . . I forgot what time it was.'

'It's OK,' said Marianne. 'I was just so worried that something might have happened. I tried to call, but there was no reply.'

'No, I've been . . . out in the barn doing a bit of carpentry.'

'It's easy to forget the time,' said Marianne with a smile.

'Thanks,' said Joakim. 'Thanks for bringing them home.'

'No problem, I live in Rörby anyway.' Marianne waved and went back to her car. 'See you Monday.'

When she had reversed out of the courtyard Joakim went inside, feeling ashamed of himself. He could hear voices from the kitchen.

Livia and Gabriel had already taken off their boots and outdoor clothes and thrown them down in two separate heaps. They were sitting at the kitchen table sharing a clementine.

'Daddy, you forgot to come and get us,' said Livia as he walked in.

'I know,' he said quietly.

'Marianne had to drive us home.'

She didn't sound cross, more surprised at the devi-ation from the normal routine.

'I know,' he said. 'I didn't mean for that to happen.'

Gabriel was eating his clementine segments, apparently unconcerned, but Livia gave her father a long look.

'I'll make us something to eat,' said Joakim, and went quickly over to the larder.

Pasta with tuna sauce was a favourite, and he boiled some water for the pasta and warmed the sauce. Several times he glanced out of the window. The barn loomed up on the far side of the courtyard like a black castle.

It had secrets. A hidden room without a door.

A room which, for a moment, had been filled with the scent of Katrine. Joakim was sure he had felt her presence; the smell of her had poured out through the hole in the wall, and he had been unable to defend himself.

He wanted to get into that room, but the only way seemed to be to attack the thick planks of wood with a saw or crowbar. But then the carved names would be destroyed, and Joakim could never do that. He had too much respect for the dead.

When the temperature dropped below freezing, the cold began to creep into the house as well. Joakim relied on the radiators and tiled stoves on the ground floor, but there were strips of coldness along the floor and around some of the windows. On windy days he searched for draughts along the floor and walls, then blocked the gaps by loosening sections of the outer panelling and pushing flax fibre in between the timbers.

The first weekend in December the thermometer hovered around minus five when the sun was shining, but dropped down to minus ten in the evening. On the Sunday morning Joakim looked out of the kitchen window and discovered that there was a layer of black ice out at sea. The open water was now several hundred yards away. The ice must have formed by the shore during the night, then slowly crept around the headland and out towards the horizon.

'We'll soon be able to walk across the water to Gotland,' he said to the children as they sat at the breakfast table.

'What's Gotland?' said Gabriel.

'It's a big island further out in the Baltic.'

'Can we walk there?' asked Livia.

'No, I was just joking,' said Joakim quickly. 'It's too far away.'

'But I want to.'

It was impossible to joke with a six-year-old – she took everything literally. Joakim looked out of the kitchen window and an image came into his mind of Livia and Gabriel walking out on to the black ice, going further and further out. Then suddenly it cracked, a black hole opened up and they were pulled down . . .

He turned to Livia. 'You and Gabriel must never go out on to the ice. Not under any circumstances. You can never be sure it will hold.'

That night Joakim called his former neighbours in Stockholm, Lisa and Michael Hesslin. He hadn't heard a word from them since the night they left Eel Point.

'Hi, Joakim,' said Michael. 'Are you in Stockholm?'

'No, we're still on Öland. How are things?'

'Fine. Good to hear from you.'

And yet Joakim thought Michael sounded wary. Perhaps he was embarrassed over what had happened the last time they met.

'You're feeling OK?' said Joakim. 'And what about work?'

'Everything's going really well,' said Michael. 'Lots of exciting projects. Things are a bit hectic right now, coming up to Christmas.'

'Good . . . I just wanted to check up, make sure everything was OK. I mean, it was a bit of a hasty departure last time you came down here.'

'Yes,' said Michael, and hesitated before going on, 'Sorry about that. I don't know what it was . . . I woke

259

up in the middle of the night and couldn't get back to sleep . . .'

He fell silent.

'Lisa thought you'd had a nightmare,' said Joakim. 'That you dreamed someone was standing by the bed.'

'Did she say that? I don't remember.'

'You don't remember who you saw?'

'No.'

'I've never seen anything strange around here,' said Joakim, 'but I've felt things sometimes. And out in the barn I've found a wall in the hayloft where people—'

'So what about the renovation?' Michael interrupted him. 'How's all that going?'

'What?'

'Have you finished the wallpapering?'

'No . . . not quite.'

Joakim was confused, until he realized that Michael had no desire whatsoever to discuss unusual experiences or bad dreams. Whatever had happened to him that night, he had closed and locked the door on the memory.

'What are you doing at Christmas?' Joakim asked instead. 'Will you be celebrating at home?'

'We'll probably go to the cottage,' said Michael. 'But we're intending to be at home for New Year.'

'Maybe we can get together, then.'

The conversation didn't last much longer. When Joakim had hung up he looked out of the kitchen window, towards the film of ice on the sea and the empty shore. The frozen desolation almost made him miss the crowded streets of Stockholm.

'There's a hidden room at Eel Point,' said Joakim to Mirja Rambe. 'A room without a door.'

'Really? Where?'

'Up in the hayloft. It's big . . . I've paced out the barn, and the floor of the loft stops almost four yards before the outside wall.' He looked at Mirja. 'You didn't know?'

She shook her head. 'The wall with all those names on it is enough for me. That's all the excitement I need.'

Mirja leaned forward on the big sofa and poured Joakim a steaming cup of coffee. Then she picked up a bottle of vodka and asked, 'A drop in your coffee?'

'No, thank you. I don't drink spirits and—'

Mirja gave a short laugh. 'Then I'll have your ration,' she said, pouring the vodka for herself.

Mirja lived in a spacious apartment close to the cathedral in Kalmar, and had invited the family over for dinner this evening.

Livia and Gabriel finally got to meet their maternal grandmother. Both were quiet and wary when they walked in, and Livia looked suspiciously at a white marble statue of the upper half of a man's body, standing in one corner. It was a while before she started talking. She had brought Foreman and two teddy bears with her, and introduced all three to her grandmother. Mirja took the children into her studio, where finished and unfinished paintings of Öland lined the walls. They all showed a flat, blossoming green landscape beneath a cloudless sky.

For someone who had hardly bothered about her grandchildren up till now, Mirja was remarkably interested in them. When they had eaten their meat-filled dumplings she worked hard to get Gabriel to come and sit on her knee, and finally succeeded. But he only stayed put for a few minutes before running off into the TV room to watch children's programmes with Livia.

'So it's just the two of us,' said Mirja, sitting down on the sofa in the main room.

'Fine,' said Joakim.

Mirja had none of her own paintings on the walls, but two of her mother Torun's pictures of the blizzard hung in the main room. Both depicted the snowstorm approaching the coast, like a black curtain about to fall on the twin lighthouses. Just like the picture at Eel Point, these were winter paintings that exuded hidden menace and the premonition of evil.

Joakim looked in vain for traces of Katrine in the apartment. She had always loved bright, clean lines, but her mother had decorated the rooms with dark, flowery wallpaper and curtains, Persian rugs and black leather sofas and chairs.

Mirja had no photographs of Katrine or her half-siblings. She did, however, have several large and small pictures of herself and a young man, perhaps twenty years her junior, with a blond goatee beard and spiky hair.

She saw Joakim staring at the pictures and nodded towards the man. 'Ulf,' she said. 'He's off playing indoor hockey, otherwise you could have met him.'

'So you're a couple?' said Joakim. 'You and the hockey player?'

A stupid question.

Mirja smiled. 'Does that bother you?'

Joakim shook his head.

'Good, because it bothers a lot of other people,' said Mirja. 'Katrine, certainly, even if she never said anything . . . older women aren't supposed to have a sex life. But Ulf doesn't seem to be complaining, and I'm certainly not.'

'On the contrary, you seem proud of it,' said Joakim.

Mirja laughed. 'Love is blind, or so they say.' She drank her coffee and lit a cigarette.

'One of the police officers in Marnäs wants to carry

262

on with the investigation,' said Joakim after a while. 'She's called me a couple of times.'

He didn't need to explain which investigation he was talking about.

'Right,' said Mirja. 'She's welcome to do that, I suppose.'

'Of course, if it provides any answers . . . but it won't bring Katrine back.'

'I know why she died,' said Mirja, drawing on her cigarette.

Joakim looked up. 'You do?'

'It was the house.'

'The house?'

Mirja laughed briefly, but she wasn't smiling. 'That damned house is full of unhappiness,' she said. 'It's destroyed the lives of every family that has ever lived there.'

Joakim looked at her, surprised by the comment. 'You can't blame unhappiness on a house.'

Mirja stubbed out her cigarette.

Joakim changed the subject. 'I'm having a visitor next week, a pensioner who knows the house. His name is Gerlof Davidsson. Have you met him?'

Mirja shook her head. 'But I think his brother lived close by,' she said. 'Ragnar. I met him.'

'Anyway . . . Gerlof is going to tell me about the history of Eel Point.'

'I can do that, if you're so curious.'

Mirja took another huge gulp of her coffee. Joakim thought her eyes were already beginning to look slightly glazed from the alcohol.

'So how did you end up at Eel Point?' he asked. 'You and your mother?'

'The rent was low,' said Mirja. 'That was the most important thing for Mum. She spent the money she earned from cleaning on canvases and oils, and she was always short of money. So we had to find places to live to fit in with that.'

'Was the place already looking shabby by then?'

'It was getting that way,' said Mirja. 'Eel Point was still owned by the state at that stage, but it was let to someone on the island for a small amount of money . . . some farmer who didn't put a penny into fixing it up. Mum and I were the only ones who were prepared to live in the outhouse in the winter.'

She drank some more of her coffee concoction.

The children were laughing loudly at something in the TV room.

Joakim thought for a while, then asked, 'Did Katrine ever talk to you about Ethel?'

'No,' said Mirja. 'Who's Ethel?'

'She was my older sister. She died last year . . . almost exactly a year ago. She was a user.'

'Booze?'

'Drugs,' said Joakim. 'Anything, really, but mostly heroin over the last few years.'

'I've never really been into drugs,' said Mirja. 'But of course I agree with people like Huxley and Tim Leary . . .'

'About what?' asked Joakim.

'That drugs can open doors in your mind. Particularly for artists like us.'

Joakim stared at her. He thought of Ethel's blank expression, and realized why Katrine had never told Mirja about her. Then he quickly finished his coffee and looked at his watch: quarter past eight. 'We'd better get back.'

'So what do you think of your grandmother, then?' asked Joakim as they drove back across the Öland bridge.

'She was nice,' said Livia.

'Good.'

'Will we be going there again?' she asked.

'Maybe,' said Joakim. 'But probably not for a while.'

He decided not to think about Mirja Rambe any more.

19

'My daughter called me last night,' said one of the elderly ladies on the sofa next to Tilda.

'Oh yes, what did she say?' asked the other elderly lady.

'She wanted to talk things through.'

'Talk things through?'

'Talk things through, yes,' said the first lady. 'Once and for all. She says I've never supported her. "You only thought about yourself and Daddy," she said. "All the time. And us kids have always been in second place." '

'That's what my son says as well,' said the other lady. 'Although with him it's the exact opposite. He rings before Christmas every year and complains and says that I gave him too much love. I destroyed his childhood, according to him. Don't you give it another thought, Elsa.'

Tilda stopped eavesdropping and looked at her watch. The weather report should be over by now, and she got up and knocked on Gerlof's door.

'Come in.'

Gerlof was sitting by the radio when Tilda went in to collect him. He had his coat on, but didn't seem to want to get up.

'Shall we go?' she said, holding her arm out ready to support him.

'Maybe,' he said. 'Where was it we were going?'

'Eel Point,' said Tilda.

'Right . . . and what exactly is it we're going to do out there?'

'Well, I suppose we're going to talk,' said Tilda. 'The new owner wants to hear some stories about the place. I said you knew lots of stories.'

'Stories?' Gerlof got up slowly and looked at her. 'So now I'm designated as some kind of canny old man, sitting in a rocking chair with twinkling eyes telling tales of ghosts and superstitions?'

'It'll be fine, Gerlof,' said Tilda. 'Just look on yourself as a spiritual mentor. To someone who is grieving.'

'Oh yes? There's no pleasure in grief, said the old man who sat weeping beside the wrong grave.'

Gerlof set off, leaning on his stick, and added, 'We'll just have to talk some sense into him.'

Tilda took his other arm. 'Shall we take the wheelchair?'

'Not today,' said Gerlof. 'My legs are working today.'

'Do we need to tell anyone we're going?'

Gerlof snorted. 'It's nothing to do with them.'

It was Wednesday, the second week in December, and they were on their way out to Eel Point for coffee. Gerlof and the owner of the manor were to meet at last.

'How are things going at work, then?' asked Gerlof as they drove through the centre of Marnäs.

'I only have one colleague at the station here in Marnäs,' said Tilda. 'And he tends to keep out of the way . . . he's usually down in Borgholm.'

'Why?'

Tilda remained silent for a few seconds. 'You tell

267

me . . . but I happened to bump into Bengt Nyberg from *Ölands-Posten* yesterday, and he told me that the new police station in Marnäs already has a nickname.'

'Oh?'

'They call it the old women's station.'

Gerlof shook his head wearily. 'That's what they used to call the railway stations on the island that only had female staff in the old days. The male stationmasters didn't think the women could do the job as well as them.'

'I'm sure they did it better,' said Tilda.

'Well, no one ever complained, as far as I know.'

Tilda drove out of Marnäs and down along the deserted road. The temperature was zero, and the flat coastal landscape seemed to have stiffened into a grey and white winter painting.

Gerlof looked out through the windscreen. 'It's so beautiful here by the sea.'

'Yes,' said Tilda. 'But you're biased.'

'I love my island.'

'And you hate the mainland.'

'No, I don't,' said Gerlof. 'I'm not some narrow-minded local patriot. But love always begins at home. Those of us who live on the island have to preserve and defend the dignity of Öland.'

Gerlof's sullen mood gradually lifted and he became more and more talkative. As they were passing the little churchyard in Rörby, he pointed towards the side of the road. 'Speaking of ghosts and superstitions, would you like to hear a story that my father told every Christmas?'

'Sure,' said Tilda.

'The father of your grandfather and my father was called Carl Davidsson,' Gerlof began. 'He worked as a servant over in Rörby when he was a teenager, and he once saw a very strange thing here. His older brother had come to visit him, and they were out walking here by the church in the twilight hour. It was around New Year, very cold and with plenty of snow. Then they heard a horse-drawn sleigh coming up behind them. His brother glanced over his shoulder, then cried out and grabbed hold of Carl's arm. He pulled him down off the road and out into the snow. Carl didn't understand what was going on until he saw the sleigh, which was coming closer along the road.'

'I know this story,' said Tilda. 'My father used to tell it.'

But Gerlof carried on, as if he hadn't heard her: 'It was a load of hay. The smallest load of hay Carl had ever seen, and it was being pulled by four tiny horses. And up in the hay little men were clambering around. They were less than three feet tall.'

'Goblins,' said Tilda. 'Weren't they?'

'My father never used that word. He just said they were little people dressed in grey clothes and hats. Carl and his brother didn't dare move, because the men didn't look friendly. But the load drove past the boys without anything happening, and once it had passed the churchyard the horses turned off the road and disappeared out into the darkness on the alvar.' Gerlof nodded to himself. 'My father swore it was a true story.'

'Didn't your mother see goblins too?'

'Yes indeed, she saw a little grey man run straight out into the water when she was young. But that was in southern Öland.' Gerlof looked at Tilda. 'You come from a family that has seen many remarkable things. Perhaps you've inherited the ability to see things?'

'I hope not,' said Tilda.

Five minutes later they had almost reached the turning for the manor, but Gerlof wanted to take a break and stretch his legs. He pointed through the windscreen to the grassy landscape on the other side of the stone wall. 'The peat bog has started to freeze. Shall we take a look?'

Tilda pulled up at the side of the road and helped Gerlof out into the cold wind. A thin layer of shining ice covered the watery patches all over the bog.

'This is one of the few old peat bogs left on the island,' said Gerlof as he looked out over the stone wall. 'Most of the others have been drained and have disappeared.'

Tilda followed his gaze and suddenly saw a movement out in the water, a black shiver between two thick tussocks of grass that made the film of ice quiver and crack.

'Are there fish in here?'

'Oh yes,' said Gerlof. 'I'm sure there are a few old pike . . . and the eels make their way here in the spring, when the streams created by the melting ice run down into the Baltic.'

'So you can catch them?'

'You can, but nobody does. When I was little I was told that the flesh of fish caught in the bog had a musty taste.'

'So where does the name come from, then – Offermossen, the Sacrificial Bog?'

'Sacrifices from the old days,' said Gerlof. 'Archaeologists have found Roman gold and silver here, and the skeletons of hundreds of animals that had been thrown into the water – lots of horses.' He fell silent, then added, 'And human bones.'

'Human sacrifices?'

Gerlof nodded. 'Slaves, perhaps, or prisoners of war. I suppose some powerful person decided that was all they were good for. As far as I understand it, they were pushed down beneath the water with long poles while they were still alive . . . then the bodies just lay there until the archaeologists found them.' He gazed out over the water and went on, 'Perhaps that's why the eels still come up here, year after year. They probably remember the taste. I mean they like eating the flesh of—'

'Enough, Gerlof.'

Tilda stepped away from the stone wall and looked at him.

He nodded. 'OK, OK, I'm just rambling. Shall we get going?'

Once they had parked the car Gerlof made his way slowly across the gravel, leaning on his stick and Tilda's arm. She let go briefly to knock on the glass pane in the kitchen door.

Joakim Westin opened the door after the second knock.

'Welcome.'

His voice was quiet and he looked even more tired than the last time she'd seen him, Tilda thought. But he shook hands with her, even smiled, and his earlier anger over the mix-up with the names seemed to have disappeared.

'I'm very sorry about your loss,' said Gerlof.

Westin nodded. 'Thank you.'

'I'm a widower myself.'

'Oh?'

'Yes, but it wasn't the result of an accident, it was a long illness. My Ellen got diabetes, then heart problems.'

'Recently?'

'No, it was many years ago,' said Gerlof. 'But of course it's still hard sometimes. The memories are still strong.'

Westin looked at Gerlof and nodded silently. 'Come in.'

The children were at pre-school, and the atmosphere

271

in the bright rooms was silent and solemn. Tilda could see that Westin had worked hard over the past few weeks. Almost the whole of the ground floor had been painted and wallpapered, and it was beginning to look like a real home.

'It almost feels like a journey back in time,' she said as they walked into the big drawing room. 'Like walking into a nineteenth-century manor house.'

'Thank you,' said Joakim.

He took it as a compliment, despite the fact that Tilda was mainly envious of the size of the room. She still wouldn't want to live out here.

'Where did you find all the furniture?' asked Gerlof.

'We searched and searched, both here on the island and in Stockholm,' said Joakim. 'Large rooms need large pieces of furniture to occupy the space. We've often looked for old pieces that we could renovate.'

'That's a good approach,' said Gerlof. 'These days people rarely set any store by their possessions. They don't repair things that are broken, they simply throw them away. It's buying things that's important, not looking after them.'

Tilda realized that he enjoyed going around old houses. For Gerlof the pleasure in seeing beautiful, well-made possessions went hand in hand with the knowledge of the hard work that lay behind them. Tilda had seen him sitting and contemplating items he owned, an old seaman's chest or a collection of linen hand towels, as if he could feel all the memories they contained.

'I imagine you get kind of addicted to this?' asked Gerlof.

'Addicted to what?' said Joakim.

'Fixing up houses.'

He was smiling, but Joakim shook his head. 'It's not

an addiction. It's not as if we want a new kitchen every year, like some families in Stockholm . . . and this is only the second house we've taken on. Before that we only fixed up flats.'

'So where was the first house?'

'Outside Stockholm, in Bromma. A beautiful detached house that we renovated from top to bottom.'

'And why did you move? What was wrong with the house?'

Joakim avoided meeting Gerlof's eye. 'There was nothing wrong . . . we really liked the house. But it's good to move up to something bigger now and again. Financially, above all.'

'Oh?'

'You take out a loan and find a run-down flat in a good location, and start renovating it in the evenings and at the weekends, while living there at the same time. Then you find the right buyer and sell it for much more than you paid. Then you take out a new loan and buy another run-down flat in an even better location.'

'And you sell that one too?'

Joakim nodded. 'Of course, it wouldn't be possible to make money out of property if the demand for places to live wasn't so high. I mean, everybody wants to live in Stockholm.'

'Not me,' said Gerlof.

'But lots of people do. Prices are going up all the time.'

'So both you and your wife were good at fixing places up?' said Tilda.

'We actually met when we both went to an open day at a flat,' said Joakim with fresh energy in his voice. 'An old lady had been living in a big apartment with a whole lot of cats. The location was perfect, but Katrine and I were the only ones who could put up with the stench, and stayed behind. We went for coffee afterwards and talked about what could be done with the place . . . it became our first project together.'

Gerlof turned and looked around the drawing room, his expression grim. 'And of course you're intending to do the same thing with Eel Point,' he said. 'Move in, renovate it, sell it.'

Joakim shook his head. 'We'd intended to stay here for many years. We wanted to rent out rooms, maybe even open a small restaurant.' He looked out of the window and added, 'We didn't really have a set plan for everything we wanted to do, but we knew we were going to be happy here . . .'

His energy had disappeared again, Tilda could see. The silence in the white room was oppressive.

After a tour of the house they sat down in the kitchen with a cup of coffee.

'Tilda said you wanted to hear some stories about the manor,' said Gerlof.

'I'd like that,' said Joakim, 'if there are any.'

'Oh, there are,' said Gerlof. 'But I suppose you mean ghost stories? Is that the kind of thing you're interested in?'

Joakim hesitated, as if he was afraid someone might be eavesdropping, then said, 'I'd just like to know if anyone else has experienced unusual things here. I've felt – or imagined I've felt – the presence of the dead at Eel Point. Both out by the lighthouses and here inside the manor. Others who have been here seem to have had a similar experience.'

Tilda said nothing, but she was thinking of the October evening when she had waited here for Westin. She had been alone here then – but it hadn't really felt that way.

'Those who have lived here in times gone by are still here,' said Gerlof, his coffee cup in his hand. 'Do you think they rest only in graveyards?'

'But that's where they're buried,' said Joakim quietly.

'Not always.' Gerlof nodded towards the expanse of ploughed fields at the back of the house. 'The dead are our neighbours everywhere here on the island, and you just have to get used to it. The countryside is full of old graves . . . tumuli containing chambers from the Stone Age, burial cairns from the Bronze Age, cists from the Iron Age and the burial grounds of the Vikings.' He turned to look out towards the sea, where the horizon had disappeared in a damp winter fog. 'And there's a churchyard out there too,' he said. 'The whole of the east coast is a graveyard for hundreds of ships that ran up on the sandbanks and were smashed to pieces, and for all the sailors who drowned. Many of those who went to sea in days gone by couldn't even swim.'

Joakim nodded and closed his eyes. 'I didn't believe in anything,' he said. 'Before we came here I didn't believe the dead could come back . . . but now I don't know what to believe. A number of remarkable things have happened here.'

Silence fell in the kitchen.

'Whatever you might feel of the dead, or whatever you think you might see,' said Gerlof slowly, 'it can be dangerous to let them rule our actions.'

'Yes,' said Joakim quietly.

'And to try to call them up . . . or ask questions.'

'Questions?'

'You never know what answers you might get,' said Gerlof.

Joakim looked down into his coffee cup and nodded. 'But I have wondered about this story that says they will return here.'

'Who?'

'The dead. When I was having coffee with the neighbours they told me a story: those who have died here at the manor return home every Christmas. I was just wondering if there were any more tales about that?'

'Oh, that's an old story,' said Gerlof. 'It's told in many places, not just here at Eel Point. The Christmas vigil of the dead, that's when those who have passed away during the year return for their own Christmas service. Anyone who disturbed them at that time had to run for their life.'

Joakim nodded. 'An encounter with the dead.'

'Exactly. There was a strong belief that people would be able to see the dead again. And not only in church. In their homes too.'

'At home?'

'According to folk beliefs, you should place a candle in the window at Christmas,' said Gerlof, 'so that the dead can find their way home.'

Joakim leaned forward. 'But was that just those who had passed away in the house,' he said, 'or other dead people as well?'

'You mean drowned sailors?' said Gerlof.

'Sailors . . . or other members of the family who have passed away somewhere else. Did they come back at Christmas as well?'

Gerlof glanced briefly at Tilda, then shook his head. 'This is just a story, you know,' he said. 'There are many superstitions surrounding Christmas. It was the turning point of the year, after all, when the darkness was at its peak and death was at its closest. Then the days grew longer again, and life returned.'

Joakim didn't say anything.

'I'm looking forward to that,' he said eventually. 'It's

so dark now . . . I'm looking forward to the turning point.'

A few minutes later they were outside, saying goodbye. Joakim held out his hand.

'You have a beautiful home out here,' said Gerlof, shaking it. 'But be careful of the blizzard.'

'The blizzard?' said Joakim. 'It's supposed to be a really big snowstorm down here, isn't it?'

Gerlof nodded. 'It doesn't come every year, but I'm pretty sure it will come this winter. And it comes quickly. You don't want to be outdoors down here by the sea when that happens. Especially not the children.'

'So how do people on Öland know when something like that is coming?' asked Joakim. 'Can you feel it in the air?'

'We look at the thermometer and listen to the weather forecasts,' said Gerlof. 'The cold has arrived early this year, and that's usually a bad sign.'

'OK,' said Joakim with a smile. 'We'll be careful.'

'You do that.' Gerlof nodded and set off towards the car, supported by Tilda, but he suddenly stopped, let go of her arm and turned around. 'One more thing. What was your wife wearing on the day of her accident?'

Joakim Westin stopped smiling. 'I'm sorry?'

'Do you remember what clothes she was wearing that day?'

'Yes – but they were nothing special,' said Joakim. 'Boots, jeans and a winter jacket.'

'Have you still got them?'

Joakim nodded, looking tired and tortured again. 'The hospital gave them to me. In a parcel.'

'Could I take a look at them?'

'You mean . . . you want to borrow them?'

'Borrow them, yes. I won't damage them in any way, I just want to look at them.'

'OK . . . but they're still all parcelled up,' said Joakim. 'I'll go and get them.'

He went back into the house.

'Can you take care of the parcel, Tilda?' said Gerlof, setting off towards the car once more.

When Tilda had started the engine and driven out through the gate, Gerlof leaned back in his seat. 'So, we had our little chat,' he said with a sigh. 'I suppose I was a bit of a canny old man after all. It's difficult to avoid it.'

A brown parcel containing Katrine Westin's clothes was lying on his knee. Tilda glanced at it. 'What was all that business with the clothes? Why did you want to borrow them?'

Gerlof looked down at his knee. 'It was just something that occurred to me when we were standing out there by the bog. About how the sacrifices were carried out there.'

'What do you mean? That Katrine Westin was some kind of sacrifice?'

Gerlof looked out through the windscreen, over towards the bog. 'I'll tell you more very soon, when I've looked at the clothes.'

Tilda pulled out on to the main road. 'This visit worried me a little,' she said.

'Worried?'

'I'm worried about Joakim Westin, and about his children. It felt as if you were sitting there in the kitchen talking about folk tales, while Westin regarded them as reality.'

'Yes,' said Gerlof, 'but I think it was good for him to talk a little. He's still grieving for his wife, which is not so strange, after all.'

'No,' said Tilda. 'But I thought he talked about her as if she were still alive. As if he was expecting to see her again.'

20

After the break-in at Hagelby vicarage and the flight through the forest, it was two weeks before the Serelius brothers came back to Borgholm. But suddenly there they were at Henrik's door one evening, at the worst possible moment.

Because by that time the quiet but rhythmic knocking in his flat had started to become intolerable, like a dripping tap that couldn't be turned off.

At first Henrik was convinced that it was coming from the old stable lantern, and after three difficult nights with the constant sound of tapping, he put it in the car. The following morning he drove over to the east coast and put the lantern in the boathouse.

But the knocking continued the next night, and now it was coming from inside the wall in the hallway. But not always the same wall – the sound seemed to move slowly behind the wallpaper.

If it wasn't the lantern, then it must be something else he had brought with him from the forest, or from that fucking death chamber he'd been crawling around in.

Unless, of course, it was something that had sneaked into his apartment through the brothers' ouija board. Those nights when they had sat around the kitchen table staring at the glass as it moved beneath Tommy's finger, it had definitely felt as if something invisible was in the room.

Whatever it was, it was getting on Henrik's nerves. Every night he wandered back and forth between the bedroom and the kitchen, terrified of going to bed and turning off the light. In sheer desperation he had called Camilla, his ex-girlfriend. They hadn't been in touch for several months, but she sounded pleased to hear from him. They had talked for almost an hour.

Henrik's nerves were at breaking point when his door-bell rang three days later, and the sight of Tommy and Freddy at the door didn't exactly make him feel any better.

Tommy was wearing sunglasses and his hands were twitching. He wasn't smiling. 'Let us in.'

It wasn't a friendly reunion. Henrik wanted money from the Serelius brothers, but they had none – they hadn't sold any of the stolen goods yet. He knew they wanted to do one more trip to the north of the island, but Henrik didn't want to.

And he didn't want to discuss any of it with them tonight, because he had a visitor. 'We can't talk now,' he said.

'Sure we can,' said Tommy.

'No.'

'Who is it?' asked Camilla from the sofa in front of the TV.

The brothers craned their necks curiously to see who the female voice belonged to.

'It's just . . . two friends,' said Henrik over his shoulder. 'From Kalmar. But they're not staying.'

Tommy lowered his sunglasses and gave Henrik a long look. It made him step outside and pull the door closed behind him.

'Congratulations,' said Tommy. 'Is this a new find, or an old one you've dug up?'

'It's the girl I used to live with,' said Henrik quietly. 'Camilla.'

'Fuck me. She took you back?'

'I called her,' said Henrik. 'But she was the one who wanted to meet up.'

'Nice,' said Tommy without a smile. 'But what shall we do now, then?'

'About what?'

'Our joint project.'

'It's over,' said Henrik. 'Apart from the money.'

'Oh no.'

'It's over.'

They stared at each other, Henrik and the brothers. Then Henrik sighed. 'We can't talk out here on the stairs,' he said. 'One of you can come in.'

In the end Freddy lumbered back out to the van. Henrik led Tommy into the kitchen and closed the door behind them. He lowered his voice. 'We're going to sort this out right now, then you can go.'

But Tommy was still more interested in Camilla, and asked loudly and clearly, 'So has she moved back in? Is that why you look so fucking tired?'

Henrik shook his head. 'That's something else,' he said. 'I'm not sleeping well.'

'I expect that'll be your conscience,' said Tommy. 'But the old bloke will be OK, they'll patch him up.'

'Who the fuck knocked him down?' hissed Henrik. 'Don't you remember?'

'It was you,' said Tommy. 'You kicked him.'

'Me? But I was behind you in the hallway!'

'You stood on the old bloke's hand and broke it, Henrik. If they find us, you're going down.'

'For fuck's sake, we're all going down!' Henrik

282

glanced towards the door and lowered his voice again. 'I can't talk any more now.'

'You want money,' said Tommy. 'Don't you?'

'I've *got* money,' said Henrik. 'I've got a job during the day, for fuck's sake!'

'But you need more,' said Tommy, nodding towards the other room. 'They're expensive to run.'

Henrik sighed. 'It's not the fucking money that's the problem, it's all the stolen stuff in the boathouse. We need to get it sold.'

'We'll sell it,' said Tommy. 'But first we're going to do one more trip . . . the last trip to the north. To the manor house.'

'What manor house?'

'The one with all the paintings. The one Aleister told us about.'

'Eel Point,' said Henrik quietly.

'That's the one. When shall we go?'

'Wait a minute . . . I was there last summer. I went just about everywhere, but I didn't see any fucking paintings. And besides . . .'

'What?'

Henrik didn't say any more. He remembered the echoing rooms and corridors at Eel Point. He had enjoyed working for Katrine Westin, the woman who lived there with her two small children. But the place itself had felt forbidding even in August, despite the fact that the Westin family had given it a thorough clean and started a massive renovation project. What would it be like there now, in December?

'Nothing,' he said. 'But I didn't see any paintings at Eel Point.'

'They're probably hidden, then,' said Tommy.

There was a faint knocking sound.

Henrik jumped, then realized it was just an ordinary

knock at the kitchen door. He went over and opened it.

Camilla was standing outside. She didn't look pleased. 'Will you be done soon? Otherwise I'm going home, Henrik.'

'We're done,' he said.

Camilla was small and slender, much shorter than the men. Tommy smiled sweetly down at her and held out his hand. 'Hi there . . . Tommy,' he said, in a quiet, polite voice Henrik had never heard before.

'Camilla.'

They shook hands so vigorously the buckles on Tommy's jacket jingled. Then he nodded at Henrik and moved towards the door. 'OK, so that's agreed then,' he said to Henrik. 'I'll call you.'

Henrik locked the front door behind Tommy, then went and joined Camilla on the sofa. They sat in silence and finished watching the film they'd started before the brothers turned up.

'Do you think I should stay, Henrik?' she asked half an hour later, when it was almost eleven o'clock.

'If you want to,' he said. 'That would be good.'

After midnight they were lying next to each other in the little bedroom, and for Henrik it was like being taken six months back in time. As if everything was as it should be. It was just fantastic that Camilla had come back; the only thing that was bothering him now was the persistent Serelius brothers.

And the knocking.

Henrik was listening for it, but all he could hear was the sound of Camilla's soft breathing. She had fallen asleep with no problem.

Silence. No noises inside the walls.

He didn't want to think about the knocking now. Or about the visit from the Serelius brothers. Or about the manor house at Eel Point.

284

* * *

Camilla had come back, but Henrik didn't dare to discuss with her exactly what their relationship was. They weren't living together, anyway. Early the next morning he got up and went off to work in Marnäs. She was still in the flat then, but when he got home it was empty. There was no reply when he rang her.

That night he lay alone in his bed again, and when he had turned out the light the noises started in the hallway. There was a knocking sound inside the walls, quiet but persistent.

Henrik raised his head from the pillow.

'Shut the fuck up!' he yelled out into the room.

The knocking paused briefly, then resumed.

WINTER 1959

*The last year of the fifties – that's when my own
story begins. The story of Mirja at the manor house at
Eel Point, and of Torun and her paintings of the
blizzard.*

*I was eighteen years old and fatherless when I arrived
at the lighthouse station. But I had Torun. She had
taught me something all girls ought to learn: never to be
dependent on men.*

Mirja Rambe

The two men my artistic mother Torun hated most
were Stalin and Hitler. She was born a couple of
years before the First World War and grew up on
Bondegatan in Stockholm, but she was restless and
wanted to venture out into the world. She loved
painting, and at the beginning of the 1930s she
went to art school in Gothenburg first of all, and
then on to Paris where, according to Torun, people
constantly mistook her for Greta Garbo. Her
paintings attracted a certain amount of attention,
but she wanted to get back to Sweden when the war
broke out, and travelled back via Copenhagen.
There she met a Danish artist and managed to fit in

286

a quick romance before Hitler's soldiers suddenly appeared on the streets.

When she got home to Sweden Torun discovered that she was pregnant. According to her, she wrote several letters to the father-to-be, my Danish daddy. It might be true. However, he never got in touch.

I was born in the winter of 1941, when fear covered the world. At that time Torun was living in Stockholm, where all the lights had been turned off and everything was rationed. She kept on moving to different rooms for unmarried mothers, poky little holes rented out by disapproving old ladies, and supported herself by cleaning for the rich folk of Östermalm. She had neither the time nor the money to be able to paint.

It can't have been easy. I know it wasn't easy.

When I first heard the dead whispering in the barn at Eel Point, I wasn't afraid. I'd experienced far worse in Stockholm.

One summer after the war, when I am seven or eight years old, I start to have problems peeing. It's terribly painful. Torun says I've been swimming too much, and takes me to a doctor with a beard on one of Stockholm's widest streets. He's nice, my mother says. He charges next to nothing to see children.

The doctor is very friendly when he says hello. He is old, he must be at least fifty, and his coat is all creased. He smells of booze.

I have to go in and lie down on my back in a special room in his surgery, which also stinks of booze, and the doctor closes the door behind us.

'Unbutton your skirt,' he says. 'Pull it up and just relax.'

I am alone with the doctor, and he is very thorough. But at last he is satisfied.

'If you tell anyone about this they'll put you away in an institution,' he says, patting me on the head.

He buttons up his coat. Then he gives me a shiny one-krona coin and we go back to Torun in the waiting room. I stagger along, my legs trembling, and I feel even more ill than I did before, but the doctor says there isn't anything serious wrong with me. I am a good girl, and he will prescribe some suitable medicine.

My mother is furious when I refuse to take the doctor's tablets.

At the beginning of the 1950s Torun takes me to Öland. It is one of her ideas. I don't think she had any connection with the island, but just as when she travelled to Paris, she longs for an artistic environment. And of course Öland is famous for its light and for the artists who have succeeded in capturing it. My mother babbles about Nils Kreuger, Gottfrid Kallstenius and Per Ekström.

I am just happy to be leaving the city where that old doctor lives.

We arrive in Borgholm on the ferry. We have all our possessions with us in three suitcases, plus Torun's package of canvases and oils. Borgholm is a neat little town, but my mother is unhappy there. She thinks the people are stiff and haughty. Besides, it's much cheaper to live out in the country, so after a year or so we move again, to a red outhouse in the village of Rörby. We have to sleep under three blankets, because it is always so cold and draughty.

I start at the local school. All the children there think I speak a kind of affected big-city talk. I don't

288

say what I think of their dialect, but I still don't make any friends.

Soon after we end up out in the country I start to draw in earnest. I draw white figures with red mouths and Torun thinks they're angels, but it is the doctor and his slashed mouth that I am drawing.

When I was born Hitler was the big bad wolf, but I grow up filled with the fear of Stalin and the Soviet Union. If the Russians want to they can conquer Sweden in four hours with their aeroplanes, according to my mother. First they will occupy Gotland and Öland, then they will take the rest of the country.

But for me, as a child, four hours is quite a long time, and I give a great deal of thought to what I would do during this last period of freedom. If the news comes that the Soviet planes are on their way I will run off to the shop in Rörby and stuff myself with as much chocolate as I can, I'll eat all they've got, then I'll grab some crayons and paper and watercolours and rush back home. Then I'll be able to cope with living the rest of my life as a communist, just as long as I can carry on painting.

We move around as lodgers from one place to another, and every room we rent stinks of oils and turpentine. Torun makes enough money to live on by cleaning, but paints in her spare time – she goes out with her easel and paints and paints.

In the last autumn of the 1950s we move again, to an even cheaper room. It is in an old building at the manor house at Eel Point. An outhouse, built of limestone, with whitewashed walls. Cool and pleasant to live in during the hot summer days, but freezing cold the rest of the year.

When I find out that we are going to live near

289

lighthouses, of course I get a whole lot of magical pictures in my head. Dark, stormy nights, ships in trouble out at sea and heroic lighthouse-keepers.

Torun and I move in one October day, and I immediately feel unwelcome there. Eel Point is a cold and windy place. Walking between the big wooden buildings feels like sneaking around some desolate castle courtyard.

The pictures in my imagination turn out to be entirely false. The lighthouse-keepers have left Eel Point, and only come to visit a few times a year – the lighthouses were converted to electricity a year or so after the war, and ten years later everything was automated. There's an old watchman, his name is Ragnar Davidsson and he lumbers around at Eel Point as if he owns the place.

A couple of months after we move in I experience my first blizzard – and almost end up an orphan at the same time.

It is the middle of December, and when I get home from school, Torun isn't there. One of her easels and the bag with her oils in is also missing. Twilight falls and it begins to snow; the wind from the sea grows stronger.

Torun doesn't come back. At first I am angry with her, then I start to feel afraid. I have never seen so much snow whirling past the windows. The flakes are not falling, they are slicing through the air. The wind shakes the windowpanes.

Half an hour or so after the storm begins, a small figure finally appears, ploughing through the snowdrifts in the inner courtyard. I hurry outside, grab hold of Torun before she collapses and help her inside, to the fire.

The bag is still hanging over her shoulder, but the easel has been swept away in the storm. Her eyes are swollen shut; grains of ice mixed with sand have blown into them, and she can hardly see. When I take off her clothes they are soaked; she is frozen stiff.

She had been sitting painting on the far side of the peat bog, Offermossen, when the clouds gathered and the storm came. She tried to take a short cut through the tussocks of grass and the thin ice of the bog, but fell into the water and had to fight her way on to firmer ground. She whispers, 'The dead came up out of the bog . . . lots of them, clawing at me, ripping and tearing . . . they were cold, so cold. They wanted my warmth.'

Torun is rambling. I get her to drink some hot tea and put her to bed.

She sleeps peacefully for more than twelve hours, and I keep watch by the window as the snowfall gradually diminishes during the night.

When Torun wakes up she is still talking about the dead who walked in the blizzard. Her eyes are scratched and bloodshot, but the very next evening she sits down at a canvas and begins to paint.

21

Just when Tilda had stopped thinking about Martin Ahlquist every morning and night, the telephone rang in her little kitchen. She thought it was Gerlof, and picked up the receiver without any misgivings.

It was Martin.

'I just wanted to see how you were. Make sure everything's OK.'

Tilda didn't speak; the pains in her stomach came back immediately. She gazed out at the empty quays in the harbour.

'Fine,' she said eventually.

'Fine, or just OK?'

'Fine.'

'Do you fancy having a visitor?' asked Martin.

'No.'

'Isn't it lonely in northern Öland any more?'

'Yes, but I'm keeping busy.'

'Good.'

The conversation was not unpleasant, but it was short. Martin ended by asking if he could ring her again, and she said yes in a very small voice. The wound somewhere between her heart and her stomach started bleeding again.

It isn't Martin who's ringing, she thought, it's his

hormones. He's just horny and wants a change from his wife again, he can't cope with everyday life . . . The worst of it was that she still wanted him to come over, preferably that very night. It was sick.

She should have posted the letter to his wife long ago, but she was still carrying it around in her bag like a brick.

Tilda worked long hours. She worked almost all the time to avoid thinking about Martin.

In the evenings she would sit for hours preparing the talks on traffic awareness or law and order that she was due to give in schools or local companies. And as often as she could, in between the talks, the foot patrols and the paperwork, she went out in her police car all over the area.

One Tuesday afternoon, on the deserted coast road, she slowed down when she saw the twin lighthouses at Eel Point. But she didn't stop; instead she turned down towards the neighbouring property where a farming family lived. Their name was Carlsson, she recalled. Her only visit there had been on that long, difficult night after Katrine Westin had drowned, when Joakim had broken down in the neighbours' hallway.

The lady of the house, Maria Carlsson, recognized her at once when she rang the doorbell.

'No, we haven't seen much of Joakim this autumn,' she said when they were sitting at the kitchen table. 'We haven't fallen out, nothing like that, but he tends to keep himself to himself. His children play with our Andreas sometimes.'

'And what about his wife, Katrine?' said Tilda. 'Did you see more of her when she was living there alone with the children?'

'She came over for coffee a couple of times . . . but I

think she had her hands full with the house. And of course we work long hours too.'

'Did you notice whether she had visitors?'

'Visitors?' said Maria. 'Well, there were a few workmen there, towards the end of the summer.'

'But did you ever see a boat there?' said Tilda. 'At Eel Point, I mean.'

Maria pushed back her fringe and thought about it.

'No, not that I remember. Nobody would have seen it from here anyway. The view is pretty much obscured.'

She pointed towards the window in the north-east, and Tilda could see that the view of the lighthouses was blocked by the big barn on the far side of the yard.

'But did you perhaps hear the sound of a boat at some point?' she ventured. 'The sound of an engine?'

Maria shook her head. 'You do hear boats chugging past sometimes when there's no wind, but I don't usually take any notice of it.'

When Tilda got outside she stopped by the car and glanced to the south. There was a group of red boathouses out on the nearest point, but not a soul in sight.

And no boats surging through the water.

She got back in the car and realized it was time to put this particular criminal investigation to bed. It had never really been an investigation anyway.

When she got back to the station she moved the file containing her notes on Katrine Westin into the tray marked NON-PRIORITY.

She had four substantial piles of paper on her desk, and half a dozen dirty coffee cups. Hans Majner's desk on the other side of the room was, in contrast, completely clear of papers. Sometimes she had the urge to dump a huge bundle of traffic reports on his desk, but it always passed.

* * *

In the evenings Tilda took off her uniform, got into her own little Ford and drove around getting to know Öland, while listening to the recordings she had made with Gerlof. Most of them sounded good, the microphone picking up both his and Tilda's voices, and she could hear that he had become more and more accustomed to talking each time they met.

It was during one of these outings that she finally found the van Edla Gustafsson had mentioned.

She had driven down to Borgholm, toured around the streets of the town for a while, then carried on south across the bridge to Kalmar. There were lots of streets there, lots of huge car parks, and she drove slowly past hundreds of vehicles without spotting a dark van. The whole thing just seemed hopeless.

After half an hour, when she heard on the local radio that there was horse racing tonight, she left the centre and headed for the racecourse. The enclosed course was illuminated with huge spotlights. There was money to be won and lost in there, but Tilda stayed in the car and drove slowly along the rows of parked cars.

Suddenly she slammed on the brakes.

She had passed a van. It said KALMAR PIPES & WELDING on the sides, and it was black.

Tilda made a note of the registration number and reversed into a parking space a little further along. Then she called the central control number, asked them to look up the plates and found that they belonged to a forty-seven-year-old man with no police record, in a village outside Helsingborg. The van had no record of traffic offences, but it had been de-registered since August.

Aha, thought Tilda. She also asked them to check out a firm called Kalmar Pipes & Welding, but no such firm was registered.

Tilda switched off the engine and settled down to wait.

'Yes, Ragnar used to fish illegally up by Eel Point,' said Gerlof in her headphones. 'He was in fishing waters belonging to other people sometimes, but of course he always denied it . . .'

After fifty minutes the spectators started pouring out through the gates. Two powerfully built men aged around twenty-five stopped by the dark van.

Tilda took off her headphones and straightened up in her seat.

One of the men was taller and broader than the other, but she couldn't make out any clear facial features. She peered through the darkness as the men got into the van, and wished she had a pair of binoculars.

The men responsible for the break-ins? Impossible to tell, of course. *They're just ordinary workmen, darling*, she heard Martin's self-assured voice saying in the back of her mind, but she ignored him.

The men drove out of the car park. Tilda started her own car and put it in first gear. The van drove away from the racecourse, out on to the main road and on towards Kalmar. Tilda followed, a couple of hundred yards behind.

Eventually they reached a high-rise apartment block not far from the hospital, and the van slowed down and pulled in by the kerb. The men got out and disappeared through a doorway.

Tilda sat and waited. After thirty seconds the lights went on in a couple of windows on the second floor. She quickly wrote down the address. If these were the burglars, then at least she now knew where they lived. The best thing would of course be to go into the flat to search for stolen goods, but her only justification for doing so was old Edla's information that the van had been on Öland. That wasn't enough.

'I've given up on the investigation into Katrine Westin's death,' said Tilda as she was having coffee with Gerlof a couple of evenings later.

'Her murder, you mean?'

'It wasn't a murder.'

'Oh yes,' said Gerlof. 'I think it was.'

Tilda said nothing, she merely sighed and took out the tape recorder. 'Shall we do one last—'

But Gerlof interrupted her. 'I saw a man almost murdered once, without anyone touching him.'

'Really?'

Tilda put the tape recorder down on the table, but didn't switch it on.

'It was out by Timmernabben, a few years before the war,' Gerlof went on. 'Two cargo ships carrying stone were moored up side by side, in perfect harmony. But aboard one was a first mate from Byxelkrok, and aboard the other an ordinary seaman from Degerhamn. They got into an argument about something, and stood yelling at each other across the gunwales. In the end one of them spat at the other . . . then it got serious. They started hurling shards of stone at one another, and in the end the guy from Degerhamn jumped up on to the gunwale to get across to the other ship. But he didn't get far, because his opponent met him with a boathook.'

Gerlof paused, drank a little of his coffee, and went on: 'Boathooks these days are pathetic things made of plastic, but this was a sturdy wooden pole with a big iron hook on one end. So when this lout came hurtling over the gunwale his shirt got caught on the hook, and he stopped in mid-air. Then he fell straight down like a stone into the water between the ships, with his shirt still tangled up on the boathook . . . and he didn't come up again, because the other man was holding him under the water.' He looked at Tilda. 'It was more or less the same as they did with those poor souls who were pushed down into the water with poles out on the peat bog.'

'But he survived?'

'Oh yes, the rest of us broke up the fight and got him out. But he only just made it.'

Tilda looked at the tape recorder. She should have switched it on.

Gerlof bent down and started rustling with some paper under the table. 'Anyway, it was that fight I was thinking of when I asked to see Katrine Westin's clothes,' he said. 'And now I've had a look at them.'

He took an item of clothing out of the paper bag. It was a grey cotton top with a hood.

'The murderer came to Eel Point by boat,' said Gerlof. 'He put in by the stone jetty, where Katrine Westin was waiting . . . and she stayed where she was, so she must have trusted him. He was holding a boathook, which of course was perfectly natural because that's what you use when you put in. But this was one of the old kind . . . a long pole with an iron hook which he twisted into the hood of her top, then he used it to drag her down into the water. Then he held her down until it was over.'

Gerlof spread the top out on the table, and Tilda saw that the hood was torn. Something sharp had ripped two inch-long holes in the grey fabric.

22

Often when Joakim looked out of the kitchen window in the evening he would see Rasputin slinking off to go hunting. But sometimes he thought he caught a glimpse of other black shapes moving out there – sometimes on four legs, sometimes on two.

Ethel?

The first few times Joakim had hurried out on to the veranda steps to get a better look, but the inner courtyard had always been empty.

The shadows lengthened around Eel Point with every evening, and Joakim felt that the sense of unease in the house was also increasing as Christmas approached. The howling of the wind rose and fell around the eaves, and there was a constant tapping and creaking in the house.

If there were some unseen visitor at the manor, it wasn't Katrine, he knew that. She was still keeping herself from him.

'You can have the clothes back,' said Gerlof, handing over the brown package to Joakim on the other side of the table.

'Did you get anything out of them?'

'Perhaps.'

'But you don't want to tell me what it was?'

'Soon,' said Gerlof. 'When I've finished thinking.'

Joakim had never visited an old people's home, as far as he remembered. Both sets of grandparents had remained at home until a ripe old age, and had spent their final days in hospital. But he was sitting here now, drinking coffee in silence in Gerlof Davidsson's room at the home at Marnäs. A candle-holder with two lit Advent candles was the only sign that Christmas was coming. A series of old objects hung on the walls: ships' nameplates, framed ships' certificates and black and white photographs of two-masted sailing ships.

'Those are pictures of my cargo ships,' said Gerlof. 'I had three different ones.'

'Are any of them still around?'

'Just one. She's at a sailing club down in Karlskrona. The other two are gone . . . one of them burned, the other sank.'

Joakim looked down at the package of Katrine's clothes, then looked out of the only window in the room. Twilight was already starting to fall.

'I have to pick up my children in an hour,' he said. 'Can we talk for a while?'

'Of course,' said Gerlof. 'The only thing on my schedule this afternoon was a talk on incontinence in the day room. It wasn't all that appealing.'

For a long time Joakim had wanted to talk to someone about what had happened in the autumn, someone who knew Eel Point. The pastor at the church in Marnäs seemed to have such rigid views, and Mirja Rambe thought too much about herself. It was only when Gerlof Davidsson came out to the house and proved himself to be a good listener that he thought he might have found the right person. A kind of father confessor.

'I never asked you when you came out to the house, but . . . do you believe in ghosts?'

Gerlof shook his head. 'I neither believe nor don't believe,' he said. 'I do collect ghost stories, but not in order to prove anything. And of course there are so many theories about ghosts . . . that they are part of the framework of old houses, or electromagnetic radiation.'

'Or just patches on the cornea,' said Joakim.

'Exactly,' said Gerlof. He was silent for a few seconds, then went on, 'Of course, I could tell you a story I've never written about in any folk-history book, but it's the only real ghostly experience I've had.'

Joakim nodded.

'I took over my first cargo ship when I was seventeen,' said Gerlof. 'I'd been at sea for a couple of years before that, saving up, and my father helped out with the finances. I knew exactly which ship I wanted to buy, a single-masted sailing ship with an engine; she was called *Ingrid Maria*, and her home port was Borgholm. The owner, Gerhard Marten, was in his sixties and had sailed cargo ships all his life. But then he developed heart problems and his doctor told him he couldn't go to sea any more. *Ingrid Maria* was for sale, and the price was 3,500 kronor.'

'That was cheap, wasn't it?' said Joakim.

'Yes, that was a good price even then,' said Gerlof, and went on: 'The evening I was due to go and hand over the money to Marten, I took a walk down to the harbour to have a look at her. It was April, and the ice had just disappeared from the sound. The sun was going down, and there was hardly anybody around in the harbour. The only person I saw was old Gerhard. He was walking around on the deck of the *Ingrid Maria*, as if he was finding it difficult to part with her, and I went aboard. I don't remember what we talked about, but I took a short walk around the deck with him, and he pointed out a few little things that would need repairing. Then he told me to look after her, and we parted company. I went ashore and walked home to my parents' house to have dinner and pick up the envelope containing the money.'

Gerlof fell silent, looking at the pictures of the cargo ships on the wall.

'At about seven o'clock I cycled over to the Marten family cottage, north of Borgholm,' he went on. 'But I arrived to find a house in mourning. Marten's wife was there, her eyes red with weeping. Gerhard Marten was dead, it turned out. He had signed the purchase agreement the night before, then walked down to the shore early in the morning with his shotgun, and shot himself in the head.'

'In the morning?' said Joakim.

'That same morning, yes. So when I met Gerhard Marten down in the harbour, he had actually been dead for a whole day. I can't explain it . . . but I *know* that I met him that evening. We even shook hands.'

'So you met a ghost,' said Joakim.

Gerlof looked at him. 'Perhaps. But it doesn't prove anything. It certainly doesn't prove that there's life after death.'

Joakim shifted in his seat and looked down at the parcel of clothes. 'I'm worried about my daughter, Livia,' he said. 'She's six years old, and she talks in her sleep. She always has done . . . but since my wife died she's started to dream about her.'

'Is that so strange?' said Gerlof. 'I dream about my late wife sometimes, and she's been dead for many years.'

'Yes . . . but it's the same dream, over and over again. Livia dreams that her mother comes to Eel Point, but can't get into the house.'

Gerlof listened in silence.

'And sometimes she dreams about Ethel, too,' Joakim went on. 'That's what worries me the most.'

'Who's Ethel?' asked Gerlof.

'She was my sister. She was three years older than me.' Joakim sighed. 'That's my own ghost story. Sort of.'

'Tell me about her,' said Gerlof quietly.

Joakim nodded wearily. It was time.

'Ethel was a drug addict,' he said. 'She died one winter's night close to where we lived . . . two weeks before Christmas, a year ago.'

'I'm sorry,' said Gerlof.

'Thank you,' said Joakim. 'I lied to you when I saw you last time . . . when you asked why we'd sold the house in Bromma and moved here. It had a lot to do with what happened to my sister. Once Ethel was dead we didn't want to stay in Stockholm.'

He stopped speaking again. He wanted to talk about this, and yet he didn't want to. He didn't really want to remember Ethel and her death. Nor Katrine's long depression.

'But you miss your sister?' said Gerlof.

Joakim thought about it. 'A little.' That sounded terrible, so he added: 'I miss her the way she used to be before . . . before the drugs. Ethel used to talk a lot, she always had so many plans. She was going to open a hair salon, she was going to be a music teacher . . . but after a while you just got so tired of it all, because none of the plans involved giving up the drugs. It was like watching someone sitting in a burning house, planning a party in the middle of the flames.'

'So how did it start?' asked Gerlof, sounding almost apologetic. 'I know so little about that world . . .'

'For Ethel it started with hash,' said Joakim. 'Weed, as they called it. It was cool to smoke at parties and

303

concerts. And life was a party for Ethel in her teens. She played the piano and the guitar – she taught me to play a little too.'

He smiled to himself.

'It sounds as if you were very fond of her,' said Gerlof.

'Yes, Ethel was happy and funny,' said Joakim. 'She was pretty too, and popular with the boys. And she partied a lot; with amphetamines she could party even more. She must have dropped twenty pounds in weight, although she was already thin. She was away more and more. Then our father died of cancer and I think it was around then she started with heroin . . . brown heroin. Her laughter grew harsher and more hoarse.'

He took a sip of his coffee and went on quickly: 'Nobody who smokes heroin thinks they're a real user. You're not a junkie. But sooner or later you switch to needles, because it's cheaper . . . you need less heroin per dose. But you still need to come up with at least fifteen hundred kronor for supplies every day. That's a lot of money, particularly when you haven't got any. So you start stealing. You take your elderly mother's money, or steal the jewellery she's inherited.'

Joakim looked at the Advent candles and added: 'On Christmas Eve, when we were sitting in my mother's house eating ham and meatballs, there was always an empty chair at the table. Ethel always promised to come, but she would be in the city centre looking for drugs. For her that was routine, just everyday life. And routines are the most difficult thing to break, however terrible they are.'

He was deep into his confession now, not even aware if Gerlof was listening any longer.

'So you know that everything has gone to hell and that your sister is in the middle of the city gathering money for drugs, and her social worker never calls back . . . but you go off to your teaching job in the morning and have dinner with the family and work on your new house in the evening, and you try not to think and feel so much.' He lowered his eyes. 'Either you try to forget, or you try to find her. My father used to go out looking in the evenings, before he got too sick. I did too. On the streets, in the squares, in the underground stations and the emergency psychiatric wards . . . We soon learned where she might be.'

He fell silent. In his mind he was back in the city, among the drug users and those sleeping rough, among all the lonely, half-dead souls who spent their nights chasing around out there.

'That must have taken a great deal of strength,' said Gerlof quietly.

'Yes . . . but I wasn't out every night. I could have looked for her more often. I could have done more for her.'

'And you could also have given up.'

Joakim nodded grimly. He had one more thing to tell Gerlof about Ethel, the most difficult thing of all to talk about.

'What was in fact the beginning of the end happened two years ago,' he said. 'Ethel had been in rehab that winter, and it had gone well. When she went in she weighed less than a hundred pounds, her body was covered in bruises and her cheeks looked completely hollow. But when she came home to Stockholm she was much healthier. She had been clean for almost three months and had put some weight on, so we let her stay in our guest room. And it worked well. She used to play a lot with Livia in the evenings. They got on really well.'

He remembered that they had begun to hope again at that time, he and Katrine. They had begun to trust Ethel. They had started to go for long walks in the evenings, leaving Ethel to look after Livia and Gabriel. And it had gone well every time.

'One evening in March, Katrine and I went to see a film,' he went on. 'When we got back to the house after a couple of hours it was dark and empty. There was only Gabriel there, sleeping in his cot with a soaking-wet nappy. Ethel had gone, and she had taken two things with her. My mobile phone and Livia.'

He stopped speaking and closed his eyes.

'I knew where she'd gone, of course,' he continued. 'The craving had returned and she had taken the underground into the city to buy heroin. She had done it so many times before. Bought a tab for five hundred kronor, injected it in some toilet and rested for a few hours, until the craving came back again. The problem this time was that she had Livia with her.'

The memories of that night came back to Joakim – ice-cold memories of growing panic. He had hurled himself into the car and driven around the areas close to the central station. He had done it before, either alone or with Katrine. But then he had been worried about what could have happened to Ethel.

This time he was terrified for Livia.

'I found Ethel in the end,' he said, looking at Gerlof. 'She was lying in the dark graveyard at Klara church. She had curled up next to a tomb and passed out. Livia was sitting beside her in thin clothes, ice cold and apathetic. I called an ambulance and made sure Ethel went into detox. Again. Then I drove home to Bromma with Livia.'

He fell silent.

'Katrine made me choose after that,' he said in a low voice. 'And I chose my family.'

'You made the right choice,' said Gerlof.

Joakim nodded, although he would still have preferred not to make that choice.

'After that night I told Ethel not to come near our house any more . . . but she did. We didn't let her in, but in the evenings, two or three times a week, she would stand at our gate in her scruffy denim jacket staring at the Apple House. Sometimes she would open our post, to see if there was any money or a cheque in the envelope. And sometimes she'd have a boy with her . . . some skeleton standing next to her, shaking.'

He paused and thought about the fact that this was one of his last memories of his sister: standing by the gate, her face deathly pale, her hair standing on end.

'Ethel used to just stand there yelling,' he said to Gerlof. 'She yelled stuff about . . . about Katrine. Sometimes about me too, but mostly about Katrine. She would roar and bawl until the neighbours started peeping through their curtains, and I would have to go out and give her some money.'

'Did that help?'

'Yes, it worked at the time, but of course it meant that she came back the next time she was broke. It became a vicious circle. Katrine and I felt . . . besieged. I would sometimes wake up in the middle of the night and hear Ethel shouting by the gate, but when I looked out the street would be empty.'

'Was Livia at home when your sister turned up?'

'Most of the time, yes.'

'Did she hear Ethel yelling?'

'I think so. She hasn't talked about it, but I'm sure she did.'

Joakim closed his eyes.

'Those were dark days . . . a terrible time. And Katrine started to wish that Ethel would die. She would talk about it late at night, in bed. Ethel might take an overdose, sooner or later. Preferably sooner. I think that's what we were both hoping for.'

'And that's what happened?'

'Yes, eventually. The telephone rang at eleven thirty one night. When it rang so late we knew it was about Ethel, it always was.'

A year ago, thought Joakim, but it felt like ten.

It was his mother Ingrid who told them the news. Ethel had been found drowned in Bromma, just below the area where their house was.

Katrine had even heard her earlier. Ethel had been standing there at the gate as usual at around seven o'clock, yelling, then the screaming had stopped.

When Katrine looked out she was gone.

'Ethel had gone down to the walkway by the shore,' said Joakim. 'She had sat down by a boathouse and pushed the needle in, then she had tumbled into the freezing water. And that was the end of her.'

'Weren't you home that night?' asked Gerlof.

'I came home later. Livia and I were at a children's party.'

'That was probably a good thing. For her sake.'

'Yes. And for a while we hoped that everything would settle down,' said Joakim. 'But I kept on waking up at night thinking that I could hear Ethel yelling out in the street. And Katrine just lost all her joy in life. We'd finished renovating the Apple House by that time and it was lovely, but she just couldn't relax there. So last winter we started talking about moving out to the country, moving south, maybe finding a place here on Öland. And in the end that's what we did.'

He fell silent and looked at his watch. Twenty past four. It felt as if he had talked more during this last hour than during the whole of the autumn.

'I have to go and pick up my children,' he said.

'Did anyone ask how all this made you feel?' said Gerlof.

'Me?' said Joakim, getting up. 'I felt terrific, of course.'

'I don't believe that.'

'No. But we've never talked about how we feel in my family. And we never really talked about Ethel's problems, either.' He looked at Gerlof. 'You just don't tell people that your sister is a junkie. Katrine was the first . . . you could say I dragged her into all this.'

Gerlof sat there in silence, apparently lost in thought.

'What did Ethel want?' he said. 'Why did she keep on coming to your house? Was it just to get the money for drugs?'

Joakim pulled on his jacket without answering.

'Not just that,' he said eventually. 'She wanted her daughter back as well.'

'Her daughter?'

Joakim hesitated. This was also difficult to talk about, but in the end he came out with it. 'There was no father . . . he died of an overdose. Katrine and I were Livia's godparents, and social services awarded her care to us four years ago. We adopted her last year . . . Livia is ours now.'

'But she's Ethel's child?' said Gerlof.

'No. Not any longer.'

23

Tilda had put in a report to headquarters in Borgholm on the black van, describing it as an 'interesting' vehicle worth looking out for. But Öland was a big place and the number of police officers out patrolling the roads was small.

And Gerlof's talk of a murderer with a boathook at Eel Point? She hadn't put in a report on that particular theory. Without any proof that there had in fact been a boat out by the point it was impossible to instigate a murder investigation – it would take more than a few holes in a top.

'I've returned the clothes to Joakim Westin,' said Gerlof the next time he called her.

'Did you tell him about your murder theory?' said Tilda.

'No . . . it wasn't the right time. He's still out of balance. He would probably believe that an apparition had dragged his wife down into the water.'

'An apparition?'

'Westin's sister . . . she was a drug addict.'

Gerlof told her the story of Joakim's sister Ethel, her heroin addiction and her habit of disturbing the peace.

'So that's why the family moved from Stockholm,' said Tilda when he finished. 'A death drove them away.'

'That was one reason. But Öland might just have tempted them as well.'

Tilda thought about how tired and worn Joakim Westin had looked when they went to see him, and said, 'I think he could do with talking to a psychologist. Or maybe a priest.'

'So I'm not up to the job of father confessor?' said Gerlof.

Almost every evening when Tilda passed a postbox on her way home from work, she was on the point of taking out the letter to Martin's wife and dropping it in the box, and yet it was still in her bag. It was as if she were carrying an axe around – the letter gave her power over a person she didn't know.

Of course she had power over Martin too. He had continued to call her from time to time, trying to make small talk. Tilda didn't know what she would say if he asked if he could come and see her again.

Two weeks had passed without a single reported break-in in northern Öland. But one morning the telephone rang in the police station. The call came from Stenvik on the west coast of the island; the man on the other end of the line spoke quietly, with a strong local dialect, and said that his name was John Hagman. Tilda recognized the name – Hagman was one of Gerlof's friends.

'I hear you're looking for people who've been breaking into houses,' he said.

'We are,' said Tilda. 'I was intending to call you . . .'

'Yes, Gerlof told me.'

'Have you seen anyone breaking in?'

'No.'

Hagman didn't say any more.

Tilda waited, then asked, 'Have you perhaps seen any *trace* of someone breaking in?'

311

'Yes. They've been here in the village.'

'Recently?'

'I don't know . . . sometime in the autumn. They appear to have been in several houses.'

'I'll come down and take a look,' said Tilda. 'How will I find you in the village?'

'I'm the only one here right now.'

Tilda got out of the police car on a gravel track in the middle of a row of closed-up summer cottages, a hundred yards or so above the sound. She looked around in the cold wind, and thought about her family. They came from Stenvik; they had somehow managed to survive in this stony landscape.

A short, elderly man in dark-blue dungarees and a brown cap came over to the car. 'Hagman,' he said.

He nodded briefly and pointed to a dark-brown one-storey house with wide windows. 'There,' he said. 'I noticed it had blown open. Same thing next door.'

One of the windows at the back of the house was ajar. When Tilda went closer, she could see that the frame was split and broken open near the catch.

There were no footprints on the veranda below the window. Tilda went over and pulled it wide open. The room inside was a mess, with clothes and tools just thrown on the floor.

'Have you got a key to this house?'

'No.'

'In that case I'll climb in.'

Tilda grabbed hold of both sides of the frame with her gloved hands and hauled herself into the darkness inside. She jumped down on to the floor of a small storeroom and flicked a switch, but no light came on. The power was turned off.

The traces left by the burglars were clearly visible, however – all the storage boxes had been pulled out and emptied on to the floor. And when she moved through into the main room she saw fragments of broken glass, just as in the vicarage at Hagelby.

Tilda went over for a closer look. Small pieces of wood lay among the glass, and it was a while before she realized it was a ship in a bottle that had been smashed on the floor.

A few minutes later, she heaved herself back out through the window. Hagman was still standing on the grass.

'They've been in there,' she said, 'and they've made a real mess . . . smashed things.'

She held out a clear plastic bag and showed him the bits of wood she had collected, the remains of the model ship. 'Is it one of Gerlof's?'

Hagman looked sadly at the bits and nodded. 'Gerlof has a cottage here in the village. He's sold ships in bottles and model boats to plenty of the summer visitors.'

Tilda pushed the bag into her jacket pocket. 'And you haven't heard or seen anything at night from these cottages?'

Hagman shook his head.

'No unusual traffic in the area?'

'No,' said Hagman. 'I mean, the owners go home to the city in August every year. In September there was a firm out here replacing some floors. But since then there hasn't—'

Tilda looked at him. 'A flooring company?'

'Yes. They worked in these houses for several days. But they made sure everything was properly locked up when they'd finished.'

'It wasn't a plumbing firm?' said Tilda. 'Kalmar Pipes and Welding?'

Hagman shook his head. 'They were laying floors,' he said. 'Young lads. Several of them.'

'Laying floors . . .' said Tilda. She remembered the newly polished floor at the vicarage in Hagelby, and wondered if she'd found a pattern. 'Did you talk to them?'

'No.'

Tilda went round the other cottages nearby with Hagman, and made a note of which ones had broken window frames.

'We need to get in touch with the owners,' she said as they walked back towards the police car. 'Have you got contact details for them, John?'

'For some of them, yes,' said Hagman. 'Those who have decent manners.'

When Tilda got back to the station she called a dozen or so owners of cottages on Öland or in the Kalmar area who had reported break-ins during the autumn.

Four of the owners she managed to get hold of had either had floors sanded or replaced in their summer cottages earlier in the year. They had used a local firm in northern Öland: Marnäs Fine Flooring.

She also called the vicarage in Hagelby; the owners were now home from hospital. Gunnar Edberg still had his hand in plaster, but he was feeling better. They had also used the firm in Marnäs to lay a new floor.

'It went really well,' said Edberg. 'They were here for five days early on in the summer. But we never saw them – we were in Norway at the time.'

'So you lent them the keys,' said Tilda, 'even though you didn't know who they were?'

314

'It's a reliable firm,' said Edberg. 'We know the owner, he lives in Marnäs.'

'Have you got his number?'

Tilda had the bit between her teeth now, and she called the owner of Marnäs Fine Flooring as soon as she finished talking to Gunnar Edberg. She quickly spelled out the purpose of her call: to find out the names of the men who had been working in northern Öland laying floors over the past year. She stressed that they weren't suspected of any crime, and that the police would appreciate it if the owner didn't mention her call to his employees.

No problem. The owner of the flooring company gave her two names, along with their addresses and ID numbers.

Niclas Lindell.

Henrik Jansson.

Both good men, he assured her. Decent, capable and conscientious. Sometimes they worked together, sometimes separately – usually for residents of the island when they were away on holiday, and in summer cottages out of season when the owners had gone home. There was plenty of work.

Tilda thanked him and asked one last question. Could she have a list of the houses where Lindell and Jansson had worked during the summer and autumn?

That information was held on a calendar on the company's computer system, the owner told her. He would print out the pages and fax them over to her.

When she had hung up Tilda switched on her own computer and checked out Lindell and Jansson's ID numbers in the police database. Henrik Jansson had been arrested and fined for driving illegally in Borgholm seven years earlier – he had driven a car at the age of seventeen without a licence. There was nothing else relating to either him or Lindell.

Then the fax machine whirred into action and the list of jobs carried out by Marnäs Fine Flooring started churning out. Tilda was quickly able to establish that of the twenty-two house-owners who had had work done on their floors, seven had reported break-ins over the past three months. Niclas Lindell had worked in two of the houses. But Henrik Jansson had worked in all of them.

Tilda felt the same excitement as the hunter in the forest when an elk appears. Then she noticed something else: during one week in August Henrik Jansson had been at the manor house at Eel Point. According to the job sheet, the work had been 'To sand floors, ground floor'.

Did it mean anything?

Henrik Jansson lived in Borgholm. According to the calendar, he was out on a job outside Byxelkrok today, and given the current situation he was welcome to carry on laying floors in peace and quiet. Tilda needed more time before calling him in for an interview with the police.

The silence was broken by the sound of the telephone ringing. She looked at the clock – it was already quarter past five. She was almost certain she knew who it was.

'Marnäs police station, Davidsson.'

'Hi, Tilda.'

And she was right.

'How are you?' said Martin.

'Fine,' she said, 'but I don't have time right now. I'm just in the middle of something important.'

'But Tilda, wait . . .'

'Bye.'

So there. She put the phone down without feeling

even the slightest bit curious about what he wanted. It felt like a liberation to realize that Martin Ahlquist had suddenly become so unimportant to her. Right now Henrik Jansson was the man in her life.

Tilda's goal was to find Henrik and arrest him – and on the way to the cells, to ask him a couple of questions. She wanted to know why he had attacked pensioners, of course – but also why he had smashed the ship in a bottle that Gerlof had made.

WINTER 1960

*The summer was unusually wet on Öland that year, and
our second winter at Eel Point was worse than the first.
Much colder, and with even more snow. In January and
February the school in Marnäs was closed every Monday,
as I recall, because the snow ploughs hadn't managed to
clear the roads after the snowfall over the weekend.*

Mirja Rambe

My mother Torun continues to paint, although her
sight never recovers after her experience out in the
snowstorm. She can only just see where she's going
by this stage, and she is no longer able to read.

Her glasses don't help much. In Borgholm we
find a kind of big halogen lamp that stands on a
sort of tripod. It shines with a dazzling white light,
making our two dark rooms in the outhouse at Eel
Point look like a film studio. In the middle of this
brilliant sunshine my mother sits painting, using the
darkest tones she is able to mix.

Torun's spatula and brushes rasp across the taut
canvas like stressed-out mice. My mother is painting
the blizzard in which she got lost the previous
winter, and she has her face so close to the canvas

318

that the tip of her nose is almost permanently dark grey. She stares intensely at the dark shadows that develop – I think when she is painting she feels as if she were still out there among the dead in the pools on the peat bog, Offermossen.

Canvas after canvas is covered in oils, but since no one wants to buy or even exhibit the paintings, she keeps the rolled-up canvases in an empty, dry room next to the kitchen in the outhouse.

I am also doing some painting, when there are colours and paper left over, but the atmosphere in the house at the end of the world still remains grim. We never have any money, and Torun can no longer see well enough to work as a cleaner.

Torun has her forty-ninth birthday at the beginning of November; she celebrates alone with a bottle of red wine, and begins to talk about the fact that her life is over.

Mine feels as if it hasn't even begun yet.

I am nineteen years old, I have left school, and I have taken over some of Torun's cleaning jobs while I wait for something better to turn up. I have missed the 1950s in every way. It is only when they are over that I come across some old copies of *Picture Journal* and find out that the fifties, apart from the death of Stalin and the fear of the atom bomb, was the decade of the teenagers, with white ankle socks, house parties and rock 'n' roll – but there wasn't much of that out in the country. Our radio was old, and usually broadcast a mixture of crackles and ghostly voices. After the blissful season when it's possible to go swimming, life on the coast is nine months of darkness, wind, long muddy tracks, wet clothes and constantly frozen feet.

The only consolation this year is Markus.

Markus Landkvist came from Borgholm in autumn
that year and moved into a little room in the manor
house at Eel Point. Markus is nineteen, one month
older than me, and is doing casual work on the
farms in the area while he waits to be called up for
his military service.

He is not my first love, but he is definitely a step
forward. Earlier romances have mostly involved
standing and staring at a boy across the schoolyard,
hoping that he will come over and pull my hair.

Markus is tall and blond and the best-looking
boy around, at least that's what I think.

'You know Eel Point is haunted?' I ask him when
we meet in the kitchen of the manor house for the
first time.

'What do you mean?'

He doesn't seem in the least afraid or even
interested, but I have made contact now and I have
to carry on: 'The dead live in the barn,' I say. 'They
whisper behind the walls.'

'It's just the wind,' says Markus.

It isn't exactly love at first sight. But we start
spending time together. I am the talkative annoying
one, Markus is the strong silent one. But I think he
likes me. I draw Markus from memory before I fall
asleep, and start to dream about leaving Eel Point
with him.

As I see it, Markus and I are the only ones here
who have any kind of life ahead of us. Torun has
given up, and the older men in the house seem
content to work during the day and to sit around
gossiping in the evenings.

Sometimes they drink home-brewed booze in the
kitchen with Ragnar Davidsson, the eel fisherman.

I can hear their laughter through the windows.

We all move in our own circles at Eel Point, and this winter I discover the hayloft above the barn. There is hardly any hay in there, but it is full of possessions that people have left behind, and I set off on a journey of discovery almost every week. There are lots of traces of families and lighthouse-keepers who have lived in the manor house; it is almost like a museum, with odds and ends to do with boats and wooden boxes and piles of old navigation charts and logbooks. I move things aside so that I can make my way further in among the treasures and the rubbish, and finally I reach the wall at the far side of the loft.

And I discover all those names, carved into the wall:

CAROLINA 1868

PETTER 1900

GRETA 1943

And many more. Almost every plank in the wall has at least one name carved into it.

I read the names and I am fascinated by all those who have lived and died at Eel Point. It feels as if they are with me up there in the loft.

My main goal in life is now to get Markus up there with me.

24

Twilight fell over sea and land in the afternoon now. The solitary street lamp out by the main road came on earlier and earlier, and Joakim walked around in his big house and tried to feel pride in what he had achieved.

The renovations on the ground floor were more or less finished. All the painting, wallpapering and furnishing was done, as far as possible. He ought to buy some more furniture, but he was short of money at the moment and had made only half-hearted attempts to find a new teaching post. But at least he had put the big eighteenth-century cupboard, the long dinner table and the tall dining chairs in the drawing room. He had hung the big round chandelier from the ceiling, and placed candlesticks in the windows.

He had managed hardly any work on the outside of the house this autumn – he had no money for scaffolding – but he had the feeling that the previous residents still appreciated the renovation indoors. When he was alone Joakim sometimes hoped that he might hear them in the house, hear their slow steps crossing the floor upstairs, their murmuring voices in the empty rooms.

But not Ethel. Ethel was not allowed to come into the

house. Thank goodness Livia seemed to have stopped dreaming about her.

'Are you coming up to me for Christmas?' asked Ingrid when she called in the middle of December.

She spoke in the same quiet, tentative voice as always, and Joakim just felt like hanging up.

'No,' he said quickly, looking out of the kitchen window.

The door to the barn was open again. He hadn't opened it. Of course it could be down to the wind or one of the children, but he sensed that it was a sign from Katrine.

'No?'

'No,' he said. 'We're intending to stay here this Christmas. At Eel Point.'

'Alone?'

Maybe not, thought Joakim. But he replied, 'Yes, unless Katrine's mother Mirja calls by. But we haven't discussed it yet.'

'Can't you—'

'We'd love to come up to you for New Year,' said Joakim. 'We can exchange presents then.'

Of course Christmas was going to be grim wherever he celebrated it.

Unbearable, without Katrine.

Early on the morning of December the thirteenth Joakim sat in darkness at the pre-school in Marnäs, watching the children celebrate the feast of St Lucia. Dressed in white with candles in their hands, smiling nervously, the six-year-olds processed into the meeting room where their parents were waiting. Several of the parents had their video cameras at the ready.

Joakim didn't need to film the children, he would

remember exactly which songs Livia and Gabriel sang. He touched his wedding ring and thought about how Katrine would have loved to see this.

The next day the first winter storm swept in over the coast, with bullet-like granules of snow rattling against the window panes. Out at sea the white-crested waves reared up. They moved rhythmically in towards the shore and smashed the thin layer of ice that had formed off the point, then they crashed over the jetty, the water foaming and swirling around the islands where the lighthouses stood.

When the storm was at its worst, tearing at the house, Joakim rang Gerlof Davidsson, the only person he knew on the island who was interested in the weather.

'So this is the first blizzard of the winter,' said Joakim.

Gerlof snorted at the other end of the line. 'This?' he said. 'This is just a slight breeze. This isn't a blizzard. But it is coming, and I think it'll be before New Year.'

The strong wind died away before dawn, and when the sun rose next morning Joakim saw that a thin layer of snow was still covering everything. The bushes outside the kitchen window were wearing white hats, and down on the shore the waves had hurled ice up to form wide banks.

Beyond these banks a new layer of ice had quickly formed out at sea, like a blue and white field criss-crossed with black cracks. The ice didn't look safe – some of the deep cracks met up in dark gaps.

Joakim peered towards the horizon, but the line between sea and sky had disappeared in a dazzling mist.

* * *

The telephone rang after breakfast. It was Gerlof's relative, Tilda Davidsson, who started off by saying that she was calling on a police matter.

'I just wanted to check something, Joakim. You said before that your wife didn't have any visitors at the house but you have had workmen there?'

'Workmen?'

It was an unexpected question, and he had to think about it.

'I heard you'd had someone laying floors,' said Tilda. 'Is that correct?'

Now Joakim remembered. 'Yes,' he said, 'but it was before I moved here. There was a guy here to rip out some old cork flooring and sand the floors in the main rooms.'

'From a firm in Marnäs?'

'I think so,' said Joakim. 'It was the estate agent who suggested them. I've probably still got the invoice somewhere.'

'We don't need that at the moment. But do you remember what he was called?'

'No. It was my wife who dealt with him.'

'When was he there?'

'In the middle of August, a few weeks before we started bringing our furniture down.'

'Did you ever meet him?' asked Tilda.

'No. But Katrine did, as I said. She and the children were here then.'

'And he hasn't been back since then?'

'No,' said Joakim. 'All the floors are finished now.'

'One more thing. Have you had any uninvited guests during the autumn?'

'Uninvited?' said Joakim, his thoughts immediately turning to Ethel.

'Anyone trying to break in, I mean,' said Tilda.

'No, we haven't had anything like that. Why do you ask?'

'There have been a number of break-ins on the island during recent months.'

'I know, I read about it in the paper. I hope you find them.'

'We're working on it,' said Tilda.

She put down the phone.

The following night Joakim woke up in bed with a start.

Ethel . . .

The same fear as always. He raised his head and looked at the clock. 01:24.

He pushed away all thoughts of Ethel. Had Livia called out? There wasn't a sound in the house, but still he got up and pulled on a sweater and a pair of jeans, without switching on the light. He went out into the corridor and listened again. He could hear the ticking of the wall clock, but not a sound came from the darkness of Livia's and Gabriel's rooms.

He went in the opposite direction, over to the windows in the hallway, and looked out into the night. The solitary lamp illuminated the inner courtyard, but nothing was moving out there.

Then he saw that the door to the barn was standing open once again. Not far, just eighteen inches or so – but Joakim was almost certain he had pulled it shut a few evenings earlier.

He would go and close it right now.

He pulled on his winter boots and went out through the veranda.

It was windy outside, but the sky was clear and full of stars, and the southern lighthouse flashed rhythmically, almost keeping pace with his heartbeat.

He went over to the half-open door and peered into the barn. It was pitch black.

'Hello?'

No reply.

Or was there? Perhaps he could hear a slow, whimpering sound somewhere inside the wooden building. Joakim reached in and switched on the light. He didn't step inside until the lights on the ceiling were on.

He wanted to call out again, but stopped himself.

He could hear something now: a quiet but regular rasping sound. Joakim was sure of it.

He went over to the steep steps. The bulb high above on the ceiling wasn't very powerful, but he began to climb upwards.

Up in the hayloft Joakim stopped again and looked at the piles of old forgotten rubbish. At some point he must clear all this out. But not tonight.

He moved in amongst the objects. He could make his way through the piles without any problem by now, he knew this labyrinth by heart and was drawn to the far side of it. Towards the wall at the far end of the loft.

That was where the rasping noise was coming from.

Joakim could see the wall now, and the names of the dead that had been carved into it. Before he had time to start reading them again, he heard a whimpering noise again, and stopped. He looked down at the floor.

First of all came the whimpering, then Rasputin yowling.

The cat was sitting by the wall, carefully washing his paws. Then he looked up at the visitor, and Joakim met his gaze; the cat almost looked pleased. And why not? He had worked hard tonight.

In front of him lay a dozen or so slender bodies with brown fur. Mice. They had been carefully ripped apart,

327

and looked as if they had been killed just before Joakim arrived.

Rasputin had placed the bloody mice in a row at the bottom of the wall.

They looked like a sacrifice.

25

'People worry too much nowadays,' said Gerlof. 'I mean, these days people call out the lifeboat as soon as it gets a little bit choppy out there. In the old days people had more sense. If the wind got up when you were a long way out, it was no problem . . . you just carried on to Gotland, pulled the boat up on to the shore then lay down underneath it and went to sleep, until the wind had blown itself out. Then you sailed home again.'

He fell silent, lost in thought after his last story.

Tilda leaned over and switched off the tape recorder. 'Fantastic. Are you OK, Gerlof?'

'Yes. Of course.'

Gerlof blinked, and was back in the room.

They each had a small glass of mulled wine in front of them. The start of Christmas week had been heralded with wind and snow, and Tilda had brought a bottle with her as a present. She had warmed the sweet red wine out in the kitchen and added raisins and almonds. When she brought the tray in, Gerlof had got out a bottle of schnapps and added a shot to each glass.

'So what are you doing at Christmas?' Gerlof asked when they had almost finished their drinks and Tilda was feeling warm right down to the tips of her toes.

'I'll be celebrating quietly, with the family,' she said. 'I'm going over to Mum's on Christmas Eve.'

'Good.'

'And what about you, Gerlof? Would you like to come with me over to the mainland?'

'Thanks, but I think I'll stay here and eat my Christmas rice pudding. My daughters have invited me to the west coast, but I can't sit in a car for so long.'

They both fell silent.

'Shall we have one last go with the tape recorder?' said Tilda.

'Maybe.'

'But it's fun to talk, isn't it? I've found out so much about Grandfather.'

Gerlof nodded briefly. 'But I haven't told you about the most important part yet.'

'No?' said Tilda, pressing the Record button.

Gerlof seemed hesitant.

'Ragnar taught me a great deal about the weather and the winds and fishing and sailing when I was a kid . . . all the important stuff. But when I got a little older, I realized I couldn't trust him.'

'No?' said Tilda.

'I realized that my brother was dishonest.'

There was silence around the table once again.

'Ragnar was a thief,' he went on. 'Nothing more than a thief. I can't make it sound any better, unfortunately.'

Tilda thought about switching off the tape recorder, but left it running. 'So what did he take?' she asked quietly.

'Well, he stole everything he could, by and large. He went out at night sometimes and stole eels from others' tanks. And I remember one time . . . when the manor house at Eel Point was having new drainpipes. There was a box left over, sitting out in the courtyard, until

330

Ragnar stole it. He didn't actually need drainpipes at the time, but he had keys to the lighthouses, so he put the box in there, and I'm sure it's there to this day. It wasn't the need that was important to him, it was the opportunity, I think. He always kept an eye open for something that was left unlocked or unwatched.'

Gerlof was leaning forward; it seemed to Tilda that he was speaking more intensely than ever.

'But surely you must have stolen something yourself at some point?' she said.

Gerlof shook his head. 'No, I haven't, actually. I might have lied a little about my cargo prices sometimes, when I met up with other skippers in port. But fighting and stealing, those are things I've never done. I just think we should all help one another.'

'That's the right attitude,' said Tilda. 'We are the community.'

Gerlof nodded. 'I don't think about my older brother too often,' he said.

'Why not?'

'Well . . . he's been gone for such a long time, after all. Many, many years. The memories have faded . . . and I have allowed them to fade.'

'When was the last time you saw him?'

The silence hung in the room, before Gerlof replied, 'It was at Ragnar's little farm, in the winter of 1961. I went out there, because he was refusing to answer the telephone. We quarrelled . . . or rather, we stood and glared at one another. That was our way of quarrelling.'

'About what?'

'We quarrelled about our inheritance,' said Gerlof. 'Not that it helped, but—'

'What inheritance?'

'Everything my mother and father left.'

'What happened to it?' said Tilda.

'A lot disappeared. But it was Ragnar who took it, he did himself proud on it . . . My brother was a real shit, in fact.'

Tilda looked at the tape recorder, but couldn't come up with a suitable response.

'Ragnar was a shit, towards me at any rate,' Gerlof went on, shaking his head. 'He emptied our parents' place in Stenvik, sold most of the contents of the house, sold the house to people from the mainland and kept the profit for himself. And he refused to discuss it. He would just stare coldly at me . . . It was impossible to get anywhere with him.'

'Did he take *everything*?' said Tilda.

'I got a few mementoes, but Ragnar took the money. Presumably he thought he would be better at taking care of it.'

'But wasn't there anything you could do?'

'Sue him, you mean?' said Gerlof. 'That isn't the way we do things here on the island. We become enemies instead. Even brothers, sometimes.'

'But . . .'

'Ragnar helped himself,' Gerlof went on. 'He was the eldest brother, after all. He took what he wanted first, then shared with me if he felt like it. So we parted on bad terms, in the autumn before he froze to death in the storm.' Gerlof sighed. ' "Let brotherly love continue," it says in St Paul's Epistle to the Hebrews, but it isn't always that easy. Of course, that's the sort of thing I end up thinking about these days.'

Tilda looked at the tape recorder again with a regretful expression. Then she switched it off. 'I think . . . I think it might be best if I delete this last part. Not because I think you're lying, Gerlof, but . . .'

'Fine by me,' said Gerlof.

When Tilda had put the tape recorder away in its

black case, he said, 'I think I know how it works now. Which buttons you have to press.'

'Good,' said Tilda. 'You obviously have a talent for technology, Gerlof.'

'Might you be able to leave it here? Until we see each other again?'

'The tape recorder?'

'Just in case I feel like talking into it some more.'

'Of course.' Tilda passed over the case. 'Talk as much as you want. There are a couple of blank tapes you can use.'

When she got back to the police station the light on the answering machine was flashing. She started to listen to the message, but when she heard Martin's voice she sighed and pressed Delete.

It was time he gave up.

26

Joakim was making one last trip with the children before Christmas. It was the first day of the Christmas break and he drove down to Borgholm with them.

There were plenty of people out shopping for Christmas presents. The Westin family went into the big supermarket on the way into town and wandered up and down the long aisles full of food, stocking up on supplies for the holiday.

'What shall we have for Christmas dinner?' asked Joakim.

'Grilled chicken and chips,' said Livia.

'Juice,' said Gabriel.

Joakim bought chicken, chips and raspberry juice, but also potatoes and sausage and ham and Christmas beer and crispbread for himself. He bought frozen minced beef to make meatballs, and when he saw that they were selling Öland eel on the fish counter, he bought some smoked pieces. It had presumably swum past just off Eel Point. He also bought a couple of pounds of cheese. Katrine had always liked to eat bread with thick slices of this particular cheese at Christmas.

It wasn't entirely sensible, but the previous week Joakim had actually bought her a Christmas present. He had been down in Borgholm looking for presents for the children, and in the window of a shop he had seen a pale-green tunic Katrine would have loved. He had gone on to the toy shop, but then went back to Danielsson's boutique and bought the tunic.

'Could I have it gift-wrapped please . . . as a Christmas present,' he had said, and the assistant had handed over a red package with white ribbons.

In the car park next to the supermarket they were selling Christmas trees wrapped in plastic. Joakim bought a big Nordman fir that was tall enough to reach up to the ceiling on the ground floor. He fastened it on to the roof of the car, then they drove home.

It was cold on the island – minus ten degrees – but there was hardly a breath of wind when they got back to Eel Point. The water was just beginning to freeze again, but there was still only a thin layer of snow on the ground. Joakim's breath billowed out in white clouds, slowly drifting away, as he carried the bags of food across the courtyard and into the house. Then he brought the tree into the warmth. Thousands of tiny insects would come in too, tucked among the branches, he knew that, but most of them were in the middle of their long winter sleep, and would never wake up.

That would be the best way to die, Joakim thought – in your sleep, without any warning.

He put the tree up in the drawing room, beneath the white ceiling. The table with its high-backed chairs was already here, but not much else. The rooms on the ground floor were feeling more and more empty as Christmas grew closer.

The Westin family spent the last two days before Christmas cleaning and getting everything ready in the house. They had two big cardboard boxes of Christmas decorations to unpack: the Christmas crib, the candlesticks, the red and white hand towels for the kitchen, the Christmas stars to hang in the windows and a goat and a pig made of straw which they placed on either side of the tree.

When all the Christmas decorations had been unpacked, Livia and Gabriel helped to dress the tree. They had both made paper decorations and wooden figures at nursery which they hung up where they could reach, on the lowest branches. On the higher branches Joakim placed tinsel and baubles and Christmas candles, with a golden star right at the top. The tree was ready for Christmas.

Finally they got out the bags of Christmas presents and arranged them under the tree. Joakim placed the gift for Katrine next to the other presents.

Everything fell silent around the tree.

'Is Mummy coming back now?' asked Livia.

'Maybe,' said Joakim.

The children had almost stopped talking about Katrine, but he knew that Livia in particular really missed her. For children the line between what was possible and what was impossible didn't exist in the same way as for adults. Perhaps it was just a question of wanting to see her enough?

'We'll have to see what happens,' he said, looking at the pile of packages.

It would be wonderful to see Katrine one last time. To be able to talk to her and say goodbye properly.

The TV weather forecasters had warned of storms and snowfall over Öland and Gotland during Christmas, but two days before the festivities began Joakim looked out of the window and saw only fine wisps of cloud in the sky. The sun was shining, it was minus six degrees and there was hardly any wind. Then he looked at the bird table outside the kitchen window, and had the feeling that a storm was on the way after all.

The table was empty. The fat balls and piles of seed were still there, but there were no birds pecking at them.

Rasputin jumped up on to the worktop next to Joakim and confirmed for himself that the bird table was empty.

The meadow leading down to the shore was equally deserted, and there were no mute swans or long-tailed ducks out at sea. Perhaps they had all sought shelter over in the forest. Birds don't need to look at a weather chart to know when a storm is on the way, they can feel it in the air.

That same morning Joakim let Livia and Gabriel sleep in until eight thirty. He would have liked to take them off to nursery so that he could be alone, but they would be at home with him for the next two weeks, however he felt about that.

'Is Mummy coming home today?' asked Livia as she got out of bed.

'I don't know,' said Joakim.

But the atmosphere in the house was different now, he could feel it, and the children seemed to sense it too. There was an air of tense expectancy in all the white-painted rooms.

He got the candles out straight after breakfast. He had bought them in a shop in Borgholm, despite the fact that you really ought to make your own Christmas candles as people had done in the kitchen at the manor house in days gone by, after the children had plaited the wicks; that made the candles personal. But these factory-made candles were all the same length and burned with an even glow in the windows, on the tables and in the circular holders suspended from the light fittings.

Living flames for the dead.

The family ate a light lunch in the kitchen in the middle of the day, when the sun was just above the roof of the outhouse. It would soon begin to go down again.

After lunch Joakim dressed the children in thick jackets and took them for a walk down to the sea. He glanced at the closed door of the barn as they walked past, but didn't say anything to the children.

They carried on down to the shore in silence. The fine, feathery cirrus clouds were still hovering above the point, but away on the horizon a storm front had begun to loom like a dark-grey curtain.

The ice was thin and frosty white by the shore, but firm and dark blue further out. The children threw pebbles and bits of ice that bounced and slid across the shining surface meeting no resistance, out towards the black cracks.

'Are you cold?' asked Joakim after a while.

Gabriel's nose was red, and he nodded gloomily.

'We'd better go home, then,' said Joakim.

This was the shortest day of the year – it was only half past two, but the sky was dark blue, like twilight on a late summer evening, as they walked back up to the house. Joakim thought he could feel the breath of the approaching snowfall on the back of his neck.

When they got back into the warmth he lit the candles again. In the evening the glow from the house would be seen all the way up to the road, perhaps even as far away as Offermossen, the sacrificial peat bog.

When Livia and Gabriel had fallen asleep that evening and everything was quiet in the house, Joakim put on his padded jacket and left the house with a torch in his hand. He was going to visit the barn. These last few weeks he had rarely managed to stay away for more than a few days at a time.

It was a clear, starry night, and the thin covering of snow in the courtyard had become hard and dry in the cold. The ice crystals crunched beneath his boots.

He stopped by the door of the barn and looked around. Dark shadows surrounded the outhouse, and it was easy to imagine that somebody was standing over there. A thin woman with a ravaged face, gazing at him with a dark expression . . .

'Stay away, Ethel,' Joakim muttered to himself as he dragged open the heavy door. He walked in and listened for the sound of yowling from Rasputin the mouser, but heard nothing.

Tonight Joakim didn't go over to the steps leading up to the hayloft. He took a walk round the ground floor first, past the empty feeding troughs and stalls where cows had once stood in a line in the winter, chewing away.

A rusty horseshoe had been nailed to the gable-end wall at the far side of the barn. Joakim went over to look at it. The ends were pointing upwards, presumably so that the luck wouldn't run out.

The light from the bulbs on the ceiling didn't quite reach this far, so he switched on his torch. When it illuminated the roof beams up above it occurred to Joakim that he must be directly underneath the hidden room in the loft. Then he lowered the torch.

Someone had swept the stone floor. Not everywhere, but in a strip next to the walls. There was no dried dung or piles of old hay there.

It could hardly be anyone other than Katrine who had swept in here.

In the right-hand corner on the gable wall, old fishing nets and thick ropes hung from a row of nails.

Several of them reached right down to the floor, like a curtain. But behind the curtain, the wall appeared to sink inwards.

Joakim took a step forward and shone the torch, and the shadow by the wall moved silently away, revealing a low opening down by the floor. Part of the wooden wall was missing, and when Joakim pushed the curtain of ropes and nets smelling of tar to one side, he could see that the stone slabs continued beyond it.

There was some kind of opening by the floor in the gable wall. It only reached up to Joakim's knees, but was at least six feet wide.

He was driven on by his curiosity, and bent down to try and see what was on the other side of the opening. All he could see was more closely packed earth, and dancing balls of fluff.

In the end he lay down on his belly and started to crawl. He took the torch with him, and wriggled under the wooden planks.

He just managed to get under the wall before he came to a stop; there was another wall in front of him, made of limestone this time. It was ice cold – it must be the outside wall. The space between was only about three feet wide. When Joakim had brushed aside some curtains of freshly spun cobwebs, he could actually stand up.

In the beam of the torch he could see that he was in a narrow space between two walls: the inner wall made of wood that he had crawled under, and the western outer wall of the barn. A couple of yards away an old wooden ladder led straight up into the darkness.

Someone had been here before him. It looked as if someone had been moving around in here, creating walkways in the hundred-year-old dust. Was it Katrine? After all, Mirja had said she didn't know anything about a hidden room anywhere at the manor.

The ladder in front of him rose almost vertically into the darkness. Joakim shone his torch upwards and saw that it led to a square hole. It was pitch black up there, but he didn't hesitate for a second. He started to climb.

Eventually he perched on the edge of the opening and heaved himself up from the ladder. He was on a wooden floor. To his left was an unpainted wooden wall. He recognized the wide planks, and knew that he had found the hidden room behind the hayloft.

He stood up and swept the torch around in front of him.

In its yellow glow he saw benches – rows of benches. Church benches.

He was at one end of something that looked like an old wooden chapel inside the loft. It was a little room dedicated to worship beneath the high, angular roof, set out with four benches and a narrow aisle alongside them. The wooden benches were dry and split and the edges were battered, completely without any kind of ornamentation; they looked as if they came from a medieval church. They must have been put here when the barn was built, Joakim realized. There was no door through which to carry them in.

There was no pulpit in the room. And no cross. High up on the wall in front of the pews was a filthy window. Below it a sheet of paper was hanging from a nail, and when he went over he saw that it was a page ripped out of a family Bible: a Doré drawing of a woman, Mary Magdalene perhaps, staring in amazement at the stone rolled away from the entrance to Jesus's tomb. The big round stone lay cast aside on the ground, and the opening to the tomb gaped above her like a black hole.

Joakim looked at the picture for a long time. Then he

turned around – and discovered that the wooden benches behind him were not empty.

In the glow of the torch he could see letters lying on them.

And dried-up bunches of flowers.

And a pair of children's white shoes.

On one of the benches lay something small and pale, and when he bent down he saw that it was a set of false teeth.

Possessions. Mementoes.

There were also several small plaited baskets containing pieces of paper. Joakim reached down and carefully picked one out. He shone the torch on it and read:

Carl, forgotten by everyone, but not by me or the Lord.
Sara

In another basket lay a yellowing postcard with a black and white picture of an angel on the front, smiling serenely. Joakim picked it up, turned it over and saw that someone had written on the back in ink, in ornate handwriting:

Tender loving thoughts of my dear sister Maria, sadly
missed. My daily prayer goes to the Lord our God that
we may soon meet again.
An unbearable loss.
Nils Peter

Joakim gently put the card back in the basket.

This was a prayer room – a sealed-up room for the dead.

A book lay on one of the benches. It was a thick notebook, Joakim saw when he picked it up. Inside was page after page of handwriting, too small and spidery to read in the darkness, and on the title page *The Book of the Blizzard* was written in black ink.

He pushed it inside his jacket.

Joakim straightened up, looked around for one last time and noticed a small hole in the wall beside the bench at the front. He went closer, and realized what it was: the hole he himself had hacked in the wall of the hayloft a few weeks ago.

He had reached through with his arm that evening, as far as he could. On the bench just below that little opening lay the object he had touched.

A folded cloth bundle.

A pale-blue, tattered denim jacket, which Joakim thought he had seen before.

When he recognized some of the small badges on the front which said RELAX and PINK FLOYD, he knew whose jacket it was. Joakim had seen it night after night when he looked out into the street from behind the curtains at the Apple House.

It was his sister Ethel's denim jacket.

WINTER 1961

I was the one who discovered the big hayloft in the barn, but I enticed Markus up the steps with me and we explored it together. It was my first romance, and perhaps my best.

But it was so short.

Mirja Rambe

In the evenings that autumn and winter Markus and I creep around with a paraffin lamp among the ropes and chains and open chests and look at old documents relating to the lighthouses.

It looks like a rubbish dump, but there are fantastic things up there – so many memories from the hundred-year-old history of the manor. All the rubbish every family and every lighthouse-keeper left behind at Eel Point seems to have ended up here in the barn sooner or later, and has been forgotten.

After a few weeks we carry all the spare blankets we can find in the house out to the barn and make a little tent out of them. We sneak out bread and wine and cigarettes and start to have picnics up there too, high above the dreariness of everyday life.

I show Markus the wall with all the carved names of those who have died. We trace the letters with our fingers and I fantasize gleefully about the tragedies that have visited Eel Point over the years.

We carve our own names into the floor of the loft instead, close beside one another.

It takes three picnics in the loft before he dares to kiss me on the mouth. He isn't allowed to do much more – the old doctor still haunts me – but I live on his kiss for several weeks.

And now I can paint Markus quite openly.

Suddenly Eel Point is not the end of the world after all. It is the centre of the world, and I start to believe and hope that Markus and I will be able to do what we want, travel wherever we want. We get through the long winter together.

The sea is cold and as usual it takes a long time for the summer to reach the island, but at the end of May the sun shines bright and clear over the meadows once again. But that is also when Markus gets ready to leave – not with me, but alone. He has been called up for one year's military service on the mainland.

We promise to write to one another. Lots of letters.

When he has packed his suitcase I go with him to the railway station in Marnäs. We stand there in silence, waiting with other residents of the island. The railway on Öland is to be closed this year, and the atmosphere in the waiting room is gloomy.

Markus has gone, but Ragnar Davidsson continues to moor his boat at Eel Point and come up to the house.

He and I actually have a number of discussions about art, even if the level is quite low. It starts one day when I come out into the hallway of the outhouse and notice that the door to the middle room is open. When I look in, Davidsson is standing there in the middle of the floor. He is looking at all the dark paintings that cover the walls.

It is obvious that this is the first time he has discovered Torun's huge collection, and he doesn't like it. He shakes his head.

'What do you think?' I ask.

'It's all just black and grey,' he says. 'Just a lot of dark colours.'

'That's what a blizzard looks like at night,' I say.

'In that case it looks like . . . crap,' says Davidsson.

'You can also look at it from a symbolic point of view,' I venture. 'It's a blizzard at night, but it also represents a soul . . . the tormented soul of a woman.'

Davidsson shakes his head. 'Crap,' he says again.

He has clearly never read Simone de Beauvoir. I haven't either, of course, but at least I've heard of her.

I make one last attempt to defend Torun, and say, 'They'll be worth a lot of money one day.'

Davidsson turns his head and looks at me as if I'm insane. Then he walks past me and goes outside.

When I go back into the other room I see Torun sitting by the window, and realize straight away that she heard the whole conversation. Despite the fact that she is almost completely blind now, she stares out of the window.

I try to talk to her about something else, but she shakes her head. 'Ragnar is right,' she says. 'It's crap, all of it.'

*   *   *

I stop going up to the hayloft once Markus has gone. It reminds me of him too much, it feels too empty.

But of course we send letters to each other. I write the most often – several long letters in reply to one of his short ones.

Markus's letters are mostly about military exercises, and they don't come very often. But this just makes me fill letter after letter with my dreams and plans. When can we see each other again? When is he on leave? When does he finish?

He doesn't really know, but promises that we will meet up. Soon.

I begin to realize that I have to get away from Eel Point, take the ferry to the mainland and Markus. But how can I leave Torun? It's impossible.

27

Henrik knew the police were looking for him. Twice during the last week a police officer had left a message on his answering machine, asking him to come to the station for an interview.

He hadn't bothered going in.

Of course he couldn't keep on playing truant like that, but he needed time to get rid of the evidence of his career as a burglar. The most tangible was of course the boathouse full of stolen goods.

'I can't have the stuff here any longer,' he said when he called Tommy. 'You have to come over and deal with it.'

'OK.' Tommy didn't sound stressed in the slightest. 'We'll bring the van over on Monday. At about three.'

'And you'll bring the money?'

'Sure,' said Tommy. 'It's cool.'

Monday was the day before Christmas Eve. Henrik was working up in Marnäs, but finished at two and drove straight down to the boathouse in Enslunda.

When he got out on to the coast road he heard that the weather forecast was predicting persistent snowfall and strong winds over Öland and Gotland that evening – and there was a storm warning for the Baltic. But the weather was still fine, the sky dark blue. A bank of grey cloud was approaching the island from the east, but Henrik would soon be back in Borgholm.

As usual there was nobody around down by the boat-house. Henrik swung the car around and reversed the last few yards down to the white boat standing on its trailer. The previous weekend he had been here with Camilla. She had wanted to look in the boathouse, but he had managed to talk her out of it. Instead they had taken the boat out of the water and removed the outboard motor. They hadn't managed to cover it with a tarpaulin, but he would do that now.

As he stepped out on to the grass and breathed in the smell of seaweed, he thought about his dead grandfather for half a second, then lifted the handle of the trailer to attach it to the tow bar on the back of his car.

The idea of hiding some of the stolen goods came to him a little bit later, as he stood inside the boathouse looking at everything they had collected during the autumn. There must have been a hundred items, large and small, antique and modern. Henrik had no real idea what was there, and he was sure the brothers hadn't either.

His boat wasn't registered anywhere, there was no way the police could know he had it. Once he had taken it to the industrial estate outside Borgholm, he could drive out there and pick up the stolen goods whenever he wanted.

Henrik decided to go for it. He picked up one of the old limestone vases, worth maybe five thousand kronor in an antique shop, and carried it out to the boat.

It was snowing now, feathery flakes floating down towards the ground.

He carefully placed the vase on the floor next to the driver's seat. Then he went back to the boathouse and picked up a box of vintage Scotch.

Eventually Henrik had carried over a dozen or so items and hidden them between the seats in the boat. The floor was almost full of stolen goods by this stage. He fetched a green tarpaulin from the boathouse, pulled it over the boat from prow to stern, and fastened it with a long nylon rope.

Done.

The snowflakes had continued to fall at a leisurely pace, forming a thin white covering on the ground.

When Henrik went back to lock the boathouse, he heard a dull roar through the soughing of the wind. He turned his head. Through the trees he could see a vehicle approaching – a dark van.

The Serelius brothers pulled in next to Henrik's boat. The doors opened and slammed shut.

'Hi there, Henrik!'

The brothers walked towards him through the snow, both smiling. They were dressed for the cold weather, in black padded jackets, boots and lined hunting caps. Tommy was wearing huge ski shades, as if he were on holiday in the mountains. The old Mauser hung over his shoulder.

He was on something, Henrik could see that despite the mirrored shades that hid his pupils. Crystal meth, no doubt. As usual he had red scratch marks on his neck, and his chin was trembling. Not good.

'And so the time has come,' said Tommy. 'Time to wish each other a Merry Christmas.'

When Henrik didn't reply, he laughed harshly. 'No, of course that's not all . . . we've come to collect the stuff as well.'

'Stuff,' said Freddy.

'The loot.'

'And the money?' said Henrik.

'Sure. We'll share it like brothers.' Tommy was

still smiling. 'What do you think we are, thieves?'

It was an old joke, but Henrik's answering smile was tense; he realized they weren't really talking about the division of the stolen goods.

He saw Freddy walk over to the boathouse and open the door wide. Then he disappeared into the darkness, but came straight back out with a television set in his arms.

'That's what we said,' said Henrik. 'Like brothers.'

Tommy went past him and walked over to the boat.

'I'm taking the boat home afterwards,' said Henrik. 'So you're moving on now?'

'Yep . . . back to Copenhagen. We're just going up to that place by the lighthouses first.' Tommy waved his hand in a northerly direction. 'To look for those paintings. Are you coming?'

Henrik shook his head. He saw that Freddy had placed the television in the van and gone back into the boathouse. 'No, I haven't got time,' he replied. 'Like I said, I have to get the boat home.'

'Yeah, yeah,' said Tommy, studying the trailer. 'Where do you keep it over the winter?'

'Down in Borgholm . . . behind a factory.'

Tommy pulled at the rope securing the tarpaulin and asked, 'Is it safe there?'

'It's in a fenced yard.'

Henrik's pulse rate increased. He should have got more ropes and knotted them tightly over the tarpaulin. In order to distract Tommy, he started talking again: 'Do you know what I saw out here back in the autumn?'

'No.'

Tommy shook his head, but didn't take his eyes off the boat.

'It was in October,' said Henrik, 'when I was here emptying the boat. I saw a motor cruiser, it must have come from the north. It put in up by the lighthouses at Eel Point. There was a man standing in the prow . . . and that evening they found her drowned, in just the same place. I've thought about it a lot.'

He was talking too much, and too quickly. But now at last Tommy turned his head. 'Who are you talking about?'

'The woman from the manor house up there,' said Henrik. 'Katrine Westin. I did some work for her last summer.'

'Eel Point,' said Tommy. 'That's where we're going. So you saw a murder there?'

'No, I saw a motor boat,' said Henrik. 'But it wasn't that easy to see . . . it was just that they found her dead afterwards.'

'Fuck,' said Tommy, not sounding particularly impressed. 'Did you tell anyone?'

'Tell who? The police?'

'No,' said Tommy, 'they would just have started asking you what you were doing out here. They might even have checked inside the boathouse and arrested you.'

'*Us*,' said Henrik.

Tommy looked at the boat again. 'Freddy told me a story on the way here,' he said. 'It was pretty cool.'

'Oh yes?'

'It's about a girl and a guy . . . they're on holiday in the USA, driving around, and at a picnic area by the road they come across a skunk. They've never seen a skunk before, and they think it's really cute. The girl wants to take it home to Sweden, but the guy doesn't think Customs will let wild animals through. So the girl suggests that she should smuggle the skunk through in her panties. "That's an idea," says the guy. "But what about the smell?" '

Tommy scratched his neck and paused before the punchline.

' "What's the problem?" says the girl. "I mean, the skunk stinks as well." '

He laughed to himself. Then he turned around and grabbed hold of the tarpaulin. 'The skunk stinks as well,' he said again.

'Just a minute . . .' Henrik began.

But Tommy didn't wait. He pulled the tarpaulin hard, over to one side. He only managed to loosen a small section from the rope, but it was enough to reveal most of the stolen goods.

'Aha,' said Tommy, looking down at the objects in the boat. Then he pointed at the ground. 'You should have swept away the tracks in the snow, Henke . . . you've been shuttling back and forth between the boathouse and the boat.'

Henrik shook his head. 'I took a few things . . .'

'A few?' said Tommy, beginning to walk towards him.

Henrik took a step backwards. 'So what?' he said. 'I've worked hard for this. I've planned every trip, and all you've done—'

'Henke,' said Tommy, 'you talk too much.'

'*Me?* You can—'

But Tommy wasn't listening; he struck out, fetching Henrik a hard blow in the stomach and making him stagger backwards. There was a rock behind him; he slumped down on it and looked at the ground.

His jacket was ripped. A narrow tear ran from the bottom of the material up towards his navel.

Tommy quickly went through Henrik's pockets and fished out the car keys. 'Sit still. I'll punch you again if you move.'

Henrik didn't move. His stomach started throbbing. The pain came in waves, and during one of them Henrik leaned forward and vomited between his legs.

Tommy took a couple of steps away from him, adjusted the gun on his shoulder and pushed the sharp screwdriver into his back pocket.

Henrik coughed laboriously and looked up at him. 'Tommy . . .'

But Tommy just shook his head. 'Do you think that's what we're really called – Tommy and Freddy? Those are our stage names.'

Henrik had run out of words. And strength. He sat there on the rock in silence.

Over by the road, Freddy was still carrying stolen goods out to the van. Eventually he closed the door. 'Finished!'

'Good.' Tommy straightened up, scratched his cheek and glanced at Henrik. 'You'll have to get the bus back . . . or whatever it is they have out here. A horse and cart?'

Henrik didn't reply. He just sat there on the rock, watching the Serelius brothers. Freddy climbed un-hurriedly in behind the wheel of the van. Tommy settled himself in Henrik's Saab.

The brothers were stealing both his car and his boat, and all Henrik could do was watch. He saw both vehicles disappear slowly towards the coast road.

Eventually he took his hand away from his stomach and looked. The tear in his grey padded jacket was coloured red now. And yet it wasn't bleeding that much, actually, just a little trickle. Henrik had given blood in Borgholm once, and they had taken a whole pint. This little drop was nothing.

A little bit of stomach ache, a slight shock and one bout of vomiting. No problem.

After a while he managed to get up from the rock. The blood throbbed in the wound with approximately the same rhythm as the waves rolling in towards the shore, but he was actually able to walk. His intestines and his liver must be OK.

Colder air had started to blow in off the sea. Henrik thought about how his grandfather had died alone out here one winter's day, but pushed the thought aside. With his hand pressed against his belly, he started to walk towards his boathouse. The door was ajar, and he stopped on the threshold.

All the stolen goods were gone. The only consolation was that Tommy and Freddy had taken the old stable lantern as well. Perhaps it was their turn to hear the knocking now.

Henrik stepped inside with difficulty, and made his way over to his grandfather's workbench. Algot's old wood axe was lying there, a small but sturdy item. And the long, slender scythe was standing in one corner. He took the axe and the scythe and went slowly back outside into the snow.

The padlock had fallen off into the snow. Henrik couldn't find it. All he could do was close the door behind him, which cost him considerable effort. Then he set off into the snow, away from the road and the boathouses and out on to the meadow by the shore.

He carried on northwards along the coast, his head bowed, walking diagonally into the strengthening wind. He was protected against the gusts by his woollen hat and padded jacket, but it made his eyes and nose smart.

Henrik ignored the cold, he just kept on walking.

The Serelius brothers, or whatever their name was, had struck him down and stolen his boat. And they had talked about going up to Eel Point.

In which case Henrik intended to meet them there.

28

Tilda rang the doorbell of Henrik Jansson's flat in Borgholm, keeping her finger there for a long time. She waited in silence along with Mats Torstensson, one of her colleagues in the town.

It was the day before Christmas Eve and this should all have been sorted out much earlier, but Henrik hadn't turned up at the police station despite the fact that he had been called in for questioning about the wave of break-ins in northern Öland. If he wasn't prepared to come in voluntarily, he would have to be picked up.

There wasn't a sound. Tilda rang again, but no one opened the door and she couldn't hear anything when she pressed her ear against it. She tried the handle – it was locked.

'Maybe he's gone away,' suggested Torstensson. 'To his mother or father, for Christmas.'

'His boss said he was supposed to be working today,' said Tilda. 'Only half a day, but . . .'

She rang the bell again, and at the same time the outside door of the apartment block slammed and they heard the sound of boots clomping up the stairs. Tilda and Torstensson turned their heads at the same time – but it was a teenage girl who was coming up the stairs, a red woollen scarf covering half her face and a bag of Christmas presents in her hand. She glanced briefly at the uniformed police officers. When she had unlocked the door opposite Henrik's, Tilda took a step towards her and said, 'We're looking for your neighbour, Henrik. Do you know where he is?'

The girl looked at the nameplate on Henrik's door. 'At work?'

'We've checked there.'

The girl thought about it. 'He could be at the boat-house.'

'Where's that?'

'On the east coast somewhere. He wanted to take me out there to go swimming last summer, but I said no.'

'Good,' said Tilda. 'Have a great Christmas.'

The girl nodded, but glared at her bag of presents as if she were already pretty tired of the whole Christmas thing.

'That's it then,' said Torstensson. 'We'll have to pick him up after the holiday.'

'Unless we bump into him on the way back,' said Tilda.

It was half past two. It was cold and grey out in the street, almost minus ten, and twilight was already falling.

'I finish in quarter of an hour,' said Torstensson as he opened the car door. 'Then I have to go shopping. I'm a little behind with the Christmas presents!' He looked at his watch. In his mind he was probably already at home with a glass of Christmas beer in front of the TV.

'I'll just call . . .' said Tilda.

Her five days of leave were also approaching, but she still didn't want to let go of Henrik Jansson.

She got in the car and called Henrik Jansson's boss

357

for the second time that day. He told her that Henrik's boathouse was at Enslunda. That was south of Marnäs, quite close to Eel Point.

'I'll drive you back to the station,' she said. 'Then I can call in at Enslunda on the way up. I'm sure he won't be there, but at least I can check.'

'I'll come with you, if you want.'

Torstensson was a nice guy and his offer was no doubt genuine, despite the Christmas stress, but she shook her head.

'Thanks, but I'll call on the way home,' she said. 'If Jansson's there I'll bring him back here and ruin his Christmas. Otherwise I'll go home and wrap presents.'

'Drive carefully,' said Torstensson. 'There's a snow-storm coming, you do know that?'

'Yep,' said Tilda. 'But I've got winter tyres.'

They drove back to the station. When Torstensson had gone inside, Tilda swung the car around and was just on her way out of the car park when the door opened again. Mats Torstensson was waving at her.

Tilda wound down the window and stuck her head out. 'What is it?'

'You've got a visitor,' he said.

'Who is it?'

'Your tutor from the academy.'

'Tutor?'

Tilda didn't understand, but she parked the car and went into the station with Torstensson. Reception wasn't manned. The Advent candles flickered in the windows; most of the police officers on the island had already started their Christmas leave.

'I caught her,' said Torstensson.

He was speaking to a broad-shouldered man who was sitting in one of the armchairs in the waiting room. The man was dressed in a jacket and a pale-grey police sweater, and smiled with satisfaction when Tilda walked in.

'I was in the area,' he said, getting up. He held out a big present wrapped in red paper. 'I just wanted to wish you a Merry Christmas.'

It was Martin Ahlquist, of course.

Tilda kept the mask in place and tried to smile. 'Hi Martin . . . same to you.'

Her lips quickly stiffened, but Martin's smile grew even broader. 'Would you like to go for a coffee?'

'Thanks,' she said, 'but I'm afraid I'm rather busy.'

She did accept the present, however (it felt like a box of chocolates), nodded to Mats Torstensson, then went out into the car park.

Martin followed her. She turned around; now she no longer had to pretend to look pleased. 'What do you think you're doing?'

'What do you mean?' said Martin.

'You keep on calling me, and now you turn up here with a present. Why?'

'Well, I wanted to see how you were.'

'I'm fine,' said Tilda. 'So you can go home . . . home to your wife and children. It's almost Christmas Eve.'

He just kept on smiling at her.

'It's all arranged,' he said. 'I told Karin I was staying over in Kalmar, and I'd be home early in the morning.'

For Martin everything seemed to be about practical problems – keeping the lies in some sort of order.

'You do that, then,' said Tilda. 'Take yourself off to Kalmar.'

'Why would I do that? I can just as easily stay over here, on Öland.'

She sighed and walked over to her car. She opened the door and threw Martin's present on the back seat. 'I haven't got time to talk now. There's a guy I have to pick up.'

She closed the door before he had time to reply. Then she started the engine and pulled out of the station car park.

Soon she saw a blue Mazda pull out behind her.

Martin's car. He was following her.

On the way north from Borgholm she wondered why she hadn't been more determined in her efforts to get rid of him. She could have spat and yelled – perhaps he would have understood those signals.

By the time Tilda reached the eastern side of the island it was half past three. The daylight was almost completely gone, the sky was dark grey and the silently falling snow had changed and become more intrusive. The snow had become aggressive, she thought. The flakes had stopped whirling around aimlessly in the air and were grouping for attack. They hit the front of the police car in dense flurries, clinging to the windows.

She turned off on to the narrow track down towards Enslunda. Martin's Mazda was still a little way behind her.

In the glow of the headlights Tilda could see that there were several tyre tracks in the snow ahead of her, and when the track ran out fifty yards or so from the sea she expected to see at least a couple of parked cars.

But the little turning area was completely deserted.

There was nothing there but a mass of fresh tracks in the snow – tracks left by heavy shoes or boots, running back and forth between the tyre tracks and one of the boathouses. The snowflakes were already beginning to cover them.

The Mazda had pulled in and stopped behind her.

Tilda put on her police cap and pushed open the

driver's door against the wind. It was bitterly cold and desolate here at the edge of the Baltic. The cold and the emptiness made the entire coast feel menacing. The waves were rolling in, and had begun to break up the covering of ice offshore.

Martin got out of his car and walked over to Tilda. 'This guy you're going to pick up . . . is he supposed to be out here?'

She just nodded. She preferred not to speak to him.

Martin started to walk purposefully over to the boat-houses. He appeared to have forgotten that he was a tutor, and no longer a police officer.

Tilda said nothing, she just followed him.

A rhythmic thudding could be heard as they drew closer – the door of one of the boathouses was banging to and fro in the wind. Almost all the footprints in the snow seemed to lead to this particular building.

Martin opened the door and peered in. 'Is this one his?'

'I don't know . . . I suppose so.'

Thieves are always afraid of other thieves, Tilda thought. They want good locks on their own houses. If Henrik Jansson had forgotten to lock up here, then something unforeseen must have happened.

She went over to Martin and peered into the darkness. There was a workbench, some old nets and other fishing tackle and tools along the walls, but not much else.

'He's not home,' said Martin.

Tilda didn't reply. She went inside and bent down. Small shiny droplets could be seen on the wooden floor.

'Martin!' she shouted.

He turned his head and she pointed at the floor. 'What do you make of this?'

He bent down. 'Fresh blood,' he said.

Tilda went outside and looked around. Someone had been injured, possibly shot or stabbed, but they had still been able to leave the area. She carried on down to the meadow by the sea, where the wind was even stronger. There were indistinct tracks in the snow – a long line of footprints leading north.

Tilda considered following the trail along the shore, facing straight into the wind and the raw chill from the sea, but the impressions would soon disappear in the falling snow.

There were only two inhabited houses within reasonable walking distance, as far as Tilda knew: the Carlsson family's farm, and, to the north-east, the manor house at Eel Point. Henrik Jansson, or whoever had made these footprints, seemed to be heading for one of them.

A fierce gust of wind gave Tilda a push, and she turned around and headed back towards the car, away from the shore.

'Where are you going?' shouted Martin behind her.

'It's confidential,' she replied, and carried on to the police car.

She got in without checking whether he was following her or not. Then she switched on her police radio and called central control in Borgholm. She wanted to report the suspected altercation by the boathouses, and to let them know that she was heading north.

There was no reply.

The snow was falling even more thickly now. Tilda started the car, turned the heat full on and switched on the windscreen wipers before slowly setting off.

In her wing mirror she saw the interior light of the Mazda come on as Martin opened the door. Then he switched on the headlights and started to follow her car along the gravel track.

Tilda increased her speed – before she looked to the east and saw that the horizon had disappeared. A grey-white wall of snow hung over the sea. It was dropping rapidly towards the coast.

29

Joakim was standing in the kitchen in the twilight, watching the thickening snowfall between the buildings. It was going to be a white Christmas at Eel Point.

Then he looked over at the barn door. It was closed now, and no footprints led towards it through the snow. He hadn't been back inside the barn since the previous evening, but couldn't stop thinking about the hidden room.

A room for the dead, with its own church benches.

Ethel's jacket had been lying there neatly folded on one of the benches, among all the other old mementoes. He had left it there.

It was Katrine who had put it there. She must have found the room during the autumn and placed the denim jacket on the bench, without telling Joakim. He hadn't even known that Katrine had the jacket.

His wife had kept secrets from him.

It was only when he called his mother that he found out she had sent the jacket to Eel Point. Until then he had assumed that Ingrid had simply placed Ethel's clothes in a box and put it in the attic.

'No, I got it down and wrapped it in brown paper,' said Ingrid. 'Then I posted it to Katrine . . . it was some time in August.'

'But why?' Joakim had asked.

'Well . . . she asked me to send it. Katrine called me last summer, wanting to borrow the jacket. She wanted to check on something, she said, and so I sent it to her.' Ingrid paused. 'Didn't she tell you?'

'No.'

'Didn't you talk to each other?'

Joakim didn't reply. He wanted to say that of course he and Katrine had talked to each other, trusted each other completely – but he remembered the strange look she had given him the night they found out Ethel was dead.

Katrine had hugged Livia and looked at Joakim with shining eyes, as if something wonderful had happened.

When darkness fell outside the kitchen window, Joakim began to prepare dinner. Serving up Christmas fare on the twenty-third of December was perhaps a little early, but he wanted to get the celebrations under way as quickly as possible.

It had been the same last year. His sister had drowned at the beginning of December, and her name had not been mentioned at all over Christmas – instead Katrine and Joakim had bought more presents and even more food than usual. They had filled the Apple House with candles and decorations.

But of course it had still felt as if Ethel were there. Joakim had thought about her every time Katrine raised her glass of alcohol-free cider to him.

He blinked away the tears, continued flicking through the recipes in *Delicious Christmas Fare*, and did the best he could in the kitchen as the shadows grew outside the window.

He fried sliced sausage and meatballs. He cut the cheese into strips, shredded the cabbage and warmed the spare ribs. He grilled the oven-baked ham, peeled the potatoes and brushed the freshly baked spiced bread with syrup and water. He dished up eel and herring and salmon, and cooked the children's specially requested meal: grilled chicken with chips.

Joakim placed dish after dish on the kitchen table, and underneath the table Rasputin got a bowl of fresh tuna.

At half past four he called Livia and Gabriel. 'Time to eat.'

They came in and stood by the table.

'Lot of food,' said Gabriel.

'It's called the Christmas table,' said Joakim. 'You take a plate and fill it up with a little bit of everything.'

Livia and Gabriel did as he said, up to a point. They took some chicken and chips, and potatoes and a little sauce, but the fish and the cabbage remained untouched.

Joakim led the way into the drawing room and the family sat down at the big table beneath the chandelier. He poured cider and wished his children a happy start to the Christmas festivities. He waited for them to ask why he had set a fourth place at the table, but they said nothing.

Not that he really believed Katrine would come back during the evening, but at least he could look at her empty place and fantasize that she was actually sitting there.

The way it should have been.

His mother had always set an extra place every Christmas. But of course Ethel never turned up either.

'Can I get down now, Daddy?' asked Livia after ten minutes.

'No,' said Joakim quickly.

He could see that her plate was empty.

'But I've eaten everything up.'

'Stay there anyway.'

'But I want to watch TV.'

'Me too,' said Gabriel, who still had a lot of food left on his plate.

'There's horse riding on TV,' said Livia, as if this were a weighty argument.

'Just stay where you are,' said Joakim, his tone harsher than he had intended. 'This is important. We're celebrating Christmas together.'

'You're stupid,' said Livia, glaring at him.

Joakim sighed. 'We're celebrating together,' he repeated, with no conviction.

The children kept quiet after that, but at least they stayed put. Eventually Livia went off to the kitchen with her plate, followed by Gabriel. Both came back with a helping of meatballs.

'It's snowing really hard, Daddy,' said Livia.

Joakim looked out of the window and saw thick flakes whirling by. 'Good. We'll be able to go sledging.'

Livia's bad mood disappeared just as quickly as it had arrived, and soon she and Gabriel were chatting about the Christmas presents under the tree. Neither of them seemed concerned about the fourth chair at the table, while Joakim kept glancing towards it all the time.

What had he been expecting? That the front door would open and Katrine would walk into the drawing room?

The old Mora clock by the wall struck just once – it was already half past five, and almost all the light had vanished outside the window.

As Joakim popped the last meatball in his mouth and looked over at Gabriel, he could see that his son was already falling asleep. He had eaten twice as much food as usual this evening, and now he was sitting there motionless, gazing down at his empty plate with his eyelids drooping.

'Gabriel, how about a little sleep?' he said. 'So you'll be able to stay awake longer tonight?'

At first Gabriel just nodded, then he said, 'Then we can play. You and me. And Livia.'

'It's a promise.'

Joakim suddenly realized that his son had probably forgotten Katrine. What did *he* remember from when he was three years old? Nothing.

He blew out the candles, cleared the table and placed the food in the fridge. Then he turned down Gabriel's bed and tucked him in.

Livia didn't want to go to sleep at such an early hour. She wanted to watch horses, so Joakim moved the small television into her room.

'Is that OK?' he said. 'I was just going to go out for a little while.'

'Where?' asked Livia. 'Don't you want to see the horse riding?'

Joakim shook his head. 'I won't be long,' he said.

Then he went and picked up Katrine's Christmas present from under the tree. He took the present and a torch into the hallway and pulled on a thick sweater and a pair of boots.

He was ready.

He stopped in front of the mirror and looked at himself. In the darkness of the corridor he was hardly visible in the glass, and got the idea that he could see the contours of the room through his own body.

Joakim felt like a ghost, one of the apparitions haunting the manor house. He looked at the white English wallpaper around the mirror and the old straw hat hanging on the wall like some kind of symbol of life in the country.

Suddenly everything seemed completely meaningless – why had he and Katrine actually carried on renovating and decorating year after year? The places where they lived had just got bigger and bigger; as soon as one project was finished they had started the next one and made every effort to get rid of any trace of the people who had lived there before. Why?

A low yowling interrupted his thoughts. Joakim turned and saw a small four-legged creature crouching on the rag rug.

'Do you want to go out, Rasputin?'

He went over to the glassed-in veranda, but the cat didn't follow him. It just looked at him, then slunk into the kitchen.

The wind whirled around the house, rattling the small windowpanes in the veranda. Joakim opened the outside door and felt the wind seize hold of it; it was coming in strong gusts now and seemed to be growing stronger all the time, transforming the snowflakes into needle-sharp shards whirling across the courtyard. He went carefully down the steps, screwing his eyes up against the snow.

The sky over the sea looked darker than ever, as if the sun had disappeared for good into the Baltic. The cloud cover over the water was a threatening shadow-play of grey and black patches – huge snow clouds in the north-east had begun to descend, moving closer to the coast.

A storm was on its way.

Joakim went along the stone pathway between the buildings, out into the wind and the snow. He remembered Gerlof's warning, that you could get lost if you went out in a blizzard – but there was only a thin covering of snow on the ground so far, and the short walk over to the barn didn't seem to pose many risks.

He went over to the broad door and pulled it open.

Nothing moved inside.

A flash of light in the corner of his eye made him stop and turn his head. It was the light from the lighthouses. The barn obscured the northern tower, but the southern lamp was flashing at him with its red glow.

Joakim walked into the barn and it felt as if the wind were pushing at his back, as if it wanted to come with him. But he slammed the door shut.

After a few seconds he switched on the lights.

The light bulbs hung there like feeble yellow suns in the dark space of the barn. They couldn't chase away the shadows along the stone walls. Through the roof he could hear the howling wind, but the framework of solid beams didn't move. This building had survived many storms.

In the loft was the wall with Katrine's name and the names of all the others who had died, but Joakim didn't go up the steps this evening either. Instead he moved on past the stalls where the cattle had stood every winter.

The stone floor in the furthest stall was still free of dust and hay.

Joakim sank down to his knees and got down on his stomach. Then he slowly wriggled in through the narrow opening under the wooden planks, the torch in one hand and Katrine's present in the other.

Inside the false wall he stood up and switched on the torch. Its beam was weak and it would soon need new batteries, but at least he could see the ladder leading up into the darkness.

Joakim listened, but everything was still silent in the barn.

He could stand here or start climbing. He hesitated. Just for a moment he considered the fact that a storm was coming, and Livia and Gabriel were alone in the house. Then he lifted his right foot and placed it on the bottom rung.

Joakim's mouth was dry and his heart was pounding, but he was more expectant than afraid. Step by step he was getting closer to the black opening in the ceiling. He didn't want to be anywhere else but where he was now.

Katrine was close, he could feel it.

WINTER 1962

*Markus came back to the island and wanted to see me,
but not at Eel Point. I had to go down to Borgholm to
meet him in a café.*

*Torun, who could hardly see the difference between
light and darkness now, asked me to buy potatoes and
some flour. Flour and root vegetables, that was what we
lived on.*

*It turned out to be a final meeting in a grey town still
waiting for winter, despite the fact that it was the
beginning of December.*

Mirja Rambe

The thermometer is showing zero, but there is no
snow in Borgholm. I am wearing my old winter coat
and feel like the country cousin I am as I walk along
the straight streets of the town.

Markus is back on the island to visit his parents
in Borgholm, and to see me. He is on leave from
the barracks in Eksjö and is wearing his grey
soldier's uniform, with stylish creases pressed in his
trousers.

The café where we have arranged to meet is full of
decent, upstanding ladies who study me as I come

in from the cold – cafés in small towns in Sweden are not the territory of young people, not yet.

'Hi, Mirja.'

Markus stands up politely as I walk over to the table.

'Hi there,' I reply.

He gives me an awkward little hug and I notice he has started using aftershave.

We haven't seen each other for several months and the atmosphere is tense at first, but slowly we begin to talk. I haven't got much to tell him from Eel Point – I mean, nothing has happened there since he went away. But I ask him about life as a soldier and whether he lives in a tent like the one we built in the loft, and he says he does when he is out on exercises. His company has been in Norrland, he tells me, and it was minus thirty degrees. To keep warm they had to pack so much snow all over the tent that it looked like an igloo.

Silence falls between us at the table.

'I thought we could carry on until spring,' I say eventually. 'If you want. I could move closer to you, to Kalmar or something, then when you come out we could live in the same town . . .'

These are vague plans, but Markus smiles at me.

'Until the spring,' he says, brushing my cheek with his hand. His smile broadens, and he adds quietly, 'Would you like to see my parents' flat, Mirja? It's just around the corner. They're not at home today, but I've still got my old room . . .'

I nod and get up from my chair.

We make love for the first and last time in the bedroom Markus had when he was a boy. His bed is too small, so we drag the mattress on to the floor and lie there. The flat is silent around us, but we fill it with the sound of our breathing. At first I am terrified that his parents will come in, but after a while I forget about them.

Markus is eager, yet careful. I think this is the first time for him too, but I dare not ask.

Am I careful enough? Hardly. I have no protection – this is something I could never have imagined would happen. And that's exactly why it's so wonderful.

Half an hour later we go our separate ways out on the street. It is a short farewell in the bitter wind, with a last clumsy embrace through the layers of clothes.

Markus goes back up to the flat to pack before he catches the ferry across the sound, and I go off to the bus station to head back northwards.

I am alone, but I can still feel his warmth against my body.

I would have liked to catch the train, but the trains have stopped running. All I can do is climb aboard the bus.

The atmosphere is gloomy among the small number of passengers, but it suits me. I feel like a lighthouse-keeper on my way to a six-month tour of duty at the end of the world.

It is twilight when I get off to the south of Marnäs, and the wind is bitterly cold. In the grocery shop in Rörby I buy food for Torun and myself, then walk home along the coast road.

I can see slate-grey clouds out at sea when I drop down on to the road to Eel Point. Strong winds are on their way to the island, and I quicken my pace. When the blizzard comes you must be indoors, otherwise things could turn out as they did for Torun on the peat bog. Or even worse.

There are no lights in most of the windows when I reach the house, but in our little room there is a warm yellow glow.

Just as I am about to go in to Torun I see out of the corner of my eye that something is flashing down by the water. I turn my head and see that the lighthouses have been switched on before the night comes. The northern lighthouse is also lit, glowing with a steady white light.

I put the bag of food down on the steps and walk across the courtyard, down towards the shore. The northern lighthouse continues to shine out.

As I stare at the tower something suddenly blows past me on the ground, something pale and rectangular.

Even before I catch up with it and pick it up, I know what it is.

A canvas. One of Torun's blizzard paintings.

'So you're back, are you, Mirja?' says a man's voice. 'Where have you been?'

I turn around. It's Ragnar Davidsson, the eel fisherman, walking towards me from the house. He is wearing his shiny oilskins, and he is not empty-handed. In his arms he is carrying a great bundle of Torun's paintings – fifteen or twenty of them.

I remember what he said about them in the outhouse: *It's all just black and grey. Just a lot of dark colours . . . looks like crap.*

'Ragnar,' I say. 'What are you doing? Where are you going with my mother's pictures?'

He walks past me without stopping, and replies, 'Down to the sea.'

'What did you say?'

'There's no room for them,' he shouts back. 'I've taken over the storeroom in the outhouse. I'll be keeping the eel nets there.'

I look at him in horror, then at the ghostly white light of the northern lighthouse. Then I turn my back on the sea and the wind and hurry back to the house and Torun.

30

The wind along the coast had increased to storm force. The gusts shook the car, and Tilda clutched the wheel tightly.

Blizzard, she thought.

The falling snow whirled across the road like a black and white film, flickering in the beam of the headlights. Tilda slowed right down and leaned closer to the windscreen so that she could make out the road ahead. The snowfall looked more and more like thick white smoke swirling in across the coast. Drifts were beginning to form everywhere that the snow was able to stick, and they quickly turned into banks.

Tilda knew how quickly it could happen. The blizzard transformed the alvar into a white, ice-cold desert and made it impossible to travel by car anywhere on the island. Even the snow scooters would sink and get stuck in the drifts.

She was on her way north now, with Martin still following her. He wouldn't give up – but she had to forget him and concentrate on looking ahead. Snowdrifts covered the road, and it was difficult for the wheels to grip the surface properly. It felt like driving through cotton wool. Tilda was looking out for the headlights of approaching cars, but everything was grey beyond the falling snow.

When she was somewhere in the region of the peat bog, the road in front of the car disappeared completely in the driving snow, and she looked in vain for markers showing where the edge of the carriageway was. Either they had already blown away, or nobody had put them out.

She noticed in her rear-view mirror that Martin's car was getting closer – and that was partly what caused her to make a mistake. She looked into the mirror for a second too long, and didn't notice the bend ahead in the darkness. Not until it was too late.

Tilda turned the wheel as the road curved to the right, but not enough. Suddenly the front wheels sank down into the snow. The police car stopped with a violent bang. A second later she felt an even bigger bang and heard the sound of breaking glass. The car was pushed forwards and stopped, stuck in the ditch by the peat bog.

Martin's car had driven into hers.

Tilda slowly straightened her back behind the wheel. Her ribs and the back of her neck seemed OK.

She floored the accelerator to try and pull back up on to the road again, but the back wheel spun around in the snow, unable to find a grip.

'Shit.'

Tilda switched off the engine and tried to calm down.

In the rear-view mirror she saw Martin open his car door and step out into the snow. The wind made him stagger slightly.

Tilda opened her door as well.

The storm came roaring across the road, and the grey-black landscape made Tilda think of the picture of the blizzard she had seen at Eel Point. When she stepped away from the car the wind grabbed hold of her and seemed to want to drag her out on to the peat bog, but she fought against it and felt her way along the side of the police car.

The front of the car was pushed right down into the ditch. The car was at such an angle that one of the back wheels, the right-hand one, was actually in the air. The whirling snow had begun to pile up against the doors and was already covering the tyres.

Tilda fought her way back along the side of the car, with her hand on her police cap to keep it in place, and made her way over to Martin. She had finally decided how she was going to treat him: not like her former tutor at the police academy, not like her former lover, but like an ordinary mortal. A civilian.

'You were too close!' she said through the wind.

'You slammed the brakes on!' he shouted back.

She shook her head. 'Nobody asked you to follow me, Martin.'

'Well, you've got a radio car,' he said. 'Call the breakdown truck.'

'Don't tell me what to do.'

She turned her back on him, but knew he was right. She would call – although presumably every breakdown truck would be working flat out tonight.

Martin got back in the Mazda and Tilda struggled back to the warmth and quiet of the police car. Once inside she used the radio to call Borgholm for the second time – and this time a rasping voice actually came back over the loudspeaker.

'Central control?' she said. '1217 here, over.'

'1217, received.'

She recognized the voice. Hans Majner was manning the radio, and he was speaking more quickly than usual.

'What's the situation?' asked Tilda.

379

'Chaos . . . more or less complete chaos,' said Majner. 'They're wondering whether to close the bridge completely.'

'Close it?'

'Overnight, yes.'

In that case the winds over the island had already reached storm force, Tilda realized – it was only in extremely bad weather that the Öland bridge was closed to traffic.

'And where are you, 1217?' asked Majner.

'By Offermossen on the eastern road,' said Tilda. 'I'm stuck.'

'Understood, 1217. Do you need help?' Majner actually sounded as if he cared as he went on, 'We'll send somebody out, but it's going to take a while. There's a lorry jammed across the road on the hill by the castle ruins, so all our cars are down there right now.'

'And the snow ploughs?'

'They're only working on the main roads . . . the drifts keep on coming back.'

'Understood. It's the same here.'

'But you're OK for a while, 1217?'

Tilda hesitated. She didn't want to mention the fact that Martin was with her.

'I haven't got any coffee, but it'll be fine,' she said. 'If it gets colder I'll just make my way to the nearest house.'

'Understood, 1217, I'll make a note of that,' said Majner. 'Good luck, Tilda. Out.'

Tilda replaced the radio microphone and stayed where she was behind the wheel. She couldn't decide what to do and looked in the rear-view mirror, but a thick blanket of snow had already covered the back windscreen.

In the end she picked up her mobile and called a number in Marnäs. She got an answer after three rings, but the wind was howling so loudly outside the car that she couldn't make out the words. She raised her voice.

'Gerlof?'

'Speaking.'

His voice sounded quiet and distant.

'It's Tilda!' she shouted.

There was a scraping noise in her ear. The reception was dire out here, but she heard his question.

'Surely you're not out driving in the blizzard?'

'Yes, I'm in the car, on the coast road. Near Eel Point.'

Gerlof said something inaudible.

'What?' Tilda yelled into her mobile.

'I said that's not so good.'

'No.'

'How are you feeling?'

'I'm fine. I've just—'

'But do you really feel fine, Tilda?' Gerlof interrupted her, speaking more loudly. 'In your heart and soul, I mean?'

'In what? What did you say?'

'Well, I'm just wondering if you might be unhappy . . . there was a letter in the bag along with the tape recorder.'

'A letter?'

But suddenly Tilda realized what Gerlof was talking about. She had thought about nothing but work and Henrik Jansson over the past few days, and had completely forgotten her private life. Now it all came back.

'That letter was not addressed to you, Gerlof,' she said.

'No, but . . .' His voice disappeared in a hiss of static, then came back: '. . . wasn't sealed.'

'Right,' she said. 'So you read it?'

'I read the first few sentences . . . and then I read a little bit at the end.'

Tilda closed her eyes. She was too tired and anxious to be angry with Gerlof for rummaging in her bag.

'You can tear it up,' was all she said.

'You want me to destroy it?'

'Yes. Throw it away.'

'OK, I will,' said Gerlof. 'But are you feeling OK?'

'I feel the way I deserve to feel.'

Gerlof said something quietly, but she couldn't make it out.

Tilda wanted to tell him everything, but she couldn't. She couldn't tell him that Martin's wife had fallen pregnant while he was still seeing Tilda. She had just been happy and contented that Martin was with her – even on the night when Karin's pains started. At midnight he had gone off to the hospital, full of excuses for missing the birth of his son.

Tilda sighed and said, 'I should have stopped it long ago.'

'Yes, yes,' said Gerlof. 'But you've stopped it now, I presume.'

She looked in the rear-view mirror. 'Yes.' Then she looked out through the windscreen. The snow had continued to rise, and she could hardly see out now. The car was turning into a snowdrift. 'I think I'd better get out of here,' she said to Gerlof.

'Can you drive through the snow?'

'No. The car's stuck.'

'Then you need to get to Eel Point,' said Gerlof. 'But be careful of your eyes as you're walking. The blizzard blows up sand and earth along with the snow.'

'OK.'

'And never, ever sit down to rest, Tilda, no matter how tired you are.'

'No, of course not. Talk to you soon,' said Tilda, switching off the mobile.

Then she breathed in the warm air inside the car one last time, opened the door and stepped out into the snow.

The wind pressed itself against her, screamed in her ears and pulled and tore at her. She locked the car and started to move along the road, as laboriously as a diver wearing lead boots on the seabed.

Martin wound down the window as she reached his car. He blinked in the wind and raised his voice. 'Is someone coming?'

She shook her head and shouted back, 'We can't stay here.'

'What?'

Tilda pointed eastwards. 'There's a house down there!'

He nodded and wound up the window. A few seconds later he got out of the car, locked it and followed Tilda.

She walked through the swirling powdery snow blowing across the road. She carried on down into the ditch and climbed over a stone wall.

Tilda led the way towards Eel Point, with Martin a few steps behind her. Progress was slow. Every time she looked up into the wind it was like being lashed with ice-cold birch twigs. She had to walk carefully, almost crouching to avoid being pushed over. Tilda was wearing only a pair of short boots on her feet, but wished she had been wearing skis. Or snow shoes.

Eventually she turned away from the wind and stretched her arms out to the dark figure behind her. 'Come on!' she shouted.

Martin had already begun to shiver and shake in the cold. He was dressed in a thin leather jacket, and had nothing on his head. The inadequate clothes were his own fault, but she reached out her hand anyway.

He took it without a word. They clung together and carried on towards the house at Eel Point.

31

Henrik Jansson was fighting his way through the blinding snow. He tucked his head down towards his chest in the roaring wind, and had only the vaguest idea of where he was.

He guessed that he had reached the meadows by the shore to the south of the lighthouses at Eel Point, but he couldn't see them. The snow scratched at his eyes.

Idiot. He should have stayed inside. He had always stayed indoors when the blizzard came.

One January weekend when he was seven years old and staying in his grandparents' cottage he had had a nightmare: a pride of roaring lions had been stalking around in his room during the night. When he woke up in the morning, the lions were gone. Everything was silent in the house, but when he got up and looked out the ground between the buildings was sparkling white.

'There was a blizzard overnight,' his grandfather Algot had explained.

The undulating snow had been almost as high as the window ledges – Henrik couldn't open the front door.

'How can you tell, Grandfather – that it's a blizzard?'

'You don't know when the blizzard is coming,' Algot had said. 'But you know when it arrives.'

And Henrik knew, there on the Baltic shore. This was

the blizzard. The gales before it started had been nothing more than a premonition.

Algot's scythe swung in the wind, weighing him down. He was forced to drop it in the snow, but hung on to the axe. He took three steps over the solid, frozen ground, hunkered down and rested. Then three more steps.

After a while he had to rest after every other step.

The thin ice cover out at sea was smashed to pieces by the strengthening waves. Henrik heard the long drawn-out rumbling, but could no longer see the sea – he could see nothing in any direction.

The pains in his stomach had abated. It might have been the effects of the icy wind, reducing the bleeding, but at the same time he felt as if his entire body were slowly becoming numb. His consciousness began to drift – sometimes it was so far away that it felt as if he were hovering next to his body.

Henrik thought about Katrine, the woman who had drowned at Eel Point. He had enjoyed sanding and replacing the floors with her. She had been small and blonde, just like Camilla.

Camilla.

He remembered her warmth as they lay in bed. But that thought quickly disappeared in the wind.

It was too late to turn back towards the boathouses at Enslunda – he didn't even know where they were any longer. And where were the fucking lighthouses? Henrik peered up into the wind, and caught a brief glimpse of a faint flashing light in the distance. So he was heading in the right direction.

Breathe in, move forward, breathe out.

Then came a hard shove from the direction of the sea that stopped him in the middle of a step. The wind had increased in strength yet again, although Henrik had thought that was impossible.

He sank to his knees. At the same time he dropped the axe in the snow, but managed to pick it up again with enormous difficulty, and tucked the shaft inside his jacket. The axe was meant for the Serelius brothers, and he mustn't lose it.

He crept north, or at least in the direction he thought was north. There was nothing else he could do; if he stopped to rest in the storm he would soon freeze to death.

'Thieves deserve to be thrashed,' he could hear his grandfather saying. 'They're good for nothing but fertilizer and fish food.'

Henrik shook his head.

No, his grandfather had always been able to trust him. The only people he had ever deceived were his teachers, some of his friends, his parents, and John, his boss at the flooring company. And the people who owned the houses. And Camilla, of course. He had sometimes lied to her when they were together, and in the end she had grown tired of him.

A screwdriver in the stomach – perhaps that was what he deserved.

Suddenly someone was clawing at him. Henrik panicked before he realized it was just long leaves from the reeds, whirling around in the wind.

He stopped, closed his eyes and curled up in the icy blast. If he just relaxed and stopped struggling, he would soon go completely numb, in his stomach and right through the rest of his body.

Was death warm or cold? Or somewhere in between?

Somewhere in his head were the Serelius brothers with their broad smiles. That got him moving again.

32

Joakim stood in the barn listening to the wind roaring over the huge roof. He could feel its power through the beams and the sheets of asbestos, but at least he was out of its reach.

He had climbed the ladder a few minutes earlier and was back in the room behind the hayloft. Everything was silent here. The angular roof high above gave him the feeling of having stepped into a church.

The batteries in his torch were almost done, but he could still make out the old church benches in the darkness. And all the old objects lying on them.

This was the prayer room for those who had died at Eel Point; this was where they gathered every Christmas. Joakim was sure of it. Would they come tonight, or tomorrow? It didn't matter, he would stay here and wait for Katrine.

Slowly Joakim moved forward along the narrow aisle beside the benches, looking at the possessions of the dead. He stopped by the front bench and shone the torch on the denim jacket lying there, neatly folded.

He had left it exactly where he found it – he had hardly dared touch it that night. He had taken the book Mirja Rambe had written into his bedroom and started to read it, but he didn't want Ethel's jacket in the house.

He was afraid that Livia would start dreaming about her again.

Joakim reached out and felt the worn fabric, as if touching it could provide answers to all his questions. When he got hold of one sleeve, something rustled and fell on the floor.

It was a small piece of paper.

He bent down and picked it up, and saw a single sentence written in ink. In the faint beam of the torch Joakim read the words, which had been pressed hard into the paper:

MAKE SURE
THAT JUNKIE WHORE
DISAPPEARS

Slowly he moved backwards, the note in his hand.
That junkie whore.

Joakim read the six words on the note several times, and realized this was not a message to Ethel. This had been written to him and Katrine.

Make sure that junkie whore disappears.

But he had never seen it before.

The paper had not been damaged by damp and the ink was black and clear, so the note couldn't have been in the pocket the night Ethel fell in the water. It must have been placed there later. Presumably by Katrine, after she had got hold of the jacket from Joakim's mother.

Joakim thought back to the nights when Ethel would stand and scream in the street outside the Apple House. Sometimes he had seen the neighbours' curtains being pulled aside. Pale, terrified faces had peered out at Ethel.

A note with an exhortation from the neighbours. Katrine must have found it pushed through the door

389

one day when she was home alone, and she had read it and realized that this couldn't go on. The neighbours had had enough of the yelling, night after night.

Everybody had had enough of Ethel. Something had to be done.

Joakim was very tired now, and sank down on the bench next to Ethel's jacket. He carried on staring at the note in his hand, until he heard a faint scraping noise through the wind.

It was coming from the opening in the floor behind him.

Someone was inside the barn.

WINTER 1962

*When the northern lighthouse is lit, someone is going to
die at Eel Point. I have heard that story, but that evening
when I got home from Borgholm and saw the white light
from the northern tower, I didn't think about it. I was
too shocked at seeing Ragnar Davidsson carrying Torun's
paintings down to the water, without taking the slightest
notice of my cries.*

*He had dropped a few rolled-up canvases in the snow,
and I tried to gather them up, but they scudded away in
the wind. All I had in my arms were two paintings when
I got back to the house.*

Mirja Rambe

With the wind at my back I race into the outhouse
porch and carry on into the middle room, despite
the fact that I know what I will see there.

Empty white walls.

Almost all of Torun's blizzard paintings have
gone from the storeroom – there are just a few
rolled up on the floor, alongside several piles of
fishing nets.

The door to our end of the house is closed, but I
know that Torun is sitting in there. I can't go in to

her, can't tell her what has happened, so I sink down on to the floor.

Over on the table are a half-full glass and a bottle. They weren't there before. I quickly go over to them, stick my nose in the glass and sniff at the clear liquid. It's schnapps – presumably Davidsson's ration to keep him warm.

Here and there around the house are similar bottles with different contents, and when I think about them I know what I am going to do.

There is no sign of Davidsson as I hurry across the inner courtyard, open the barn door and slip into the darkness. I can find my way around in there among the shadows without a light, and go further inside to the rubbish and the hidden treasures. In a corner stands a special metal container – a container on which someone has drawn a black cross. I take it back to the outhouse with me.

In the storeroom I empty out most of Davidsson's schnapps on to one of his piles of nets, which stinks of tar, then top it up with the same amount of the equally clear and almost odour-free liquid from the can.

There is a wooden cupboard in the corner; I hide the can in there.

Then I sit down on the floor again and wait.

Five or ten minutes later there is a rattling at the door. The howling of the wind increases in volume, before the noise is cut off with a bang.

A pair of heavy boots step into the porch and stamp up and down to shake off the snow; I recognize the smell of sweat and tar.

Ragnar Davidsson comes into the room and looks

at me. 'So where have you been?' he asks. 'You just took off this morning.'

I don't reply. The only thing I can think of is what I'm going to say to Torun about the paintings. She mustn't find out what has happened.

'With some boy, of course,' says Davidsson, answering his own question.

He walks slowly around me on the cement floor, and I give him one last chance. I raise my hand and point towards the shore. 'We have to go and fetch the paintings.'

'That's not possible.'

'It is. You have to help me.'

He shakes his head and walks over to the table. 'They're already gone . . . they're on their way to Gotland. The wind and the waves took them.'

He fills up the glass and raises it to his lips.

I could warn him, but I say nothing. I simply watch as he drinks – three good gulps which almost empty the glass.

Then he puts it down on the table, smacks his lips and says, 'Right, little Mirja . . . so what do you fancy doing now?'

33

Henrik woke up to find his dead grandfather standing over him like a shadow in the whirling powdery snow. Algot leaned forward and raised his boot-clad foot.

Move yourself! Do you want to die?

He felt hard blows striking his legs and feet, over and over again.

Get up! Thieving bastard!

Henrik slowly lifted his head, wiped the snow out of his eyes and screwed his eyes up as he peered into the wind. His grandfather's ghost was gone, but in the distance he could see a searchlight sweeping silently across the night sky. The blood-red glow made the veils of snow above him sparkle.

A little further away he thought he could see another light. A steady white light.

The light from the twin lighthouses at Eel Point.

Henrik had struggled along in a daze, yard by yard through the snow, but in the end he had made it. His jeans were soaking wet – it was the water that had woken him up. The storm waves were so high by now that they came crashing in over the shore, sluicing his legs with foam even though he was lying a long way up on the grass.

He got up slowly with his back to the sea. His hands

had gone to sleep, as had his feet, but he was able to move. There was a little strength left in Henrik's trembling legs, and he set off again, his arms dangling at his sides.

A rectangular wooden object shifted inside his jacket, and ice-cold steel was poking up by his throat.

It was his grandfather's axe – he remembered tucking it inside his jacket, but not why he was carrying it around.

Then it came to him: the Serelius brothers. He took the axe out and carried on going.

Two grey towers took shape through the storm. The sea below them was boiling, hurling glittering lumps of ice on to the islands where the lighthouses stood.

Henrik had arrived at Eel Point. He stopped, swaying in the wind. What should he do now?

He would go up to the house – it must be somewhere on the left. He turned off in that direction, away from the lighthouses.

With the wind at his back everything was suddenly much easier. It helped to nudge him along, up over the hard crust of snow covering the meadow. He had begun to recognize the different gusts of wind by now, how the weaker bursts were followed by sharper squalls.

After a hundred or two hundred steps he began to get an impression of broad shadowy shapes ahead of him.

A wooden fence suddenly blocked his way, but he found an opening. On the other side the buildings of Eel Point rose up like great ships in the night, and Henrik moved into the shelter between the gable ends.

Made it.

The manor house enfolded him in its dark embrace. He was safe.

The wind in the courtyard was like a caress compared with the way it had been down by the sea, but there was a lot more snow between the buildings. It came swirling down from the roofs like powder, melting on his face, and the drifts were almost up to his waist.

Henrik could just glimpse the veranda of the main house through the curtains of snow, and he ploughed over to it and eventually reached the steps. He stopped on the bottom step, caught his breath and looked up.

The door had been broken open. The lock was smashed and the frame appeared to have been split.

The Serelius brothers had been here.

Henrik was too cold to be cautious now; he staggered up the steps, pulled open the veranda door and more or less fell headlong over the threshold on to a soft rag rug. The door closed behind him.

Warmth. The storm was shut out, and he could hear his own wheezing breath.

He let go of the axe and began to move his fingers tentatively. At first they were like ice, but when the warmth and the feeling slowly began to return to his hands and toes, the pain came. The wound in his stomach started to throb again.

He was wet and tired, but he couldn't just lie here.

Slowly he got up and staggered through the next doorway. It was dark around him, but here and there he could see the glow of small yellow lamps and candles. The wallpaper was fresh and white, the ceilings had been repaired and painted – a lot had happened since he was last here.

He turned left and suddenly found himself in the big kitchen. He had replaced and polished the floor in here last summer. A grey and black cat was sitting looking out of the window, and the faint aroma of fried meatballs lingered in the air.

Henrik spotted the sink and staggered over to it.

The tap water was only lukewarm, but still it burned

his frozen hands. He gritted his teeth as the nerves warmed up, but after holding his fingers in the running water for a few minutes, he was able to move them.

The cat turned to look at him, then returned its gaze to the snowstorm.

On the worktop stood a block containing stainless steel kitchen knives. Henrik grabbed the handle of the biggest one and pulled it out.

With the carving knife in his hand he went back into the main house.

He tried to remember the layout of the rooms, but had difficulty in picturing it. Suddenly he was standing in a long corridor, in the doorway of a small room.

A child's room.

A little girl of about five or six, with blonde hair, was sitting up in bed. She was holding a white cuddly toy and a red sweater in her arms. A small television stood on the floor in front of her, but it was switched off.

Henrik opened his mouth, but his head was completely empty.

'Hello,' was all he said.

His voice was hoarse and rough.

The girl looked at him, but said nothing.

'Have you seen anyone else here?' he asked. 'Any other . . . nice men?'

The girl shook her head. 'I just heard them,' she said. 'They were clomping around and they woke me up. I was scared to go out.'

'Good,' said Henrik. 'You need to stay in here. Where are your mum and dad?'

'Daddy went out to Mummy.'

'And where's your mummy?'

'In the barn.'

Before Henrik had time to think about that response,

the girl pointed at him and asked, 'Why have you got a knife?'

He looked down. 'Don't know.'

It felt very strange to see himself clutching a big knife. It looked dangerous.

'Are you going to cut some bread?'

'No.'

Henrik closed his eyes. The feeling was beginning to return to his feet now, and it hurt.

'What are you going to do?' said the girl.

'I don't know . . . but you need to stay here.'

'Can I go into Gabriel's room?'

'Who's Gabriel?'

'My little brother.'

Henrik nodded with some effort. 'Of course.'

The girl quickly jumped out of bed, still holding the cuddly toy and the sweater, and scampered past him.

Henrik gathered his remaining strength and turned around. He heard the door close in the next bedroom along. He went in the other direction, to look for the Serelius brothers. Had he been along here before? He must have been.

Down along a corridor, back to the front of the house.

He listened for noises apart from the wind, and for a few seconds he thought he could hear a rhythmic banging from the upper floor – a loose shutter, perhaps. Then the house was silent again.

A dark, flat object was lying in a corner out in the hallway. Henrik went closer. He saw that it was the ouija board, thrown on to the floor, split across the middle with considerable force. The little glass lay beside the board like a cracked egg.

Henrik went back out to the veranda, where the air was cooler. The snow was sticking to the window panes,

398

but he could just make out movements in the courtyard. He bent down in silence and picked up his grandfather's axe.

Two shadows were moving out there. They slowly came closer through the snow, and Henrik could see that one of them was holding a dark object. A gun?

He wasn't sure if it was the brothers, but raised the axe anyway.

By the time the outer door was opened he had already swung it.

34

Tilda staggered forwards, heading straight for the blinding wall of swirling snow. Martin was still by her side, but neither of them was talking. It was impossible in the storm.

They were out in a field, but the few times Tilda tried to look up to work out where they were heading, granules of snow flew into her eyes like burning sparks. She had lost her police cap; it had been ripped off by the wind and disappeared. She felt as if her ears were frozen solid.

One small encouraging sign was that the storm had briefly carried with it the aroma of burning wood. She guessed that it came from an open fire or stove, and realized they were close to a house – presumably Eel Point.

A rectangular snowdrift appeared in front of them, but when Tilda tried to plough through it, she came to a sudden stop. It was a stone wall.

She slowly clambered over the snow-covered stones, and Martin followed her. On the other side the ground was flatter, as if they were walking along a little track.

Suddenly Tilda heard a creaking noise further along the wall, followed by a grinding squeal and a dull thud. After a minute or so they reached a couple of huge white drifts with square contours. Two parked vehicles were standing there rocking in the wind, half-buried in the snow.

Tilda brushed away the snow along the side of the taller vehicle and recognized it. It was the dark-coloured van with KALMAR PIPES & WELDING on it.

Further along by the wall lay a boat on a trailer, lying on its side. It looked as if it had been picked up and tipped over by the wind. The boat was still securely tied to the metal frame, but the tarpaulin covering it had split. An extraordinary collection of objects lay scattered in the snow: loudspeakers and chainsaws alongside old paraffin lamps and wall clocks. They looked like stolen goods.

Martin shouted something, but Tilda couldn't hear what he said. She made her way slowly along the side of the van and tried the doors. The driver's door was locked, but when she went round to the other side and tried the passenger door, it flew open with a crash.

Tilda climbed in to catch her breath.

Martin stuck his head in behind her, with snow in his hair and eyebrows. 'How are you doing?' he asked.

Tilda massaged her frozen ears and nodded wearily. 'OK.'

The air inside the van was still warm, and she was finally able to breathe normally. She looked behind the seats and saw that the back of the van was full of even more items, all piled on top of one another. There were jewellery boxes and cartons of cigarettes and cases of alcohol.

As she turned back to Martin she discovered that the brown panel inside the passenger door had come loose. White plastic was protruding beneath the panel – it was a packet of some kind.

'A hiding place,' she said.

Martin looked. Then he got hold of the plastic and pulled, and the whole panel came away and fell off into the snow. Behind it was a secret cache, full of more packets. Martin took out the top one, made a small slit in it with his car key and put his finger against the gap. He licked the powder off his finger and said, 'It's metamphetamine.'

Tilda believed him – he had taught her group about different types of narcotics. She pushed a couple of the packets in her pocket. 'Evidence,' she said.

Martin looked at her as if he wanted to add something, but Tilda didn't want to hear it. She unfastened her holster and took out her SIG-Sauer. 'There are bad guys around here,' she said. Then she clambered past Martin out into the gale and began to make her way along the track once again.

When she had left the vehicles and the boat behind her, she caught her first glimpse of the beam from the lighthouse: a sweeping glow that only just managed to penetrate through the snowstorm.

They had almost reached Eel Point now. Tilda could see the main house, with faint lights shimmering in the windows. They were candles, she realized. And Joakim Westin's car was parked in front of the house beneath a pile of snow.

The family must be at home. In the worst-case scenario they were being held hostage inside by the thieves – but Tilda didn't want to think along those lines.

The big barn appeared in front of her. She struggled to cover the last few steps to the red wooden wall, and at last found some shelter from the wind. It was a considerable achievement – she breathed out and wiped the melting snow off her face with the sleeve of her jacket.

Now all she had to do was see who was in the house, and what state they were in.

She unzipped her jacket and pulled out her torch. With her pistol in one hand and the torch in the other she pressed herself against the wall of the barn, moved slowly forwards and peeped around the corner.

Snow – all she could see was snow. White curtains sweeping down from the roof, and whirlwinds of snow swirling between the buildings.

Martin came up behind her out of the darkness, his back bent, and took shelter by the wall. 'Is this where we were heading?' he yelled.

Tilda nodded and took a deep breath. 'Eel Point,' she said.

The main house was about ten yards from the barn. The lights were on in the kitchen, but there was no sign of anyone.

She started moving again, away from the barn and out into the inner courtyard, which was completely covered in snow. It came up to her waist in some places, and she had to force her way through the drifts. She carried on towards the house, her gun at the ready.

There were fresh tracks in the snow here. Someone had recently plodded across the courtyard and walked up the stone steps.

When Tilda reached the veranda, which was in darkness, she looked at the door.

It had been broken open.

She moved slowly up the steps. Then she grabbed hold of the handle, opened the door cautiously and moved on to the top step.

Then something slender and metallic grey came whirling through the opening. She closed her eyes but didn't manage to duck or raise her arm in time.

403

Axe, was all she was able to think before it hit her in the face.

There was a crunching noise from her own head, then a burning pain seared all the way up her nasal bone.

She could hear Martin shouting in the distance.

But by then she had already begun to fall backwards, down the steps and back out into the snow.

35

The murderer had stepped out of the shadows among the trees, walked over to Ethel and whispered, 'Do you want to come with me? If you just keep quiet and come with me I'll show you what I've got in my pocket . . . No, it isn't money, it's something even better. Come down to the water with me and you can have a fix of heroin from me, completely free. You've got your own needle and spoon and lighter, haven't you?'

Ethel had nodded.

Joakim shivered and pushed the dream-pictures out of his head. A rumble like thunder shook him.

He woke up properly and looked around him. He was sitting on the front row in the prayer room, with Katrine's Christmas present on his knee.

Katrine?

It was almost completely dark. The torch had gone out and the only light came from the single bulb in the loft, seeping in through the narrow gaps in the wall.

And the rumbling noise? The barn hadn't been struck by thunder or lightning – it was the storm, roaring its way in over the coast.

The blizzard had reached its peak.

The stone walls on the lower floor were immovable,

but the rest of the barn was shaking in the wind. The sound of the air being forced in through the cracks rose and fell like a siren around Joakim.

He looked up at the roof beams above his head and thought he could see them trembling. The storm-force winds came pouring in over Eel Point like black waves, making the wooden walls creak and bang.

The blizzard was tearing the barn apart. That's what it felt like.

But Joakim thought he could hear other sounds too. Rustling noises from inside the room – slow footsteps crossing the wooden floor. Restless movements in the darkness. Whispering voices.

The church benches had begun to fill up behind him.

He couldn't see who the visitors were, but felt a growing chill in the room. There were many of them, and they were starting to sit down.

Joakim listened, his body tense, but remained where he was.

It was quiet on the church benches now.

But someone was walking slowly along the aisle beside them. He heard careful noises in the darkness, the scraping sound of footsteps from a figure passing all the benches behind him.

Out of the corner of his eye he saw that a shadow with a pale face had stopped beside his bench, and was standing there motionless.

'Katrine?' whispered Joakim, without daring to turn his head.

The shadow slowly sat down beside him on the bench.

'Katrine,' he whispered again.

Tentatively he groped in the darkness and his fingers brushed against another hand. It was stiff and ice-cold when he took hold of it.

'I'm here now,' he whispered.

There was no reply. The figure bent its head, as if in prayer.

Joakim also lowered his eyes. He looked down at the denim jacket beside him and carried on whispering. 'I found Ethel's jacket. And the note from the neighbours. I think . . . Katrine, I think you killed my sister.'

And still there was no reply.

WINTER 1962

So we sat there in the outhouse staring at one another,
Ragnar Davidsson the eel fisherman and I.

I was extremely tired by this time. The blizzard was on
its way, but I had managed to rescue only a few of
Torun's oil paintings, half a dozen canvases that were
lying on the floor next to me. Davidsson had thrown the
rest into the sea.

Mirja Rambe

Davidsson has refilled his glass with schnapps. 'Sure
you don't want some?' he asks.

When I clamp my lips together he takes a deep
draught from the glass. Then he puts it down on the
table and smacks his lips.

He seems to get various inappropriate ideas when
he looks at me, but before he has time to select one
of them, his guts are suddenly twisted into a knot
in his belly. That's what it looks like to me, anyway
– his body jerks, he bends over and presses his arms
against his stomach.

'Shit,' he mumbles.

Davidsson tries to relax. But then he suddenly
goes rigid again, as if he has suddenly thought of
something.

'Oh shit,' he says, 'I think . . .'

He falls silent and looks to one side, still thoughtful – then the whole of his upper body jerks in a violent attack of cramp.

I sit there motionless, staring at him; I don't say a word. I could ask if he's not feeling well, but I know the answer: the poison in the glass has finally begun to work.

'It wasn't schnapps in that glass, Ragnar,' I say.

Davidsson is in a lot of pain now; he is leaning against the wall.

'I put something else in there.'

Davidsson manages to get to his feet and staggers past me towards the door. This suddenly gives me a burst of fresh energy.

'Get out of here!' I yell. I pick up an empty metal bucket standing in a corner and hit him on the back with it. 'Out!'

He does as I say, and I follow him out into the snow and watch him aim for the fence. He manages to find the opening, and carries on down towards the sea.

The southern lighthouse is flashing blood-red through the falling snow; the northern tower is dark now.

In the darkness I can see Ragnar's open motor boat bobbing in the sea out by the jetty. The waves are breaking along the shore with a long drawn-out roaring sound, and I ought to try and stop him, but I stay where I am, just watching as he teeters out along the jetty and loosens the ropes. Then he stops, bends over again and vomits into the water.

He drops the rope and the waves begin to play with the boat, nudging it away from the jetty.

Ragnar seems to be feeling too ill to bother about

409

the boat. He glances out to sea, then begins to stagger inland instead.

'Ragnar!' I yell.

If he asks me for help he can have it, but I don't think he can hear me. He doesn't stop when he reaches the shore, but sets off northwards. Heading for home. Soon he has disappeared in the darkness and the snow.

I go back to the outhouse and Torun. She is still awake, sitting in her chair by the window as usual.

'Hi, Mum.'

She doesn't turn her head, but asks, 'Where is Ragnar Davidsson?'

I go and stand by the fire and sigh.

'He's gone. He was here for a while . . . but now he's gone.'

'Did he throw out the paintings?'

I hold my breath and turn around.

'The paintings?' I say, a lump forming in my throat. 'Why do you think he would do that?'

'Ragnar said he was going to throw them out.'

'No, Mum,' I say. 'Your canvases are still in the storeroom. I can fetch—'

'He should have done it,' says Torun.

'What? What do you mean?'

'I asked Ragnar to throw them in the sea.'

It takes four or five seconds for me to understand what she's saying – then it's as if a membrane breaks inside me and dangerous fluids begin to mingle in my brain. I see myself rushing over to Torun.

'Fucking sit here, then, you fucking old cow!' I scream. 'Sit here till you die! You fucking blind old . . .'

I hit her over and over again with the palm of my

410

hand, and Torun can do nothing but take the blows. She doesn't see them coming.

I count the blows – six, seven, eight, nine – and I stop hitting her after the twelfth.

Afterwards both Torun and I are breathing loudly, almost wheezing. The mournful howling of the wind can be heard through the windows.

'Why did you leave me with him?' I ask her. 'You should have seen how dirty it was, Mummy, and the stench of him . . . you shouldn't have let me go in there, Mummy.'

I pause for a moment.

'But you were blind even then.'

Torun stares rigidly ahead, her cheeks red. I don't think she has any idea what I'm talking about.

And that was the end for me at Eel Point. I left and never came back. And I stopped speaking to Torun. I made sure she got a place in a care home, but we never spoke again.

The next day the news came that the evening ferry between Öland and the mainland had capsized in the waves. Several passengers had died in the icy waters. Markus Landkvist was one of them.

Another victim of the storm was Ragnar Davidsson, the eel fisherman. He was found dead on the shore a day or so later. I felt no guilt over his death – I felt nothing.

I don't think anyone ever lived in the outhouse again after Torun and me, and I don't think anyone really lived in the main house again, apart from the odd month in the summer. Sorrow had permeated the walls.

Six weeks later, when I had moved to Stockholm to start at the art school, I found that I was pregnant.

Katrine Månstråle Rambe was born the following year, the first of all my children.

You had your father's eyes.

36

'Hello?' Henrik shouted to the figure down in the snow. 'Are you OK?'

It was a stupid question, because the body below him was lying motionless with a bloody face. The snow had already begun to cover it.

Henrik blinked in confusion; it had all happened so quickly.

He thought he had spotted the Serelius brothers outside. When the first of them opened the veranda door Henrik had thrown his grandfather's axe as hard as he could, and it had hit the intruder on the head. With the blunt edge – not with the blade, he was sure of that.

He stayed in the doorway of the veranda. In the glow of the outside light he suddenly saw that it was a woman he had hit.

A few yards behind her stood a man, as if he were frozen solid in the whirling snow. Then he strode forward and knelt down.

'Tilda?' he shouted. 'Wake up, Tilda!'

She moved her arms feebly and tried to raise her head.

Henrik walked out on to the steps, with his back to the warmth of the house and the cold and wind in his face, and discovered that the woman was wearing a dark-coloured uniform.

Police. She had almost disappeared in a huge billowing drift at the bottom of the steps. A thin stream of dark blood was pouring out of her nose and down around her mouth.

For a few seconds everything stood still, except for the falling snow.

The pains in his belly came back.

'Hello?' he said again. 'How are you?'

No one replied, but the man picked up the axe and came over to the steps. 'Drop it!' he yelled at Henrik.

Behind the man the woman suddenly coughed and started vomiting violently in the snow.

'What?' said Henrik.

'Drop it now!'

The man was talking about the kitchen knife, Henrik realized. He was still clutching it in his hand.

He didn't want to drop it. The Serelius brothers were around somewhere, he needed to be able to defend himself.

The woman had stopped vomiting. She put her hand to her face, felt her nose cautiously. The snowflakes were landing on her shoulders and her nose, and the blood had congealed into black patches on her face.

'What's your name?' asked the man on the steps.

The woman raised her head and shouted something to Henrik through the howling wind, the same thing over and over again, and eventually he was able to make out what it was. His own name.

'Henrik!' she was shouting. 'Henrik Jansson!'

'Drop the knife, Henrik,' said the man. 'Then we can talk.'

'Talk?'

'You're under arrest for robbery with violence, Henrik,' the woman went on from her snowdrift. 'And breaking and entering . . . and criminal damage.'

Henrik heard what she said, but didn't reply; he was too tired. He took a step backwards, shaking his head. 'All that stuff . . . that was Tommy and Freddy,' he said eventually.

'What?' said the man.

'It was those fucking brothers,' said Henrik. 'I just went along with them. But it was much better with Mogge. I never thought . . .'

There was a sudden tinkling noise, just a couple of inches from his right ear. A short, solid sound in the wind. Henrik turned his head and saw that a black, uneven hole had appeared in one of the small panes of glass in the veranda windows.

Was it the storm? Perhaps the storm had smashed the glass. Henrik's second confused thought was that the pistol had been fired at him, despite the fact that the policewoman was no longer holding it.

But when he looked out through the whirling snow, over towards the barn, he discovered that there was someone else there.

A dark figure had stepped out of the half-open door of the barn and was standing there in the snow, legs apart. In the glow from the outside light Henrik could see that the figure was holding a slender stick in its hands.

No, not a stick. It was a gun, of course. Henrik couldn't make it out properly, but he thought it was an old Mauser.

A man in a black hood. Tommy. He shouted something across the courtyard, then the gun in his hands jerked. Once. Twice.

No panes of glass broke this time – but the face of the man in front of Henrik contorted suddenly, and he went down.

37

Tilda saw it all so clearly when Martin was shot.

It was after the axe had hit her. She almost wished she had lost consciousness then, but her brain remained awake, registering everything. The pain, the fall, and the pistol spinning out of her hand.

When she landed on her back the snow received her like a soft bed.

She stayed where she was. Her nose was broken, warm blood was pouring down into her mouth and she was completely exhausted after the trek through the storm.

I've done my bit tonight, she thought. Enough.

'Tilda!'

Martin was calling her name, bending over her. Behind him she saw a man step out from the veranda and look down at her. He was holding a big knife in his hand and shouting something, but she couldn't make out a word.

Everything stopped for a little while. Tilda sank down into a warm drowsiness before the nausea hit her. She turned her head to the side and threw up into the snow.

Tilda coughed, raised her head and tried to pull herself together. She saw Martin go over to the man and shout to him to drop the knife.

It was Henrik Jansson up there on the steps, the man responsible for the break-ins, the man she'd been looking for.

'Henrik?'

Tilda called his name several times, her voice thick, while at the same time trying to recall all the things he was suspected of.

She didn't hear his reply. She did, however, hear the gunshot.

It came from the barn on the other side of the courtyard and sounded like a dull bang with no echo. The bullet hit the veranda, a pane of glass broke next to Henrik.

He turned his head and looked at the hole in confusion.

Martin carried on up the steps towards him. He was moving calmly and speaking firmly to the perpetrator, like the police instructor he was. Henrik backed away.

Neither of them had heard the shot, Tilda realized.

As she opened her mouth to warn them, there were several more bangs.

She saw Martin jerk on the steps. His upper body contorted, his legs gave way. He collapsed and landed heavily in the snow just a few yards from Tilda.

'Martin!'

He was lying there with his back to her, and she began to crawl towards him, keeping her head down. She could hear a faint moaning sound through the wind.

'Martin?'

Breathing, bleeding, shock. That was the list she had learned to check in cases of stabbing or gunshot wounds.

Breathing? It was difficult to see in the storm, but Martin hardly seemed to be breathing.

She dragged his upper body into the recovery position, ripped open his jacket and blood-stained sweater and finally found the small entry hole – high up and just to the left of the spine. The hole looked deep and the blood was still flowing. Had the bullet hit the main artery?

He shouldn't be left out here, but there was no way Tilda could get him into the house. There was no time.

She unbuttoned her right jacket pocket and took out a pressure bandage pack.

'Martin?' she called again, at the same time pressing the bandage against the bullet hole as firmly as she could.

No reply. His eyes were open, unblinking in the snow – he had gone into shock.

Tilda couldn't find a pulse.

She pushed his body on to its back again, leaned over him and began pressing on his chest with both hands. One firm push, wait. Then a firm push again.

It didn't help. He no longer seemed to be breathing, and when she shook him his body was completely lifeless. The snow was landing in his eyes.

'Martin . . .'

Tilda gave up. She sank down beside him in the snow, snivelling blood up her nose.

Everything had gone completely wrong. Martin wasn't even supposed to be here. He shouldn't have come with her to Eel Point.

Suddenly she heard two more bangs from the direction of the barn. Tilda kept her head down.

The pistol? She had dropped it when she fell in the snow.

The SIG-Sauer was made of black steel – she ought to

be able to see it in all this whiteness, and she began to feel around with her hands. At the same time she peeped cautiously over the drifts.

A figure was moving through the snow. He had a black hood over his head and a gun in his hands. The man clambered over a snowdrift and when he realized that Tilda had seen him, he shouted something into the wind.

She didn't answer. Her hand was still burrowing in the snow – and suddenly it felt something hard and heavy down there. At first the object just slid away, but then she managed to get hold of it.

She pulled the gun out of the snow.

She banged the barrel a couple of times to get the snow out of it, undid the safety catch and aimed in the direction of the barn.

'Police!' she yelled.

The masked man said something in reply, but the wind ripped his words to shreds.

'Ubba . . . ubba,' it sounded like.

He slowed down and stooped slightly, but carried on through the snowdrifts towards her.

'Stand still and drop the gun!' Tilda's voice became shrill and small, she could hear how weak it sounded, but still she went on: 'I'll fire!'

And she did actually fire, a warning shot straight up into the night. The bang sounded almost as weak as her voice.

The man stopped, but didn't drop his gun. He dropped to his knees between two snowdrifts, less than ten yards away. He raised the gun and aimed it at her again, and Tilda fired two shots at him in rapid succession.

Then she ducked back behind the drifts, and at almost the same moment the light went out. The lamps in the windows and the lantern in the inner courtyard went out at the same time. Everything went black.

The blizzard had caused a power cut at Eel Point.

38

So Ethel went down the dark paths, down among the trees by the walkway along the shore. Down to the water, where the lights of the houses and streets of Stockholm glittered in the blackness.

There she sat down obediently in the shadow of a boat-house and got her reward. Then she just had to do the usual: melt the yellow-brown powder in the spoon, draw it up into the syringe and insert it into her arm.

Peace.

The murderer waited patiently until Ethel's head was drooping and she was just beginning to doze off . . . then went over and gave the unresisting body a hard shove. Straight down into the winter water.

Joakim was still sitting slumped on the bench, motionless. There was no light in the prayer room, and yet it wasn't completely dark. He could make out the wooden walls, the window and the drawing of Jesus's empty tomb. There was a faint, pale glow around him, as if from a distant moon.

The storm continued to howl over the roof.

He was not alone.

His wife Katrine was sitting beside him. He could see her pale face out of the corner of his eye.

And the benches behind him had filled up with visitors. Joakim could hear the faint sound of creaking, just like when the congregation in a church is impatiently waiting to go up and take communion.

They started to get up.

When Joakim heard this he stood up too, with the unpleasant feeling of being in the wrong place on the wrong night. Soon he would be discovered – or unmasked.

'Come on,' he whispered. 'Trust me.'

He pulled at Katrine's cold hand and tried to get her to stand up, and in the end she obeyed him.

He heard creaking steps approaching. The figures behind him had begun to move out into the narrow aisle. There were so many of them when they were gathered together. More and more shadows seemed to fill the room.

Joakim couldn't get past them. All he could do was stay where he was in front of the bench – there was nowhere to go now. He stood completely still, not letting go of Katrine's hand.

The air grew colder around them, and Joakim shivered. He could hear the rustling sound of old fabric, and the floor creaked faintly as the chapel's visitors spread out around him.

They wanted so much warmth that he was unable to give them. They wanted to take communion. Joakim was freezing now, but still they pressed forward to reach him. Their jerky movements were like a slow dance in the narrow room, and he was drawn along with them.

'Katrine!' he whispered.

But she was no longer with him. Her hand had slipped from his grip and they were separated by all the movement in the room.

'Katrine?'

She was gone. Joakim turned around and tried to push his way through the crowd to find her again. But no one helped him, everyone was standing in his way.

Then suddenly he heard something more than the wind through the cracks in the barn: someone shouting, then several dull bangs. It sounded as if someone were shooting with a rifle or a pistol – like a volley of shots somewhere down below the hayloft.

Joakim stiffened and listened. He could no longer hear any other sounds, no voices or movements inside the room.

The pale light that had been seeping through the wall from the bulb in the loft suddenly went out.

The electricity had gone, Joakim realized.

He stood still in the pitch darkness. It felt as if he were completely alone now, as if all the others in the room had gone away.

After several minutes a flickering light began to glow somewhere in the barn. A pale yellow glow that rapidly increased in strength.

39

Tilda blinked away the drops of melted ice flakes from her eyes and cautiously pressed a fistful of snow against her throbbing nose. Then she got up slowly on unsteady legs, her pistol in her right hand. Her head was aching just as much as her nose, but at least she was able to stand upright.

The manor was in complete darkness now, and the soft drifts between the buildings had turned into hills with blurred contours. Beyond them the barn rose up, like a cathedral in shadow. The electricity seemed to have gone at Eel Point – perhaps throughout the whole of northern Öland. It had happened before, when a tree blew down on to one of the main power lines.

Martin was lying motionless a couple of yards away from Tilda. She couldn't see his face, but his lifeless body was already well on the way to being covered by the snow. She took out her mobile and called the emergency number. It was busy. She tried the police station in Borgholm, but couldn't get through there either.

When she had put the mobile away she glanced around the inner courtyard, but couldn't see the man who had shot at her. She had returned his fire – had she hit him?

She looked over towards the steps. There was no sign of Henrik Jansson either. Keeping her pistol trained on the barn, Tilda moved backwards until she bumped into the bottom step. Her eyes slowly became accustomed to the darkness. She moved quickly up the steps to the house, bending low, and peered in through the open door.

The first thing she saw inside the veranda was a pair of boots. A dark figure dressed in outdoor clothes was half-lying on the rag rug just inside the door. He was breathing heavily.

'Henrik Jansson?' said Tilda.

There was silence for a few seconds.

'Yes?' he said eventually.

'Don't move, Henrik.'

Tilda crept through the doorway, keeping her pistol trained on him. Henrik stayed where he was, gazing wearily at the gun, and made no attempt to get away. He was clutching the edge of the rug with one hand; the other was pressed against his stomach.

'Are you hurt, Henrik?' she asked.

'I've been stabbed . . . in the stomach.'

Tilda nodded. More violence. She wanted to scream and swear at someone, but instead she picked up his knife, hurled it out into the snow, then checked his trousers and jacket. No more weapons.

She took a sterilizing pack out of her pocket along with the second and last bandage and passed them over to Henrik. 'Martin's lying out there,' she said quietly. 'He's been shot. He didn't make it.'

'Was he a policeman?' said Henrik.

Tilda sighed. 'He used to be. He's a tutor at the police training academy.'

Henrik opened the sterilizing pack and shook his head. 'They're crazy.'

426

'Who, Henrik? Who shot Martin?'

'There are two of them,' he said. 'Tommy and Freddy.'
Tilda looked at him suspiciously and he shrugged his
shoulders. 'That's what they call themselves . . . Tommy
and Freddy.'

Tilda remembered the two men at the races in
Kalmar.

'So you broke in here together? You're partners?'

'We were.' He pulled up his sweater and began to wipe
the wound in his stomach. 'It was Tommy who did this.'

'What are they carrying, Henrik?'

'They've got a hunting rifle. An old Mauser. I don't
know if they've got anything else.'

Tilda bent down and held the compress while Henrik
tied the pressure bandage.

'Now lie down on your stomach,' she said.

'Why?'

'I'm going to put the handcuffs on.'

He looked at her. 'If they shoot you they'll come after
me next,' he said. 'Am I supposed to sit here in handcuffs, waiting for them?'

Tilda thought it over for a few seconds, then hung the
cuffs back on her belt.

'I'll be back.'

She turned and jumped down from the steps, crouching between the drifts as she took a last glance at
Martin's body. With her knees and back bent, she began
to move through the snow, over towards the barn. She
blinked to see more easily through the snowflakes and
stayed on the alert as she moved forward, all the time
expecting to be shot at.

A long, billowing snowdrift ran along a couple of
yards from the barn, and behind it she found traces
of the gunman. A pair of boots had been trampling
around, and there was the outline of someone who had

been lying down in the snow. But both the man and his gun were gone, and she couldn't see any sign of blood.

He must have gone back inside the barn.

Tilda thought about Martin's blood-covered back and stayed where she was, out in the courtyard. The broad doorway gaped like the opening of a cave. She didn't want to go in there.

A little further away to the right was another entrance – a narrow door made of wooden planks, painted black. She began to move slowly towards it, pressed against the stone wall, the fine snow whirling down and melting on the back of her neck.

When Tilda reached the door she grabbed the handle and pulled the door open as far as she could before the snow stopped it.

She peered inside.

Pitch black. The electricity was still off.

With her pistol at the ready she moved inside on to the earth floor, straight into the darkness and silence. She stayed by the wall for a while, listening for sounds; her nose was beginning to throb again. It was impossible to tell if anyone was lying in wait for her in the shadows.

The storm was more distant in here, but high above her the great roof squeaked and creaked. After a minute or so she started moving again, silently and cautiously. There was no snow to contend with, of course, but the floor was uneven – sometimes it was earth, sometimes stone.

When she saw a broad shadow looming up ahead of her she almost aimed her pistol at it – until her boot hit an enormous rubber tyre. Above the tyre was a bonnet with the logo McCORMICK. Tilda had bumped into an old tractor – a rusty monster on wheels that must have been parked there for years.

428

She crept silently past it. When she saw old tins of paint and piles of planks on the floor, she realized she was in a storeroom at the eastern end of the barn.

A faint thud came from somewhere in the barn. She turned her head quickly – but nothing moved behind her.

There were two of them in here, Henrik had said. Oddly enough, Tilda had the feeling that there were in fact many more people here in the barn – figures keeping watch in the shadows around her. It was a vague but unpleasant feeling, and she was unable to shake it off.

Her eyes were beginning to grow accustomed to the darkness, and she could see the stone wall opposite.

Suddenly she heard a faint tinkling sound to her left. From inside the barn.

A second or so later it grew a little lighter around her, and she saw that there was a doorway in the wooden wall beside her. It ought to lead into the barn. The light was coming from the barn; a flickering, dancing glow. Tilda caught the smell of smoke and suspected she knew what had happened. She hurried to the door and looked into the barn.

A fire was burning next to the steep wooden staircase a few yards away, leading up to the hayloft, and there was the acrid smell of paraffin mixed with smoke. Someone had gathered a big heap of old hay, then smashed a burning bottle of paraffin against the floor. The fire had taken hold by now, and the flames had already begun licking at the planks of the staircase.

A tall man was standing beneath the loft on the far side of the fire. He was about the same age as Henrik and was holding a black hood or cap in one hand; he didn't appear to have noticed her. The man's gaze was fixed on the growing flames and his face was shiny. He looked excited.

A framed oil painting was propped against a wooden pillar beside him, but there was no sign of any gun.

Tilda looked around one last time – no one was lurking behind her – then she took a deep breath and stepped out into the barn. She was holding the pistol with both hands.

'Police!' she shouted. 'Stand still!'

The man looked up and gazed at her, more surprised than anything.

'Get down on the floor!'

The man remained standing, his mouth open.

'My brother's looking for a way out,' he said. 'Round the back.'

Tilda moved forward until she was only two paces from the man. He moved backward and to one side, towards the door, and Tilda followed him.

'Down on the floor!'

If he didn't give up, would she shoot him? She didn't know. But she was aiming straight at his head.

'Lie down!'

'OK, OK . . .' The man nodded and got down on his stomach, with some effort.

'Hands behind your back!'

Tilda was by his side and had unhooked the handcuffs from her belt. She quickly grabbed his wrists, pulled them back and slipped on the cuffs. He was secure now, lying on the stone floor, and she was able to search him. He had a mountain knife in his trouser pocket, but that was the only weapon. And pills, lots of pills.

'What's your name?'

He seemed to be considering the question.

'Freddy,' he said eventually.

'Your real name.'

He hesitated.

'Sven.'

Tilda found that difficult to believe, but merely said, 'OK, Sven, just keep calm.'

When she got up she could hear the crackling of the fire. The flames had nowhere to go along the stone floor, but had got a hold on the staircase and were climbing up towards the edge of the loft.

Tilda couldn't see a fire blanket or extinguisher, nor any buckets she could use to carry water.

She pulled off her uniform jacket and beat at the steps, but the flames simply moved aside and grew. The fire seemed to want to reach up towards the storm – more than half the staircase was burning now.

Could she try to kick the whole staircase away from the edge of the loft? She raised her foot and took aim – then she saw a shadow approaching out of the corner of her eye. She spun around.

It was a tall man wearing jeans and a sweater, hurrying towards the staircase out of the darkness of the barn. He stopped and looked at the fire, then at Freddy and finally at Tilda.

She almost didn't recognize him – but it was Joakim Westin.

'I can't put it out!' she yelled. 'I've tried . . .'

Westin just nodded. He seemed calm, as if there were worse things in the world. 'Snow,' he said. 'We have to smother it.'

'OK.'

But where had Westin come from? He looked pale and tired, but didn't seem particularly surprised to have visitors. Even the fire didn't seem to bother him much.

'I'll get a shovel.'

He turned towards the barn door.

'Can you manage without me?' asked Tilda.

Joakim simply nodded, without stopping.

431

Tilda left the burning staircase. She had to go back into the darkness.

'Stay where you are,' she said to Freddy. 'I'm going to find your brother.' But she stayed in the doorway of the inner room, waiting for Joakim to come back. It took perhaps half a minute, then he was back with a huge shovelful of snow.

They nodded to each other and Tilda went into the storeroom where the tractor was. Behind her she could hear the fire hissing as Joakim began to put it out.

She had raised her pistol again.

The shadows and the cold surrounded her once more. She thought she heard movements ahead of her, but could see nothing. She kept close to the northern wall, where the small windows set in the thick stone were completely covered in snow. Then a door appeared, and Tilda went through it.

The room on the other side was large and even colder. Tilda stopped. The feeling that she wasn't alone in the darkness came back. She lowered her pistol, listened and took a step forward.

A shot rang out.

She ducked, without knowing if she'd been hit or not. Her ears were ringing from the report; she coughed quietly and breathed in the dry air. She waited.

Nothing else happened.

When Tilda finally looked up into the darkness she saw another closed door four or five yards away. It was a way out – but there was someone standing in front of it. A man.

It was Freddy's brother, Tommy. It couldn't be anyone else. He had rolled the balaclava up to his forehead and his pale face bore a resemblance to Freddy's. He had an old rifle over his shoulder.

Tilda steadied the hand holding the pistol, aiming at Tommy.

'Drop the gun.'

But Tommy just stood there like a sleepwalker, almost as if someone were holding on to him. His eyes were lowered and his right hand was resting on the door handle, as if he were on his way out, but his legs seemed to be incapable of movement.

'Tommy?'

He didn't reply.

A narcotic-induced psychosis? She walked slowly over to Martin's murderer, afraid but resolute. Then she silently reached out to his shoulder and carefully unhooked the rifle. She saw that the safety catch was on, and dropped it on the floor behind her.

'Tommy?' she said again. 'Can you move?'

When she nudged his arm he suddenly gave a start and came to life.

He fell backwards, the iron handle was pushed down and the door opened. It *flew* open, torn back by the storm. He tumbled out into a snowdrift, got up and staggered away.

Tilda raced after him over the low stone step, out into the gale. She could see swaying tree trunks a dozen or so yards away.

'Tommy!' she shouted. 'Stop!'

Her voice was ripped to shreds by the wind, and the man ahead of her didn't stop. He had picked up speed through the snow; he shouted something over his shoulder and fled, heading straight for the forest.

Tilda fired a warning shot, up into the storm, then dropped on one knee. She raised her pistol and took aim, keeping her finger on the trigger.

She knew she could hit him in the legs. But she

couldn't bring herself to shoot someone who was running away.

Tommy had reached the low-growing trees on the edge of the forest. The covering of snow was thinner there, and he was able to move faster. After fifteen or twenty steps he was a grey shadow in the forest. Then he was gone.

Shit.

Tilda remained outside for several minutes, but saw no other movements in the darkness apart from the whirling snow. It was still blowing in across the coast, and when she began to lose the feeling in her fingers she turned her back to the wind. She went over and picked up the Mauser in the doorway.

On her way back to Joakim she decided to go along the outside of the barn, despite the fact that the wind and the cold had almost finished her off by this stage. But she didn't want to risk meeting anyone else in there, in those black rooms.

40

Dousing the fire with snow had worked, but by the time Joakim finally managed to put the flames out, almost the entire staircase up to the loft was charred, and thick curtains of smoke hung from the roof beams.

Joakim coughed in the dry air and sat down at the bottom of the smoking staircase with aching legs. He was still holding the snow shovel he had fetched from the house.

He couldn't even think any more, didn't have the strength to wonder where all these uninvited guests had come from tonight, or to ponder what had happened up there in the room with the church benches. He realized that Gerlof Davidsson was right: a veil of forgetfulness was already beginning to obscure his memories of this night.

Had he really met Katrine up there? Had she confessed that she had drowned his sister?

No. Katrine hadn't said that.

Joakim contemplated the tall man lying over by the wall. He had no idea who he was or why he was wearing handcuffs, but if police officer Tilda Davidsson had caught him, then certain conclusions could be drawn.

Almost at that same moment he thought he heard fresh shots from somewhere outside the barn. Joakim listened, but when he heard nothing more he looked back at the man on the floor. 'Was it you who started all this?' he asked.

After a few seconds a quiet reply came from the floor. 'Sorry.'

Joakim sighed. 'I'll have to build a new staircase to the loft . . . some time.'

He leaned back, then remembered that Livia and Gabriel were still in the house, alone.

How could he have left them?

There was a sudden scraping noise over by the barn door, and when he turned his head he saw Tilda come stumbling in from the storm, covered in snow. She had her pistol in one hand, and an old hunting rifle in the other.

She sank down over by the wooden wall and breathed out.

'He's gone,' she said.

Freddy looked up from the floor.

'Gone?' said Joakim.

'He ran into the forest,' said Tilda. 'He disappeared. But at least he hasn't got a rifle now.'

Joakim got up. 'I have to see to my children,' he said, walking towards the door. 'Will you be OK on your own for a while?'

Tilda nodded, but remained on the floor, her head drooping. 'If you go through the veranda . . . there are people there. Two men.'

'Injured?' said Joakim.

Tilda lowered her eyes. 'One's injured . . . and one's dead.'

Joakim didn't ask any more questions. When he glanced at her one last time she had taken out her mobile and started to key in a number.

He walked out into the billowing snow dunes in the

inner courtyard, bending low against the wind. Eel Point didn't seem so big tonight – the buildings seemed to be cowering like a pack of frightened dogs beneath the blizzard. The onslaught of the wind was ripping off slates and whirling them up over the roof, where they disappeared into the darkness.

Joakim went inside the veranda and closed the door. A man was lying stretched out on the rug. Dead? No, he was just deeply asleep.

The storm was making the windows on the front of the house rattle, and the putty and frames holding the panes were creaking, but they were still holding.

Joakim walked into the house, but stopped in the hallway.

He could hear creaking noises in the corridor.

Hoarse breathing.

Ethel was there.

She was standing in front of the doors to the children's rooms. She had come to collect her daughter. Ethel was going to take Livia away with her.

Joakim didn't dare go up to her. He simply bent his head and closed his eyes.

Trust me, he thought.

He opened his eyes and went on into the house.

The corridor by the bedrooms was empty.

41

Tilda had vague memories of being helped up the steps to the veranda late that night. It was still cold outside, but it felt as if the wind from the sea was beginning to subside. It was Joakim Westin who was walking beside her, supporting her along a newly cleared track. High banks of snow rose up on either side of them.

'Did you call for help?' he asked.

She nodded. 'They said they'd get out here as soon as they could . . . but I don't know when that will be.'

They passed a snowdrift with a piece of material sticking out. It was a leather jacket.

'Who's that?' asked Joakim.

'His name was Martin Ahlquist,' said Tilda.

She closed her eyes. There would be many questions about this night – about what had gone wrong, what she had done right and what she ought to have done differently – but she was bound to ask herself more questions than anyone else would. But she just didn't have the strength to think about that right now.

The house was quiet. Joakim led her through the corridors to a big room where a mattress made up into a bed lay on the floor. There was a tiled stove nearby; it was warm, and she lay down and relaxed. Her nose was aching and was still full of blood – she couldn't breathe with her mouth closed.

The wind was howling around the house. But at last she fell asleep.

Tilda slept deeply, but was woken occasionally by a throbbing pain in her head and with memories of Martin's body in the snow – and by a spine-chilling fear of being back out there in the darkness of the barn, where pale arms with long fingers reached out for her. It took time to relax.

Some time before dawn a shadow leaned over her. She gave a start.

'Tilda?'

It was Joakim Westin again. He carried on talking, slowly and clearly, as if he were addressing a small child.

'Your colleagues called, Tilda. They're coming soon.'

'Good,' she said.

Her voice sounded thick through her broken nose. She closed her eyes and asked, 'And Henrik?'

'Who?'

'Henrik Jansson,' said Tilda. 'The guy on the veranda. How's he doing?'

'Pretty good,' said Joakim. 'I put a fresh pressure bandage on.'

'Tommy? Did he come back?'

'He's gone . . . the police are going to look for him when they get here.'

Tilda nodded and went back to sleep.

An indefinable amount of time later she was woken by a droning noise and quiet voices, but she hadn't the strength to wonder what was going on.

Then she heard Joakim's voice again.

'The cars can't get through, Tilda. They've borrowed an all-terrain carrier from the army.'

Soon after that the room was filled with voices and movement, and she was helped up out of bed, somewhat roughly.

The warm air suddenly disappeared – she was out in the cold again, but now there was barely a breath of wind. She was walking along a path that had been cleared of snow, with white mounds all around her.

Christmas Eve, she thought.

A door closed, another opened, she was placed on a bunk beneath a weak light bulb. Then she was left in peace.

Silence fell.

She was lying in an army carrier and she could see a body below her on the floor, wrapped in a plastic sack. It wasn't moving.

Then someone beside her coughed. Tilda raised her head and saw another figure lying a few yards away with a grey blanket over its legs. The body moved slightly. It was a man. He was lying on his back with his head turned away from her, but she recognized his clothes.

'Henrik,' she said.

No reply.

'Henrik!' she shouted, despite the fact that it made her ribs hurt.

'What?' asked the man, turning his head towards her.

And she finally got to see his face clearly: Henrik Jansson, flooring contractor and burglar. He looked just like any other twenty-five-year-old man, but his face was exhausted and chalk-white.

Tilda took a deep breath. 'Henrik, your fucking axe broke my nose.'

He was silent.

Tilda asked, 'Have you done anything else I should know about?'

Still he didn't reply.

'There was a death here on the point in the autumn,' she went on. 'A woman drowned.'

She heard Henrik move.

'Some people heard a boat down by the point on the day she died,' said Tilda. 'Was it your boat?'

Then Henrik suddenly opened his eyes.

'Not mine,' he said quietly.

'Not yours?' said Tilda. 'Another boat?'

'But I did see it,' said Henrik.

'Did you, indeed?'

'I was standing by the landing stage the day she died.'

'Katrine Westin,' said Tilda.

'She had a visitor,' he went on. 'In a big white boat.'

'Did you recognize it?'

'No, but it was bigger than mine, built for longer trips . . . a small yacht. It moored by the lighthouses and someone was standing there. I think it was her . . .'

'OK.'

Tilda suddenly realized she just didn't have the strength to talk any more.

'I *saw* it,' said Henrik.

Tilda met his eyes. 'We can talk about it later,' she said. 'I'm sure you'll be having plenty of interviews.'

Henrik just breathed out with a heavy sigh.

Silence fell in the carrier again. Tilda just wanted to close her eyes and doze off, so that she could escape the pain and thoughts of Martin.

'Did you hear anything in the house last night?' Henrik suddenly asked.

'What?'

A door slammed. Then the carrier's engine roared into life, and the vehicle moved off.

'Knocking noises?'

Tilda didn't understand what he meant.

'I didn't hear anything,' she said through the noise of the engine.

'Me neither,' said Henrik. 'No knocking. I think it was down to the lantern . . . or the board. But it's all quiet now.'

He'd been stabbed and was well on his way to ending up in jail, but Tilda still thought he sounded relieved.

42

On the morning of Christmas Eve it was still dark at Eel Point. The power hadn't been restored, and outside the windows huge banks of snow rose up.

Three police officers and a search dog had arrived in the all-terrain carrier during the night and searched all the buildings without finding Martin Ahlquist's murderer. Joakim let them carry on. At about three o'clock, when they had left for the hospital with Tilda Davidsson and the man who had been stabbed, he actually managed to sleep for a few hours.

For the first time in several weeks he slept peacefully, but when he woke up at around eight in the silent house he couldn't get back to sleep. The rooms were still pitch black, so Joakim got up and lit a couple of paraffin lamps.

An hour later a stronger light penetrated the snow-covered windows. It was the sun, rising over the sea. Joakim wanted to see it, but had to go upstairs, open the window on the landing and knock aside one of the shutters in order to be able to look out towards the sea.

The coast had been transformed into a winter landscape with a deep-blue sky above sparkling snow dunes. The red walls of the barn looked almost black against the dazzling snow. There was an Arctic silence all around the place. There wasn't a breath of wind – perhaps for the first time since Joakim moved in. The blizzard had blown itself out. Before moving on it had hurled up a three-foot-high wall of sea ice down by the shore.

Joakim looked towards the shore. He had read about old lighthouses that tumbled into the sea during fierce storms, but the twin lighthouses had survived the blizzard. The towers rose above the banks of ice.

Joakim lit fires in the tiled stoves at around nine, driving the cold out of the house. Then he woke the children.

'Happy Christmas,' he said.

They had fallen asleep with their clothes on in Gabriel's bed. That was how he had found them when he came in from the barn the previous night. He had covered them with blankets and let them sleep on.

Now Joakim was ready for questions about what had happened during the night, about the noise of shooting and all the rest of it, but Livia merely stretched.

'Did you sleep well?'

She nodded. 'Mummy was here.'

'Here?'

'She came in to see us while you were gone.'

Joakim looked at his daughter, then at his son. Gabriel nodded slowly, as if everything his sister said was true.

Don't tell lies, Livia, Joakim wanted to say. Mummy can't have been here.

But instead he asked, 'So what did Mummy say?'

'She said you'd come soon,' said Livia, looking at him. 'But you didn't.'

Joakim sat down on the side of the bed. 'I'm here now,' he said. 'I'm not going to disappear again.'

444

Livia looked at him suspiciously and got out of bed without a word.

Joakim woke Freddy, who was a quiet, calm young man without his brother. There hadn't been room for him in the carrier, so Freddy had stayed behind, handcuffed to one of the radiators in the hallway.

'Still no sign of your brother,' said Joakim.

Freddy nodded wearily.

'What were you actually looking for?'

'Anything . . . valuable paintings.'

'By Torun Rambe?' said Joakim. 'We've only got one. Were you looking for more in the barn?'

'There were no more in the house,' said Freddy. 'They were somewhere else, the board said. So we went out and set fire to the staircase.'

Joakim looked at him. 'But why?'

'Don't know.'

'Are you going to do it again?'

Freddy shook his head.

Tilda had given Joakim the keys to the handcuffs, and he decided to show a little good faith and trust this Christmas Eve. He released Freddy from the radiator.

When the power came back at about eleven, Freddy settled down in front of the television to watch Christmas programmes while he waited for the police to come and pick him up. With a mournful expression he gazed at cartoons about Santa, live broadcasts showing people dancing around Christmas trees, and cookery programmes from some snow-covered mountain chalet.

Livia and Gabriel sat down beside him. None of them spoke, but there was still a kind of Christmas community spirit, and they all seemed to relax.

Joakim went and sat in the kitchen with the

445

notebook he had found next to Ethel's jacket. For an hour he read Mirja Rambe's dramatic accounts of life at Eel Point. And the story of what had happened to her there.

At the end there were some blank pages, then a couple that had been written by someone other than Mirja.

Joakim looked more closely and suddenly recognized Katrine's handwriting. Her notes were scrawled, as if she had been in a great hurry. He read them several times, without fully understanding what she meant.

At twelve o'clock Joakim prepared Christmas rice pudding for everyone.

The telephone was working, and the first call came after lunch. Joakim answered and heard Gerlof Davidsson's quiet voice.

'So now you know what a real blizzard is like.'

'Yes,' said Joakim, 'we certainly do.'

He looked out of the window and thought about last night's visitors.

'It was expected,' said Gerlof. 'By me, anyway. But I thought it would come a bit later. How did you cope?'

'Pretty well. All the buildings are still standing, but the roofs are damaged.'

'And the road?'

'Gone,' said Joakim. 'There's just snow.'

'In the old days it used to take at least a week to get through to some properties after a blizzard,' said Gerlof. 'But it's quicker these days.'

'We'll be fine,' said Joakim. 'I did as you said and bought plenty of tinned stuff.'

'Good. Are you and the children alone now?'

'No, we still have one guest here. We did have several

visitors, but they've gone . . . it's been quite a difficult Christmas.'

'I know,' said Gerlof. 'Tilda called me this morning from the hospital. She'd been catching burglars out at your place.'

'They came here to steal paintings,' said Joakim. 'Torun Rambe's paintings . . . they'd got it into their heads that they were here somewhere.'

'Oh?'

'But we only have one painting here. Almost all the others were destroyed, but not by Torun or her daughter Mirja. It was a fisherman who threw them in the sea.'

'When was that?'

'Winter 1962.'

'Sixty-two,' said Gerlof. 'That was the year my brother Ragnar froze to death on the coast.'

'Ragnar Davidsson – was he your brother?' said Joakim.

'My older brother.'

'I don't think he froze to death,' said Joakim. 'I think he was poisoned.'

Then he told Gerlof what he had read in Mirja Rambe's book about her last night at Eel Point, and about the eel fisherman who set off into the storm.

Gerlof listened without asking any questions. 'It sounds as if Ragnar drank wood spirit,' was all he said. 'It's supposed to taste like ordinary schnapps, but of course it makes you ill. It kills you, in fact.'

'I suppose Mirja saw it as some kind of fair punishment,' said Joakim.

'But did he really destroy the paintings?' said Gerlof. 'I'm just wondering. If my brother got hold of something, he kept it. He was too mean to destroy things.'

Joakim was silent. He was thinking.

447

'There was something else, before I forget,' said Gerlof. 'I've recorded something for you.'

'Recorded?'

'I've been sitting here doing some thinking,' said Gerlof. 'It's a tape with a few ideas about what happened at Eel Point. You'll get it when they start delivering the post again.'

Half an hour after Gerlof had hung up, the police called from Kalmar to say they would be coming to collect the suspect from Eel Point – if Joakim could just find them a piece of flat, open ground near the house where a helicopter could land.

'We've got plenty of flat ground around here,' said Joakim.

Then he went out and cleared a square in the field behind the house, hacking away the ice so that a black cross in the frozen ground marked the spot. When he heard a throbbing sound in the south-west he went in and interrupted Freddy's viewing.

'Are those your cars?' Joakim asked as they were waiting out in the field. He pointed to a couple of curved mounds of snow on the road down to Eel Point. A few blunt metal corners were protruding from the drifts.

Freddy nodded. 'And a boat,' he said.

'Stolen?'

'Yeah.'

Then the helicopter swept in over the field and it was impossible to talk any more. It hovered for a moment, whirling white clouds up from the ground, before landing in the centre of the cross.

Two police officers wearing helmets and dark jumpsuits climbed out and came over to them. Freddy went along with them, without making any kind of protest.

'Are you all OK here now?' shouted one of the police officers.

Joakim simply nodded. Freddy waved, and he waved back briefly.

When the helicopter had vanished in the direction of the mainland, Joakim ploughed back through the snow, over towards the road and the two snow-covered vehicles. He brushed away the snow from the sides of the larger of them, a van. Then he peered inside.

Someone was sitting in there, motionless.

Joakim seized the handle and opened the door.

It was a man, curled up as if he had desperately tried to preserve his warmth in the driver's seat. Joakim didn't need to feel the man's pulse to realize he was dead.

The key was in the ignition and it was switched on. The engine must have been ticking over until it stopped some time during the night, and the cold began to creep back into the van again.

Joakim closed the door gently. Then he went back to the house to call the police and tell them the last burglar had been found.

43

The wind stayed away and the sun carried on shining over Eel Point for the next few days.

The snow didn't start to thaw, but now and again a piece of the white edging hanging from the roofs came loose and fell soundlessly into the drifts on the ground. The garden birds were back outside the kitchen window, and on the morning of the twenty-sixth the isolation from the outside world was broken when a truck with a huge plough in front of it drove over from Marnäs. It kept going in a straight line out along the coast road, but looked as if it were rolling along through a white sea.

When he got out the blower and starting blowing away the snow leading from the house, Joakim's goal was to reach the ploughed main road in an hour. It took more than two hours, but after that they could get out easily once again.

Joakim put new batteries in his torch and went out on to the veranda steps and over to the barn.

The staircase leading to the loft was black and in pieces after the fire, but there was no sign of any smoke anywhere.

He looked over towards the other end of the barn. He hesitated, but then went across and crawled in under the false wall. Inside the hidden room he switched on the torch and listened for sounds from the upper floor, but there was nothing. Then he climbed up the ladder.

Pale sunlight filtered in through the cracks in the wall as he pulled himself up into the prayer room. Everything was quiet. The letters and mementoes still lay on the old wooden benches, but no one was sitting there.

He started to move along the rows. When he reached the front he saw that both the Christmas present for Katrine and Ethel's jacket were still there. But the parcel had been opened. The tape had been pulled away and the paper folded to one side.

Joakim left the parcel where it was; he didn't dare look to see if the green tunic was gone. Instead he picked up Ethel's denim jacket for the first time – and suddenly his fingers felt a small, flat object sliding around inside the fabric.

Joakim had placed the denim jacket in a plastic bag when Inspector Göte Holmblad arrived in his own car, two days after Christmas.

By this time an ambulance and a breakdown truck had already been to Eel Point and taken away the body of the last suspect. The scene-of-crime team had also been there, digging for bullets in the snow. On the local radio news Tommy had been reported as one of two deaths at the house during the snowstorm, although he wasn't mentioned by name. The storm over northern Öland was already being referred to as 'the Christmas blizzard', and was classed as one of the worst snowstorms since the Second World War.

Holmblad got out of the car and wished Joakim compliments of the season.

'Thanks, same to you,' he said. 'And thank you for coming.'

'I'm actually on leave until New Year,' said Holmblad. 'But I wanted to see how you were getting on out here.'

'Everything's very calm now,' said Joakim.

'I can see that. The storm has passed.'

Joakim nodded and asked, 'And Tilda Davidsson . . . how's she doing?'

'Pretty good, considering,' said Holmblad. 'I spoke to her yesterday. She's left hospital and is at home with her mother at the moment.'

'But she was here alone? It wasn't a colleague who . . .'

'No,' said Holmblad, 'it was her tutor from the police academy – a father of two, it's a real tragedy. He shouldn't really have been here.' The inspector looked thoughtful, and added, 'Of course, things could have gone very badly for Davidsson too, but she coped very well.'

'She did,' said Joakim, opening the door to the house. 'I've got a few things I'd really like to show you – would you like to come in for a while?'

'Certainly.'

Joakim led the inspector into the kitchen, where he had cleared the kitchen table.

'There,' he said.

On the table lay the bag containing Ethel's denim jacket, and the items he had found in the jacket. There was the handwritten note – and a small gold case that had been tucked inside the lining of the jacket.

'What's this?' said Holmblad.

'I'm not sure,' said Joakim. 'But I hope it's evidence.'

When Holmblad had left, Joakim took a rucksack and went down through the snow to the northern lighthouse.

On the way there he glanced over towards the forest in the north. Most of the trees seemed to have survived the storm, apart from a few of the older pines closest to the shore, which were lying on the ground.

The white tower sparkled against the dark-blue sky. Before he even set off along the stone jetty he could see that it would be difficult to get inside it. The waves had crashed over the islands during the blizzard, and both lighthouses were encased in chalk-white ice. It looked like plaster that had set, extending around the lower part of the tower in an Arctic embrace.

Joakim put his rucksack down outside the door and unzipped it. He took out the keys to the lighthouse, along with a large hammer, a spray can of oil for the lock, and three Thermos flasks full of boiling water.

It took him almost half an hour to get rid of all the ice around the door and undo the lock. It was still only possible to open the door a little way, but Joakim managed to squeeze through the gap. He had the torch with him, and switched it on when he got inside.

Every little sound the soles of his shoes made on the cement floor echoed up into the tower, but he didn't hear any footsteps on the stairs. If some old lighthouse-keeper was still up there Joakim didn't want to disturb him, so he stayed downstairs.

Just a chance, Gerlof Davidsson had said. *My brother Ragnar had the keys to the lighthouses, so there's just a chance that they might be there.*

There was a small wooden door leading into the space under the staircase, a storeroom on the ground floor of the lighthouse. Joakim opened the door and walked in, stooping low.

A calendar from 1961 hung on the stone wall. Petrol cans, empty booze bottles and old lanterns stood on the floor. The collection of objects in here made him think of all the old stuff piled high in the hayloft. But this was a little more organized, and along the curve of the outside wall stood several wooden boxes.

The lids weren't secured. Joakim lifted up the closest one and shone the torch into the box. He saw metal pipes – sections of old drainpipes approximately three feet long – piled up at the bottom of the box. They would have been fixed together and put up around the house at Eel Point several decades earlier, if Ragnar Davidsson hadn't stolen them and hidden them in the lighthouse.

Joakim put his hand in and carefully lifted out one of the pipes.

44

'Where are we going?' asked Livia as they drove away from Eel Point the day before New Year's Eve, with the car packed full.

She was still in a bit of a bad mood, Joakim noticed.

'We're going to see your grandmother in Kalmar, then we're going up to see your other granny in Stockholm,' he said. 'But first of all we're going to visit Mummy.'

Livia didn't say any more. She just rested her hand on Rasputin's cat basket and looked out at the white landscape.

Fifteen minutes later they pulled up at Marnäs church. Joakim parked, took a bag out of the car and opened the wooden gate.

'Come on,' he said to the children.

Joakim hadn't been there many times during the autumn – but it felt better now. A little better.

There was just as much snow in the churchyard as everywhere else along the coast, but the main pathways had been cleared.

'Are we going far?' asked Livia as they walked along the side of the church.

'No,' said Joakim. 'We're almost there now.'

At last they were standing in a row in front of Katrine's grave.

The gravestone was covered in snow, like all the others in the churchyard. There was only one corner showing, until Joakim bent down and quickly swept it clean with his hand, so that the inscription could be seen.

KATRINE MÅNSTRÅLE WESTIN, it said, along with her dates.

Joakim took a step backwards and stood between Livia and Gabriel.

'This is where Mummy is,' he said.

His words didn't make time stop, but the children stood motionless beside him.

'Do you think it . . . looks nice?' asked Joakim in the silence.

Livia didn't reply. It was Gabriel who reacted first.

'I think Mummy will be cold,' he said.

Then he walked cautiously up to the grave in his father's footsteps and silently began to brush away all the snow. First of all from Katrine's headstone, then from the ground below it. A bunch of shrivelled roses appeared. Joakim had placed them there on his last visit, before the snow came.

Gabriel seemed happy with the result. He rubbed his nose with his gloved hand and looked at his father.

'Well done,' said Joakim.

Then he took a grave lantern out of the plastic bag. The ground was frozen, but it was still possible to push it down firmly. Inside he placed a thick candle. It would burn for five days, into the new year.

'Shall we go back to the car?' Joakim asked, looking at the children.

Gabriel nodded, but bent down and started to tug at something lying beneath the snow next to Katrine's headstone. It was a piece of pale-green fabric, stiff and

456

frozen to the ground. A sweater? The strip Gabriel had hold of looked like a sleeve.

Joakim felt a sudden icy chill down his back. He took a step forward.

'Leave that, Gabriel,' he said.

Gabriel looked at his father and let go of the material. Joakim bent down quickly and covered it with a layer of snow.

'Shall we go?' he said.

'I want to stay for a little while,' said Livia, her gaze fixed on the headstone.

Joakim took Gabriel by the hand and walked back to the main path. They waited there for Livia, who was still standing looking at the grave. After a few minutes she joined them and the family walked back to the car in silence.

Gabriel fell asleep in his seat after just a few minutes.

Livia didn't start talking to Joakim until they were back on the main road, and she didn't mention Katrine. She asked how many days of the holiday were left, and talked about what she was going to do when pre-school started again. Just small talk, but Joakim was happy to listen to her.

They arrived in Kalmar at about twelve o'clock and rang Mirja Rambe's doorbell. She hadn't made a special effort to clean up the apartment for Christmas – quite the opposite, the piles of books on the dusty parquet floor had grown even higher. There was a Christmas tree in the main room, but it had no decorations on it and the needles had already started to fall.

'I had intended to come out and see you all on Christmas Day,' said Mirja as she met them in the hallway. 'But I didn't have a helicopter.'

Ulf, Mirja's young boyfriend, was at home and

seemed really pleased to see them, especially the children. He took Livia and Gabriel into the kitchen to show them some toffee that he was in the middle of making on the stove.

Joakim took *The Book of the Blizzard* out of his bag and gave it back to the author. 'Thanks for the loan,' he said.

'Was it any good?'

'Yes,' said Joakim. 'And I understand some things much better now.'

Mirja Rambe leafed through the handwritten pages in silence. 'It's a book of facts,' she said. 'I started writing it when Katrine told me you were going to buy Eel Point.'

'Katrine wrote a couple of pages at the end,' said Joakim.

'About what?'

'Well . . . it's a kind of explanation.'

Mirja placed the book on the table between them. 'I'll read it when you've gone,' she said.

'I did wonder about one thing,' said Joakim. 'How could you know so much about the people who'd lived at Eel Point?'

Mirja gave him a forbidding look.

'They used to talk to me when I lived there,' she said. 'Have you never talked to the dead?'

Joakim couldn't answer that one.

'So it's all true?' he said instead.

'You can never be sure of that,' said Mirja. 'Not when it comes to ghosts.'

'But all the stuff you were involved in . . . did that actually happen?'

Mirja lowered her eyes. 'More or less,' she said. 'I did meet Markus one last time down at the café in Borgholm. We talked . . . then I went back to his place. His parents were out. We went up to the flat, and he pulled me down on to the floor. Not exactly a romantic seduction, but I let him do it – I mean, I thought it proved that we . . . that we were a couple. But when Markus got up afterwards and I'd pulled my crumpled skirt back on, he wouldn't look me in the eye. He just said he'd met someone else on the mainland. They were getting engaged. Markus referred to what we'd done in his room as saying goodbye.'

There was silence in the room.

'So your boyfriend Markus was Katrine's father?'

Mirja nodded. 'He was a young man on his way out into the world, who closed the chapter involving me in an appropriate way. Then he moved on.'

'But he didn't die in a ferry accident, did he?'

'No,' said Mirja. 'But he should have done.'

They fell silent again. Joakim could hear Livia laughing in the kitchen. It sounded like a lighter version of her mother's laugh.

'You should have told Katrine who her father was,' he said. 'She had the right to know.'

Mirja merely snorted. 'We get by . . . I didn't know who my father was either.'

Joakim gave up. He nodded and stood up. 'We've brought some Christmas presents,' he said. 'I need some help to carry them up.'

'Ulf will help,' said Mirja. 'Are the presents for me?'

Joakim looked over at her studio, with all its bright summer paintings.

'Oh yes,' he said. 'Lots of presents.'

Five hours after leaving Mirja's apartment Joakim and the children arrived in Stockholm. It was almost as cold there as on Öland. The area where Ingrid Westin lived was quiet and calm. She was the direct opposite of Mirja

459

Rambe; her house had been cleaned to within an inch of its life ready for New Year.

'I've got a job,' Joakim told her as they were having dinner.

'On Öland?' said Ingrid.

He nodded. 'They called yesterday. I'm going to be filling in as a craft teacher down in Borgholm from February. I can carry on working on the house in the evenings and at weekends. I want to make the outhouse and the upper floor look nice so that people can stay there.'

'Are you going to have summer visitors staying?' said Ingrid.

'Maybe,' said Joakim. 'We need more people at Eel Point.'

Afterwards they exchanged Christmas presents in Ingrid's little living room.

Joakim handed her a large, long package. 'Happy Christmas, Mum,' he said. 'Mirja Rambe wanted you to have this.'

The package was almost three feet long and was wrapped in brown paper. Ingrid opened it and looked enquiringly at him. It was one of the sections of drain-pipe Ragnar Davidsson had hidden in the lighthouse.

'Look inside,' said Joakim.

Ingrid turned one end of the pipe to face her. She peered inside, then reached in and pulled out a rolled-up canvas. She opened it out carefully and held it up in front of her. The oil painting was large and dark, and showed a foggy winter landscape.

'What's this?' said Ingrid.

'It's a blizzard painting,' said Joakim. 'By Torun Rambe.'

'But . . . is it for me?'

Joakim nodded.

'There are lots more – almost fifty of them,' he said. 'A fisherman stole the canvases and hid them inside one of the lighthouses at Eel Point. And that's where they've been for more than thirty years.'

Ingrid gazed at the big painting in silence.

'I wonder what it's worth?'

'That doesn't matter,' said Joakim.

In the evening Livia and Gabriel went outside to make snow lanterns with their grandmother.

Joakim went upstairs. He went past the closed door of the room that had been Ethel's many years ago, and into the room that had been his own bedroom when he was a teenager.

All the posters and most of the furniture had gone, but there was a bed and a bedside table and an old tape player. The black plastic casing was cracked from falling on the floor during some party, but it still worked. It was possible to open the slot.

Joakim inserted a cassette. It had arrived at Eel Point in the post a couple of days earlier. It was from Gerlof Davidsson.

He settled down on his old bed and pressed Play so that he could hear what Gerlof had to say.

45

At about three o'clock on New Year's Eve Joakim took the underground to Bromma to wish his dead sister a Happy New Year, and to try to talk to her murderer.

He stopped to buy a small bunch of roses in a flower shop by the station. Then he set off along the street, following the route past the wooden houses above the water. They looked like forts, he thought. The sun had just gone down and the lights were glowing in many windows.

After a few hundred yards he reached the street where the Apple House lay, and went up to the closed gate. He gazed at his former home. It looked empty but there was a light on in the hallway, possibly to deter burglars.

Joakim bent down and propped the bunch of flowers against the electricity box by the fence. He stood there for a few moments thinking of Ethel and Katrine, then turned away.

The neighbouring house further along the street had the lights on in most of the rooms. It was the Hesslins' huge house – the pride of the neighbourhood.

Joakim remembered Michael Hesslin had mentioned on the telephone that the family would be home for New Year. He went up to the gate, along the garden path and rang the doorbell.

Lisa Hesslin opened the door. She looked pleased when she saw who it was. 'Come in, Joakim,' she said. 'And Happy New Year!'

'Same to you.'

He walked in, on to the thick carpet in the hallway.

'Would you like some coffee? Or a glass of champagne, perhaps?'

'That won't be necessary,' he said. 'Is Michael home?'

'Not at the moment . . . but he's only gone over to the petrol station with the boys to buy some more fireworks.' Lisa smiled. 'They let off all the ones we had between Christmas and New Year. I'm sure he'll be back soon, if you can wait.'

'Sure.'

Joakim moved into the main room, which had a view of the bare trees and the ice on the bay down below the house.

'Would you like to read something?' he asked Lisa.

'What?'

'This note.'

Joakim reached into the inside pocket of his jacket and took out a copy of the note he had found in Ethel's denim jacket in the hayloft. He handed it over to Lisa.

She took it and read: 'Make sure that junkie—'

She stopped abruptly and looked enquiringly at Joakim.

'Carry on,' he said. 'Wasn't it you who wrote it and gave it to Katrine?'

She shook her head.

'Then it must have been Michael.'

'I . . . I can't imagine that.'

Lisa handed back the note. Joakim took it and stood up.

'Can I put your stereo on?' he said. 'I've got something I'd like you to listen to.'

463

'Of course. Is it music?'

Joakim went over and inserted the cassette. 'No,' he said. 'It's just talking, actually.'

When the cassette started he took a couple of steps backwards and sat down on the sofa directly opposite Lisa. There was a rattling noise from the speakers, then Gerlof Davidsson's tinny, slightly grumpy voice came through.

'Right, let's see . . . I've borrowed a tape recorder from Tilda, and I think it's running now. I've been thinking a great deal about the death of your wife, Joakim. If you don't want to be reminded of it you should stop listening now. But as I said, I couldn't stop thinking about it.'

Lisa looked dubiously at Joakim, but Gerlof's voice went on: 'I think someone killed Katrine: a person who left no traces of themselves on the sandy shore, and therefore must have come from the sea. I can't tell you the name of Katrine's murderer, but I believe he's a powerfully built, middle-aged man. He lives or has a house in southern Gotland, and there he keeps a big boat with an inboard motor. The boat must have been big and fast to be able to cover a day trip between the islands, but at the same time light enough to be able to come into the jetty at Eel Point, where the water is no more than three feet deep. He must have—'

'Joakim, who's actually talking here?' said Lisa.

'Just listen,' said Joakim.

'. . . and aiming for the twin lighthouses as you approach Öland isn't particularly difficult,' Gerlof went on. 'But how did the murderer know your wife was going to be home alone that day? I think Katrine knew him. When she heard the sound of the engine approaching across the water, she went down to the shore. The murderer was standing in the prow holding the murder weapon in his hand when she came out on

464

to the jetty. But your wife wasn't suspicious, because he was holding something almost everyone uses when they moor a boat.'

Gerlof coughed quietly and continued: 'The murder weapon was a wooden boathook, long and heavy and with a big iron hook on one end. I've seen them used in fights at sea. It's easy to grab the opponent's clothing with the hook. Then you pull, and the victim loses balance and falls into the water. If you want to drown someone, then of course all you have to do is hold the hook beneath the surface of the water. There are no fingerprints, no major injuries. All that is visible afterwards is the odd small tear in the clothing. There are holes like that in your wife's clothes.'

Gerlof stopped again, before finishing off his recording: 'Well, that's what I think happened, Joakim. This won't make things any easier for you in your grief, I know that. But we all feel better when questions have been answered. You're welcome to come over for coffee again some time. Now I'm going to switch this off . . .'

The crackling voice on the tape fell silent, and all that could be heard from the speakers was a faint hissing sound.

Joakim went over and took out the tape. 'That's it,' he said.

Lisa had got to her feet. 'Who was that?' she asked again. 'Who was talking?'

'A friend. An old man,' said Joakim, slipping the tape into his pocket. 'Nobody you know . . . but is it true?'

Lisa opened her mouth, but seemed unable to find any words. 'No,' she said. 'Surely you don't believe all that?'

'Was Michael at your cottage on Gotland when Katrine died?'

'How should I know? It was back in the autumn . . . I don't remember.'

'But when was he there?' said Joakim. 'I mean, he must have gone down there some time to take the boat out of the water. Mustn't he?'

Lisa looked at him without replying.

'I was here in Stockholm the evening Katrine drowned,' said Joakim, 'and I remember noticing there were no cars in your driveway. Nobody was home.'

He got no reply.

'Does Michael have a calendar we could look at?' asked Joakim. 'Or a diary?'

Lisa turned her back on him. 'That's enough now, Joakim . . . I need to make a start on dinner.'

She went over to the front door, opened it and looked at him.

Joakim said nothing. Before he left the house he stopped next to the photographs on the wall and looked closely at one of them: a picture of Michael Hesslin on board his white motor cruiser. He was standing behind the shining gunwale in the prow, waving at the camera. There was no sign of any boathook.

'Nice boat,' said Joakim quietly.

He left, and she quickly closed the door behind him. Joakim heard the lock click into place.

He sighed and went out into the street, but stopped when he heard a faint noise carried on the air. It was the hum of a car engine.

When it turned into the street Joakim saw that it was Michael's car.

Michael drove up to the garage, switched off the engine and got out with four long fireworks under his arm. His two boys jumped out of the back seat and ran off towards the house, each clutching their own bag of firecrackers.

'Joakim, you're back!' said Michael, coming out into the street. 'Happy New Year!'

He held out his hand, but Joakim didn't take it. Instead he asked, 'What did you dream about that night at Eel Point, Michael? You woke up screaming . . . Did you see ghosts?'

'Sorry?'

'You killed my wife,' said Joakim.

Michael was still smiling, as if he hadn't heard properly.

'And the previous year you lured Ethel down to the water,' Joakim went on. 'You gave her a fix of heroin, then you pushed her into the water.'

Michael stopped smiling and lowered his out-stretched hand.

'She was spoiling the idyll,' said Joakim. 'And perhaps junkies might give the neighbourhood a bad name. But I'm sure murder suspects are even worse.'

Michael simply shook his head slightly, as if his former neighbour were beyond all help. 'So you're going to try and set me up for murder?'

'I can help,' said Joakim.

Michael looked at his house and started to smile again. 'Forget it.'

He walked straight past Joakim as if he didn't exist.

'There's proof,' said Joakim.

Michael kept on walking towards the gate.

'Your business cards,' said Joakim. 'Where did you keep them?'

Michael stopped. He didn't turn around, but stood there listening.

Joakim moved closer and raised his voice. 'Thieving is always a problem with users. They're always looking for something they can pick up. So when my sister went down to the water with you, she took the opportunity to steal something from you . . . something valuable out of your jacket pocket.'

Joakim took a Polaroid photograph out of his pocket. It was a picture of a small object inside a clear plastic bag. A flat case, gold coloured, with the words HESSLIN FINANCIAL SERVICES engraved on the front.

'Your case was hidden inside Ethel's jacket,' he went on. 'Is it made of gold? I'm sure my sister thought it was.'

Michael didn't reply. He took a final quick look at Joakim and the photograph before going through the gate.

'I've already given this to the police, Michael,' said Joakim. 'I'm sure they'll be in touch.'

He felt a bit like Ethel, standing there yelling out in the street, but it didn't matter any longer.

He stood there and watched Michael disappear up the path.

His rapid footsteps gave him away. Joakim could imagine what the new year would be like for Michael: constantly watching from the window, sweating as he waited for a police car to pull up on the street all of a sudden. Two police officers getting out, opening the gate, ringing the bell on the imposing front door.

In the houses further down the street, the curtains would be discreetly pulled to one side by curious neighbours. What was going on?

'Happy New Year, Michael,' Joakim shouted as Michael opened the front door and went inside.

The door slammed shut.

Joakim was alone on the street again. He breathed out and lowered his eyes. Then he set off back towards the underground station, but stopped for one last time at the gate of the Apple House. The bunch of roses he had propped up against the electricity box had fallen over in the wind – he propped it up again.

He stood for a moment, thinking of his sister.

I could have done more for her, he had said to Gerlof.

Joakim sighed and took a final look along the street.

'Are you coming?' he asked.

He waited for a few seconds, then set off again, back to his little family to celebrate New Year.

Far away in the east the first fireworks could be seen over Stockholm. The rockets drew narrow white lines against the night sky, before they burst into a shower of light then went out, like ghostly lighthouses.

COMMENTARY ON *THE BOOK OF THE BLIZZARD*
by Katrine Westin

I've read your book now, Mum. And since there are some blank pages left at the end, I'm going to write down some comments before I give it back to you.

You tell a lot of stories in this book. You claim my father was a young soldier, Markus Landkvist, who died when the ferry to the mainland capsized in a blizzard in the winter of 1962 – but there has never been such a ferry disaster here. At least no one on the island that I have spoken to knows anything about it.

I'm used to it, of course. I mean, I've heard other stories about my father in the past – that he was a classmate of yours at art school, that he was the son of an American diplomat, that he was a Norwegian adventurer who ended up in jail for robbing a bank before I was born. You've always liked crazy stories.

And did you really poison an old fisherman when you lived here? Did you really hit your half-blind mother Torun and leave her to her fate one stormy winter's night?

It's possible – but you've always rearranged things and made things up. You've always been allergic to the reality of everyday life, to duties and responsibilities. Growing up with a parent like that isn't easy – whenever I talked to you I always had to try and work out what had actually happened.

One thing I promised myself: that my own

children would grow up in a much calmer, more secure environment than I did.

Joakim's sister hated me because I took care of her daughter, but she couldn't do it herself. You ought to see what drugs really do to people, Mum, you with your romantic notions about that kind of thing.

Ethel's hatred just grew and grew. But she could have stood outside our house yelling for ten years, I still wouldn't have let her take care of Livia again.

People living around us were sick and tired of Ethel and the trouble she caused. I had a feeling something was going to happen, it was in the air. But I did nothing that evening when I saw a neighbour go up to Ethel by the gate. And I couldn't feel any sorrow when she was found dead in the water – but I know it's different for Joakim. He misses his sister. If someone hurt her, he wants to know who it was.

I don't have all the answers yet, but the man who took Ethel down to the water has promised to come over to the island today to give them to me. I'm going down to the point to meet him.

Your book can stay here on the bench for the time being, along with Ethel's jacket.

Just like you, I like sitting here in the darkness of the barn, Mum. It's peaceful in here.

So far I have kept this hidden room to myself. I'm going to show it to Joakim now he's moved here. There's plenty of room for both of us.

This is a remarkable room, full of the memories of people who once lived at Eel Point. They are gone now. They passed the responsibility for the house and the land to us and disappeared. All that is left are names, dates, and short poems on postcards.

That's what we will all be one day.

Memories and ghosts.

ACKNOWLEDGEMENTS

There are many beautiful lighthouses along the coasts of Öland, and there are also cult sites where animals and people were once sacrificed. But Eel Point and its surroundings are freely invented, as are all the characters in this novel.

A book about Öland which has been particularly important to me during the writing of the novel is *Fåk – öländsk ovädersbok [Blizzard – a book of bad weather on Öland]* by Kurt Lundgren.

Thank you to Anita Tingskull, who showed me her beautiful home in Persnäs, and to Håkan Andersson, who showed me the fine royal estate in Borgholm. Thanks to Cherstin Juhlin and to Kristina Österberg, who is the daughter of a lighthouse-keeper. Thanks also to three residents of Stockholm: Mark Earthy (who found my maternal grandfather Ellert's loading quay), Anette C. Andersson and Anders Wennersten.

Thanks to the Gerlofsson family on Öland; above all, my mother Margot and her cousins Gunilla, Hans, Olle, Bertil and Lasse and their families.

Among those working professionally with *The Darkest Room* I would especially like to thank Lotta Aquilonius, Susanne Widén, Jenny Thor and Christian Manfred.

Hugs to Helena and Klara, my father Morgan, and my sister Elisabeth and her family.

Johan Theorin

THE BLIZZARD

On the following pages Johan Theorin writes about the blizzard, the storm that is so typical of Öland, and introduces some atmospheric winter pictures from the island. The original Swedish title of the novel is *Nattfåk* - Night Blizzard.

The Swedish word for blizzard, *fåk*, comes from an old Swedish verb, *fyka*, which is used to describe snow or sand being driven along violently by the wind. There is a similar word in Norwegian, *fok* or *fokk*. When the blizzard moves in across Öland, the prevailing wind is often coming from the north or north-east, and the cold which the wind brings with it feels as if it comes straight from Siberia.

The blizzard has claimed many lives over the years. In the past it was difficult to find shelter from the wind in the empty, treeless landscape, and those who were out at sea or on the alvar when the storm came were soon blinded by the swirling snow and sand which the wind carried with it. They would sometimes wander far out onto the ice and drown, or they might end up covered in snow, freezing to death in a snowdrift.

If the snow came up against an obstacle of some kind, it would quickly build up in drifts that could be several metres high. In the old days, Öland could lose touch with both the mainland and Gotland for several days when the blizzard struck. All the roads would be blocked by snow. The properties out in the country had to cope as best they could, often running out of food and wood.

473

The snowstorm also caused considerable destruction when waves and blocks of ice driving in across the shores smashed boathouses and stone walls. Cargo boats tore themselves loose from their moorings in the harbours, and out on the Baltic Sea, many vessels drifted helplessly in the stormy waves or were smashed to pieces on the coast. Once the storm had abated, many islanders would walk along the shores searching the wreckage; this was a very popular activity.

The windmills on Öland were totally exposed to the storms. On New Year's Eve in 1905, a terrible blizzard moved in across the island, and among other things, the storm tore away the rope securing the sails of a windmill in the village of Dödevi, and they began to turn. It was impossible to stop the sails in the strong wind, and eventually the friction between the millstones made the whole windmill catch fire and burn to the ground.

A hundred years later, respect for the blizzard remains. In February 2009, the rescue services on Öland carried out a training exercise involving a storm scenario in which two metres of snow had covered the island, and only all-terrain vehicles could get through along the roads.

Johan Theorin
January 2010

WINTER PICTURES FROM ÖLAND

The railway on Öland was affected by the blizzard, but the train still got through (year unknown).

From Borgholm district picture archive, Nilsson-Foto

The ruins of Borgholm castle one winter in the early 1920s.
From Borgholm district picture archive, Nilsson-Foto

Mounds of snow on Slottsgatan in Borgholm around 1925.
From Borgholm district picture archive, Nilsson-Foto

Chopping ice in Borgholm harbour. On the left is the fishing
boat "Sophie" from Kårehamn, approximately 1930.
From Borgholm district picture archive, Nilsson-Foto

Clearing snow on Kolstadsgatan outside
Borgholm, winter 1958 (next page).
From Borgholm district picture archive,
photo by Allan Bernving

The ship Dovre ran aground in a winter storm in 1911, in an inlet (or *vik*) outside Borgholm which was later named Dovreviken.

From Borgholm district picture archive, Nilsson-Foto